WILD FRANCE

A TRAVELLER'S GUIDE

EDITED BY
DOUGLAS BOTTING

INTERLINK BOOKS
An imprint of Interlink Publishing Group, Inc.
NEW YORK

First American edition published 2000 by
INTERLINK BOOKS
An imprint of Interlink Publishing Group, Inc.
99 Seventh Avenue • Brooklyn, New York 11215 and
46 Crosby Street • Northampton, Massachusetts 01060

Copyright © 1992, 2000 Sheldrake Holdings Ltd

Library of Congress Cataloging-in-Publication Data
Botting, Douglas
    Wild France : a traveller's guide / edited by Douglas Botting.
        224p. 21.0 x 14.9cm. — (Wild guides)
    Includes bibliographical references and index.
    ISBN 1-56656-333-X (pbk.)
    1. Natural history—France Guidebooks. 2. Natural areas—France Guidebooks. 3. France Guidebooks. I. Title. II Series: Wild guides (Interlink Books)
QH147.B68   1999
508.44—dc21   99-39121
                                                      CIP

Printed in Hong Kong

EDITOR: SIMON RIGGE
Deputy Editors: Lisa Cussans, Malcom Day, Nicholas Lim, Laura Smith-Spark, Sam Thorne
Picture Editor: Karin B. Hills
Art Direction & Book Design: Ivor Claydon, Bob Hook
Assistant Editors: Roger Boulanger, Sean Connolly, Judith Harte, Anita Peltonen, Chris Schüler, Caroline Smith
Picture Researchers: Eleanor Lines, Elizabeth Loving
Researcher & Marketing Assistant: Olivier Occelli
Senior Editorial Assistants: Sarah Bolton, Francisca Kellett
Editorial Assistants: Elodie Bonnet, James Moss, Katie Rigge, Tracey Stead, Sarah Tudge
Production Manager: Hugh Allan
Production Controllers: Rebecca Bone, Smita Dey
Line Illustrations: Syd Lewis
Cartographers: Swanston Graphics Ltd, Donna Dailey
Indexers: Indexing Specialists

Front cover: The rocky escarpments of the Dentelles de Montmirail loom over La Roque-Alric in Provence.

To order or request our complete catalog, please call us at **1-800-238-LINK** or write to:
Interlink Publishing
46 Crosby Street • Northampton, MA 01060
E-mail: interpg@aol.com
Website: www.interlinkbooks.com

THE GENERAL EDITOR

DOUGLAS BOTTING was born in London and educated at Oxford. He has travelled to Brazil, South Yemen, the Sahara, Arctic Siberia and to many European wild places. His travel books include *One Chilly Siberian Morning, Wilderness Europe* and *Rio de Janeiro*. He has recently written a biography of the author and conservationist Gerald Durrell.

CONTRIBUTORS

MICK HAMER wrote the chapters on Brittany and Normandy, the Alps, Central France, and the Loire and Burgundy. He is a journalist, writer and environmentalist and, as well as contributing to many national newspapers and magazines, has worked for several years for Friends of the Earth.

ROBIN NEILLANDS wrote the chapter on the Pyrenees. He is a journalist, travel writer and author of over 40 books. In his travels he has canoed down the Zambezi, cycled from Turkey to Jerusalem and walked across France from the English Channel to the Mediterranean.

ANDREW SANGER wrote the chapter on the Western Mediterranean. Having travelled world-wide, he settled for a number of years in Languedoc. He is the author of several travel books and a frequent contributor to the travel pages of many national newspapers.

KEITH SPENCE wrote the chapter on the Atlantic Coast and specializes in travel, the environment and conservation. A regular contributor to national newspapers and magazines, he is particularly concerned with increasing public interest in the environment through project work.

DAVID STUBBS wrote the chapter on the Eastern Mediterranean and Corsica. He is an ecologist who has been involved in European wildlife projects, particularly in France, and is now a consultant specializing in ecological surveys and wildlife habitat assessments. He is the author of several scientific papers and was the overall consultant for *Wild France*.

GILLIAN THOMAS wrote the chapter on the North-East. She is a travel writer and a regular contributor to national newspapers and magazines in Britain, and has worked for the BBC in Paris. She has long been concerned about environmental issues, on which she has written for *The Times Educational Supplement*.

CONTENTS

ABOUT THE SERIES

What would the world be, once bereft
Of wet and of wildness? Let them be
  left,
O let them be left, wildness and wet;
Long live the weeds and the wilderness
  yet.

Gerard Manley Hopkins: Inversnaid

These books are about those embattled refuges of wildness and wet: the wild places of Europe. But where, in this most densely populated sub-continent, do we find a truly wild place?

Ever since our Cro-Magnon ancestors began their forays into the virgin forests of Europe 40,000 years ago, the land and its creatures have been in retreat before *Homo sapiens*. Forests have been cleared, marshes drained and rivers straightened: even some of those landscapes that appear primordial are in fact the result of human activity. Heather-covered moorland in North Yorkshire and parched Andalusian desert have this in common: both were once covered by great forests which ancient settlers knocked flat.

What then remains that can be called wild? There are still a few areas in Europe that are untouched by man — places generally so unwelcoming either in terrain or in climate that man has not wanted to touch them at all. These are indisputably wild.

For some people, wildness suggests conflict with nature: a wild place is a part of the planet so savage and desolate that you risk your life whenever you venture into it. This is in part true but would limit the eligible places to the most impenetrable bog or highest mountain tops in the worst winter weather — a rather restricted view. Another much broader definition considers a wild place to be a part of the planet where living things can find a natural refuge from the influence of modern industrial society. By this definition a wild place is for wild life as well as that portmanteau figure referred to in these pages as the wild traveller: the hill walker, backpacker, bird-watcher, nature

lover, explorer, nomad, loner, mystic, masochist, *aficionado* of the great outdoors, or permutations of all these things.

This is the definition we have observed in selecting the wild places described in these books. Choosing them has not been easy. Even so, we hope the criterion has proved rigid enough to exclude purely pretty (though popular) countryside, and flexible enough to include the greener, gentler wild places, of great natural historical interest perhaps, as well as the starker, more savage ones where the wild explorers come into their own.

These are not guide-books in the conventional sense, for to describe every neck of the woods and twist of the trail throughout Europe would require a library of volumes. Nor are these books addressed to the technical specialist — the caver, diver, rock climber or cross-country skier, the orchid-hunter, lepidopterist or beetlemaniac — for such experts will have data of their own. They are books intended for the general outdoor traveller — including the expert outside his field of expertise (the orchid-hunter in a cave, the diver on a mountain top) — who wishes to scrutinize the range of wild places on offer in Europe, to learn a little more about them and to set about exploring them off the beaten track.

One of the great consolations in the preparation of these books has been to find that after 40,000 years of hunting, clearing, draining and ploughing, Cro-Magnon and their descendants have left so much of Europe that can still be defined as wild.

Douglas Botting

WILD FRANCE: AN INTRODUCTION

France is a country that has the best of both worlds: sophisticated civilization and vast expanses of wild terrain. In spite of being a thoroughly modern nation, with fast, efficient communications, it has preserved much of its traditional rural landscape. As everywhere in Europe, nature is continually retreating in the face of development, but in an area over twice as large as the United Kingdom, supporting roughly the same number of people, France still provides welcome respite for those in search of timeless countryside.

One of the great joys of France is the freedom to wander off into the wild places, to 'take to the *maquis*' and forget about mankind. To walk for hours through stately oak and beech forests or across Provençal hills cloaked in thorny *garrigue* is to experience an environment that has existed for hundreds of years. Wild places, be they mountain tops or marshes, are the lungs of a nation. They provide space and tranquillity. They offer a sense of balance and perspective, and the satisfaction of knowing that, for all the centuries of human activity, nature still thrives as abundantly as ever.

There are few places that are totally natural or free of any history of human influence. All the great forests have been managed for timber or hunting or even for browsing livestock. Wetlands are controlled, grasslands cut or grazed, crops are grown, but all in a sustainable, small-scale manner. For the most part French farmers have retained their ancestral landscape of small fields, thick hedges, wooded hills and meandering rivers. Their philosophy is one of tradition, of harmonious coexistence. From the *bocage* country of Normandy, across sparsely populated central France to the Mediterranean hills of cork-oak forests and olive groves, you still get the impression that nature reigns and man simply harvests.

Elsewhere, however, are to be found huge prairie fields, the intensive farmland of the later 20th century. Here it is man who dominates and nature that is subdued. But even in the industrial north-east or in the heavily cultivated Paris and Aquitaine basins, you can still find green oases where wildlife flourishes in exuberant defiance of the surrounding monocultures.

After hours of monotony driving south through the cereal belt of the north-east, you arrive at Laon, a pleasant town backed by wooded hills and heathlands, the beginning of the old country. Beyond these hills, the steep escarpments of the Oise valley are the hunting ground of red kites and buzzards. Similarly, the dense, broad-leaved woodland of the Chevreuse valley comes as a pleasant surprise after a train journey through Paris' southern suburbs. Deer and boar still roam these rolling hills.

Sometimes the contrasts are even sharper. On one occasion I stopped at a motorway rest area, somewhere between Auxerre and Beaune. At the edge of the car park, I climbed over a fence and immediately found myself in an ancient flower meadow. A pale blue carpet of pasque flowers spread before me and Duke of Burgundy fritillary butterflies were everywhere on the wing. Yellowhammers and lesser whitethroat sang from nearby bushes and the patchwork countryside stretched out across the valley as far as one could see.

Nature should not be hurried. All you need is a map, binoculars and a willingness to use your full range of senses. Wilderness is not an empty view. Everywhere the landscape is a mixture of innumerable sights, sounds and smells. In the intense heat of the Provençal summer, the scenery fades into a hazy blur, but all around is the incessant rasping call of the *cigale* (cicada), and the air is full of the heady aromas of myrtle, lavender and thyme. In the great high forests further north, the rich leaf litter gives off a distinctive musty smell and on calm days the tall columns of mature trees seem to exude a silent force. You are completely dominated by the living forest, yet there may be no active sign of life. You can walk for ages without seeing a bird. But

WILD FRANCE

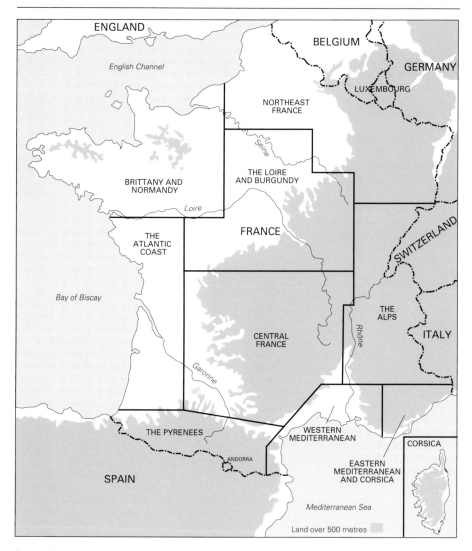

listen closely — far away a woodpecker may be tapping at some dead bough, and a thin, almost inaudible high-pitched note tells you a goldcrest or a treecreeper is nearby.

From the subtle charms of lowland rural areas, or the tranquillity of the meandering Loire, to the Atlantic coast lashed by the elements, or the high mountains fashioned from millennia of glacial activity or volcanic eruptions, France has an impressive list of wild places to offer. Every region has its special character and notable features. Each has its devotees, notably the contributors to this book.

We are not offering you an encyclopaedic coverage of all France's wild areas. There are simply too many for any reasonable volume to do justice to them all. Moreover, despite the ravages of modern life, there are still vast areas for the enquiring traveller to discover independently. What we want is to give you a taste of the natural charm of our chosen regions and, we hope, a desire to explore them for yourself.

6

THE KEY TO FRANCE'S WILD PLACES

WILD HABITATS

An appreciation of habitats is essential for anyone interested in experiencing a whole range of wild species in their natural environment. In turn, to understand the nature and distribution of the various major wildlife habitats of France, it is necessary to look at the principal influencing factors of climate and geology.

A simplified survey shows a country composed of ancient rocks, usually forming mountain chains, which, in the case of the Massif Central, are topped with volcanoes. Younger rocks make up the Alps, Jura and Pyrenees, and between all these lie the sedimentary basins and transition zones such as Languedoc and Burgundy.

Contrasts in vegetation can be traced to differences in substrate, or underlying rock type. In some areas this substrate is composed of sedimentary rocks which were formed under the sea. These chalk and limestone areas support a typically calcium-loving vegetation such as ash, wych elm and field maple, dogwood, wayfaring tree and spindle. In other areas siliceous soils, formed from crystalline and metamorphic rocks, favour a calcium-avoiding flora, such as the ericaceous heaths in the north and cork-oak and maritime-pine forests in the south.

Over these foundations lies a network of riverine or glacial river valleys, the latter group including some of the great names of Europe: Seine, Loire, Rhône and part of the Rhine. Further variation has been created over the millennia by the actions of volcanoes and glaciers in the mountain regions and by sea and wind erosion around France's 5,500 km (3,500 miles) of coastline.

France lies at the cross-roads of three principal European climatic belts. The west and north are influenced by the moist and cool Atlantic climate, which can extend up to 150 km (90 miles) from the coast. In the south and extending up the Rhône valley into central France is the Mediterranean belt, characterized by hot dry summers and plenty of sunshine throughout the year. In the north-east continental climatic influences take over, producing a huge temperature range between summer and winter, with all seasons being predominantly dry.

Mountains and uplands: In mountain regions the different altitudes and aspects of the slopes support vegetation characteristic of different climatic types, thereby often providing isolated refuges for rare Arctic-Alpine species such as marmot, ibex, chamois, alpine accentor and snow finch. In the Cévennes and in some of the Préalpes, or Alpine foothills in Haute-Provence, the southern slopes endure hot Mediterranean conditions and are clothed with evergreen-oak and pine forests, while the shaded northern slopes are more typical of cooler temperate climes and support beech and deciduous oak forests.

Forest and shrubland: France is one of Europe's most wooded countries, with trees covering some 27% of the total land area. Beech and oak dominate across vast areas, while in the north-east hornbeam is very common. The Jura and Alps support some of the finest fir forests, while the low-lying Landes de Gascogne are the home of the stone pine. In the Mediterranean south there are still some fine evergreen-oak and cork-oak forests. Cork oaks do not provide a dense canopy, so plenty of light is able to penetrate through to the ground and promote a vigorous field and shrub layer known as *maquis*. Over the years, these areas have been ravaged by fierce fires that spread rapidly across large stretches of countryside, with the result that a drier scrub vegetation known as *garrigue* has become established. Forest of one kind or another shelters much of France's rich mammal fauna, from the rare Pyrenean brown bear to the widespread and universally hunted wild boar. The forest is home to innumerable birds, including birds of prey such as goshawk and honey buzzard.

Wetlands: The wetlands, including lakes, swamps, marshes and rivers, are of great interest for the richness of their plant and bird life. The Camargue with its marvellous flocks of flamingoes is probably the most famous, but the regional nature parks of Brotonne, Normandie-Maine and Armorique also offer the possibility of great discoveries.

Coast and islands: The French coast, with its sea shores, estuaries, cliffs and sand dunes, offers a variety of spectacular wild places, some of them — for example, the Baie du Mont St-Michel — internationally renowned. Off the wild Brittany coastline lie islands such as the Sept Iles and the Iles d'Ouessant, which are home to impressive colonies of breeding birds including choughs and fulmar as well as migratory species such as ring ouzel and wheatear.

PROTECTED AREAS AND NATURE CONSERVATION

Nature conservation has a long history in France and indeed the French claim to have created the first reserve in the world. As early as 1861 a decree was passed confirming the protected status of approximately 125 hectares (308 acres) of the Forêt de Fontainebleau. Nowadays large parts of the French countryside are categorized under different forms of protected area status and it is useful to have a rough idea of the meaning of each.

Parcs nationaux: These are by far the largest protected areas in the country, usually covering several tens of thousands of acres. Seven have been created to date and with the exception of the smallest, Port-Cros island off Hyères, and the newest, on Guadeloupe, they are all located on the French mainland in remote mountain areas with few inhabitants. National parks are decreed by the state and consist of two zones: a central zone and a buffer zone. Within the central zone, all plant and animal life is strictly protected. The buffer zone is not governed by such stringent laws, but there is an emphasis on integrating local culture and tourism with the preservation of the natural environment.

Parcs naturels régionaux: More numerous than national parks — there are currently 36 regional nature parks in France — and providing less stringent protection for wildlife (hunting and fishing are generally allowed), these parks afford some control over development. They are generally formed at the initiative of local communities and interested conservation groups.

Réserves naturelles: Nature reserves are decreed by the state in order to protect important and fragile natural sites or threatened species of flora and fauna. There are more than 140 in France covering about 146,000 ha (361,000 acres). Most can be visited and several have specially marked nature trails.

Arrêté de biotope: Sites which provide critically important habitats for protected species can be notified as 'Arrêté de Biotope'. The initiative usually comes from local conservation groups. Such sites are characteristically small, well-defined areas which do not require management or supervision.

Sites naturels classés: This is one of the original forms of protection decreed by the state to ensure protection for sites of outstanding natural beauty which can range in magnitude from Mont Blanc to a single specimen tree. It is unusual for this form of protection to be accorded for a site's ecological value and it is principally used as a landscape designation. There are some 3,000 classified natural sites in France.

Le Conservatoire du littoral: In 1975 the Conservatoire was established to protect sites of outstanding natural beauty along the coast and around inland lakes. Relying on public funds and voluntary contributions, the organization has to date acquired more than 400 sites covering a total of 54,000 ha (133,000 acres). Footpaths leading into these areas are marked by the Conservatoire's blue-thistle emblem, the *chardon bleu des dunes*.

While on paper much of France's rich natural store of flora and fauna is protected, the lack of a statutory authority charged with the enforcement of protection measures means that these laws are not always effective. The success of conservation depends somewhat precariously on the devoted but all too often underfunded efforts of voluntary organizations, and on support from the international conservation community.

The landscape of nature conservation has improved to some extent in recent years, the French government responding to the ever-increasing urgency of environmental issues (and to mounting international and European pressure to address these issues more effectively) by redefining and strengthening the role of national and regional departments within the Ministry of the Environment.

However, progress is still slow. Divisions within the government on green issues combined with the strength of lobbies representing industry and commerce and the popularity of hunting in France ensure that the environment is still vulnerable to the many damaging effects of modern life.

Fortunately, areas of France and species of fauna in need of special protection are now also covered by international classifications, the most important of which are: ZICO (an EU directive establishing special protection for birds), Ramsar (an international wetlands convention), Man and the Biosphere (MAB: a UNESCO programme of research and training intended to develop the basis, within the natural and social sciences, for rational use and conservation of the resources of the biosphere) and World Heritage Site (a UNESCO convention for preserving the world's cultural and natural heritage).

EXPLORING WILD FRANCE

France is a very accessible country and is criss-crossed by innumerable tracks and paths. Many of these routes lead to isolated cultivations, while others just trail off into the forest or *maquis* for no obvious reason. For the most part they need to be searched out, as they are not marked as public footpaths.

For the serious walker, France has an excellent network of marked long-distance paths, the Grandes Randonnées, or GRs. They provide one of the best ways to penetrate the soul of rural France. The Fédération Française de la Randonnée Pédestre (see USEFUL ADDRESSES, p215) publishes a range of topographic guides full of practical information about the GRs. For guides and advice on how to prepare for long walks you can also contact the Centre d'Information Sentiers et Randonnée (see USEFUL ADDRESSES, p215). There are also several rambling associations which organize group excursions along the GRs.

Walking is not the only means of experiencing wild France at close quarters. There are associations which organize expeditions for cyclists, horse-riders, cross-country skiers, canoeists and the less energetic who wish to take canal and river tours by barge. There are also many exciting sailing itineraries along the French coast, including one along the Brittany coastline and another around Corsica.

RULES OF THE WILD

The Mountain code: learn the use of map and compass. Know the weather signs and local forecast. Plan a route within your capabilities and leave time to get down before dark. Know simple first aid and the symptoms of exposure. Know the mountain distress signals. To give a signal for help, give six blasts on a whistle and/or six flashes with a torch. Wait one minute. Repeat. To answer a signal for help, give three blasts on a whistle and/or three flashes with a torch. Repeat. Take a bearing on the signal and move towards it while continuing to signal. Never go alone. Leave written word of your route and estimated time of return, and report when you get back. Take warm/weatherproof clothing and survival bag. Take map and compass, torch and food. Wear climbing boots. Stay alert all day. Be prepared to turn back if the weather deteriorates or if any member of your party is becoming slow or exhausted. *If there is snow on the hills*, always have an ice-axe for each person. Carry a climbing rope. Know the correct use of rope and ice-axe. Learn to recognize dangerous snow slopes. Lack of space precludes a detailed description of equipment and techniques recommended for travellers in wild places. If in doubt refer to one of the many manuals on the subject.

TO THE READER

Organization: Each chapter is divided into exploration zones containing a first-person narrative description, followed by a fact-pack which gives practical information backed up with postal, e-mail and web-site addresses, telephone and fax numbers and lists of maps and further reading. This hybrid arrangement avoids cluttering the author's personal narrative with guide-book detail, but at the same time ensures that you can find practical references instantly when you want them.

Eagle symbols: The eagle symbols used in this book indicate the wildness quality of the exploration zone to which they refer. This scale is based on a number of factors, including remoteness, ruggedness, spaciousness, uniqueness, wildlife interest, natural beauty and the author's subjective reactions. Three eagles is the highest rating, no eagles the lowest.

Updating: We would welcome readers' comments and corrections for incorporation in subsequent editions. Please write to The Editor, Wild Guides, Sheldrake Press, 188 Cavendish Road, London SW12 0DA, or send an e-mail to: mail@sheldrakepress.demon.co.uk.

Non-liability: Both writers and publishers have gone to great pains to point out the hazards that may confront the traveller in certain places described in *Wild France*. We cannot under any circumstances accept any liability for mishap, loss or injury sustained by any person venturing into any of the wild places listed in this book.

Maps: We recommend the Michelin 1:200,000 *Tourist and Motoring Atlas of France* for initial route-planning and orientation. The small-scale IGN *Serie Verte* 1:100,000 maps listed in the fact-packs for individual exploration zones are useful for working out how to approach an area. Once you get in closer you will need the IGN 1:50,000 or 1:25,000 maps listed in each fact-pack; the suffix OT or ET refers to *ouest* (west) or *est* (east). Contact IGN headquarters (see USEFUL ADDRESSES, p215) for stockists.

CHAPTER 1

Brittany and Normandy

I have been to many parts of Brittany and Normandy over the years. On each occasion I explored particular places: *calvados* country, the Côte d'Emeraude west of Mont St-Michel and the megaliths at Carnac. Until now I had never made the journey west in one go, from Paris through Normandy and Brittany to Finistère (the 'end of the earth'), although I had made the parallel journey from London to the West Country (and Land's End) on dozens of occasions. The cultural links between England's West Country and Brittany and Normandy are well known, but making this trip for the first time, I was surprised by the physical similarities of their coasts and hinterlands.

First come the chalky hills of Normandy and, meandering through them, the River Seine, which emerges into the English Channel at Le Havre. On a chalk plateau, enclosed on three sides by one of the great bends in the river, is the Forêt de Brotonne, which provides a rare glimpse of how the area must have looked in its pristine state.

As you progress westward, you come to the *bocage* (copse) country, with hedged fields reminiscent of Hampshire and Dorset, although less affected by mechanized farming. Near Alençon the rocks change from chalk to granite, a transition that in Britain occurs around Somerset and Devon. Once part of a great mountain range, these ancient granite rocks have been eroded over millions of years into gently rolling hills.

The Parc Naturel Régional de Brotonne was created in 1974 to protect the lower reaches of the Seine from the menace of industrial pollution. The park is dominated by Atlantic beech woodland.

They are the source of the Caen stone from which many English cathedrals were built after the Norman Conquest. Now they are given over to orchards and pasture. South of the city of Caen, around Thury-Harcourt, the rocky landscape has been dubbed Suisse Normande; its rugged outcrops offer an exciting challenge to climbers.

To experience really wild countryside, however, you must continue into Brittany. This is the western extremity of France, a jagged finger pointing, like Cornwall, far out into the Atlantic.

In Roman times Brittany was known as Armorica. The name comes from the Celtic word 'Armor', which means 'the country by the sea'. The Celtic name for the forested interior was 'Argoat' ('the country of the wood'). As recently as a hundred years ago, the Argoat woods stretched from Rennes in the east to Carhaix in the west. This large tract of land sheltered many wild animals — the last wolf in Brittany was killed as late as 1891. Most of the forest has since been felled, for timber or farmland, but there are still a few wild places to be found. Some of the upland moors, such as the Monts d'Arrée, remain bare and uncultivated, and two fragments survive of the ancient oak and beech forest of Argoat: Huelgoat, south of Morlaix, and the Paimpont to the south-west of Rennes. The Paimpont was once known as the Forêt de Brocéliande, and it was here that Chrétien de Troyes, one of the greatest French medieval poets, situated Merlin's lair in his series of chivalrous epics about King Arthur and the knights of the round table.

Numerous rivers cut valleys through the granite plateau of Argoat on their way down to the coast, where they form deep estuaries. The rise in water levels since the last Ice Age has flooded the lower valleys, and the inlets, known as *abers*, provide safe harbours for Brittany's many fishing fleets.

The tide plays an important role in the life of coastal Brittany, which has the largest variation between high and low water in western Europe. In the Baie de Mont St-Michel the water level difference can reach 50 feet (15 metres): the sight of the incoming sea racing over several miles of sand is spectacular. Along this coast the sea used to power many tidal mills, and their ruins are a common sight.

There are many birds still to be seen on these westerly coasts. Choughs for example, now rare in Britain and much reduced in Normandy, are comparatively common in Brittany. They even have a role in the Arthurian legend. According to tradition, when Arthur returns to resume his rightful crown, it will be in the form of a chough.

The Atlantic salmon is still found in unpolluted rivers.

GETTING THERE

By air: international airports at Le Havre, T: 02 35 54 65 00, Rennes, T: 02 99 29 60 00, and Nantes, T: 02 40 84 80 00. Internal flights to Brest, Caen, Lorient, Quimper and Rouen. Contact Air France, T: 08 02 80 28 02, www.airfrance.com, or the French airports web-site: www.aeroport.fr.

By sea: there is an enormous choice of cross-Channel services from England to Normandy and Brittany. P&O Stena Line, T: 02 35 06 39 03, www.postena.com, has a Newhaven-Dieppe service. Brittany Ferries, T: 08 03 82 88 28, www.brittany-ferries.com, has Poole-Cherbourg, Portsmouth-Ouistreham/St-Malo and Plymouth/Cork-Roscoff services. P&O European Ferries, T: 08 03 01 30 13, www.poef.com, has Portsmouth-Cherbourg/Le Havre services. Irish Ferries, T: 02 33 23 44 44, www.irish-ferries.ie, links Rosslare in Ireland with Cherbourg and Roscoff. Condor Ferries, T: 02 99 20 03 00, www.condor ferries.co.uk, and Emeraude Lines, T: 02 99 40 48 40, www.emeraudelines.com, have frequent services from the Channel Islands to St-Malo.

By car: most areas of interest are within easy driving distance from the Channel ports. From Paris, motorists have a hefty drive up A11 to Rennes and Nantes, A13 to Rouen and Caen or N12 towards Alençon.

By rail: TGV services from Paris to Rennes, Brest, Quimper (in Brittany), Rouen, Le Havre, Cherbourg (in Normandy), Nantes and St-Nazaire. Trains to Brittany leave from Paris-Gare Montparnasse; to Normandy from Paris-Gare St-Lazare. Contact SNCF, T: 08 36 35 35 35 (French)/39 (English), www.sncf.fr.

By bus: Eurolines, T: 08 36 69 51 51, www.eurolines.fr, has services to Rennes, Le Mans and Nantes. Tourist offices will provide local travel information.

WHEN TO GO

Brittany and Normandy are extremely popular summer destinations but are relatively quiet for much of the rest of the year when the weather is fairly cold, damp and overcast. In winter, there is a profusion of wildfowl around the coast, offering excellent bird-watching opportunities.

WHERE TO STAY

There is a wide range of accommodation in the area, mainly concentrated around the coast; local tourist offices provide brochures and lists. Advance bookings are recommended in summer. See USEFUL ADDRESSES (p215) for a list of national accommodation agencies.

ACTIVITIES

Walking: the area is good walking country, bisected by numerous footpaths (long-distance or otherwise); waterproof clothing is advisable.

Cycling: the Fédération Française de Cyclotourisme (see USEFUL ADDRESSES, p215) publishes *La France à Vélo* series, which includes *Bretagne* and *Normandie*. Formules Bretagne in Paris, T: 01 53 63 11 53, offers several itineraries for cycle tours in Brittany. For long-distance cycle routes, see IGN map No. 906, *VTT & Randonnées Cyclos*.

Riding: the Fédération Française d'Equitation (see USEFUL ADDRESSES, p215) publishes a free comprehensive booklet, *Tourisme Equestre en France*, listing clubs and stables. Contact the Association Régionale de Tourisme Equestre for Brittany, 33 rue Laënnec, 29710 Ploneis, T: 02 98 91 02 02, F: 02 98 91 16 56; for Basse-Normandie, Le Presbytère, 50160 Breton-Ville, T: 02 33 56 76 84, F: 02 33 56 76 84; and for Haute-Normandie, 381 rue Pierre et Marie Curie, 76480 Duclair, T/F: 02 35 37 09 12.

Climbing: there are climbing opportunities around Thury-Harcourt in Suisse Normande, south of Caen. Further information from the Thury-Harcourt tourist office, 2 pl St-Sauveur, T: 02 31 79 70 45.

Fishing: salmon, trout and pike are just some of the fish found in Brittany's rivers. Contact Le Conseil Supérieur de la Pêche (see USEFUL ADDRESSES, p215).

Watersports: the Centre Régional de Nautisme in Granville (Normandy), T: 02 33 91 22 60, is one of the largest centres in France for sailing, wind-surfing and other watersports.

Adventure holidays: Loisirs Accueil (see USEFUL ADDRESSES, p215) provides information and booking services for outdoor holidays in Brittany, while the Union Nationale des Centres Sportifs de Plein Air (see USEFUL ADDRESSES) offers activity holidays at several centres in Brittany and Normandy.

FURTHER INFORMATION

Tourist offices: Comité Régional du Tourisme de Bretagne, 1 rue Raoul Ponchon, 35069 Rennes, T: 02 99 36 15 15, F: 02 99 28 44 40, www.brittanytourism.com.

CRT de Normandie, 14 rue Charles Corbeau, 27000 Evreux, T: 02 32 33 79 00, F: 02 32 31 19 04, www.normandy-tourism.org.

CRT de Pays de la Loire (see p145).

Maison de la France web-site, www.maison-de-la-france.fr, has links to all local tourist offices.

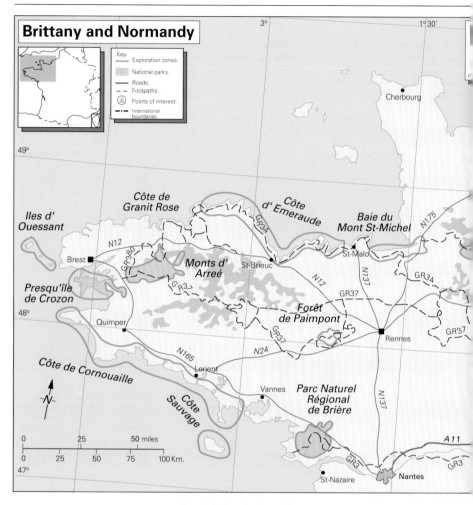

Brittany and Normandy

Key
— Exploration zones.
⬜ National parks.
— Roads.
– – Footpaths.
Ⓐ Points of interest.
–••– International boundaries.

Cherbourg

49°

Côte de Granit Rose

Iles d' Ouessant

Côte d' Emeraude

Baie du Mont St-Michel

N175

N12

Brest

GR380

Monts d' Arreé

St-Brieuc

St-Malo

N137

GR34

GR34

Presqu'île de Crozon

GR37

N12

GR37

48°

Quimper

Forêt de Paimpont

Rennes

GR37

GR37

N165

N24

Côte de Cornouaille

Lorient

Vannes

Parc Naturel Régional de Brière

N137

–N–

Côte Sauvage

A11

0   25   50 miles

0   25   50   75   100 Km.

GR3

GR3

47°

St-Nazaire

Nantes

Forêt de Brotonne & Marais Vernier

A mixture of woodland and marsh lying north-east of Caen; parc naturel regional 65,500 ha (162,000 acres)

I first saw the Forêt de Brotonne as a schoolboy, back in 1962. Spring was late that year and the trees were not fully in leaf. The family I was
14

staying with thought I would be disappointed, but my memory of the forest — of the young trees sprouting their first milk-green leaves — is still vivid.

Twenty-seven years later I went back. This time spring was early, the foliage more advanced. Of the mature trees, the chestnuts and silver birches were the first to come into leaf. Climbing a small hill above the forest, I could look down over the tree-tops and pick out the silver birches, showing green amid leafless oaks and beeches.

The forest is home to a variety

of wildlife, including foxes and deer. However, even before the trees are fully in leaf it is difficult to see any sign of these mammals, possibly because they have been driven to seek cover by the hunts that regularly beat the thicket.

The meandering river Seine encloses the forest on three sides. Further downstream, the river's next bend encircles the horseshoe-shaped Marais Vernier. This is a world apart from its surroundings: 2,000 ha (4,900 acres) of marshland dissected by drainage channels

and dykes. These waterways are lined by alders and willows and a variety of herbaceous plants, such as marsh valerian and flowering rush. Shady copses also provide ideal conditions for the spectacular royal fern.

In this botanical paradise lurks a wealth of wild animals. Frogs and viperine snakes inhabit the tussocky mounds of rushes, and there are many species of aquatic birds. Four pairs of white storks breed here, and black storks can be seen on migration during August. The corncrake also survives here, a bird now very rare in Normandy though only a few decades ago its persistent rasping call was one of the traditional night-time sounds of the *bocage*.

Before you go *Maps:* IGN 1:100,000 Nos. 7 and 8; IGN 1:25,000 Nos. 1811 OT & ET and 1911 OT. **Getting there** *By car:* the A13 skirts the southern bank of the Seine, D982 the northern. If you arrive on D982 take D490, which crosses the Pont de Brotonne and continues into the forest; from A13 take D313 or D139. For Marais Vernier, take A131 off A13 and turn left on D103, which cuts straight through the marsh. *By rail:* SNCF Paris-Le Havre service stops at Rouen and Yvetot; Evreux-Honfleur service stops at Pont-Audemer. *By bus:* CNA, T: 02 35 52 92 00, has buses from Rouen to Caudebec and Caudebec to Le Havre. Société Joffet, T: 02 35 62 15 21, has Rouen-Pont-Audemer service. **Where to stay:** Rouen is the best of the larger towns and has an interesting old centre. Other options are Caudebec-en-Caux, Duclair and La Mailleraye-sur-Seine, or the pleasant old town of Pont-Audemer, about 10 km (6 miles) from the forest. **Activities** *Walking:* Grande Randonnée routes traverse the forest (GR2, GR211, GR23 and GR23A); GR23 also skirts the Marais Vernier. Local tourist offices have details of more leisurely walks. *Cycling:* bicycles can be hired in many local villages and are an ideal way to explore the area. The Eventail de Seine-Maritime long-distance route passes through the park. *Riding:* try the Association d'Attelage de Brotonne in Notre-Dame-de-Bliquetuit, T: 02 35 37 10 24, or Les Attelages du Marais-Vernier in Le Marais-Vernier, T: 02 32 42 93 89. *Field studies:* CEDENA, T: 02 32 56 94 87, organizes nature walks and camping trips in summer. **Further information** *Tourist offices:* Caudebec-en-Caux, quai Guilbaud, T: 02 35 96 20 65; Pont-Audemer, pl Maubert, T: 02 32 41 08 21; Rouen, pl de la Cathédrale, T: 02 32 08 32 40, www.mairie-rouen.fr. *Park offices:* 76940 Notre-Dame-de-Bliquetuit, BP 13, T: 02 35 37 23 16, www.parcs-naturels-regionaux.tm.fr.

Office Nationale des Forêts (ONF), chemin de la Bretèque, Houppeville, 76230 Bois-Guillaume, T: 02 35 12 24 24.

Parc Régional Normandie-Maine

Region of hedged fields, orchards and forested hills; parc naturel régional *ZICO* *45,200 ha (112,000 acres)*

The park of Normandie-Maine begins where the chalk of the Parisian basin ends, close to the towns of Alençon and Argentan. The landscape is varied, a mixture of ridges crowned with forests and cultivated valleys reminiscent of the Dorset countryside. The rolling farmland is mostly small hedged fields, source of the region's famous butter and cheese, and orchards, which produce cider, *calvados* (apple brandy) and *poiré* (a perry).

About a fifth of the park is upland woods: the main forests are the Ecouves, Andaines and Monaye. Deciduous trees include oak and beech, pines have been planted on poorer soils and there are coppices of trees such as hazel and ash. In the south-west of Ecouves, the Butte-Chamont (378 m/1,240 ft) offers beautiful views.

Before you go *Maps*: IGN 1:100,000 Nos. 17-19; IGN 1:25,000 (OT & ET) Nos. 1515-16, 1615-16 and 1715-16.
Getting there *By car:* N12 runs from Paris to Alençon. *By rail:* from Paris-Gare Montparnasse to Alençon, Argentan, Briouze and Flers-de-l'Orne via Le Mans, or Paris-Vaugirard direct to Briouze. *By bus:* buses run between Briouze and Bagnoles, Argentan and Flers, and from railway stations to towns throughout the park.
Where to stay: the spa town of Bagnoles-de-l'Orne lies in the

centre of this sprawling park, but it's on the expensive side. Other convenient bases are Alençon, Sées, Carrouges, La Ferté-Macé or Domfront.
Activities *Walking:* GR22 and GR36 cut through the park. Details of less strenuous walks from the park office. *Cycling:* rent bicycles at railway stations of Alençon, Argentan, Bagnoles, Flers and Sées. The Paris-Brest, Randonnée des Avaloirs and Ecureuils du Domfrontais long-distance routes pass through the park. *Canoeing:* the park's 2 rivers,

the Mayenne and Varenne, are good for canoeing. Contact Alençon Canoë-Kayak Club, T: 02 33 32 03 06/02 33 26 13 96.
Outdoor sports: contact the Office Municipal des Sports in Alençon, T: 02 33 26 50 05.
Further information *Tourist offices:* Alençon, pl Lamagdaleine, T: 02 33 26 11 36, www.ville-alencon.fr; Bagnoles-de-l'Orne, pl du Marché, T: 02 33 37 85 66; Domfront, 12 pl de la Roirie, T: 02 33 38 53 97. *Park office:* Le Chapitre, BP 05, 61320 Carrouges, T: 02 33 81 75 75.

Baie du Mont St-Michel

Tidal bay enclosing a wetland environment of international importance
Ramsar, ZICO, World Heritage Site

The bay of Mont St-Michel lies at the bottom of the Cotentin Peninsula. It is best known for the town of the same name, which perches on a rocky outcrop in the middle of the bay and can be reached only at low tide. This beautiful complex of Romanesque and Gothic buildings, clustered beneath the soaring spire of the medieval abbey, attracts hordes of tourists, especially in summer.

The crowds can be avoided by withdrawing to the landlocked cliffs on the edge of the

bay, or to the intervening expanse of salt-marsh, which lies within sight of the mount.

The marshes are bisected by an old sea wall. On the landward side of the wall is an area of reclaimed marshland known as *les polders*. On the seaward side you encounter a landscape of grass and sea lavender. Farther out are mud-flats which, in spring, teem with busy colonies of oystercatchers, shelduck and curlew.

The best time to visit, though, is in winter, before the wading birds migrate to their summer breeding grounds. There are estimated to be up to 150,000 birds here at this time of year, around half of them migrants. Huge flocks of waders, especially lapwing, golden plover, gulls and ducks, colonize the bay, and in hard winters rare visitors such as whooper swans can be seen. The relative winter warmth also attracts the white-fronted goose, which the French know as the *oie rieuse*, or 'laughing goose'. The bay is a major breeding ground for shelduck, while the island of Landes, at the western end, is Brittany's only nesting place for cormorants. This wealth of bird life attracts predators, including buzzards and peregrine falcons.

The best time to see many of the birds is when the tide comes in. Because of the huge variation between high and low tide marks in the bay, the water sweeps across the flats with such terrific force that the wading birds take to the air *en masse*. These vast flocks wheeling and diving in perfect unison are one of Brittany's great natural spectacles.

The turnstone is a common migrant wader on the rocky shores of the Atlantic coast.

BEFORE YOU GO
Maps: IGN 1:100,000 No. 16; IGN 1:25,000 No. 1215.

GETTING THERE
By sea: a convenient crossing is Portsmouth to St-Malo on Brittany Ferries (see p13).
By car: take N12 followed by N176 from Paris.
By rail: infrequent trains to Pontorson-Mont St Michel from Paris-Gare St-Lazare via Lison or Caen, or from Gare Montparnasse via Folligny.
By bus: a connecting bus runs from Pontorson railway station to Mont St-Michel.
By bicycle: there is a Paris-Mont St-Michel cycle route.

WHERE TO STAY
The most convenient towns are Pontorson and Dol; Hôtel de France in Pontorson, T: 02 33 60 29 17, is good value for money. Camping du Mont St-Michel, T: 02 33 60 09 33, is 2 km (1½ miles) from the mount. Other options include St-Malo, Avranches, St-Jean-le-Thomas, Fougères and St-Lô.

ACTIVITIES
Walking: GR22, GR34 and GR223 pass through the area, the first 2 along the sea wall.
Cycling: this flat marshy area is ideal for cycling; rent bicycles at the railway stations in Pontorson and Dol.
Riding: treks organized by Annette and Jean-Pierre Jouvin in St-Senier-sous-Avranches, T/F: 02 33 60 52 67. For carriage and boat trips from Pontorson to Mont St-Michel, T: 02 33 60 68 00.

Watersports: for sailing excursions contact the Ecole de Voile in Jullouville, T: 02 33 51 44 34, or the Centre Régional Nautique in Granville (see p13). Canoeing trips can be organized through Canoë-Club d'Avranches, T: 02 33 68 19 15.

FURTHER INFORMATION
Tourist offices: Avranches, 2 rue du Général de Gaulle, T: 02 33 58 00 22; Dol, 3 grande rue des Stuarts, T: 02 99 48 15 37; Mont St-Michel, Corps de Garde des Bourgeois, T: 02 33 60 14 30; Pontorson, pl de l'Eglise, T: 02 33 60 20 65; St-Lô, pl du Général de Gaulle, T: 02 33 05 02 09; St-Malo, espl St-Vincent, T: 02 99 56 64 48.
 Maisons de la Baie at Vivier-sur-Mer, T: 02 99 48 84 38, and Courtils, T: 02 33 89 66 00.

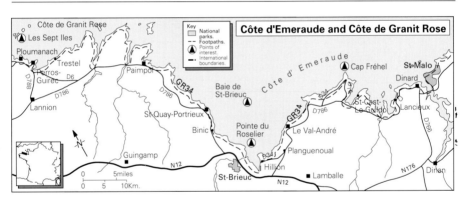

Côte d'Emeraude and Côte de Granit Rose

Côte d'Emeraude & Côte de Granit Rose

Brittany's dramatic northern coastline
ZICO

The port of St-Brieuc lies between two of the best-known ranges of cliffs in Brittany. To the east, the Côte d'Emeraude ('emerald coast') runs towards Dinard and St-Malo. Its most northerly point is Cap Fréhel, a headland jutting out into the English Channel. The view from here is spectacular — on clear days you can see the Channel Islands. To the west, the Côte de Granit Rose ('pink granite coast') stretches beyond the Pointe du Roselier and up to Perros-Guirec. At sunset, the glister of the pink granite cliffs is mesmerizing, especially when a slight haze reddens the setting sun.

 The road out of St-Brieuc west to the coastal footpath is not particularly alluring. It starts by following a long line of suburban villas, narrows, then descends quite steeply between two hedges to reach the first Grande Randonnée signpost. At the bottom of the hill lies the Gouet estuary. The path runs alongside the river then ascends to the coastal cliffs. At last, maritime Brittany opens up before you. There are good views across the Baie de St-Brieuc. If you come past when the tide is out you can walk down on to the beach, which is covered with an array of shellfish: cockles (gathered by local residents), clams, scallops, whelks and oysters, as well as sea lettuce and wrack.

The well-trodden coastal path eventually breaks free of the seaside suburbs near the Pointe du Roselier. On this point stands a curious stone furnace, once used to warm up cannonballs for the guns guarding the entrance to the estuary. From here, on a clear day, you have a good view across the bay to Cap Fréhel, the northernmost headland of the Côte d'Emeraude, and beyond: a great place from which to see the tide race in.

Cap Fréhel is also a bird reserve: fulmars and guillemots nest on the cliff ledges; along the coastal paths you can see skylarks, chats and, in summer, swallows. Along the cliff-tops the trees are covered in remarkable encrustations of lichen. The interior of the Cap Fréhel reserve is a diverse heathland, home to most of the small mammals known in Brittany; among the birds is that characteristic denizen of heaths, the Dartford warbler. Through the seasons the vegetation displays ever-changing masses of colour, which reach a peak in late summer.

Lying off this dramatic coastline, near Perros-Guirec, is the bird reserve of Les Sept Iles (actually five islands and a collection of miscellaneous rocks). Only the largest of the islands, the Ile aux Moines ('monks' island'), is open to the public, but it affords distant views of the colonies of gulls, guillemots, cormorants and puffins and the only gannet colony in France. You might glimpse a razorbill (*petit pingouin*) or, on the slabs of rock, a few grey seals at rest.

BEFORE YOU GO
Maps: IGN 1:100,000 Nos. 13, 14 and 16; IGN 1:25,000 Nos. 0515 & 0615 ET, 0714 & 0814 OT, 0916, and 1016 & 1116 ET.

GETTING THERE
By sea: the most convenient ferry crossings are run by Brittany Ferries – from Portsmouth to St-Malo (at the eastern end) or from Plymouth to Roscoff (at the western end). Irish Ferries has a Rosslare-Roscoff service (see p13).
By car: D786 more or less follows Brittany's northern coastline; a detour up D34 to Cap Fréhel is rewarding.
By rail: TGV services run from Paris-Gare Montparnasse to Rennes, Lamballe, St-Brieuc, Guingamp and Plouret-Trégor. Connecting trains link Rennes with Dol and St-Malo, while a local service runs from Dol to Dinan and Lamballe.
By bus: most places on the north coast can be reached by buses, which connect with trains at railway stations.

WHERE TO STAY
The main centres along this lengthy coastline are Dinard, St-Brieuc, Paimpol, Perros-Guirec, Lannion, Morlaix and Roscoff. Local tourist offices will provide further details of all available accommodation.

ACTIVITIES
Walking: GR34 follows the entire length of the coastline from Mont St-Michel to Roscoff. GR34C follows the valley of the Rance from Dinan to Dinard. Other offshoots of GR34 also offer inland detours.
Cycling: you can rent bicycles at the railway stations of Dinard, Lamballe, Lannion, Morlaix, Roscoff, St-Brieuc and St-Malo. For organized tours, contact the Ligue de Bretagne de Cyclotourisme, T: 02 99 45 00 86, or Formules Bretagne (see p13).
Riding: details of equestrian centres on the coast from Association Départementale de Tourisme Equestre des Côtes d'Armor, Salle Bagatelle, 22190

Plerin, T/F: 02 96 73 12 38.
Watersports: the Centre Nautique in Roscoff, T: 02 98 69 72 79, caters for a wide range of activities.
Adventure holidays: Loisirs Accueil Côtes d'Armor, Maison du Tourisme, 29 rue des Promenades, 22010 St-Brieuc, T: 02 96 62 72 15, F: 02 96 62 72 25, will provide a booking service.

FURTHER INFORMATION
Tourist offices: Lamballe, pl du Martray, T: 02 96 31 05 38; Lannion, quai d'Aiguillon, T: 02 96 46 41 00; Morlaix, pl des Otages, T: 02 98 62 14 94; Paimpol, pl de la République, T: 02 96 20 83 16; Roscoff, 46 rue Gambetta, T: 02 98 61 12 13, www.sb-roscoff.fr; St-Brieuc, 7 rue St-Gouéno, T: 02 96 33 32 50, www.cybercom.fr/ stbrieuc; St-Malo, esplanade St-Vincent, T: 02 99 56 64 48.

The Baie du Mont St-Michel is noted for large flocks of lapwings and plovers.

Monts d'Arrée

Ridge of granite hills, with heath, wetland and forest; part of the Parc Naturel Régional d'Armorique (172,000 ha/425,000 acres)

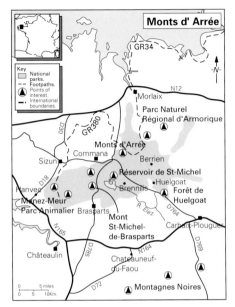

The morning frost still clung to the grass as we headed south from Morlaix, along the valley which leads up into the Monts d'Arrée. As we climbed, the sun began to melt the frost and clouds of mist hung in the combes and hollows. Locals intending a trip up into these hills say they are 'going into the mountains', an exaggeration which has the ring of bar-room talk after several draughts of the local cider.

According to an old legend, two thousand years ago the Monts d'Arrée were covered with forest. When Christ was born, God commanded all the trees to go immediately to Bethlehem to welcome him. But the plants did not have the spirit for the journey and refused to go, all except the pine tree, and some heather and gorse. In anger, Heaven decreed that the trees should shrivel where they stood, which — so the legend says — is why the region is so barren.

Formed about 600 million years ago, the Monts d'Arrée are a continuous spine of granite hills, peaking at Mont St-Michel-des-Brasparts (391 metres/1,282 feet). They separate the rolling Leon peneplain in the north from Cornouaille in the south. The landscape is a mixture of open pasture, heath and some woodland, studded with granite outcrops. At the foot of St-Michel de la Motte-Cronon (387 metres/1,270 feet) is a vast wetland valley, the Yeun Elez. This sheltered peat basin, surrounded by sharp schist and quartzite ridges to the north and blunted peaks in the south, is said to house the legendary doors of 'cold hell'.

At the heart of these sombre hills lies the forest of Huelgoat. The word is Breton for high forest — it is a relic of the Argoat, the ancient forest that once covered the whole Brittany peninsula. Yew and larch mingle with oak, beech and silver birch, while ivy

shrouds many of the trees. Despite the age of Huelgoat, many of its trees are not well founded, due to slow erosion of the forest's granite platform. The soil is stony, and many trees have roots which grow around rocks that protrude above the ground. The great storm that swept up the Channel in October 1987, devastating southern England, also tore across this exposed corner of Brittany. It cut a swathe through Huelgoat, leaving thousands of uprooted trees in its wake. Fortunately, helped by a replanting programme, the forest is recovering.

The wildlife is rich and varied. Buzzards, woodpeckers, jays and other common birds live in the forest. Salmon and otters revel in the clean waters of the rivers, and beavers have been reintroduced (see p29).

This ancient wood naturally has its own legends. Dahud, the daughter of a 6th-century Breton king called Gradlon, was in the habit of throwing her lovers off a rock near Huelgoat. King Arthur is supposed to have slept in a cave somewhere in the forest. And there is a Gallo-Roman hill-fort, which, inevitably, has come to be called Le Camp d'Artus ('Arthur's camp') — although its links with the legend are tenuous at best.

BEFORE YOU GO
Maps: IGN 1:100,000 Nos. 13-15; IGN 1:25,000 (OT & ET) Nos. 0616-18 and 0717-18.

GETTING THERE
By car: all roads in Brittany lead to Rennes. N12 follows the north coast around to Morlaix and Brest, while N24 joins the southern coast road, heading west to Quimper. From Morlaix, D769 cuts through the forest of Huelgoat on its way to Carhaix-Plouguer, while D785 provides scenic mountain views before reaching Quimper. D764 links Carhaix with Huelgoat.

By rail: TGV services from Paris-Gare Montparnasse to Guingamp, Morlaix and Quimper. From Guingamp a branch line runs to Carhaix. Change at Quimper for Rosporden and Châteaulin.

By bus: SNCF runs 2 buses a day from Morlaix to Huelgoat and on to Carhaix. From Carhaix, daily buses run to the railway stations at Rosporden and at Châteaulin, via Châteauneuf-du-Faou.

WHERE TO STAY
Carhaix, Châteaulin and Morlaix are the nearest sizeable towns. In Huelgoat, the lakeside Hôtel du Lac, T: 02 98 99 71 14, is a pleasant lunch stop out of season. Local tourist offices have details of accommodation in the area.

ACTIVITIES
Walking: GR37 and GR380 cross the park; GR380 can be picked up at Morlaix or Sizun.

Cycling: cycle-hire outlets at the railway stations of Châteaulin, Morlaix and Quimper and in Brasparts and Carhaix. The Paris-Brest long-distance route passes through the mountains.

Riding: many riding centres offer treks into the mountains. Try the Centre de Loisirs Equestres in La Feuillée, near Huelgoat, T: 02 98 99 78 46; or the Centre Equestre et Poney Club in Brasparts, T: 02 98 81 47 34. For general information, contact the Comité Départemental de Tourisme Equestre du Finistère, in Ploneis (see p13).

Fishing: Châteauneuf-du-Faou, in the Black Mountains, is well known for its salmon fishing. Contact the local tourist office or the Finistère fishing federation, 1 rue de Poher, Quimper, T: 02 98 53 16 61.

Museums: near the village of Commana, on D764, there is a museum of 19th-century life at the watermills of Kerouat, T: 02 98 68 87 76. The 420-ha (1,000-acre) animal park at Ménez-Meur, Hanvec, has a herd of *aurochs* (a recreation of the region's ancient breed of domestic cattle), plus deer and wild boar. The Maison de la Rivière, de l'Eau et de la Pêche, T: 02 98 68 86 33, at the mills of Vergraon (near Sizun) features an experimental fish farm for salmon and trout.

FURTHER INFORMATION
Tourist offices: Brest, 1 pl de la Liberté, T: 02 98 44 24 96; Châteauneuf-du-Faou, T: 02 98 81 83 90; Châteaulin, quai Cosmao, T: 02 98 86 02 11; Carhaix-Plouguer, rue Brizeux, T: 02 98 93 04 42; Huelgoat, pl Alphonse Penven, T: 02 98 99 72 32; Morlaix, pl des Otages, T: 02 98 62 14 94; and Quimper, pl de la Résistance, T: 02 98 53 04 05.

Park office: (Armorique) 15 pl aux Foires, BP 27, 29590 Le Faou, T: 02 98 81 90 08, F: 02 98 81 90 09, www.parcs-naturels-regionaux.tm.fr.

Iles d'Ouessant

Group of islands including maritime and bird reserves; part of the Parc Naturel Régional d'Armorique
ZICO

Just beyond Finistère lie the Iles d'Ouessant. They were first named the Western Isles around 330 BC by Pytheas, a Phoenician navigator, who was sailing up the Atlantic coast in search of tin. The name has stuck — and in English has become corrupted to Ushant.

The islands are geologically similar to the Finistère cape. They sit on the shallow continental shelf like crumbs broken off from the granite plateau of the mainland and left in mid-ocean. The water around them is not very deep and is often rough and choppy. Big Atlantic rollers, which have built up strength over three thousand miles, get up suddenly when they hit the continental shelf, making sailing conditions treacherous. To make matters worse for those who brave the waves, reefs abound in the shallows, sometimes erupting from the watery spray like giants' teeth. One of the better-selling lines in the tourist shops of Finistère is a poster map of the local coastline depicting the many wrecks which the sea has claimed.

The sea is the key to the climate of the Iles

d'Ouessant. They are warm in winter — February can be warmer here than on the Riviera — and cool in summer because they are completely exposed to the prevailing westerly winds.

The islands are, for the most part, blessedly deserted and all but two — Ouessant and Molène — are uninhabited. The ferry is small, and can carry no more than two cars at a time. Given that the main road on Ouessant, the largest of the islands, is only about six kilometres (four miles) long, taking a car is pretty pointless. Even on fine summer days when the ferries are full the island is never unpleasantly overrun. There is a fair-sized settlement at Lampaul, the main town; it has four hotels, though few of their visitors stray far from the main road.

Ouessant is a flat-topped island with dramatic cliffs all round, rising offshore like a raised game pie. Its central plateau, averaging up to sixty metres (180 feet) above sea-level, offers easy walking and cycling. For walkers, there are few paths and you will have to find your own way across the mats of heather and mossy grass. On the other hand, there are very few fences or walls to negotiate and the bouncy turf is guaranteed to put a spring in your heels.

The Iles d'Ouessant, where Atlantic waters meet the Channel, are renowned for their fulmar, shag, oystercatchers and kittiwake.

The islands' cliffs are a wonderful boon for connoisseurs of the sea: from vantage points along the cliff-tops you can study the ocean's moods, from its wilder rages to peaceful calms when waves gently lap the seaside rocks.

The archipelago is a convenient stopping-off point for migrating birds such as ring ouzel and wheatear, although nesting places on the cliffs are limited because the waves sometimes get so high as to make the lower reaches of the rock-face uninhabitable. The ornithological centre has a list of 350 different species which have been spotted on the islands, including many rare birds such as the yellow-browed warbler, the squacco heron and the whiskered tern.

The islands' few trees and shrubs tend to nestle in hollows out of the wind, or grow low to the ground; this undergrowth shelters a large population of rabbits. The larger islands provide grazing for a breed of dwarf sheep. In summer, the sun brings out lizards to laze on the dry stone walls which divide the fields.

BEFORE YOU GO
Map: IGN 1:25,000 No. 0317.

GETTING THERE
By air: there is a plane service from Brest to the main island of Ouessant in summer; contact Finist'air, T: 02 98 84 64 87.
By sea: Penn Ar Bed, T: 02 98 80 24 68, has ferries from Brest and Le Conquet. Finist'mer, T: 02 98 89 16 61, has faster boats from Le Conquet.

WHERE TO STAY
There are 4 hotels in Lampaul: Duchesse Ann, T: 02 98 48 80 25; Le Fromveur, T: 02 98 48 81 30; L'Océan, T: 02 98 48 80 03; and Roc'h Ar Mor, T: 02 98 48 80 19. There is also a camp-site, T: 02 98 48 85 65, and a youth hostel, T: 02 98 48 80 06, on Ouessant and rooms on the island of Molène. You are advised to book ahead.

ACTIVITIES
Walking: this is lovely walking country; there are no marked paths, but none is needed.
Cycling: Ouessant's size, scarce traffic and flattish countryside make for ideal cycling. There are rental shops at the port.
Riding: contact Ty Crenn, T: 02 98 48 86 54.
Fishing: contact Stang Ar Merdy, T: 02 98 48 86 54.
Watersports: there are several clubs on the island. For diving contact Ouessant Subaqua, T: 02 98 48 83 84 (open July-Aug).
Bird-watching: contact the Centre Ornithologique, T: 02 98 48 82 65. Trips to Molène (July-Aug), T: 02 98 49 07 18.
Museum: the Ecomusée d'Ouessant, T: 02 98 48 86 37, shows how the island's hardy inhabitants lived in the 19th century (closed Tues).

FURTHER INFORMATION
Tourist office: Lampaul, pl de l'Eglise, T: 02 98 48 85 83.

The Presqu'île de Crozon features sheltered beaches backed by marram-covered dunes.

Presqu'île de Crozon

Peninsula girt by high cliffs and topped with moorland, known for its remarkable dune system; part of the Parc Naturel Régional d'Armorique
ZICO

The Presqu'île de Crozon, or Crozon Peninsula, is a long arm of wind-swept land extending into the Atlantic between the Aulne estuary and the bay of Douarnenez. Moors alternate with open fields, now often abandoned. Villages with low rows of houses aim their gables into the prevailing winds. At the landward end rises a range of hills, the highest of which, Ménez-Hom (330 m/1,080 ft), affords fine views along the length of the peninsula. At the seaward end, the Presqu'île de Crozon splits into three long fingers: the Cap de la Chèvre pointing south, the Pointe de Penhir leading west, and the Pointe des Espagnols stretching north towards the harbour of Brest.

Along the southern coast, you can see the story of the earth's crust outlined in the tortured folds of the cliffs. Formed in the Precambrian period, they contain fossils of seaworms and other creatures dating back to

the birth of life on earth.

The Crozon peninsula is part of the Parc Naturel Régional d'Armorique, which extends westwards to the Iles d'Ouessant and eastwards to the Monts d'Arrée. The coastline boasts a remarkable dune system; in places, the Atlantic winds have swept the sand into mounds and ridges which rise up to 30 m (100 ft) above the underlying rocks. As the dunes have gradually been colonized by marram grass and sea spurge, they have become more stable.

The bulk of the tourists drive out of Camaret-sur-Mer to the point of Penhir. A far better alternative is to forsake the car and take the cliff-top walk along the south of the peninsula, from Penhir to the main road near Kerloch. Although the path is well trodden, it offers some spectacular vantage points looking out over the Atlantic, away from the roar of the road and the smell of exhaust fumes.
Before you go *Maps:* IGN 1:100,000 No. 13; IGN 1:25,000 Nos. 0418 ET and 0518 OT. **Getting there** *By sea:* ferries connect Brest with Camaret-sur-Mer on the peninsula. Contact Penn Ar Bed ferries, T: 02 98 80 24 68. *By car:* N12 leads to Brest. From here take the N165 to Châteaulin. Alternatively, take N164 from Rennes to Châteaulin. From Châteaulin, take D887 towards Morgat. From Quimper take N165 and D887. *By rail:* TGV services from Paris-Gare Montparnasse to Brest and Quimper, both on the main line from Paris. Local trains run between Brest and Quimper, stopping at Châteaulin. *By bus:* during the week buses run from Quimper

up the spine of the peninsula to Camaret-sur-Mer. There are also buses from Brest to Camaret, but the ferry is quicker. A connecting bus runs between Crozon, Camaret-sur-Mer, Le Fret and Morgat.
Where to stay: the best bases are Quimper or Châteaulin, although Douarnenez and Locronan are more rural alternatives for those with cars. Brest was rebuilt after World War II and is now rather soulless, though it is convenient. **Activities** *Cycling:* bicycles are available from the railway stations at Brest, Châteaulin and Quimper. *Museums:* the Maison des Minéraux in Crozon, T: 02 98 27 19 73, has exhibitions on geology. Oceanopolis in Brest, T: 02 98 34 40 40, www.galeode.fr/oceanopolis, has fascinating displays on Brittany's marine life. **Further information** *Tourist offices:* Brest, pl de la Liberté, T: 02 98 44 24 96; Camaret-sur-Mer, 15 quai Kleber, T: 02 98 27 93 60; Châteaulin, quai Cosmao, T: 02 98 86 02 11; Crozon, blvd Pralognan, T: 02 98 27 07 92; Douarnenez, 2 rue Docteur-Mével, T: 02 98 92 13 35; Quimper, pl de la Résistance, T: 02 98 53 04 05.

Côte de Cornouaille & Côte Sauvage

Brittany's craggy southern coastline; important bird reserves
Ramsar, ZICO

Past the Pointe du Raz, the Breton coast becomes a south-facing one. This is where the Côte de Cornouaille begins. Its wild and isolated cliffs are cut by deep inlets, which often

The praying mantis is one of the curiosities of the rich insect fauna of the Forêt de Paimpont.

harbour small fishing villages.

Pointe du Raz on Cap Sizun is something of a tourist trap, although its spectacular chasms and sinkhole are worth seeing. Venture a bit further and you come to the bird reserve at Goulien, which shelters an impressive selection of sea-birds including razorbills, guillemots, shags, cormorants, kittiwake and stormy petrel.

Twelve kilometres (eight miles) offshore lies the bleak and wind-swept Ile de Sein. This island is celebrated in France for an episode of extraordinary patriotism during World War II. When Charles de Gaulle broadcast his now famous call for resistance against the German occupation, the 'Appel du 18 Juin, 1940', the island's able-bodied men, all 150 of them, joined him in exile in London. They initially formed fully a quarter of the Free French fighters.

From Pointe du Raz, the coast curves steeply down to Pointe de Penmarch. Although this stretch is favoured by yachtsmen, old fishing ports such as Concarneau manage to retain a distinctly Breton maritime flavour and visitors are still likely to hear the ancient Breton language spoken. Thirty kilometres (20 miles) inland, on the estuary of the River Odet, lies Quimper, former capital of the old duchy of Cornouaille.

Beyond Cornouaille, the coast known as the Côte Sauvage stretches down to the Gulf of Morbihan, close to Vannes. At the beginning of this section, you get dramatic views across to the cliffs of the Ile de Groix. The island's most dramatic sight is a chasm called the Trou de l'Enfer ('hole of hell'). A small fishing community coexists on the island with a bird reserve.

Farther east the coast attracts more visitors. The Gulf of Morbihan's megaliths are famous, especially those at Carnac which are impossibly overrun with tourists. The tumulus on the island of Gavrinis offers an interesting alternative. South of the island stand some megaliths which are only revealed at low tide.

Belle Ile, lying 15 km (10 miles) off the Quiberon headland, is also worth a visit. It is best avoided during August, at the height of the tourist season, but at other times of the year you can still enjoy the solitude and calm that once made the island a favourite haunt of the French artist, Claude Monet.

Before you go *Maps:* IGN 1:100,000 Nos. 13 and 15; IGN 1:25,000 Nos. 0419 ET, 0519 OT & ET, 0620 ET, 0720 ET, 0821-22 OT and 0921 OT. *Guide-books: La Bretagne de la Pointe du Raz à l'Estuaire de la Loire,* by Marcel Bournerias, in the series *Guides Naturalistes des Côtes de France* (Editions Delachaux et Niestlé). **Getting there** *By sea:* 3 companies have boats from Concarneau to Iles de Glénan (contact tourist office for details). CMN, T: 02 97 50 06 90, has ferries from Quiberon to Belle Ile and from Lorient to Ile de Groix. Penn Ar Bed, T: 02 98 70 70 70, operates between Audierne and Ile de Sein. Several companies offer boat trips around the Gulf of Morbihan from Quiberon and Vannes (contact tourist offices for details). *By car:* D765 and D784 run from Quimper towards the Pointe du Raz; from here D2, D44, D783, D24, D152, D781 and D768 more or less skirt the coastline down towards Lorient and Quiberon. *By rail:* TGVs from Paris-Gare Montparnasse to Quimper, stopping at Vannes, Auray and Lorient. A local service runs from Auray to Quiberon, the port for Belle Ile.

Ancient stone megaliths abound throughout the Gulf of Morbihan.

By bus: buses run from Quimper to Audierne, Pointe du Raz, St-Guénolé, Lesconil and Concarneau. **Where to stay:** there are hundreds of hotels along the coast, though Auray and Vannes are good bases. **Activities** *Walking:* GR34 runs along the coast from Pointe du Raz as far as Lorient. *Cycling:* bicycles are available from SNCF stations at Auray, Lorient, Quiberon, Quimper and Vannes. Les Trois Vallées and Rennes-Vannes long-distance routes run along parts of the coast. *Riding:* contact ADTE du Morbihan, 4 rue Cadoudal, 56390 Grand Champ, T: 02 97 66 40 46, F: 02 97 66 40 46. *Bird-watching:* the Réserve de Goulien at Cap Sizun, T: 02 98 70 13 53 (open 1 Apr-31 Aug), contains cliffs and islands rich in bird life. **Further information** *Tourist offices:* Audierne, 8 rue Victor Hugo, T: 02 98 70 12 20; Concarneau, quai d'Aiguillon, T: 02 98 97 01 44; Quiberon, 14 rue de Verdun, T: 02 97 50 07 84, www.quiberon.com; Quimper, pl de la Résistance, T: 02 98 53 04 05; Rosporden, rue Hippolyte-le-Bas, T: 02 98 59 27 26/02 98 66 99 00; Vannes, 1 rue Thiers, T: 02 97 47 24 34.

CDT du Morbihan, 56009 Vannes, T: 02 97 54 06 56, www.morbihan.com.

Forêt de Paimpont

Ancient woodland near Rennes
8,000 ha (20,000 acres)

The forest of Paimpont is one of only two surviving remnants — the other being Huelgoat in the Monts d'Arrée — of the ancient forest of Argoat, which once covered vast tracts of Brittany. In the Middle Ages the forest was known as Brocéliande, and provided the backdrop to the love affair between Queen Guinevere and Lancelot of the Lake described in Chrétien de Troyes' Arthurian romances.

It is difficult to escape the legends. Joseph of Arimathea, one of Christ's disciples, was said to have come to Brittany with the Holy Grail and lived among the beeches and the oaks in the forest. The magician, Merlin, was also reputed to have lived here: the forest contains sites known as Merlin's Step and Merlin's Tomb. And in the Val sans Retour ('valley of no return'), the witch Morgana (Morgan le Fay), Merlin's great enemy, supposedly trapped unwary youths at the Rocher des Faux Amants ('rock of the false lovers').

Brush away the fables and the forest loses much of its romance. Many trees were cut down to fulfil the demand for wood during World War I and the poor rocky soil has largely prevented the oak, chestnut and beech wood from re-establishing itself, except in a few favourable locations. More recently, foresters have planted Scots pines instead of the traditional broad-leaves.

Nevertheless, the forest's flora is of great interest. Although the acidic soils cannot support a great variety of species, the range of micro-habitats in the

forest — rocky outcrops, ravines, dry and wet areas — has led to a fascinating mosaic of rich vegetation. The fauna holds some surprises as well, with green woodpeckers, normally forest birds, living alongside chats on the heathlands and reed and sedge warblers in the marshes. The insect life includes two notable species: the praying mantis and the *Ephippigère*, a form of bush cricket more typical of southern climes.

Before you go *Maps:* IGN 1:100,000 No. 16; IGN 1:25,000 (OT & ET) Nos. 1018-19. **Getting there** *By car:* the forest lies north of N24, which runs from Rennes to Lorient. Turn right just after Plélan on to D38, which leads to the Abbaye de Paimpont. Then take D40, which wends into the forest; at the crossroads is the start of GR37. *By rail:* TGV service from Paris-Gare Montparnasse to Rennes. The best option is to rent a bicycle from Rennes station, take it by train to Montfort-sur-Meu, and cycle to Paimpont from there. *By bus:* Eurolines service to Rennes (see p 13). Service from Rennes to Paimpont operated by TIV buses, T: 02 99 30 87 80. **Where to stay:** Rennes, Montfort, Plélan and Paimpont all have hotels. *Outdoor living:* camp-site at Paimpont, T: 02 99 07 89 16/02 99 06 90 74. **Activities** *Walking:* GR37 runs from Montfort through the forest to Plélan, and back into the forest again, along the Val sans Retour. **Further information** *Tourist offices:* Paimpont, 5 esplanade de Brocéliande, T: 02 99 07 84 23; Rennes, 11 rue St-Yves, T: 02 99 67 11 11.

La Brière, the second largest marshland in France after the Camargue, consists of an intricate network of reed-fringed channels, where eels are common.

La Brière

The European beaver, once threatened with extinction in France, is steadily increasing in numbers thanks to strict protection measures.

Area of almost impenetrable marshland, lying 40 km (25 miles) north-west of Nantes; parc naturel régional
Ramsar, ZICO
40,000 ha (99,000 acres)

To be in the middle of Brière marsh is like being becalmed at sea. The reeds and meadows stretch out languidly towards the horizon. Imperceptible gusts of wind ripple the water and shiver the rushes. In the far distance a couple of hills, islands in this expanse of marsh, float like shadows, their church spires piercing the thick haze.

Brière is the second largest wetland area in France after the Camargue, neighbouring the Morbihan Gulf and Vilaine estuary to the north, the Guérande salt-marsh to the west and, to the south, the Loire estuary and Lac de Grand-Lieu. The marshland is difficult to penetrate and so has retained much of its austere beauty: Alphonse de Châteaubriant described it as 'a great wild marsh, filled with the silence of man and the song of birds.' A few tracks cross the park but by far the easiest way to get around — and in winter the only way — is in a flat-bottomed punt, known locally as a *chaland* and used mainly for eel-fishing.

The difficulty in moving around is in fact a blessing in disguise, for the real enjoyment of the marsh lies in just sitting and waiting for the wildlife to show. On a hot and humid spring day, I watched as a water vole appeared from its hide to sniff the air. Fortunately, I was upwind. It swam around for a few minutes, inspecting its domain, before spotting me and disappearing underwater with a plop.

On the opposite bank, gregarious geese herded a gaggle of fluffy brown goslings. It is one of nature's quirks that two or three adult geese will look after the offspring of several parents: a kind of goosey kindergarten. Suddenly alerted, this kindergarten decamped amidst blasts from adult foghorns, running swiftly across the meadow marsh to the relative safety of the next water course. The source of the danger was flying above in the form of two large herons. Though their main diet is fish, they are not averse to the odd gosling or duckling. A third heron stood fishing in the middle of a shallow waterway, spearing its prey with its beak, tossing the fish up for its final journey and swallowing it on the way down.

BEFORE YOU GO
Maps: IGN 1:100,000 No. 24; IGN 1:25,000 Nos. 1022 OT & ET and 1023 OT.
Guide-books: the park publishes an ornithological map and booklets on the flora and fauna of the Brière.

GETTING THERE
By air: La Baule-Escoublac, T: 02 40 60 23 83, and Nantes, T: 02 40 84 80 00, are the nearest airports.
By car: main roads enclose the park. N165 from Nantes to Vannes is the border on the north-east side while D773, N171 and D774 circle the park to the east, south and west.
By rail: TGV service to St-Nazaire from Paris-Gare Montparnasse. Local trains to Pontchâteau from Nantes.
By bus: Eurolines service to Nantes (see p13).
By bicycle: the Paris-La Baule long-distance route passes through the park.

WHERE TO STAY
St-Nazaire is not an attractive place to stay, as the old town was destroyed in 1943. Other large towns with a wide range of hotels are La Baule, Nantes and Redon.
Two *auberges rurales* accommodate visitors to the park: Auberge de Kerhinet in Kerhinet, T: 02 40 61 91 46, and Auberge 'Les Typhas' in St-Lyphard, T: 02 40 91 40 30. Contact park or tourist offices for further details of accommodation in the area.

ACTIVITIES
Walking: GR3 winds through the park. Brière tourist office (see below) has details of guided walks and itineraries for shorter walks.
Cycling: the quiet roads that cross the marsh are ideal for cycling. You can rent bicycles at the station in St-Nazaire. Brière tourist office has details of 5 cycle routes in the area and local hire outlets.
Riding: try the Centre Equestre de Brière in St-Lyphard, T: 02 40 91 44 41, or Le Sabot d'Or in St-Nazaire, T: 02 40 61 95 20. Contact the Comité Départemental de Tourisme Equestre d'Ille et Vilaine, Le Feuillet, 35250 St-Sulpice-la-Forêt, T: 02 99 66 28 00.
Fishing: contact Loire-Atlantique fishing federation in Nantes, T: 02 40 73 62 42.
Boating: 7 guided tours through the Brière canals on traditional punts, known as *chalands*, are recommended by the Brière tourist office and excursions can be booked through them.
Museums: numerous attractions include an ecomuseum at Kerhinet featuring a restored *briéron* village, T: 02 40 61 95 24; a deer farm at La Madeleine-de-Guérande, T: 02 40 42 95 01; and an animal park at St-Malo-de-Guersac, T: 02 40 91 17 80.

FURTHER INFORMATION
Tourist offices: La Baule, 8 pl de la Victoire, T: 02 40 24 34 44, www.labaule.tm.fr; St-Nazaire, pl François Blancho, T: 02 40 22 40 65. Brière, 38 rue de la Brière, La Chapelle-des-Marais, T: 02 40 66 85 01, F: 02 40 53 91 15.
Park office: 177 Ile de Fédrun, St-Joachim, T: 02 40 91 68 68, F: 02 40 91 60 58, www.parcs-naturels-regionaux.tm.fr.

THE BEAVER

Despite its considerable size, up to 80 cm (2½ ft) long and 30 kg (66 lb) in weight, the European beaver is not easy to see. It is discreet, wary of humans and almost exclusively nocturnal, spending the day in its bank-side lodges. It is vegetarian, eating leaves and aquatic plants. The beaver's dams are relatively modest constructions compared to the vast building works of its North American cousins.

Although the beaver's only natural enemies are dogs and foxes, its fur is prized; trapping nearly killed it off. It was one of the first animals in France to be protected, in 1905.

Despite the protection measures taken, the beaver had virtually disappeared from France thirty years ago. There were just a few colonies left on tributaries of the Rhône. In the early 1970s, beavers were reintroduced to Brittany just south of Huelgoat on the River Elez and on the Roudouhir, near Hanvec. The colonies have spread naturally ever since. This pattern of recovery has been repeated elsewhere in France and the country's beaver population is now estimated at somewhere between 5,000 and 10,000. Beaver colonies are concentrated mainly along the Loire and Rhône, in Brittany and in the Cévennes.

CHAPTER 2

The North-East

Friends smiled knowingly when I told them I was off to check out the wild side of North-East France: they had visions of me whiling away the small hours in the night-spots of deepest Pigalle. When I explained that my task was to explore other forms of wildness, they looked blank. They doubted whether the area had anything in the way of natural wonders to discover. Recalling the urban sprawl of Paris and the heavy traffic of the Channel ports, I initially shared some of these concerns.

I needn't have worried. My search was rewarded by a surprisingly wide variety of landscapes. I drove from seaside to mountains along straight roads lined with tall poplars and plane trees, across wide rolling plains and wooded ridges. Vast areas of the North-East are forested, particularly Alsace and the Meuse.

On the Channel coast, the flowers and grasses of the dunes provide a fascinating contrast to the brilliant alpine plants of the *chaumes*, the high pastures in the Vosges mountains. There are added curiosities such as the gnarled old beeches in the forests of the Montagne de Reims or the pink seaweed that grows, amazingly, 400 kilometres (240 miles) from the sea on the salty marshes of Lorraine. Amid the vast expanses of farmland, milky white cows stand knee-deep in meadows of wild flowers and wide verges left uncut at the roadside are speckled with brilliant red poppies.

The coastal bays, inland lakes and *étangs* (shallow lakes) attract many bird species as they migrate across Europe. In the Ardennes, on the Belgian border, birds of prey such as hawks, red kites

The sun rises over the Vosges, a haven for some of France's rarest and most secretive wildlife, with red and roe deer, and both pine and beech martens.

30

The delicate yellow flowers of the cowslip are a welcome springtime sight in wild pastures.

and buzzards circle over the forests, swooping for food along the meandering valleys of the Meuse and Semoy.

Admittedly, the North-East is unspoiled only in patches. Apart from the great conurbation of Paris, the area also encompasses the flat industrial northern plain and the broad sunny hillsides whose chalky soil has been covered since the 12th century in one of France's best-known and most valuable crops — the vines of Champagne.

To the south of the wine-growing region is the 'wet' part of Champagne, so called because of its many lakes and rivers. You really feel out in the country — *en province* — amongst its half-timbered villages, earth-brown beamed cottages, barns and churches. General de Gaulle described it as a 'countryside pervaded with quiet, vast, corrupt and sad horizons, woods, fields, pastures and wild spots set against ancient hills'.

The Vosges mountains in Alsace, on France's eastern border with Germany, were the largest stretch of wildness I discovered in the North-East. While less extensive and lower than the Alps and less remote than the Pyrenees, they are nonetheless one of France's most beautiful mountainous areas. Boars, wild-

cats and martens still roam the forests, and the dense beech-wood heights also provide cover for falcons, chamois and the rare, turkey-like capercaillie.

Alsace was occupied by Germany from 1870 to the end of World War I and again during World War II, despite the construction of the reputedly impregnable Maginot Line in the 1930s. It still retains curious Germanic place names and red-roofed villages, making it seem removed from the rest of France.

In fact the whole of the North-East echoes with memories of war. Over the centuries, the armies of Caesar, Charlemagne, Napoleon and Hitler have all marched across the wide plains and ridges of Champagne, Lorraine and Picardy, where the open countryside provides ideal conditions for battle. Villages perch grandly on hilltops overlooking the vast expanses where battles once raged and carefully tended cemeteries filled with endless rows of white crosses bear testament to some of the 20th century's bloodiest conflicts.

Though the scars of battle have now healed, the countryside and its wildlife were changed in the process. Woods were felled for the war effort, and the fragile dunes along the coast were trampled by the Allied armies arriving from Britain. Now farmers have become the main threat to the environment. So much marshland has been drained to make way for crops that special areas such as the canals and marshes of the Ried, the old flood plain of the Rhine at the foot of the Vosges, have all but disappeared. This agricultural development had a devastating effect on Alsace's storks, whose arrival in March was traditionally a sign of good luck. By the early 1980s, the population had dwindled to only three pairs but an extensive rehabilitation programme has since raised numbers to around 700.

Tourism is also taking its toll, particularly in the Vosges, where ski resorts have been developed. Around Paris, there are inevitable pressures on land for visitor attractions as well as housing and industry. Sadly, cavalier attitudes towards building restrictions are doing nothing to enhance the environment, particularly in areas such as the superb natural forests north of the capital. On the bright side, the demand for drinking water in Paris has led to the creation of huge reservoirs in Champagne, which are now a favourite stop-over for thousands of cranes migrating between Scandinavia and North Africa.

GETTING THERE
By air: the main international airports are Paris-Charles de Gaulle, T: 08 36 25 05 05 (French)/01 48 62 22 80 (English), www.adp.fr, and Paris-Orly, T: 01 48 75 15 15. International flights also go to Lille, T: 03 20 49 68 68, and Strasbourg, T: 03 88 64 67 67.
By sea: Hoverspeed, T: 08 00 90 17 77, www.hoverspeed.co.uk, has Dover-Calais and Folkestone-Boulogne crossings. SeaFrance Sealink, T: 01 44 94 40 40, www.seafrance.co.uk, and P&O Stena, T: 01 44 51 00 51, www.postena.com, have Dover-Calais car-ferry services.
By car: from Paris, A1 runs north through Lille, with A26 branching off near Arras for Calais and A25 at Lille for Dunkerque. The A16 runs through Amiens and Boulogne to link up with the Channel Tunnel at Calais. East from Paris, A4 cuts through Reims and Metz to Strasbourg.
By rail: Eurostar, T: 08 36 35 35 39, www.eurostar.com, has London-Paris and London-Ashford-Lille passenger services through the Channel Tunnel. Eurotunnel, T: 03 21 00 61 00, www.eurotunnel.com, carries cars between Folkestone and Calais. TGVs run from Paris-Gare du Nord to Lille, Calais and Boulogne. Services run from Paris-Gare de l'Est to Strasbourg, Nancy and Metz. Contact SNCF (see p13).
By bus: Eurolines (see p13) has services to Paris, Lille, Reims, Strasbourg, Amiens, Colmar, Metz and Nancy. Busabout, www.busabout.com, has buses to Calais and Paris. Tourist offices will provide details of local and regional services.

WHEN TO GO
Thousands of migratory birds stop over along the coast or on inland reservoirs in spring and autumn. Wild flowers are in bloom Mar-Nov, but are most abundant in spring. The region has a temperate climate, although some mountain roads in the Vosges are impassable when there is heavy snow.

WHERE TO STAY
Local and regional tourist offices publish free brochures. Reservations are not usually necessary except in the peak of summer and, in the Vosges, during the skiing season.

ACTIVITIES
Walking: several Grande Randonnée footpaths cross the North-East, including the GR Littoral along the northern coast from Abbeville to the Belgian border, GR12 through Champagne to Luxembourg and GR5 through Alsace and Lorraine. The 8 *parcs naturels régionaux* in the area all have marked nature trails and paths.
Cycling: bicycles are available at railway stations, camp-sites and cycle shops. Three *La France à Vélo* brochures (see p13) cover the region: *Nord, Flandres, Artois, Picardie*; *Champagne-Ardennes*; and *Vosges, Alsace, Lorraine*. For long-distance routes, see IGN map No. 906, *VTT & Randonnées Cyclos*.
Riding: contact the Fédération Française d'Equitation (see USEFUL ADDRESSES, p215) for riding clubs in the region.
Fishing: to obtain permits, enquire at tourist offices and town halls, or contact the Conseil Supérieur de la Pêche (see USEFUL ADDRESSES, p215).
Watersports: there is sailing and wind-surfing on the Orient and Der-Chantecoq lakes and on the Madine *étang* in Lorraine; also on the sea at the Baie de la Somme and around Le Touquet. You can canoe on the rivers in the Ardennes.
Skiing: cross-country pistes are marked out when the snow is adequate in the Ardennes and the Vosges; there are also some downhill runs in the Vosges.

FURTHER INFORMATION
CRT de Nord-Pas-de-Calais, 6 pl Mendès France, 59800 Lille, T: 03 20 14 57 57, F: 03 20 14 57 58, www.cr-npdc.fr.

CR de Picardie, 11 Mail Albert 1er, BP 2616, 80026 Amiens, T: 03 22 97 37 37, www.cr-picardie.fr.

CRT de Champagne-Ardenne, 15 av du Maréchal Leclerc, BP 319, 51013 Châlons-en-Champagne, T: 03 26 21 85 80, www.tourisme-champagne-ard.com.

CRT de Lorraine, 1 pl Gabriel Hocquard, BP 81004, 57036 Metz, T: 03 87 37 02 16, F: 03 87 37 02 19, www.cr-lorraine.fr.

CRT d'Alsace, 6 av de la Marseillaise, BP 219, 67005 Strasbourg, T: 03 88 25 01 66, www.tourisme-alsace.com.

Côte d'Opale & Baie de la Somme

Surprisingly secluded coastline renowned for migrating birds; includes Parc Naturel Régional du Nord-Pas-de-Calais Ramsar, ZICO

The easily accessible coastline around the Channel ports of Calais and Boulogne, known as the Côte d'Opale, is as busy a spot for migratory birds as for people and boats. As cross-Channel tourists rush to and from their ferries, few are aware of the grass-topped cliffs, sandy beaches and wide estuaries that lurk just beyond the docks.

Even before you set foot in France there is plenty to see by scanning the swirling flocks of gulls and bobbing masses of red-necked grebe, eider and long-tailed ducks as your ferry slips in to Boulogne harbour. For those that have the knowledge to tell the species apart, there is always the chance of spotting something unusual, such as a glaucous gull

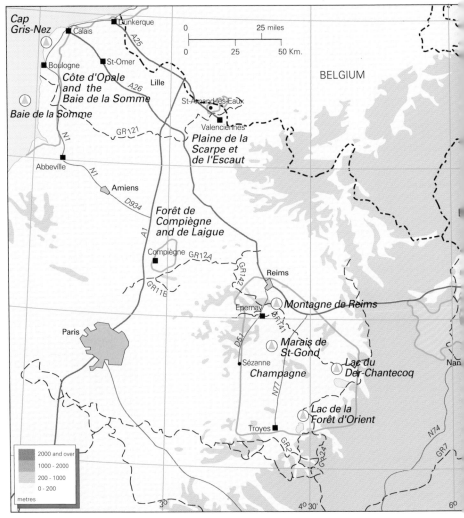

in winter or little gull in late summer.

After landing in Boulogne, you face a difficult choice of either turning left for the impressive white cliffs of Cap Gris-Nez and Cap Blanc-Nez and some of the best migrant bird-watching along the Channel coast, or right for the salt marshes and estuarine wildlife of the Canche and the Somme. To the east, Dunkerque may seem less than enticing, but again you would be wrong. Even the stark, forbidding east jetty of the new port provides one of the best vantage points for watching migrant sea-birds —

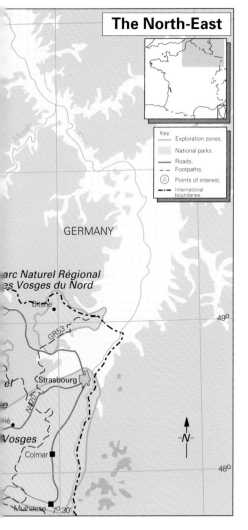

The North-East

Key
— Exploration zones.
— National parks.
— Roads.
- - Footpaths.
Ⓘ Points of interest.
-·-· International boundaries.

GERMANY

arc Naturel Régional
es Vosges du Nord

Bitche

GR53

Strasbourg

N420

Vosges

Colmar

Mulhouse 7° 30'

-N-

49°

48°

divers, grebes, skuas and ducks — while the Braek dyke is noted for its wintering flocks of snow bunting, and all sorts of rarities which turn up in the adjacent lagoon.

Just beyond Dunkerque is a small nature reserve at La Dune Marchand, covering 110 hectares (270 acres) and containing sand dunes, maritime scrub and scattered dune slacks (damp hollows). The site offers a classic example of natural dune formation, ranging from the wind-buffeted seaward frontal dunes of golden sand, stabilized by marram grass and impressive tufts of sea spurge, to the so-called grey dunes, with their luxuriant carpet of lichens and mosses. Here you can find relics of glacial times such as sand pansy and early forget-me-not dotted around the open areas, which nestle between dense thickets of sea buckthorn, creeping willow and wild privet. But the most exciting features of this little reserve are another group of glacial relict flowers growing in the dune slacks, and even in old bomb craters; these include three species of rare orchid — fen orchid, musk orchid and marsh helleborine — as well as the delicate mauve flowers of autumn gentian and the inaptly named grass of Parnassus, which, with its five-petalled white flowers, resembles saxifrage more than it does grass.

The Grande Randonnée Littoral runs along the cliff tops and dunes from the Belgian border in the north-east to the Baie d'Authie south of Le Touquet: it is widely regarded as the most beautiful coastal footpath in France, offering glorious Channel views and wide inland vistas of rolling farmland. At several points you can scramble down rocky paths to the sea.

The Parc Naturel Régional du Nord-Pas-de-Calais covers the coast south from Calais to Le Touquet, as well as the inland canals and marshes around St-Omer. The most striking feature of this coastline is the band of dunes that stretches for two kilometres (more than a mile) inland in places. Having survived the ravages of two world wars and haphazard building development, the dunes are now protected within the park.

The shallow bays between Calais and the Somme have a wide variety of vegetation, and are home to many species of sea-bird all year long. The cliffs, dunes and marshes farther north along the coast are also rich habitats. Cap Gris-Nez, half-way between Calais and Boulogne, ranks as one of the most ecologically interesting sites in northern France, with an abundance of shrews, voles, field mice, harvest mice and even the rare dormouse. Newts and the rare natterjack toad can be seen where the cliffs have crumbled. The area is also notable for its tiger beetles, fast-running insects with huge eyes and jaws. And if you get bitten, take comfort from the possibility that you have nourished a very rare species of horsefly known to occur here!

The towering cliffs of Cap Gris-Nez and Cap Blanc-Nez provide grandstand views of the great seasonal peaks in European bird traffic. There are few spectacles more impressive than wave after wave of migrant birds looming out of an October morning mist, and from such a vantage point you can almost feel part of this great avian transit. Winter brings fieldfares and redwings, skylarks, starlings and chaffinches, while in spring you can wave the swallows *bon voyage* on their way to Britain.

The Baie de la Somme, south of the Côte d'Opale, is another remarkable spot for birds. You can see flotillas of northern ducks out on the river or in the lagoons, and innumerable small brown waders resting on some slightly elevated mud bank. The birds are often too far away to identify but you can simply savour the peculiar ambience of the estuary, a natural larder for millions of migratory wildfowl and waders.

The bay is particularly impressive when the tide recedes, leaving small rivulets and miles of sand, mud-flats and salines. From the steep pebbly beach by Le Hourdel at the southern end of the bay, you can watch as the on-rushing tide quickly submerges the sandbanks beneath a vast expanse of water.

Towering sand dunes offer some visual relief from these tidal flats on the north side of the bay, which is part of the large, privately owned Marquenterre bird reserve. Nature trails have been marked out to guide visitors to some excellent vantage points for observing a wide selection of the hundreds of species of birds which pass through the bay each year. The trails also wind their way into the dunes, which extend up the coast to the north as far as the eye can see.

BEFORE YOU GO
Maps: IGN 1:100,000 No. 1; IGN 1:25,000 Nos. 2202-06.
Guide-books: *La Manche de Dunkerque au Havre* in the *Guides Naturalistes des Côtes de France* series by Marcel Bournerias (Editions Delachaux et Niestlé).

GETTING THERE
By sea: there are frequent cross-Channel services from Dover and Folkestone to Boulogne and Calais by car ferry, hovercraft or SeaCat (see p33 for details).
By car: the A26 to Calais branches off the A1 from Paris. The A16 coast road runs from the Belgian border through to Abbeville at the head of the Somme canal. The N1 runs from Amiens to Boulogne.
By rail: Eurotunnel (see p33) operates between Folkestone

and Calais. TGV services run from Paris-Gare du Nord to Calais, Boulogne and Dunkerque. Local trains go along the coast from Abbeville to Calais, stopping at all the main towns in between.
By bus: there are regular services in and between the main resorts on the coast and inland to St-Omer, Montreuil and Abbeville.

WHERE TO STAY
The area has a good range of places to stay, from well-appointed hotels such as the 4-star Westminster in Le Touquet, T: 03 21 05 48 48, to *chambres d'hôtes* (bed and breakfast), hostels and farms. In the 2-star category and well placed for seeing the coast or exploring inland is the Hostellerie du Château des Tourelles in the village of Le

Wast, T: 03 21 33 34 78. Boulogne has a youth hostel, T: 03 21 80 14 50.
Outdoor living: La Bien-Assise camp-site, T: 03 21 35 20 77, is in an attractive *château* setting at Guines and also has pine chalets.

ACTIVITIES
Walking: you can join the 148-km (90-mile) GR Littoral anywhere from the Belgian border to Conchil-le-Temple. Several other long-distance paths (GR5A, 120, 121, 123, 124, 127 and 128) run inland. Contact the Pas-de-Calais ramblers' association in Angres, T: 03 21 72 67 33, for details of shorter walks.
Cycling: the Tour du Pas-de-Calais long-distance route can be picked up at Calais or Wimereux.
Riding: CDTE du Pas-de-

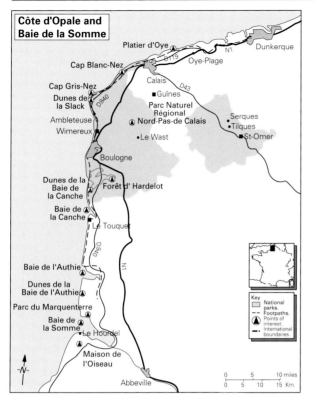

Côte d'Opale and Baie de la Somme

Boulogne, T: 03 21 30 99 99, is one of the largest marine visitor centres in Europe, featuring exhibitions and interactive displays.

FURTHER INFORMATION
Tourist offices: Abbeville, pl Amiral Courbet, T: 03 22 24 27 92; Boulogne, quai de la Poste, T: 03 21 31 68 38; Calais, 12 blvd Clemenceau, T: 03 21 96 62 40; Le Touquet, pl de l'Hermitage, T: 03 21 06 72 00, www.letouquet.com; St-Omer, pl Foch, T: 03 21 98 08 51.
 CDT du Pas-de-Calais, 24 rue Désille, Boulogne, T: 03 21 83 32 59, www2.pas-de-calais.com.
Park offices: Nord-Pas-de-Calais, Audomarais section, Le Grand Vannage, rue des Alpes, 62510 Arques, T: 03 21 98 62 98; Boulonnais section, Manoir du Huis-Bois, 62142 Le Wast, T: 03 21 83 38 79, www.parcs-naturel-regionaux.tm.fr.
 Dune Marchand nature reserve, Direction de l'Environnement, Lille, T: 03 20 63 57 57.

Calais, 78 blvd Jean Moulin, Béthune, T: 03 21 57 32 97, will provide details of local equestrian centres.
Fishing: all along the coast, people fish in the sea with lines, particularly at the bays of the Somme and Canche. Deep-sea fishing is possible from Boulogne. Contact the Pas-de-Calais fishing federation, 2 résidence de France, rue Emile Zola, BP 241, 62400 Béthune, T: 03 21 01 18 21.
Watersports: the sandy beaches, particularly between Le Touquet and the Somme, are ideal for wind-surfing and sailing. Canoeing is available on the Canche estuary at Etaples. Contact Baie de Canche watersports, T: 03 21 05 12 77. There are barge cruises on the Audomarois canals around St-Omer. Several

leave from the *base nautique* in Arques, T: 03 21 98 35 97; the park office (Audomarais section) has details of others.
Adventure holidays: contact Loisirs Accueil Pas-de-Calais, 24 rue Désille, 62200 Boulogne-sur-Mer, T: 03 21 83 32 59, who can book activity holidays.
Ornithology: tableaux of birds set against seascape backgrounds are displayed at the Maison de l'Oiseau at Lanchères near St-Valéry, T: 03 22 26 93 93; open daily Mar to mid-Nov. The Parc Ornithologique du Marquenterre, T: 03 22 25 03 06, has trails and guided walks in an extensive wooded park; open daily mid-Mar to mid-Sept, weekends Oct-Mar. There is an annual bird festival in Abbeville in early April.
Museum: Nausicaa in

Plaine de la Scarpe et de l'Escaut

Forest, marsh and reclaimed coal-mining land on the Belgian border; parc naturel régional
ZICO
43,240 ha (106,846 acres)

One of the least likely places I expected to find nature in the wild was France's industrial zone along the border with Belgium. Yet the plain of the canalized rivers Scarpe and Escaut has woods, marshes, ponds and streams where visitors can feel buried in the depths of the countryside.
 This coal-mining area stretches for 40 km (25 miles) east to west, and 15 km (10

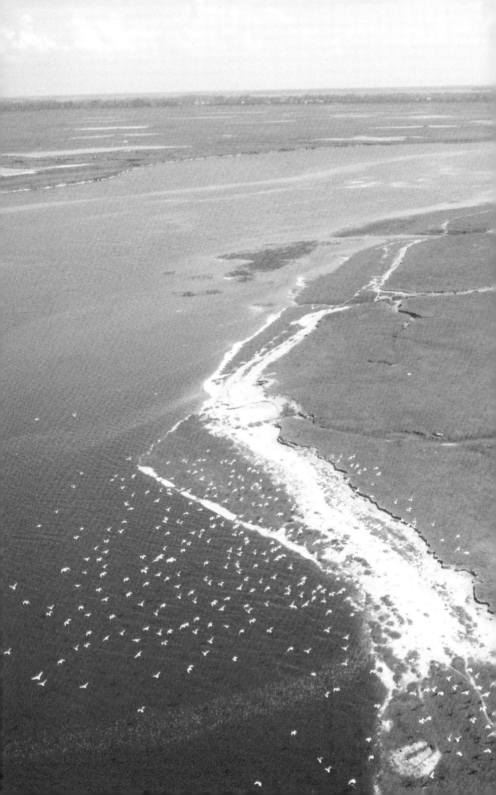

miles) north to south. The mines have now closed and nature has been able to take over again. Today the area comprises three main habitats: woodland (mostly oaks, pines and beeches), farmland and marshy ponds. At the centre is the old spa town of St-Amand-les-Eaux. The wide variations in both the acidity of the soil and the humidity have attracted an enormous diversity of wildlife, particularly birds and insects.

Having crunched my way up a black gritty path on a disused slag heap beside the Mare à Goriaux, I surveyed a scene as wild as any in France: a lake, which has grown, thanks to mining subsidence, from three marshy ponds, bordered by alder and willow. Its banks are thickly lined with reeds, bulrushes and water-lilies, providing a haven for waterfowl

The tidal estuary of the Somme is a vast desolate landscape but also home to countless thousands of wetland birds.

and insects, while the shallow waters conceal carp, bream and perch. On the flat top of the slag heap, young birches flourish and in spring the woods are carpeted with anemones, as well as bluebells and blueberries. Sweet-smelling lily of the valley appear by May. The warm gritty coal also provides a home for insects and small sea-birds such as the ringed plover, which likes to nest in the coal pebbles because they resemble the shingle of a beach.

Over 200 species of bird have been observed here since the park was created. Wild duck, grebe and heron thrive on the lake, while all around you can see and hear finches, larks, peewits, screech owls and nightingales.

In the autumn and spring, the lake and woods become a dormitory for large numbers of migratory birds, such as hen harrier, black kite, tern, sandpiper and swallow. If you are really lucky, in spring you might see an osprey swooping

Early morning frost sparkles in the winter landscape on the margins of the Forêt de Compiègne.

on to the water, although its stay in the area is always brief. Every October, wild duck reappear, in some years as many as 2,000.

The Forêt de Raismes-St-Amand-Wallers, the largest area of woodland in the park, was largely replanted with firs after substantial felling during World War I. However, an avenue of 180-year-old beeches remains, regally lining one of the roads through the forest. Acacias were also planted to improve the soil, which now supports oak, hornbeam and hawthorn. In five special botanic reserves there are the diminutive carnivorous sundew, broom and mosses.

Before you go *Maps:* IGN 1:100,000 Nos. 2 & 4; IGN 1:25,000 Nos. 2505-06 ET and 2605-06 OT & ET. **Getting there** *By car:* the nearest town, Valenciennes, 5 km (3 miles) south of the park boundary, is

39

on the A2, which branches off the A1 Paris-Lille road. A23 (Valenciennes-Lille) passes near the Mare à Goriaux, while D169 (Valenciennes-Tournai) and D935 also cross the park. *By rail:* Eurostar (see p33) and TGV services to Lille. Frequent local trains from Lille to Valenciennes. *By bus:* a half-hourly service, Ligne 4H, runs from Valenciennes station to the edge of the Forêt de Raismes and to the Centre d'Amaury, at Hergnies (see *Adventure holidays* below). **Where to stay:** there are several hotels in St-Amand-les-Eaux, including the 2-star Grand Hôtel de Paris, T: 03 27 48 21 00, or, near the Forêt de Raismes, the Hôtel Thermale, T: 03 27 48 50 37, a grand spa establishment with a pool and casino. The hostel at Le Luron in St-Amand-les-Eaux, T: 03 27 48 01 20, was once a hunting lodge. *Outdoor living:* try Camping Mont des Bruyères, T: 03 27 48 56 87, in the forest near St-Amand-les-Eaux (open Mar-Nov). **Activities** *Walking:* trails wind through the Forêt de Raismes, around the Mare à Goriaux and beside the lake and canals at the Amaury centre. GR121 crosses the park. *Cycling:* bicycles for hire at St-Amand-les-Eaux, Beloeil and Raismes. There are several cycle routes through the forest. *Riding:* ADTE du Nord, 23 rue de Bazinghien, 59000 Lille, T: 03 20 09 76 22, will provide details of riding centres. *Adventure holidays:* the Centre d'Amaury in Hergnies, T: 03 27 25 28 85, has activities such as sailing, wind-surfing, canoeing, fishing and cycling. Alternatively, contact Loisirs Accueil du Nord, 6 rue Gauthier du Châtillon, 59013 Lille, T: 03 20 57 59 59. *Field studies:* the Maison de la Forêt in Raismes, T: 03 27 36 72 72, has displays and organizes excursions into the forest.

40

> ## BEECH FORESTS OF NORTHERN FRANCE
> The beech is most at home in central Europe, but it forms the major component of many of the great forests of northern France. Typically the trees have been subject to selective felling, leaving great stands of towering, even-aged trees. Beech occurs mostly on shallow, porous soil, which does not support much undergrowth. Together with the very low light penetration to the ground in high summer, this soil type makes for a very open, if rather dark, interior. The straight, grey trunks stretching up to the high canopy impart a mysterious feeling, like being in some natural cathedral. Bird life is hard to track down, being mostly hidden in the upper canopy, but where there are mixed stands with hornbeam and oak and great rides cut through the forest, you may catch a glimpse of some of the raptors, such as goshawk, sparrowhawk or honey buzzard.

Further information *Tourist office:* St-Amand-les-Eaux, Grand Place, T: 03 27 22 24 47. *Park office:* Le Luron, 357 rue Notre-Dame-d'Amour, St-Amand-les-Eaux, T: 03 27 19 19 70, F: 03 27 19 19 71.

Forêt de Compiègne & Forêt de Laigue

Dense forests located 80 km (50 miles) north of Paris; former royal hunting grounds, now preserving their rich wildlife

The ancient forests that surround Paris are among the most attractive in France. Despite the millions who live in the area and seek recreation outdoors, these forests are often remarkably wild. Footpaths, bridleways and cycle tracks lead into thick woods where the silence is disturbed only by the rustling of leaves. The beech and oak Forêt de Compiègne is one of the largest forests in the country, covering 14,458 ha (35,700 acres). It is also less frequented than those nearer the capital. Across the

River Aisne is the Forêt de Laigue, which covers another 3,827 ha (9,450 acres).

Sturdy wooden signposts, painted white with small pointers, caught my eye as I drove into the forest along the avenue des Beaux-Monts, which leads from the imposing Château de Compiègne. The *poteaux* (posts) stand reassuringly at every crossing along the many straight, sandy tracks leading through the forest. Their presence dates from the middle of the 19th century. Once, when out on a hunting expedition, the Empress Eugénie, wife of Napoléon III, got hopelessly lost — not surprising as the leafy alleyways all look remarkably similar. To prevent a repetition, the Emperor immediately ordered the posts to be erected. Though some are now rather dilapidated, if you look closely you can see that each bears a red spot. Stand with your back to the spot and the way ahead always leads to Compiègne.

Both forests were at the heart of the vast Sylvacestes woods that covered the entire area in Roman times; due to their proximity to the capital, successive French kings jealously preserved them for hunting. The oldest oak woods in the Beaux-Monts area, on the northern side of the forest, were planted by François I during the 16th century. During the 18th and 19th centuries, 3,000 more hectares (7,400 acres) of oaks were planted, together with pines in places where the soil is poorer. Beeches predominate in the hillier parts, where the forest trails are particularly pleasant for walking; in spring, sunlight streams through the branches, lighting up a vibrant jumble of wild flowers in the undergrowth.

The highest points, from which there are remarkably lovely views, are called *monts* (mountains), yet rise to no more than 120 m (400 ft)! At the lowest levels there are small tranquil lakes where fishing is allowed. Their reedy banks provide a haven for large numbers of wild ducks, herons and a regular passage colony of migrant waterfowl. The trees are also home to a wide range of birds, but when walking through the serried columns of the high beech forest you are likely to experience a blanketing silence; the occasional robin or chaffinch may call, but specialities such as the woodpeckers, owls and raptors remain unheard. Wild boar and roe and red deer are common in the remoter parts of the forests, particularly on the Mont des Singes in Laigue; they are still hunted from September to March.

In spring the ground is carpeted with wild anemones and bluebells, while the Laigue's south-east-facing slopes are covered in sweet-smelling lily of the valley. In autumn, the beech forests turn a stunning amber.

Pretty villages of shuttered stone cottages with stepped slate roofs have grown up in a handful of clearings, the most famous of which is Clairière de l'Armistice ('Armistice clearing'). It was here that Marshal Foch, Commander-in-Chief of the Allied Forces, headed the delegation which, on 11th November 1918, signed the Armistice ending World War I. The ceremony took place in a railway carriage. A statue of Foch surrounded by a simple circle of firs commemorates the historic event and a similar brown polished Wagon-Lits carriage provides the centre-piece of a small museum in which documents, newspapers and photographs are on display. **Before you go** *Maps:* IGN 1:100,000 No. 9; IGN 1:25,000 No. 2511 OT. **Getting there** *By car:* 80 km (50 miles) north of Paris, N31 leads from the A1 into Compiègne. The D932, D332, D973 and N31 lead into the Forêt de Compiègne; D85 crosses it. D130 crosses the Forêt de Laigue. *By rail:* there are regular services to Compiègne from Paris-Gare du Nord. *By bus:* regular bus services operate throughout the area from Compiègne. *By bicycle:* the Paris-Lille long-distance route runs through the forest. **Where to stay:** Compiègne has a good selection of hotels at various prices. The 2-star Hôtel de Flandre, T: 03 44 83 24 40, is near the station and overlooks the River Aisne. More central is the 2-star Hôtel de France in rue Eugène-Floquet, T: 03 44 40 02 74. There are also rural *gîtes d'étape* situated on walking and cycling routes. *Outdoor living:* camping is permitted in designated areas. Try Terrain av Baron-R-de-Soultrait, T: 03 44 20 28 58 (open Mar-Nov). **Activities** *Walking:* the 2 forests are criss-crossed by marked trails, including GR12 from Paris to Belgium. There is a 10-km (6-mile) nature circuit around Mont St-Pierre. *Cycling:*

The fragrant lily of the valley is a characteristic spring flower of beech woodland.

marked tracks run through the forests. A popular excursion is to Pierrefonds, a round trip of about 25 km (15 miles) from Compiègne. Bicycles available at Compiègne railway station. *Riding:* there are bridle paths in the forests; riders are not allowed on footpaths. Contact Poney Club de Compiègne, T: 03 44 85 63 63. *Fishing:* permits for the Aisne and Oise rivers and forest ponds from Oise fishing federation, 10 rue Pasteur, Compiègne, T: 03 44 40 46 41. *Museums:* the Château de Compiègne is a former royal palace now open to the public, T: 03 44 38 47 00. Armistice museum, T: 03 44 85 14 18. *Exhibition:* there is a small information centre with displays on wildlife and trees in the Maison Forestière des Etangs St-Pierre, open Mon-Sat. Contact ONF Compiègne, T: 03 44 40 02 75, who also organize nature walks. **Further information** *Tourist offices:* Compiègne, pl de l'Hôtel de Ville, T: 03 44 40 01 00, www.mairie-compiegne.fr; Pierrefonds, pl de l'Hôtel de Ville, T: 03 44 42 81 44.

Champagne

Varied landscape, ranging from the vast vineyards of 'dry' Champagne to the lakes and forests of the 'wet' part; contains parcs naturels régionaux of Montagne de Reims and Forêt d'Orient
Ramsar, ZICO, World Heritage Site

The sturdy green vines that have made Champagne famous stretch in ruler-straight lines over hillside after hillside in the 'dry' northern part of the region, where the soil is predominantly chalk.

Centuries ago, before the planting of the vines, these chalk hills were considered a wasteland. Now only the inaccessible military training grounds lend any clue to how the natural landscape looked. Areas not turned over to cultivation have been planted with conifers. Nevertheless, conditions in the open, cultivated areas are still favourable for two of Europe's most exciting 'steppe' birds — the stone curlew and little bustard. Despite their size, they are almost impossible to pick out, being perfectly camouflaged against the grey and brown stony ground. Much commoner are grey partridge and quail, to be heard but rarely seen, together with crested larks and corn buntings, typical of arable France.

Reference literature proclaims that more than 30,000 hectares (75,000 acres) of vineyards on Champagne's chalky ridges are dedicated to producing 330 million bottles of France's most sought-after wine each year. This fact left me pessimistic about finding any corner of the precious soil unturned, let alone wild. Yet between the towns of Epernay and Reims, the hilly forests of the Montagne de Reims, decreed a *parc naturel régional* in 1976, provide a sharp contrast to the vineyards. The area is not so much a mountain as a plateau, the highest point being 228 metres (750 feet) at Mount Sinai, which affords a spectacular view over the

Poppies grow wild in the Champagne region in defiance of farmers' efforts.

Champagne plain. The indigenous beech and elm forests are interspersed with plantations of firs, while tiny villages nestle in clearings in the folds of the hills.

The ancient beech woods at Verzy, on the north-eastern side of the Montagne de Reims, are a particular curiosity. They are known to have existed since the 6th century, when reference was made to them in the annals of the local St-Basles abbey. The most venerable trees, mutations of the common beech, are probably more than 500 years old. Over time their branches have become so intertwined they form a domed ceiling, while the thick gnarled trunks, with their grotesque bumps and twists, are like the nightmarish visions of a Disney cartoon.

Bilberries carpet the undergrowth, while in the marshy areas thrives sundew with its curious round carnivorous leaves. Roe and red deer populate the woods, along with a small number of wild boar: many more boar used to come here from forests farther north but the arrival of nearby *autoroutes* has restricted these migrations.

'Wet' Champagne, which lies to the south of the vineyards, is a very different landscape. As you approach, leaving the dry lands behind, the soil turns from chalk to clay, creating a greener, lusher vegetation, also largely agricultural, but punctuated with oak woods, lakes and marshes.

The St-Gond marshes once covered the plain to the south of Epernay but now only small patches survive. Laced with rivulets and canals, the boggy land has been greatly exploited for peat. However, the marshes that still exist beside the road from Bannes to Joches are rich in wildlife, particularly birds: little owls, nightjars, great grey shrikes and several species of woodpecker, including wryneck. In these few remaining marshy fragments the elegant hen harrier and Montagu's harrier still cling on, but only just. The tall plantations of poplars are the place to stop and look for golden orioles — or rather, listen, for despite their gaudy plumage they usually remain well concealed.

The creation of huge reservoirs, such as the Lac d'Orient and the Lac du Der-Chantecoq near St-Dizier, has changed the countryside of 'wet' Champagne considerably since the 1960s. Forests, farmland and villages have disappeared underwater and tourists have begun to come to Champagne for beach holidays! At the same time, the Lac d'Orient and Lac du Temple are protected within the Parc Naturel Régional de la Forêt d'Orient and parts of the lakes have areas protected as ornithological reserves (though in summer the birds are adversely affected by all the leisure activities and the lower water levels). Red kites nest in the ash woods around the lakes; other common nesters include the great crested grebe and, to a lesser extent, shoveller ducks, pochards and teal. The dense woodland of the Forêt d'Orient is also known to support up to 350 different types of mushroom.

Since its creation in 1974, the Lac du Der — France's largest stretch of inland water with a perimeter of 77 kilometres (46 miles) — has become one of the country's major stop-over sites for migrating cranes. In autumn and spring, around 80,000 cross France on a 200-kilometre (125-mile) front on their migration route between Sweden and Spain. Champagne has always figured on the route, but now around 40,000 cranes rest at the Lac du Der and as many as 6,000 have been known to winter there.

The chanterelle (*Cantharellus cibarius*) is a highly prized and tasty mushroom. Its vivid orange trumpets are abundant in broad-leaved deciduous forests.

BEFORE YOU GO
Maps: IGN 1:100,000 Nos. 5, 9, 10 & 22.

GETTING THERE
By car: the A4 Autoroute de l'Est from Paris crosses the Montagne de Reims, as do N51 and D9. The N19 runs beside Orient lake and forest between Troyes and Bar-sur-Aube; the D1, D11 and D79 are scenic routes through the forest and lakes. The Der-Chantecoq lake lies due west of D384, 18 km (10 miles) south of St-Dizier.
By rail: there are direct services from Paris-Gare de l'Est to Reims, Epernay, Troyes and Châlons-en-Champagne with connections to St-Dizier.
By bus: STDM, T: 03 26 65 17 07, has a TransChampagne service from Reims to Troyes. There is a service from Troyes to the Forêt d'Orient, T: 03 25 71 28 42; for Der-Chantecoq there are buses from St-Dizier to Eclaron and Braucourt.

WHERE TO STAY
There is a choice of hotels in Troyes, Reims, St-Dizier and Epernay, as well as *auberges* throughout the area. The *auberge* Le Cheval Blanc, T: 03 26 72 62 65, is near the dam of Der-Chantecoq in the village of Giffaumont-Champaubert.
Youth hostels: in St-Dizier, St-Julien-les-Villas and Vendeuvre-sur-Barse.
Outdoor living: Camping de la Presqu'île de Champaubert, T: 03 25 04 13 20, is one of several camp-sites beside the Der-Chantecoq lake. Near Reims is the Airotel de Champagne camp-site, rte de Châlons-sur-Marne, T: 03 26 85 41 22.

ACTIVITIES
Walking: marked trails traverse the Forêt d'Orient, including the GRP offshoot of the GR2 path and a walk that passes the spot where the Order of the Knights Templar settled in the

The golden oriole is hard to spot high up in the dense woodland canopy, despite the bright plumage of the males.

13th century. GR14, 141 and 142 cross the Montagne de Reims, where there are also several shorter routes, which give a taste of the local villages, views, wildlife and architecture. There are short walks in the Verzy and Hautvillers woods.
Cycling: information on cycle hire and itineraries is available from park offices. The Bouchon du Champagne route tours the countryside around Reims.
Riding: contact ARTE for Champagne-Ardenne, 3 impasse de la Bionnerie, 51170 Ville-en-Tardenois, T: 03 26 61 88 96, F: 03 26 61 88 97.
Watersports: several clubs are based on the lakes, offering sailing, water-skiing, wind-surfing and scuba diving. Fishing is allowed on Lac d'Orient and Lac du Der. Contact the Giffaumont-Champagne tourist office for activities on the Lac du Der.
Reserves/museums: in the Forêt d'Orient, an animal reserve has red and roe deer and wild boar; several bird sanctuaries have observation points beside each lake. There is a bird and fish museum at Outines on the Lac du Der-Chantecoq, T: 03 26 74

00 00. The museum village of Ste-Marie-du-Lac, T: 03 26 72 63 25, features half-timbered buildings typical of the Champagne countryside. There is an exhibition on the natural history of the Montagne de Reims at the Maison du Parc in Pourcy, and a museum devoted to forestry, La Maison du Bûcheron, in the village of Germaine, T: 03 26 59 44 44.

FURTHER INFORMATION
Tourist offices: Châlons-en-Champagne, 3 quai des Arts, T: 03 26 65 17 89; Epernay, 7 av de Champagne, T: 03 26 53 33 00; Reims, 12 blvd Général Leclerc, T: 03 26 77 45 00, www.tourisme.fr/reims; Sézanne, pl de la République, T: 03 26 80 51 43; St-Dizier, 4 av de Belle Forêt-sur-Marne, T: 03 25 05 31 84; Troyes, 16 blvd Carnot, T: 03 25 82 62 70, www.ot-troyes.fr. Maison du Lac du Der-Chantecoq, Giffaumont-Champaubert, T: 03 26 72 62 80.
Park offices: Montagne de Reims, 51480 Pourcy, T: 03 26 59 44 44, F: 03 26 59 41 63; Forêt d'Orient, 10220 Piney, T: 03 25 43 81 90.

Parc Régional de Lorraine

Unique area of forests, salt ponds and grassy hillside oases near Strasbourg;
parc naturel régional
Ramsar, ZICO
208,000 ha (514,000 acres)

There I was, 400 km (250 miles) from the sea in the heart of Lorraine, yet a small patch of saltwort was growing beside other marine plants in a sandy dell. Its tiny distinctive leaves, spiky and a delicate pink colour, looked decidedly out of place so far from the coast.

This is just one of the remarkable quirks of nature found in the extensive Parc Naturel Régional de Lorraine, which is divided into two sections on either side of the River Moselle. The salt beneath the soil, on the vast plain between the Moselle to the west and the Vosges in the east, rises to the surface in several places at shallow *mares salées* (salt ponds), which evaporate in summer. Most plants cannot tolerate the salinity, so only those that thrive by the sea grow here. On the edge of the village of Marsal, a short trail enables visitors to observe these plants in a small botanical reserve. The reserve is designed to protect them from not only people, but also the hardier reeds and grasses that would otherwise overwhelm them.

Lorraine is also notable for its *pelouses calcaires*. These are patches of grass on sheltered hillsides where the limestone is topped by a thin layer of comparatively poor sandy soil, which supports an exceptional variety of exotic and rare wild flowers. A typical example lies

near the village of Génicourt-sur-Meuse, where you can follow a marked trail at the foot of a disused quarry. Twenty different varieties of wild orchid bloom here between May and September, when their delicate and exquisitely marked petals mingle with over 30 other varieties of flower. Broom, hawthorn and hazel grow around them, as well as saplings of oak and birch.

Another characteristic of Lorraine, particularly on the eastern side, is its large shallow *étangs* (lakes). Though too big to be called ponds, they are never more than waist-deep, so the water warms through to the bottom in summer. Some *étangs* are used for watersports, but others are kept strictly for the birds and fish. Their still waters and reed fringes offer an attractive stopping point for all kinds of birds of passage: black storks, black-winged stilts and, in winter, the very rare white-tailed eagle are among the specialities.

Of the 500 species of birds seen in France, around 320 have been sighted at the Etang de Lindre; 120 actually nest here, including the elusive and now rare bittern. Otters occur here, too, but rarely show themselves. Surrounded by woods and fields, the habitat is varied and wonderfully undisturbed as public access is severely restricted; most of the lake is surrounded by privately owned farmland with no roads across. A good spot from which to observe the bird life is the old dam in the village of Lindre-Basse at the western end, where you can walk for a short distance beside the water. At the other end there is a hide at Guermange.

Another superb wetland site is the Etang de Gondrexange. Like many others in the region, it is noted as a place for migrant birds in autumn and

winter, but for many people the most magical time is spring, when the dawn chorus is in full voice, pouring across the still waters from the dense forests and reed beds. The rich symphony of bird calls is dominated by two virtuosi — the nightingale and the golden oriole — but if you pay closer attention you may be rewarded with the short and simple song of the collared flycatcher, which can be heard in only a few places in France.

Before you go *Maps:* IGN 1:100,000 Nos. 11 and 12; IGN 1:25,000 Nos. 3213-15, 3313-

15, 3514-15, 3614-15 OT.
Getting there *By car:* the east-west A4 and north-south A31 cross Lorraine through Metz. *By rail:* main-line services from Paris-Gare de l'Est to Metz and Nancy. Local services from Metz to Sarrebourg. *By bus:* there is a network of local services radiating from Metz and Nancy, but you cannot rely on being able to get one to every small village; few buses run on Sun. **Where to stay:** accommodation of all standards is available in Nancy or Metz, and there are many smaller towns and villages with

1- and 2-star hotels. Pont-à-Mousson on the Moselle lies between the 2 sections of the regional park. Sarrebourg and Dieuze are convenient for the east side, St-Mihiel for the west. *Outdoor living:* camp-sites include Camping de la Base de Plein Air de St-Mihiel, T: 03 29 89 03 59, and Camping Les Mouettes at Gondrexange, T: 03 87 25 06 01. **Activities** *Walking:* the regional park organizes nature walks throughout the summer; themes include bird-watching, the *mares salées* and the *pelouses calcaires.* GR5 crosses

Open water, marshland and forest support abundant, varied wildlife in the Etang de Gondrexange.

the east section of the park and runs along the edge of the western section. There is a trail to the *mare salée* at Marsal, a marked woodland walk at Mulcey and a nature trail beside the *pelouse calcaire* at Génicourt-sur-Meuse. *Riding:* contact ARTE de Lorraine, 1 rue Eugène Vallin, 54000 Nancy, T: 03 83 37 02 72. *Fishing:* carp, pike and eels are plentiful in the *étangs*; fishing permits from local tourist offices. *Adventure holidays:* the St-Mihiel activity centre, T: 03 29 89 03 59, runs courses in canoeing, caving and archery; it also organizes walking and biking excursions. Loisirs Accueil Moselle, 1 rue du Pont Moteau, 57036 Metz, T: 03 87 37 57 80. *Museums:* there is an *écovillage* at Ville-sur-Yvon, T: 03 82 33 91 70, which offers a tour of a typical Lorrainian village, as well as the Ste-Croix animal park near Rhodes, T: 03 87 03 92 05. **Further information** *Tourist offices:* Pont-à-Mousson, pl Duroc, T: 03 83 81 06 90; Metz, pl d'Armes, T: 03 87 55 53 76; Nancy, pl Stanislas, T: 03 83 35 22 41; St-Mihiel, rue du Palais de Justice, T: 03 29 89 06 47. *Park office:* Domaine de Charmilly, chemin des Clos, 54702 Pont-à-Mousson, T: 03 83 81 12 77, www.parcs-naturels-regionaux.tm.fr.

Massif des Vosges

Wild high point — literally — of the North-East, with wooded mountains rising to 1,400 m (4,600 ft) above the Rhine valley; includes Parc Naturel Régional des Ballons des Vosges (288,000 ha/712,000 acres) ZICO

The Vosges massif is the most extensive area of wildness in North-East France. It stretches about 100 kilometres (60 miles) from north to south and 50 kilometres (30 miles) across, rising to 1,424 metres (4,672 feet) at Le Grand Ballon. The mountainsides are thickly wooded, mostly up to their softly rounded beech-wood summits, and dotted with small glacial lakes and bogs.

The high forest is home to the large turkey-like capercaillie, a shy bird. At mating time the males put on a big show in the clearings, ruffling their feathers, cooing and strutting. Unfortunately, the approach of unwanted spectators rather cools their ardour and they wander off without finishing the job in hand.

Because foliage is dense, it takes skill and patience to spot any wildlife in the Vosges, though there is plenty around. Six species of tits nest in these high forests, as well as Europe's two smallest songbirds, the gold- and fire-crests. Honey buzzards arrive in the forests in June, and there are sparrowhawks and goshawks, as well as speckled Tengmalm's owls. Hazelhens thrive in areas of young conifers, burrowing in to the winter snow for food. Red and roe deer are increasing in number, and there are good populations of pine and beech martens. Chamois

have also been reintroduced here.

The thickness of the forest makes panoramic views hard to come by, though you get glimpses down over pristine valleys and lakes as you twist around hair-pin bends when negotiating mountain passes such as the Col de la Schlucht. Most spectacular is the Route des Crêtes, which follows the ridges along the north-south backbone. The views are particularly dramatic at the south

Tengmalm's owl has recently spread from upland forest to beech woodland.

end of the route, where the road is highest: on a clear day you can see right across the Rhine plain to the Black Forest in Germany. Half-way along the road, at Hohneck, 1,362 metres (4,468 feet) high, a small botanical garden of alpine plants has been laid out. The garden features typical flowers from mountainous areas around the world, such as wild orchids and the yellow gentian, whose big cauliflower-like leaves are traditionally used to make *schnapps*.

Flowers thrive on the sunny mountaintops where trees have been felled to create grassy summit pastures, or *chaumes*, another feature of the Vosges. These clearings, warmed by the dry wind known as the *foehn*, are reputed to date back to the 7th century, when Irish monks settled in the village of Munster (named after their homeland) and wanted grass for their cattle in summer. Farmers have done the same ever since, though the custom is becoming less popular because it is uneconomic compared with modern farming methods. As a result the *chaumes* are under threat from the encroaching trees. The Gazon du Faing *chaume* near La Valtin is among several areas that have been designated as nature reserves under the auspices of the Parc Naturel Régional des Ballons des Vosges, created in 1989.

Bogs are another famous characteristic of the Vosges, though they are small compared with those in, say, Scotland. But what they lack in size, they make up for in numbers on both hilltops and slopes. Andromeda, a protected species from the heather family,

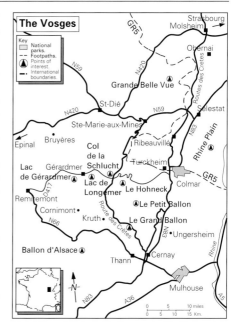

thrives in these marshy wet areas, as do all the four vacciniums (wild bilberry, blueberry, cowberry and cranberry) and also sundew, one of the carnivorous *Drosera* species.

The natural habitats of the Vosges are threatened mainly by skiing and viticulture. Many mountainsides have been taken over by ski resorts and pistes, while the east-facing slopes of the Vosges have for centuries been anything but wild: here the vineyards that produce Alsace's famous wines stretch for miles above the flood plain of the Rhine.

Despite its industrial image, the wide, flat Rhine valley retains many areas of ecological interest. Most notable is the Ried, an area of lush meadows on alluvial deposits along the valley floor, which are flooded in spring and autumn. These water meadows are a source of great botanical interest, with even minor variations in elevation sufficient to reveal distinct differences in the flora. The Ried has a number of plants in common with Siberia, but the most characteristic species are the low, delicate spikes of green-winged orchids and the Chiltern gentian.

A RETURN TO THE PAST

For centuries regarded locally as a sign of good luck (and fertility), white storks are being reintroduced to Alsace at several breeding centres. Numbers decreased drastically in the 1980s due to the draining of marshes along the Rhine, hunting in North Africa (their winter destination) and the erection of power lines, but recently they have risen again to around 700. Young birds are kept in the breeding centres for their first three years to curb their migratory instinct; afterwards, they are content to winter in the area. It is good to see them nesting in the church spires and chimney pots again.

(*Overleaf*) A typical winter landscape graces the Lac du Forlet in the Vosges mountains.

BEFORE YOU GO
Maps: IGN 1:100,000 No. 31; IGN 1:25,000 Nos. 3518-19, 3616-21 and 3715-21.

GETTING THERE
By car: several main east-west roads cross the Vosges; these are steep and twisting in the mountains. The north-south routes are slower but extremely scenic; these include the Route du Vin, through the vineyards and wine-making villages, and the Route des Crêtes between Ste-Marie-aux-Mines and Cernay. For details of the wine route, contact Maison des Vins d'Alsace in Colmar, T: 03 89 20 16 20, www.alsacewine.com. Drivers can rely on even the narrowest, most remote mountain roads being in good condition.
By rail: there are main-line services to Strasbourg, Colmar

The capercaillie, a retiring and secretive bird of the forested uplands, nevertheless exhibits a spectacular mating display.

and Mulhouse, with connections into the Vosges as far as Metzeral, Kruth, Cornimont and Bruyères. Services run between Strasbourg, Lunéville, Sélestat and St-Die.
By bus: towns and villages in the main valleys are served by buses at least once a day.

WHERE TO STAY
The area has a good choice of hotels and inns, particularly in Gérardmer, Ribeauville and Turckheim. Farmhouses in the valleys offer accommodation, a centuries-old tradition, and there are self-catering *gîtes*.
Outdoor living: many villages have a municipal camp-site; these include Munster, T: 03 89 77 31 08, Turckheim, T: 03 89 27 02 00, and Obernai, T: 03 88 95 38 48.

ACTIVITIES
Walking: there are marked trails in the forests and across the open pastures. The Club Vosgien in Strasbourg, T: 03 88

32 57 96, organizes walking tours and sells IGN maps already marked-up with the area's GR routes. GR5 follows the north-south ridges, passing the alpine botanical garden at Hohneck. GR53, 531, 532 and 533 also cross the region.
Cycling: the Raid Vosgien, Randonnée des Vosges and Randonnée des Ballons Vosgiens cross the mountains.
Riding: ARTE d'Alsace, Maison des Associations, 6 rte d'Ingersheim, 68000 Colmar, T: 03 83 37 02 72, F: 03 89 23 15 08, will provide details of equestrian centres.
Watersports: the lakes at Gérardmer and Xonrupt-Longemer have boats for hire. There is canoeing on the region's many rivers; contact the Ligue d'Alsace de Canoë-Kayak, 15 rue de Genève, Strasbourg, T: 03 88 21 10 66.
Ballooning: for an aerial view of the Vosges, contact Aérovision in Munster, T: 03 89 77 22 81.
Skiing: contact the Comité Régional de Ski des Vosges in Mulhouse, T: 03 89 43 25 50.
Adventure holidays: contact Loisirs Accueil Haut-Rhin, 1 rue Schlumberger, 68007 Colmar, T: 03 89 20 10 62/60.
Ecology: there is a stork reintroduction centre in Hunawihr, T: 03 89 73 72 62.
Exhibitions: the largest *ecomusée* in France is at Ungersheim, T: 03 89 74 44 74; it features 42 furnished old Alsatian buildings.

FURTHER INFORMATION
Tourist offices: Colmar, 4 rue des Unterlinden, T: 03 89 20 68 92, www.tourisme.fr/COLMAR; Gérardmer, pl des Déportés, T: 03 29 27 27 27, www.ville-gerardmer.fr; Strasbourg, 17 pl de la Cathédrale, T: 03 88 52 28 28.
Park office: Ballons des Vosges, 1 cour de l'Abbaye, 68140 Munster, T: 03 89 77 90 34, F: 03 89 77 90 30.

Vosges du Nord

Secluded hills with varied flora and fauna on site of the ill-fated Maginot Line; parc naturel régional Biosphere Reserve, World Heritage Site 122,000 ha (300,000 acres)

Driving through the pretty northern Vosges, I wondered how it had managed to escape an invasion by tourists. Its soft misty horizons of wooded hillsides dotted with curiously shaped sandstone rocks and ruined medieval castles are not really spectacular, but they have a certain charm and beauty. One answer is that it is relatively tucked away in the far north-eastern corner of France. Another might be that the region has physical and cultural characteristics that seem curiously un-French.

With ubiquitous huge piles of logs for winter fires and meadows of wild flowers, the Vosges du Nord has a distinctly alpine feel, yet the cliffs and soil are red, more reminiscent of the Mediterranean. Place names are Germanic, reflecting the fact that Alsace was under German jurisdiction from 1870 to the end of World War I. The ugly concrete fortifications near the German border, which once formed part of the Maginot Line, built between the two world wars, also add to the sense of being in a frontierland.

The fact that the Parc Naturel Régional des Vosges-du-Nord has been designated a Biosphere Reserve reflects the wealth of its flora and fauna.

Beech, Scots pine and oak predominate in the 72,000 ha (177,900 acres) of woodland which form an important part of the park. Twice as I drove along, a deer hurried across the road just in front of me. Wild boar are also common, but sightings of wildcats and martens are rare. The wealth of game animals reflects the tight hunting controls, a relic of German influence. In holes on the sandstone cliffs, several pairs of peregrine falcons are nesting; one of the places where they can be seen is the rocky crags of Erbsenfelsen. Tengmalm's owl is also known to nest hereabouts.

The plants that thrive in the park are extremely varied, ranging from delicate pink alpine laurels and the curious round-leaf sundew to the rare lily-like water arum and wood's grape-fern. The variety of flora reflects the diversity of habitats in the park, ranging from moors and sandy grasslands to marshes and peat bogs.

In a well-placed hide in the bushes and reeds around the pretty lake at Baerenthal, there is an identification chart showing 27 species of bird and the best spots to look out for them. It includes those that nest here, such as kingfishers, great crested grebe and coots; those that winter here, such as teal and tufted duck; and migrants, such as grey herons and occasionally ospreys.

Before you go *Maps:* IGN 1:100,000 No. 12; IGN 1:25,000 Nos. 3613-14 ET, 3713-14 ET, 3814 ET and 3914 OT. *Guide-books:* park headquarters have guides to the deer, birds and castles; it also has leaflets on the wildlife and walking trails. **Getting there** *By car:* the A4 runs along the south of the area between Metz and Strasbourg; N62 crosses it from Haguenau to Bitche. *By rail:* main-line service from Paris-Gare de l'Est to Saverne, or there are services from Strasbourg to Sarreguemines with connections to Bitche, Niederbronn and Haguenau. *By bus:* hourly services operate between some villages, including Ingwiller and La Petite-Pierre. **Where to stay:** the main tourist centres are Bitche and Niederbronn-les-Bains, where the 3-star Muller, 16 av de la Libération, T: 03 88 63 38 38, is renowned for its cuisine. *Outdoor living:* there is a campsite in Baerenthal, T: 03 87 06 50 73, and others in Bitche, Saverne, Oberbronn and the Etang de Hanau. **Activities** *Walking:* contact Club Vosgien, T: 03 88 32 57 96, which organizes walking tours. GR53 crosses the Vosges du Nord via La Petite-Pierre and Oberbronn; GR531 and 532 also cross the park. There are marked nature trails at Geyerstein near La Petite-Pierre and around the lake at Hanau. Bird hide at the Etang de Baerenthal, T: 03 87 06 50 26; collect the key from the town hall, 8am-12pm or 2-6pm. *Cycling:* the Raid Vosgiens long-distance route passes through the park. *Riding:* contact ADTE du Bas-Rhin, 4 rue des Violettes, 67201 Echbolsheim, T: 03 88 77 39 64, for details of equestrian centres. *Adventure holidays:* contact Loisirs Accueil Bas-Rhin, 9 rue du Dôme, BP 53, 67061 Strasbourg, T: 03 88 15 45 85/88. *Exhibitions:* there are displays on water, sandstone and forest in the castle at La Petite-Pierre, T: 03 88 01 49 59, and on the flora and fauna at the Maison de la Forêt at Etang de Hanau. *Field studies:* the regional park has a programme of excursions with themes such as natural history, archaeology and history. **Further information** *Tourist offices:* Bitche, Hôtel de Ville, T: 03 87 06 16 16; Niederbronn-les-Bains, 2 pl de l'Hôtel-de-Ville, T: 03 88 80 89 70. *Park office:* 67290 La Petite-Pierre, T: 03 88 01 49 59, F: 03 88 01 49 60, www.parcs-naturels-regionaux.tm.fr.

CHAPTER 3

The Alps

Over 200 million years ago dinosaurs lived out their last days in a temperate region by the edge of an ocean known as Tethys, which covered the area where the Alps now stand. The movement of giant continental plates on the surface of the earth spelt the end for this ancient sun trap, and the dinosaurs living there. The land mass south of Tethys pushed north, causing the sea to dry up as the Alps buckled and heaved upwards.

Evidence that these mountains were once sea bed shows itself even to the casual hiker. Walking in the Ecrins national park one day, I turned over some limestone at the side of the path. On the other side of the stone was a fossil ammonite, an extinct marine creature related to the modern nautilus and squid. When this creature died the area was sea, yet the hardened rock that retained its outline was now nearly a kilometre above sea level. Ammonites were a common feature of this ancient seascape and I was struck by the thought that I held 200 million years of history in my hand.

Even though I have travelled through the Alps on countless occasions, their soaring peaks and dramatic scenery never fail to inspire me. The mountains tower above the valleys, dwarfing people, fields and entire towns. A patchwork of meadows and woods covers the lower slopes, but your gaze is drawn quite naturally to some distant summit high above the tree-line where the rocks stand raw and naked, offering you a rude and majestic slice of nature.

The mountain range is shaped like a

The Massif de la Chartreuse, whose impressive limestone cliffs dominate the dense mixed forest lying below, is home to many rare species such as the wildcat, eagle owl and raven.

MOUNTAIN SAFETY

The Alps are a genuinely wild place and can present dangers to those who venture into them without taking sensible precautions. The weather can change quickly in the mountains; even in summer it is possible to get stranded by mist and fog and exposure can be a serious hazard. Always take a waterproof and warm clothing, walking boots with moulded rubber soles (smooth soles can be lethal), food, maps and a compass. A whistle could save your life by attracting attention if you get into difficulties.

Always tell someone where you are going and how long you intend to be, especially if walking alone.

crescent moon around the north of Italy, forming a natural boundary with neighbouring France, Switzerland, Austria and Yugoslavia. France has the highest peak in the range, Mont Blanc, which at 4,807 metres (15,760 feet) is Western Europe's highest mountain.

The French Alpine region divides fairly naturally into five parts: the warm, dry Alpes Maritimes at the southern end of the range; the higher western Alps, containing the Ecrins and Queyras massifs, and the Pennine Alps, encompassing the Mont Blanc massif; the Jura, further north, pushed up by the opposing pressures of the Alps and Massif Central; and the Préalpes, a chain of foothills lying to the west.

The physical and mental challenge of crossing this formidable natural barrier has fired both the classical and modern imagination. In 218 BC, Hannibal astounded the ancient world by marching some 30,000 troops and 38 elephants across on his way to Rome. Snowfall and landslides hindered their passage and most of the elephants perished, but the army still managed to make the journey in only fifteen days. When following either of the two routes that historians believe Hannibal may have taken — the valley of the Durance river, which passes Briançon, or the more northerly Genèvre pass — one cannot help but wonder at this feat.

Conditions in the Alps can be harsh and at altitudes above 3,300 metres (10,000 feet) the snow is likely to be permanent. Glaciers have carved out deep valleys, often creating what are known as 'chimneys': needles of hard rock more resistant to glacial erosion than softer rocks around them. Lower down, rich sub-Alpine flora and fauna exist in milder conditions amongst woods of pine, larch and beech.

For centuries the height of the Alps kept 'civilization' at a distance and helped to preserve the region's natural habitats, but in recent times hunting and skiing have taken their toll. The Alpine ibex, once common throughout the mountains, was hunted to extinction in the Ecrins and Vercors over a hundred years ago. It was hunted not only for its meat but also for one particular bone, whose cruciform shape had acquired mystical value as a talisman. Over the last thirty years, new ski lifts and access roads have encroached into areas previously left for wildlife. However, the creation of three national parks and three regional parks during the same period has helped redress the balance and has allowed the revival of ibex and other Alpine specialities.

Another characteristic Alpine mammal is the marmot, a ground-based relative of the squirrel similar to the American groundhog, which lives, like the ibex and chamois, above the tree-line. When alarmed, marmots emit a shrill whistle, warning friends and family of impending danger, which often comes in the shape of a golden eagle overhead. This majestic bird (the French call it the *aigle royale*) still nests in the more remote parts of the Alps; marmots form part of its staple diet.

GETTING THERE
By air: international airports are at Lyon-Satolas, T: 04 72 22 72 21, and Nice, T: 04 93 21 30 30. Internal services also go to Mulhouse, Grenoble and Chambéry. Contact Air France (see p13).
By car: the A6 Autoroute du Soleil is as much for skiers as for sun worshippers; exit on to A36, near Beaune, for Besançon and the Jura, or A40, near Mâcon, for the Haute Savoie. Farther south, A43 from Lyon leads to Grenoble. N85 heads north out of Nice through the Alpine foothills to Gap and Grenoble.
By rail: Eurostar, T: 08 36 35 35 39, www.eurostar.com, operates the 'ski train' from London to Moutiers and Bourg St-Maurice. TGV services run from Paris-Gare de Lyon to Lyon, Grenoble, Chambéry, Modane, Bourg-St-Maurice, Annecy and St-Gervais (for Mont Blanc). Lyon and Grenoble are the best places to pick up local connections.

By bus: Eurolines, T: 08 36 69 51 51, www.eurolines.fr, has services to Besançon, Aix-les-Bains, Annecy, Chambéry, Chamonix, Grenoble, Valence, Lyon and Nice. Busabout, www.busabout.com, has buses to Lyon, Chamonix and Nice. Tourist offices will provide details of local services.

WHEN TO GO
The Alps make a spectacular destination whatever the time of year, whether for summer hill-walking or winter skiing.

WHERE TO STAY
Both road and rail networks tend to follow the valleys, where most of the towns are sited. See individual exploration zones for details of the best places to set up base. Accommodation can be booked through local tourist offices and national agencies (see USEFUL ADDRESSES).

ACTIVITIES
Walking: you must expect some stiff climbs in the Alps, though no special equipment is needed to walk on a Grande Randonnée (GR). Contact the Rhône-Alpes rambling association at 14 rue de la République, Grenoble, T/F: 04 76 54 87 85, for details of long- and short-distance and glacier walks.
Cycling: the Fédération Française de Cyclotourisme (see USEFUL ADDRESSES) publishes the *La France à Vélo* series, which includes *Bourgogne, Franche-Comté, Rhône-Alpes* and *Provence-Côte d'Azur*. There are several long-distance cycle routes in the Alps; see IGN map No. 906, *VTT & Randonnées Cyclos.*.
Riding: contact the Association Régional de Tourisme Equestre for Rhône-Alpes, Maison du Tourisme, 14 rue de la République, 38019 Grenoble, T: 04 76 44 56 18, F: 04 76 63 15 85; and for Provence, 29 pl Roger Salengro, 84300 Cavaillon, T: 04 90 78 04 49, F: 04 90 78 33 73.
Climbing: the Club Alpin Français at 38 rue Thomassin, Lyon, T: 04 78 42 09 17, will provide information on climbs and refuges.
Caving: the massifs of Chartreuse and Vercors are famous sites for cavers. See individual exploration zones for details.
Fishing: get information on restrictions, licences and departmental fishing federations from Le Conseil Supérieur de la Pêche (see USEFUL ADDRESSES).
Aerial sports: a wide range of aerial sports is available in the Alps, from ballooning to paragliding. Contact the Ligue Rhône-Alpes de Vol Libre in Chambéry, T: 04 79 85 17 82. Further information is in individual exploration zones.
Adventure holidays: the Loisirs Accueil Service (see USEFUL ADDRESSES) offers a range of activity holidays; see individual exploration zones.
Skiing: there are many resorts offering all kinds of skiing. Visit French skiing web-sites: www.skifrance.fr or www.ski-nordic-france.com; or contact the Bureau Information Montagne, 14 rue de la République, Grenoble, T: 04 76 42 45 90.

FURTHER INFORMATION
Tourist offices: CRT Rhône-Alpes, 104 rte de Paris, 69260 Charbonniers-les-Bains, T: 04 72 59 21 59, F: 04 72 59 21 60, e-mail: rhonealpes.tourisme @wanadoo.fr.
   CRT de Franche-Comté (see p77).
   CRT de Provence-Alpes-Côte d'Azur (see p167).

FURTHER READING
E. Anchisi, *200 Randonnées Botaniques dans les Alpes*, and J-P. Schaer, *Guide du Naturaliste dans les Alpes* (Editions Delachaux & Niestlé).

The agile and alert marmot is an inhabitant of Alpine pastures.

Alpes de Provence

Barren hills and plateaux with heavily wooded valleys in the foothills of the Alps
ZICO

My introduction to the Alpine foothills was unforgettable. For a youth from the south of England, the scenery was remarkable: Telegraph Hill and Windmill Hill were but molehills compared to these 5,000-foot monsters. And these were not even the Alps proper.

I hitched a lift just east of Avignon for the south coast. My driver chose a cross-country route through the Alpes de Provence because it was, at the time, the shortest route. The road climbed and wound its way through the foothills and its switchback turns should have dictated a relatively slow speed. My driver, however, was intent on averaging 60 miles an hour. He took each bend as though he were driving in the 24-hour marathon at Le Mans: on the inside, regardless of whether that meant driving on the right or the left of the road.

I spent the drive gripping my seat feverishly, eyes screwed shut, and, needless to say, the scenery rather passed me by. *Autostop*, I concluded, was not the best way to see France. I promised myself that the next time I came here I would make the journey in a more sedate fashion.

It took me 20 years to keep this promise. The train from Nice to Digne, known locally as *le train des pignes*, has many qualities. Speed is not one of them. But there is plenty of time to examine the *pignes* (pine cones) during the three-and-a-half-hour journey. For the last two hours into Digne, the ride is one of the most spectacular in Europe, passing bluffs, canyons and ravines, and layers of rock thrown up at crazy angles. However, the view from the train, as it winds through the densely wooded valleys, is misleading. Up on the hills the land is arid and there are few trees: this is one of the barest, most deserted parts of the Alpine foothills.

BEFORE YOU GO
Maps: IGN 1:100,000 Nos. 60 & 61; IGN 1:25,000 Nos. 3339, 3439, 3340-41 and 3541-42.

GETTING THERE
By car: N85 runs from Grenoble to Gap and Digne-les-Bains. The scenic and historic Route Napoléon from Golfe-Juan to Grenoble passes through Sisteron, Château-Arnoux and Digne: contact the Association Nationale des Elus de la Route Napoléon, T: 04 93 40 32 00, www.route-napoleon.com, for details.
By rail: SNCF trains link Grenoble with Sisteron, Château-Arnoux, St-Auban and Gap. The Chemins de Fer de la Provence runs *le train des pignes* to Digne from Nice (station is 10 mins from SNCF in Nice).
By bus: connecting bus from Château-Arnoux railway station to Digne.

WHERE TO STAY
Digne is the most central base, though Sisteron and Seyne lie on GR6 (see below). Château-Arnoux is another possibility. Tourist offices have details of the many camp-sites and *gîtes* in the area.

ACTIVITIES
Walking: GR6 runs from Sisteron to Seyne, north of Digne. There are a number of other paths leading into the hills from stations on the Nice-Digne railway.
Cycling: rent bicycles at the railway station at Digne.
Riding: trekking is available at La Fénière, quartier Champarlaud, Peipin, T: 04 92 62 44 02. Further information from Association Départementale de Tourisme Equestre des Alpes de Haute-Provence, ferme du Petit St-Martin, Gaubert, 04000 Digne, T: 04 92 31 27 50.

Fishing: contact the Alpes-de-Haute-Provence fishing federation in Digne, T: 04 92 32 25 40.
Adventure holidays: the Vallée de l'Ubaye in the north of the region offers a wide range of outdoor sports: from skiing at the resorts of Le Sauze and Pra-Loup to rafting and canoeing on the River Ubaye. Contact the Maison de la Vallée de l'Ubaye in Barcelonnette, T: 04 92 81 03 68, www.ubaye.com.
Museum: there is an excellent geological museum in Digne, T: 04 92 36 70 70, featuring 600 fossil ammonites.

FURTHER INFORMATION
Tourist offices: Digne, pl du Tampinet, T: 04 92 36 62 62; Pra-Loup, T: 04 92 84 10 04, www.praloup.com; Sisteron, pl de la Mairie, T: 04 92 61 12 03.
For taped weather forecasts, T: 08 36 68 02 04.

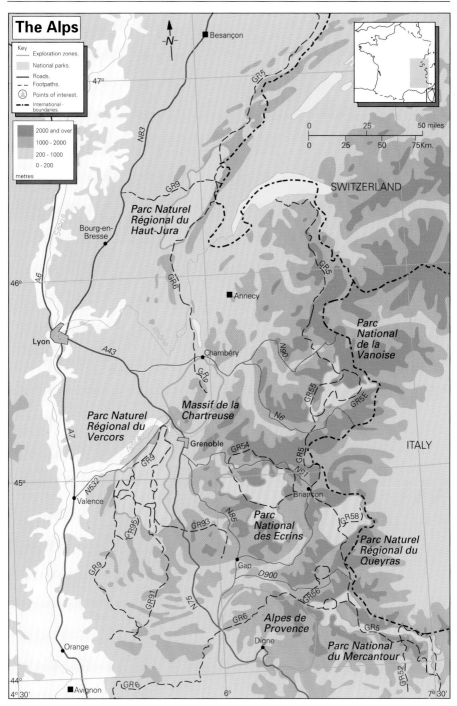

The Alps

Key
- Exploration zones.
- National parks.
- Roads.
- Footpaths.
- Points of interest.
- International boundaries.

2000 and over
1000 - 2000
200 - 1000
0 - 200
metres

0   25   50 miles
0   25   50   75Km.

Besançon

SWITZERLAND

GR5

N83

Parc Naturel
Régional du
Haut-Jura

GR9

Bourg-en-
Bresse

GR6

Annecy

GR5

Parc
National
de la
Vanoise

Lyon

A43

Chambéry

N90

GR9

GR55

GR5E

ITALY

Massif de la
Chartreuse

N6

Parc Naturel
Régional du
Vercors

GR9

Isère

Grenoble

GR54

N91

GR5

Valence

N532

Briançon

GR58

GR95

GR93

N85

Parc
National
des Ecrins

Parc Naturel
Régional du
Queyras

GR9

Gap

D900

GR56

GR91

N75

Alpes de
Provence

GR6

Orange

Digne

GR5

Parc National
du Mercantour

GR52

Avignon

GR6

4° 30'   6°   7° 30'

47°
46°
45°
44°

Saône

Rhône

—N—

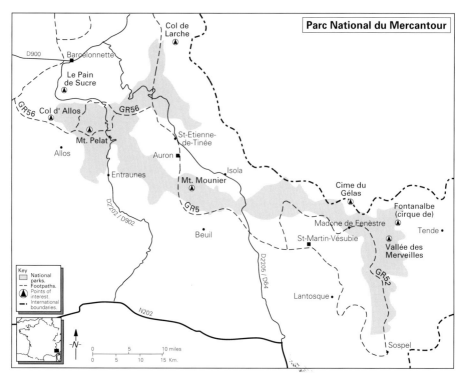

Massif du Mercantour

Sunny, arid parc national *stretching from the high Alps to the Alpes Maritimes*
ZICO
68,500 ha (169,265 acres)

It was the way you could almost smell the heat that brought the memories back. My companion and I were sitting down for a picnic near the southern end of the Parc National du Mercantour. This is where the park takes on a Mediterranean feel: the soil is dry and everywhere the vegetation shows signs of the heat. The grass is coarse and sparse and interspersed with succulents, plants that speak eloquently of the need to hang on to water. Pine trees grow where they can, severally and in copses. Only the crowns of snow on distant peaks serve to remind you that you are in the Alps.

We sheltered under some conifers to keep cool, and I unpacked my lunch: half a baguette, a lump of cheese and a tomato. Twenty years ago, on my first trip through the Alps, I had enjoyed the same lunch on an Alpine hillside just a few miles away. Then, the ingredients for my sandwich had cost one franc; now they cost ten. That's inflation for you. The other difference was that 20 years ago it was enough food for the day. Now I looked forward to a large evening meal as well. That's middle age for you! I thought back nostalgically to my first 'epic' voyage when I had had to sleep rough because I was broke, fancying myself as the hero of a Jack Kerouac novel.

The smell that brought these memories back is particularly hard to define. Every breath of wind smells fresh and different as the tang of the pines and cypresses mixes with the scent of herbs. Nearby, too, is Grasse, centre of the French perfume industry. I can't help thinking that some exotic scent may have floated up from the perfumeries and, much diffused, added to the heady mixture I inhaled on both occasions.

The Parc National du Mercantour is a long thin slice of the Alpes Maritimes that stretches for 80 kilometres (50 miles) along the Italian border. The French government designated Mercantour a national park in 1979, then only the sixth area to achieve that status. Across the Italian border is the Alpi Marittime (formerly Argentera) natural park. Were it not for the national boundary that separates them, these two parks could be considered as one.

Despite being so close to the tourist traps of the Riviera, the park has no permanent inhabitants. This makes it a refuge for wildlife. In recent years ibex have been reintroduced successfully, joining the indigenous marmots and mountain hares — in 1998, over 400 ibex were counted, compared to only 30 in 1963. Numbers of chamois have also risen dramatically from 400 originally to over 7,000, and wolves have crossed the Italian border to re-establish themselves in the park, after an absence of over 50 years. Thirty-nine pairs of golden eagles nest here and the bearded vulture was reintroduced in 1993.

The richness of Mercantour's animal life is equalled by its flora; about 40 species of plant found in the park are endemic to this part of the Alps. At the southern end of the park, barely 16 kilometres (10 miles) from the Mediterranean, holm oaks can be found at altitudes below 700 metres (2,300 feet) and olive trees are grown on terraces near the bottom of the slopes. At the northern end of the park, rhododendron heathland flourishes at more than 2,500 metres (8,000 feet), above the pine tree-line.

The park also has two notable archaeological sites. In the Vallée des Merveilles (Valley of Marvels) and the Cirque de Fontanalbe, both near Tende, there is a collection of more than 100,000 open-air rock engravings in grey-green schist, dating from the early Bronze Age (about 1800 to 1500 BC). Archaeologists are still puzzling over why these prehistoric people retreated to such a remote, inhospitable place.

BEFORE YOU GO

Maps: IGN 1:100,000 No. 61; IGN 1:25,000 Nos. 3540, 3640-41, 3741 and 3841.

GETTING THERE

By air: Nice is the nearest airport (see p57).
By car: from Gap D900 runs up the valley to Barcelonnette at the park's northern end; D2204 from Nice leads to Sospel at the southern end. Several scenic roads cross the park: D2205 runs from N202 to Isola and on to St-Etienne-de-Tinée (it meets D64, which joins D900 near Barcelonnette); while D2202 climbs to 2,300 m (7,400 ft) before hugging the northern edge of the park and dropping down to Barcelonnette.
By rail: trains run from Nice to Sospel and on to Tende; Sospel is only 33 km (20 miles) from Nice but an hour by train. From the station it's a 5-km (3-mile) walk up D2568 or GR52

to the park's southern tip.
By bus: there are buses from both Gap and Digne to Barcelonnette, as well as a service from Digne to Allos.

WHERE TO STAY

Barcelonnette is the nearest town of any size, though Sospel is a much prettier base. Closer to the park are St-Etienne-de-Tinée, Auron, Entraunes, Isola, Beuil, St-Martin-Vésubie and Lantosque.
Outdoor living: camping is allowed only outside the park.
Refuges: the park information office has a list of refuges; or contact the Club Alpin Français des Alpes-Maritimes at 14 av Mirabeau, 06000 Nice, T: 04 93 62 59 99.

ACTIVITIES

Walking: GR52 runs up the southern spine of the park from Sospel to St-Martin-Vésubie. GR5 crosses the park from St-

Sauveur-sur-Tinée to join up with GR56, which loops through the northern sector of the park from the Col d'Allos to Col de Larche. In addition there are more than 600 km (360 miles) of local footpaths.
Cycling: rent bikes in Sospel. The Randonnée du Mercantour, the Tour des Alpes Maritimes and Côte d'Azur-Léman long-distance cycle routes all pass through the park.
Riding: the Association Régional de Tourisme Equestre Provence-Côte d'Azur, Mas de la Jumenterie, 318 rte d'Azur-Cézaire, 06460 St-Vallier-de-Thiey, T: 04 93 42 62 98, F: 04 93 42 64 73, will provide information.
Canoeing: the Roya is navigable Mar-Oct; information from tourist office at Tende.
Skiing: the massif of Sanguinière is excellent for cross-country skiing. Contact

Alpes de Haute-Provence Ski de Fond in Digne, T: 04 92 31 57 29.

Nature walks: during summer, park officials organize walks to study Mercantour's natural history. Guides can also be arranged through the Bureau du Val des Merveilles in Tende, T: 04 93 04 77 73.

Museum: the Musée des Merveilles in Tende, T: 04 93 04 32 50, has displays on the history and geology of the Val des Merveilles and organizes field trips in the summer.

FURTHER INFORMATION

Tourist offices: Barcelonnette, pl Frédéric Mistral, T: 04 92 81 04 71; Sospel, blvd de la 1ère D.F.L., T: 04 93 04 18 44; Tende, T: 04 93 04 73 71.

Park offices: headquarters in Nice, 23 rue d'Italie, T: 04 93 16 78 88, www.parcsnationaux-fr.com; other offices at Barcelonnette, T: 04 92 81 21 31; St-Etienne-de-Tinée, T: 04 93 02 42 27; St-Martin-Vésubie, T: 04 93 03 23 15; and Tende, T: 04 93 04 67 00.

For taped weather forecasts, T: 08 36 68 02 04.

Massif du Queyras

Mountain stronghold above the Durance valley; parc naturel régional
60,000 ha (148,000 acres)

Most Alpine valleys are today covered in development of one form or another: quarries and industry vie with tourist chalets for each square foot of valley soil. Climbing into the mountains is often the only

Snow lingers late in the year on the peaks of the Massif du Queyras.

way to get to the wilder areas, so I set off from the Durance valley up an ill-frequented forest path. As I strode along, I heard a sudden movement and spotted the tail of a marmot disappearing into the undergrowth. In more touristy areas of the Alps, the marmots will eat cake out of your hand, like squirrels in a suburban park, but my marmot clearly had not seen many tourists.

The mountains of the Queyras have always served as a natural fortress. In times gone by they have offered safety to marauders, and provided a base from which to prey on travellers using the trade route along the Durance valley. Indeed, the Gauls may well have attacked Hannibal's army from the dominant position that these mountains afford. The fort at Château-Queyras was for a while the centre of Europe's first republic – or *escarton* – in the 14th century, though the price of independence was not cheap: each *escarton* had to pay an annual rent of 4,000 golden ducats to the dauphin of France.

During the industrial revolution Queyras lost many of its inhabitants to the growing towns and cities. By the 1960s the population of the 600 sq km (230 sq miles) that now constitute the regional park had dropped to fewer than 2,000, a quarter of the number that lived here a century before. With so little human interference, the mountains became a stronghold for wildlife. The chamois counts among the park's larger mammals and some half a dozen pairs of golden eagles are said to nest here. A wide variety of game birds can be found in the park, including the ptarmigan which, like the mountain hare, changes colour in winter. The Spanish

---

COUNTRYSIDE CARE

To protect this fragile environment the park rules forbid camping (other than overnight stops for hikers), making fires, picking flowers or digging up plants. Motor vehicles are also forbidden (other than on public roads) and cigarettes must be extinguished carefully.

---

moon moth, closely related to tropical silk moths, adds a touch of exoticism to the park's insect life.

Away from industrial pollution, the Alpine air in Queyras is so clear that distant snowy peaks seem to be situated in the next valley. The quality of light is remarkable, especially when the sun shines bright, although there is a price to be paid for this visual clarity: even at high altitudes, climbing can be fearfully hot work. In summer, nothing can be more welcome than the occasional cooling breezes that ripple the leaves of the trees, giving them a fleeting iridescence.

Before you go *Maps:* IGN 1:100,000 No. 54; IGN 1:25,000 Nos. 3536 OT, 3537-38 ET and 3637 OT. **Getting there** *By car:* D902 runs south from Briançon through the park and out of its western boundary to Guillestre; D5 runs to St-Véran and D205 cuts through to the Italian border; D947 leads to Château-Queyras and Abriès, with some good views. Be warned that many park roads swiftly turn into unpaved tracks. *By rail:* TGV service from Paris-Gare de Lyon to Briançon; the park boundary is 6 km (4 miles) away. There are regular services from Briançon to Mont-Dauphin and Guillestre. *By bus:* connecting

---

services from Mont-Dauphin station to Guillestre, Château-Queyras, Ceillac, Abriès, Arvieux, Molines, St-Véran and Vars-les-Claux. **Where to stay:** you have a choice of hotels in Briançon, Mont-Dauphin, Guillestre and Vars-les-Claux. Inside the park try Ceillac, Château-Queyras, Molines-en-Queyras, St-Véran, Abriès, Aiguilles or Arvieux. The park office at Guillestre has a list of camp-sites and refuges. **Activities** *Walking:* GR5 from Briançon crosses the park from north to south; GR58 makes a tour of the park. Local tourist offices have details of less energetic hikes and guided walks. For mountain guides, call the Bureau des Guides in Molines, T: 04 92 45 85 87. *Cycling:* the Côte d'Azur-Léman cycle route passes over the Col d'Izoard – the high point of the Tour de France – on the park's northern boundary. There are cycle hire shops in Abriès, Aiguilles and Ceillac. *Riding:* many forest and riverside trails; details from local tourist offices and the CDTE des Hautes-Alpes, 05150 Rosens, T/F: 04 92 66 60 73. *Climbing:* Ceillac lies at the foot of La Font Sancte (3,387 m/11,000 ft), a noteworthy challenge. Contact Gilles Cremades in Ceillac, T: 04 92 45 05 74. *Fishing:* there is excellent trout fishing on the river Guil; contact Le Cognarel in Molines, T: 04 92 45 81 03. *Canoeing:* in summer you can canoe or raft down the Guil and Durance. Contact Arc Boutant in Aiguilles, T: 04 92 46 75 11; Quey'raft in Château-Ville-Vieille, T: 04 92 46 86 61; or Le Cognarel in Molines, (see above). *Skiing:* 120 km (75 miles) of downhill piste and 200 km (125 miles) of cross-country piste. Such sports as dog-sledging, skating and diving in frozen lakes are also available. *Ecology:* Val d'Escreins communal reserve along the southern border of the park has an exceptionally rich collection of flora. **Further information** *Tourist offices:* Briançon, porte Pignerol, T: 04 92 21 08 50; Ceillac, Mairie, T: 04 92 45 05 74; Guillestre, pl Salva, T: 04 92 45 04 37, www.guil.fr.com; Molines-en-Queyras, T: 04 92 45 83 22; St-Véran, pl du Tour, T: 04 92 45 82 21. *Park office:* Guillestre, av de la Gare, T: 04 92 45 06 23, www.parcs-naturels-regionaux.tm.fr.

The Queyras central reservation service, T: 04 92 46 76 18, www.queyras.com, has a booking service for accommodation and activities.

For taped weather forecasts, T: 08 36 68 04 04.

Massif des Ecrins

Majestic mountains in the high Alps, some 50 km (30 miles) south-east of Grenoble; parc national ZICO
92,000 ha (226,900 acres)

The first and only person I saw the day I climbed the mountains of the Ecrins was a lean, grey-haired man in his fifties. Nothing unusual about this, but his outfit was odd: swimming trunks and a short-sleeved pullover, which seemed superfluous on such a hot day. He stopped and chatted amiably to me.

He was clearly a true lover of nature, for he lived in a cabin in a remote spot 8 km (5 miles) from the nearest village. At this altitude (1,600 m/5,250 ft), the snow would lie waist-high at his cabin door during winter, so he would retreat to another cabin further down the mountain until the spring. Neither of his

two homes had electricity or a telephone, and gas lamps and wood fires were his only sources of light and heat. I couldn't help feeling I'd run into the modern French equivalent of Henry David Thoreau, who, despairing of progress, retreated into the woods to find inspiration for his writing. When we parted, he wished me a 'bonne promenade'; I wished him a 'bonne vie', thinking to myself somewhat enviously that he already had precisely that.

The mountains of the Ecrins were designated a national park in 1973; a central and buffer zone were set up following the formula established by the Parc National de la Vanoise (see p72). Proud peaks dominate the skyline, and are snow-capped throughout the year. Three river valleys mark the park boundary: the Romanche to the north, Drac to the west and Durance to the south. The Barre des Ecrins, west of Briançon, is the highest point of the park at 4,102 m (13,460 ft). The next highest peaks stand in the granite Massif de Pelvoux, which comprises the northern half of the park.

Glaciers radiate outwards from the highest summits, melting to flow into the rivers below. However, despite the fact that ice covers about one tenth of the park, something like half the plant species of France are to be found here, reflecting the climatic variations within the Ecrins massif.

The fauna, as in other Alpine mountains, includes marmots, chamois and the mountain hare. The park boasts one of the largest established populations of golden eagles in France; 37 pairs have been counted. Between 1990 and 1995, ibex were reintroduced here, using animals taken from the Parc National de la

The Spanish moon moth is also known as the *papillon d'Isabelle*.

Vanoise: the population is now estimated at around 200. Other specialities include the black grouse and Tengmalm's owl. **Before you go** *Maps:* IGN 1:100,000 No. 54; IGN 1:25,000 Nos. 3336, 3436 ET and 3437 OT & ET. **Getting there** *By car:* N85 from Grenoble runs along the edge of the park's buffer zone to Gap; from here N94 circles the central zone (the park itself) on the southern side around to Briançon. Alternatively, N91 forks off N85 at Vizille, south of Grenoble, and runs around the north of the central zone. A number of secondary roads lead into the buffer zone but stop at the boundary of the central zone. *By rail:* TGV service from Paris-Gare de Lyon to Briançon via Gap, Embrun, Mont-Dauphin and Argentière. *By bus:* SNCF runs buses from Gap to Embrun, Mont-Dauphin and St-Crépin; the last is useful to hikers as GR54 passes by the station. **Where to stay:** Gap, Briançon, Mont-Dauphin and Embrun are the main towns, and offer a range of accommodation. Good bases in the buffer zone include St-Maurice-en-Valgaudemar, Freissinières, Puy-St-Vincent, Pelvoux, St-Antoine, Vallouise and Villar-Loubière. *Refuges:* there are 42 refuges and 68 *gîtes* in the

park. Details from park offices, or Club Alpin Français at 6 av René-Froger, Briançon, T: 04 92 20 16 52. **Activities** *Walking:* GR54 passes through the park; pick up the path at Mont-Dauphin or St-Crépin. GR50 skirts the park buffer zone, north of Briançon. *Adventure holidays:* there are several UCPA centres near the park; La Durance in Châteauroux-les-Alpes, T: 04 92 43 22 39, and Les Orres, T: 04 92 44 01 40, offer weekend activity breaks. *Viewpoints:* the Glacier Blanc and popular Serre Chevalier can be reached by cable car from Chantemerle, on N91. *Museum:* there is an animal and mineral museum at Bourg d'Oisans, T: 04 76 80 27 54. **Further information** *Tourist offices:* Briançon, porte Pignerol, T: 04 92 21 08 50; Embrun, pl Général-Dosse, T: 04 92 43 72 72, www.embrun. net; Gap, 12 rue Faure du Serre, T: 04 92 52 56 56;

The 'Demoiselle Coiffée' is a remarkable geological feature in the limestone mountains of the Queyras.

Goats roam freely among scattered rocks and scrub vegetation of the Alpes de Provence.

Guillestre, pl Salva, T: 04 92 45 04 37, www.guil-fr.com. *Park offices:* headquarters at Gap, Domaine de Charance, T: 04 92 40 20 10; other offices at Vallouise, T: 04 92 23 32 31; Oisans, T: 04 76 80 00 51; Valbonnais, T: 04 76 30 20 61; and Valgaudemar, T: 04 92 55 25 19.

Taped weather forecasts, T: 08 36 68 04 04.

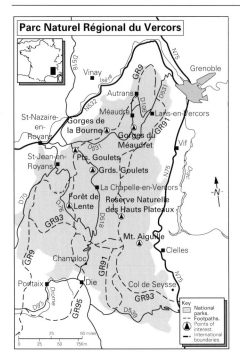

Parc Naturel Régional du Vercors

Massif du Vercors

*Mountainous plateau on the western side
of the Alps;* parc naturel régional
ZICO
175,000 ha (430,000 acres)

The day had started in much the same way as many others on the trip. My companion and I had been dogged by poor weather, and now the weather forecasters were on strike. 'It won't make the weather any different,' said the hotel-keeper.

We stopped to have lunch early, about half an hour short of our target, the Col de Seysse, in order to watch the weather. The pass itself could be seen, we reckoned, for only about five minutes in every thirty. The question was, were we going to attempt to reach it? Eventually we decided we would, but, fearing a total loss of visibility later on, we located a water course to follow back

down if we became engulfed in cloud.

As we walked up the valley the thick cloud only rarely thinned out enough to yield a glimpse of the majestic col. Patches of blue sky appeared then vanished in swirls of mist. Fifty metres (150 feet) below the col visibility was just as poor as it had been earlier, but as we reached our destination, it was as though a curtain had been raised. Nature had laid on a *coup de théâtre*, seemingly for our benefit.

Where we had come from, the mountains were wreathed in low, dark cloud. But on the other side of the col, above the ridges of the Vercors, the sky was clear and the valleys beneath were bathed in brilliant summer sunshine. An amazing show was going on overhead. The low cloud was being sucked up our valley, racing like a flock of lemmings at 65 kilometres (40 miles) per hour or more, only to be vaporized instantaneously by the fierce heat on the col. The view was quite simply spectacular.

The Parc Naturel Régional du Vercors, created in 1970, lies to the south and west of Grenoble. The valleys of the Drac, Drôme and the Isère are the natural boundaries of this roughly triangular tract of mountains. The centre-piece of the park is the 17,000-hectare (42,000-acre) high plateau of Vercors, the largest nature reserve in France.

The edge of the plateau is a masterpiece of nature. Where it is cleanly cleft, the cliffs resemble a medieval fortress. These dramatically sculpted rock-faces are accompanied by such quirks of erosion as Mont Aiguille, 'needle mountain', which protrudes from the plateau like a peninsula over the sea of sylvan hills below. The plateau is composed of limestone, which has become so eroded that its surface now looks like coarse foam rubber. Rain rapidly drains through fissures in the rocks, so that the plateau acts as a huge reservoir. Internal erosion has created a vast network of labyrinthine tunnels and caves which helped to shelter resistance fighters during the last war and which can still be explored today.

The Vercors once provided an ideal habitat for bears, lynx and wolves, but sadly all are now extinct in the park. Grenoble's natural history museum contains the skull of the last Alpine bear, killed in these mountains in 1921. Nevertheless, the mountain hare can still be found here, as can the marmot. In 1989, the park authorities undertook the ambitious project of reintroducing ibex and in 1994 the population passed 100. Other specialities include the black grouse (the symbol of the park), chamois, *mouflon* from Corsica, the peregrine falcon and the griffon vulture, reintroduced in 1996.

BEFORE YOU GO
Maps: IGN 1:100,000 No. 52; IGN 1:25,000 (OT & ET) Nos. 3136 and 3235-37.

GETTING THERE
By car: the eastern edge of the park is only 5 km (3 miles) from Grenoble, on the A51 *autoroute*. South of Grenoble, N75 follows the park boundary. The southern edge of the park is more or less described by D539 and D93. One of the more spectacular drives through the park runs from D531 turn-off on N532, near St-Nazaire-en-Royans. The road skirts the Gorges de la Bourne before turning off on to D106 for a tour of the Gorges du Méaudret; it rejoins D531 for the descent into Grenoble.
By rail: TGV services run from Paris-Gare de Lyon to Valence and Grenoble, local services to Romans, St-Hilaire-du-Rosier, Die, Clelles-en-Trièves and Monestier-de-Clermont.
By bus: there are regular buses from Grenoble to villages in the park — Autrans, Lans-en-Vercors and Villard-de-Lans are all points to pick up GR9.

WHERE TO STAY
The Bon Accueil at St-Maurice-en-Trièves, T: 04 76 34 72 28, is cheap, comfortable and convenient. Grenoble and Valence are the area's largest towns, Romans-sur-Isère the next town down the scale.
Outdoor living: tourist offices have lists of camp-sites.
Refuges: contact CAF d'Isère, 32 av Félix-Viallet, 38000 Grenoble, T: 04 76 87 03 73; or CAF Grenoble-Oisans, 14 rue de la République, Grenoble, T: 04 76 42 49 92.

ACTIVITIES
Walking: GR9, GR91, GR93 and GR95 run through the park. Pick up GR9 and GR91 off D106, just over the river from Grenoble; join GR95 at Die, where it runs north to link with GR93.
Cycling: the Etoile Crestoise route passes through the park.
Riding: La Renardière, at Villard-de-Lans, T: 04 76 95 13 10, offers everything from children's lessons to organized tours; try also Le Vercors à Cheval in La-Chapelle-en-Vercors, T: 04 75 48 20 47.
Caving: the high plateau of the Vercors is a centre for caving. Details from Maison de l'Aventure, La-Chapelle-en-Vercors, T: 04 75 48 22 38.
Aerial sports: the Aéroclub du Royans in St-Jean-en-Royans, T: 04 75 48 61 29, offers a range of activities. Voyage, Aventure et Baptême in Villard-de-Lans, T: 04 76 95 06 62, organizes ballooning expeditions.
Skiing: there are 300 km (190 miles) of downhill pistes and 900 km (560 miles) of cross-country pistes. The main resort is Lans-en-Vercors.
Viewpoint: the Col de Seysse, on GR93, offers a spectacular view over the Vercors plateau.
Sightseeing: a summer-only tourist train runs from the SNCF station at St-Georges-de-Commiers, T: 04 76 72 57 11. Small train, large spectacle, says the advertising.

FURTHER INFORMATION
Tourist offices: Autrans, rte de Méaudre, T: 04 76 95 30 70; La Chapelle-en-Vercors, pl Pietri, T: 04 75 48 22 54; Die, pl St-Pierre, T: 04 75 22 03 03; Grenoble, 14 rue de la République, T: 04 76 42 41 41; Lans-en-Vercors, pl de l'Eglise, T: 04 76 95 42 62; Valence, parvis de la Gare, T: 04 75 44 90 40.
Park office: chemin des Fusillés, 38250 Lans-en-Vercors, T: 04 76 94 38 26, F: 04 76 94 38 39, www.pnr-vercors.fr.
Weather reports, T: 08 36 68 04 04.

Massif de la Chartreuse

Small, well-wooded sub-alpine massif of high plateaux, deep gorges and mid-sized peaks; parc naturel régional 69,000 ha (170,000 acres)

In a word association game it would be hard to avoid linking Chartreuse with the alcoholic drink of the same name. This sweet green liqueur was created in 1604 by the monks of Grande Chartreuse, the first monastery of the Carthusian order, founded by Saint Bruno in 1084. In the tradition of medieval alchemy, the drink was considered an elixir, the substance tirelessly sought after for its promise of everlasting life. Nowadays it probably holds only the promise of an everlasting hangover! The original recipe requires 130 aromatic and medicinal plants, most of which can be found growing in the abundantly wooded, lozenge-shaped Massif de la Chartreuse.

Chartreuse is the smallest of the *massifs préalpins* which form the foothills of the Alps. Its limestone plateaux have been moulded over time by glaciers and water and, like Vercors, they have many grottoes and underground passages to explore.

Unfortunately the massif has taken a battering from the fast-growing skiing industry. Despite this encroachment, and the proximity of Chambéry and Grenoble, Chartreuse has some lovely, unspoilt scenery consisting of a mixture of wooded escarpments interlaced with valleys and waterfalls. Its highest peak, Chamechaude (2,082 m/6,830 ft) is relatively low by Alpine standards but the views from the top over the Chartreuse and Vercors massifs more than compensate for the lack of altitude.

Before you go *Maps:* IGN 1:100,000 No. 53; IGN 1:25,000 Nos. 3333 and 3334 OT. **Getting there** *By car:* 3 roads enclose the massif: A41, N6 and A48. *By rail:* TGV services to Chambéry and Grenoble. Two railway lines take the same route as the main roads around the park. Take a local train from Grenoble to either Chambéry or Moirans, get off at an intermediate station and hike from there. *By bus:* buses run infrequently from Grenoble to St-Laurent-du-Pont, Les Echelles, Le Sappey, Voiron and St-Pierre-de-Chartreuse. *By cable car:* the quickest way out of the valley is via the cable car (*la téléphérique*) from the riverside up to the forest overlooking Grenoble. **Where to stay:** despite its size Grenoble is a pleasant base; Hôtel Royal is comfortable and quiet, T: 04 76 46 18 92. Towns in the massif include Les Echelles, St-Laurent-du-Pont, Le Sappey-en-Chartreuse, St-Pierre-de-Chartreuse and St-Pierre-

d'Entremont. Lists of camp-sites, *gîtes* and *chambres d'hôte* available from local tourist offices. **Activities** *Walking:* GR9 runs along the spine of the massif. *Cycling:* the Tour de Savoie passes through the park. *Caving:* excellent caving in La Dent de Crolles; contact Thierry Guérin, T: 04 76 88 68

96, Daniel Bruyère, T: 04 76 88 69 98, or 10 Pôles Passion, T: 04 76 88 61 00, in St-Pierre-de-Chartreuse; or Frédéric Perez, T: 04 76 88 84 16, in Le Sappey. *Skiing:* main centres are Le Sappey, Les Entrements, La Ruchère, St-Hilaire-du-Touvet, St-Hugues, Le Planolet and St-Pierre-de-Chartreuse.

Sightseeing: the Chartreuse distillery in Voiron, T: 04 76 05 81 77, is open to visitors. La Correrie, a museum which presents the life of a monk, is situated near the monastery, between St-Laurent-du-Pont and St-Pierre-de-Chartreuse, T: 04 76 88 60 45. **Further information** *Tourist offices:* Chambéry, 24 blvd de la Colonne, T: 04 79 33 42 47, www.chambery.com; Challes-les-Eaux, av du Chambéry, T: 04 79 33 42 47; Les Echelles, rue Stendhal, T: 04 79 36 56 24; Grenoble (see p69); St-Pierre-de-Chartreuse, T: 04 76 88 62 08; Le Sappey-en-Chartreuse, T: 04 76 88 84 05. *Park office:*

Mist-shrouded peaks tower above glaciers in the Ecrins.

St-Pierre-de-Chartreuse, T: 04 76 88 75 20, F: 04 76 88 75 30, www.gni.fr/parc_chartreuse. Chartreuse tourist association, T: 04 76 88 64 00.

Taped weather forecasts, T: 08 36 68 02 04.

Massif de la Vanoise

Remote parc national *running south of the Isère valley to the Italian border*
ZICO
53,000 ha (130,000 acres)

The rule of thumb when walking uphill is that the temperature drops one degree Fahrenheit (half a degree Celsius) for every 300 feet (90 metres) climbed. It did not feel like it. Europe was in the middle of a June heat wave — the English newspapers were already bringing out their 'Phew!' headlines — which meant a very sweaty climb. Relief came above the tree-line when we stumbled across a running brook, fed by the melting snow above us. We splashed ourselves with the cool water and replenished our bottles.

The reward for the climb was the view. Sheer mountains and scree soared up from the green expanse of valley floor. On one side plunged a deep ravine, audible before it was visible because of the gurgling of the

Chamois (top) and Alpine ibex (below) inhabit the high rocky slopes of the Alps. Once in danger of extinction, the rarer ibex numbers around 4,500 in the whole of France.

waters at its rocky bottom. The mountains on the far side of this divide were topped with snow. I had to pinch myself. This was summer; the sun was burning hot; that was snow. The surrounding peaks, sharp points that prodded the sky, were among the grandest in the French Alps. White clouds hung over some of the highest ones, making it hard to discern where the cloud ended and the snow began. Looking back down into the valley was something of a culture shock. That was where we had come from, but it was hard to identify with the low landscape and the tapestry of pastures that seemed so small and insignificant from such a height.

The Parc National de la Vanoise was the first of the French national parks. The idea for its establishment dated from the 1930s, when naturalists wanted to create a reserve to help protect the Alpine ibex. Italy had already created a national park (the Parco Nazionale del Gran Paradiso) on its side of the border, but the ibex had no protection from the hunters' bullets once they crossed the French border.

Arguments between naturalists, who wanted a large park, and locals, who wanted a small one which did not unduly restrict their activities, were not resolved until well after World War II. The compromise between these two positions set a pattern for subsequent parks. When the Vanoise was created in 1963, it had a central zone (the park itself) where there were strict regulations to minimize human disturbance of the environment, and a less stringently protected buffer zone encircling it.

Today there is no permanent human habitation in the central zone, while the 1,450-square kilometre (560-square mile) buffer zone — nearly three times as large — has fewer than 30,000 inhabitants. Together with the Gran Paradiso, the park forms the largest protected area in Western Europe.

The Vanoise supports a rich fauna, including around 1,500 ibex (the most important colony in France) and 5,000 chamois. When the park was set up, the numbers were 40 and 400 respectively. Since 1989, the ibex has been successfully reintroduced in other parts of the Alps — notably in the Ecrins and Vercors parks (see p65 and p69) — using animals taken from the Vanoise.

Unlike the park's flora, which is at its most luxuriant at the Alpine pasture level, the bird life becomes more spectacular as you climb to the higher zones. The upper forests are home to vast numbers of chaffinches and dunnocks, while one zone up at the sub-Alpine level the main species to look for are ring ouzel, nutcracker, redpoll and black grouse. Farther up still, in the grasslands, live water pipits, rock thrushes and wheatears, and above the snow-line, ptarmigan, alpine accentor and snow finch. In a recent census, twenty pairs of golden eagles were counted in the park.

In summer the Vanoise is a popular walking centre and the paths within easy reach of a road are well-trodden. The more distant parts of the park, where unaffected by ski resorts, are still quite wild.

The blue thistle, or queen of the Alps, is one of the many delights of the abundant and varied flora to be found higher in the Alpine meadows.

BEFORE YOU GO
Maps: IGN 1:100,000 No. 53; IGN 1:25,000 (OT & ET) Nos. 3532, 3534, 3633-34.

GETTING THERE
By car: from Chambéry or Grenoble take the A43 or N6 turn-off from the A41 *autoroute*. N6 splits near St-Pierre-d'Albigny; N90 follows the valley of the River Isère to Bourg-St-Maurice, on the northern edge; N6 dives down to Modane, in the south.
By rail: Eurostar runs to Moutiers and Bourg St-Maurice (see p57). TGV services from Paris-Gare de Lyon go to Chambéry, Bourg-St-Maurice and Modane.
By bus: Transavoie, T: 04 79 05 01 32, runs buses from Modane to Lanslebourg, Bessans and Bonneval-sur-Arc. There are also buses from Bourg-St-Maurice to Val d'Isère and Les Arcs; and from the SNCF station at Moutiers to Pralognan and Val-Thorens.

WHERE TO STAY
Bourg-St-Maurice is on the expensive side; Modane is scruffier and cheaper. Bonneval-sur-Arc, Bessans, Pralognan-la-Vanoise and Val d'Isère are other options.
Refuges: there are around 60 refuges in the park; reserve in advance from the park office.

ACTIVITIES
Walking: GR55 runs from Val d'Isère up some stiff inclines to Pralognan-la-Vanoise, joining GR5 near Modane. GR5 runs from Val d'Isère to Modane along a less strenuous route.
Climbing: CAF de Vanoise-Tarentaise, Pralognan-la-Vanoise, T: 04 79 08 22 07.
Adventure holidays: contact Loisirs Accueil in Savoie, Maison du Tourisme, 24 blvd de la Colonne, 73024 Chambéry, T: 04 79 85 01 09.

FURTHER INFORMATION
Tourist offices: Bonneval-sur-Arc, T: 04 79 05 95 95; Bourg-St-Maurice, pl Gare, T: 04 79 07 04 92; Modane, pl Replaton, T: 04 79 05 22 35; Pralognan-la-Vanoise, T: 04 79 08 79 08; Val d'Isère, T: 04 79 06 06 60.
Park office: 135 rue du Dr-Julliand, 73007 Chambéry, T: 04 79 62 30 54, F: 04 79 96 37 18, www.vanoise.com.

Taped weather forecasts, T: 08 36 68 02 73.

ALPINE FLOWERS

The wild flowers of the Alpine meadows are delightful. Exotic species such as the lady's slipper orchid thrive alongside saxifrage, buttercups and dandelions. These meadows have not been farmed for many years, resulting in a staggering profusion of flowers: green meadows are set ablaze by the violet, trumpet-shaped gentian, yellow anemone and blue thistle, known as *la reine des Alpes* (queen of the Alps). The three national parks contain nearly half of all the plant species found in France and, by forbidding their extraction, the parks aim to protect them within their natural habitat.

Haut-Jura

A range of lush, wooded mountains 50 km (30 miles) north-west of Geneva; includes Parc Naturel Régional du Haut-Jura 76,000 ha (188,000 acres) ZICO

The mountains of the Jura are composed of sedimentary rock, mostly limestone or chalk. Originally, there was a plain here, but during the formation of the Alps it was squashed between an irresistible force and an immovable object: the Alps to the south and the solid Massif Central to the west. The result was that the rocks of the Jura were folded into mountains that resemble a ruffled rug on the floor.

The Jura limestone is riddled with underground caverns whose chambers have been found to have a curious effect on the mountains' water courses. The true source of the River Loue, for example, was only discovered in 1901, when a young Frenchman caught a whiff of *anise* on the air; the river reeked of Pernod! The Pernod distillery, on the upper reaches of another river, the Doubs, had had a large spillage several days earlier. When the Loue became infused with Pernod too, it was the first anyone knew of an underground connection between the two rivers.

The name Jura comes from a 2,000-year-old Gaulish word and means 'forest'. The language may now be extinct, but the description still fits. Benefiting from the area's heavy rainfall (this is the wettest region in France, although it does have a dry spell in summer), the Jura mountains are heavily forested; even the highest peaks, which are half the height of the Alps, have a covering of oak and beech, interspersed with Scots pine. The densely wooded gorges that cut through the Jura make for spectacular scenic drives and train journeys.

The Jura has another rather better known

The gently rolling lower slopes of the Jura mountains provide excellent walking country.

etymological association: in 1830, a distinctive line of fossils was discovered in the Jura chalk, inspiring geologists to name the Jurassic period after these mountains. As movie-goers will know, this was the age of the dinosaurs. The Jurassic period — the central period of the Mesozoic era — took place about 200 million years ago. As the Jura sediments were laid down, they became a repository for the remains of fish and dinosaurs. An abundance of fossils has emerged, especially in the hills of Le Bugey, to the south of the park near Marchamp.

The Jura has some notable living species as well: it is one area of France where the lynx can still be seen. This wild cat had become extinct in the Alps by the end of the last century and is dangerously close to extinction in the French Pyrenees. However, since being reintroduced in Switzerland, these rare and beautiful creatures do sometimes cross the border into France.

Another curiosity of the Jura massif is its large number of bogs. This is surprising because much of the massif is composed of limestone, which is porous and does not normally hold surface water. The bogs exist in damp hollows, which were originally gouged out by glaciers in the last Ice Age. Their survival has been attributed by scientists to a combination of the unusual glacial relief, pockets of clay which impede drainage, exceptionally humid microclimates and spaghnum moss, which is able to live on rainwater. The spaghnum moss eventually decomposes into peat, which allows such carnivorous plants as the sundew and blue-flowered butterwort to grow. Other wet habitats on the Jura plateau are dominated by sedges, home to tree pipits, whinchats and snipe, as well as the Apollo butterfly.

At the western border of the massif, the famous geological site of Cirque de Baume-les-Messieurs contrasts with the rather Nordic atmosphere of the plateau by imparting a Mediterranean feel to the scenery. Here a forest of white oak and box nestles comfortably under the towering limestone cliffs, supporting a typically sub-Mediterranean bird fauna, including the short-toed eagle, Alpine swift, crag martin, rock bunting, ortolan and Bonelli's warbler.

BEFORE YOU GO
Maps: IGN 1:100,000 Nos. 37, 38 and 44; IGN 1:25,000 (OT & ET) Nos. 3327-28.

GETTING THERE
By car: N83 from Bourg-en-Bresse to Lons-le-Saunier and Besançon runs roughly parallel to the Jura mountains. At right angles to this run the roads that cross the mountain range into Switzerland: D72, N5, N78 and A40. It is the turnings off these roads that take you into the heart of the mountains. D437 north of St-Claude and D984 from Bellegarde to St-Laurent along the Swiss border are notably scenic.
By rail: TGV services run from

In France the mountain hare is confined to the Alps, where, in winter, its coat turns almost totally white, with the exception of the ears which remain black.

Paris-Gare de Lyon to Dole, Bellegarde, Bourg-en-Bresse and Vallorbe. Local trains go to Besançon, St-Laurent, Morbier, Morez, Pontarlier and St-Claude.

By bus: regular buses run from Morez to La Cure, on the Swiss border, from St-Claude to La Cure and from Morez to Bois d'Amont. Buses from St-Claude also run to Clairvaux.

WHERE TO STAY
St-Claude is relatively central; most of the better hotels lie on the outskirts. Champagnole, Lons-le-Saunier, Pontarlier and Poligny are other convenient bases.

ACTIVITIES
Walking: GR5 crosses the north of the park and meets GR9 near Les Rousses. From here GR5 heads east towards Evian while GR9 cuts west through the middle of the park. Ancillary routes, centred on St-Claude, also tour the park.
Cycling: the railway stations at Bourg-en-Bresse, Besançon, Pontarlier and St-Claude rent out bicycles. The Raid Jurassien, Randonnée du Jura and Randonnée du Haut-Bugey long-distance cycle routes run through the area.
Riding: you can get details of equestrian centres from Association Régionale de Tourisme Equestre de Franche-Comté, Haras National, 52 rue de Dôle, 25000 Besançon, T: 03 81 52 67 40, F: 02 81 51 55 64; Comité Départemental de Tourisme Equestre du Jura, Creps de Chalain, 39130 Doucier, T: 03 84 87 28 28, F: 03 84 25 76 05.
Climbing: contact CAF du Haut-Jura in St-Claude, T: 03 84 45 58 62.
Fishing: the streams here offer some of the best trout fishing in France. The lakes have tench, bream and carp. Contact Jura fishing federation in Dole, T: 03

The Apollo butterfly, a rare inhabitant of the Massif Central and the Alps, is prized for its dramatic beauty.

84 79 18 19.
Canoeing: contact the Comité Départemental de Canoë-Kayak for Jura, BP 139, 39101 Dole, T: 03 84 79 75 08; or for Doubs, Résidence les Arcades, 25410 St-Vit, T/F: 03 81 87 59 69, who will put you in touch with local clubs.
Skiing: there is a 210-km (130-mile) cross-country piste from Villers-le-Lac to Hauteville-Lompnes; contact Grande Traversée du Jura, T: 03 84 52 58 10, or Haut-Doubs Ski de Fond in Pontarlier, T: 03 81 39 23 16. IGN produce a 1:50,000 map called *Ski de Fond — Massif du Jura*. The main ski resort is Métabief-Mont d'Or.
Adventure holidays: contact Loisirs Accueil Jura, 8 rue Louis Rousseau, 39000 Lons-le-Saunier, T: 03 84 87 08 88.
Nature walks: guided walks can be arranged through the Centre Permanent d'Initiation à l'Environnement du Haut-Jura in La Pesse, T: 03 84 42 85

96; the Bureau des Accompagnateurs du Haut-Jura, also in La Pesse, T: 03 84 41 60 70; and the Bureau des Accompagnateurs du Haut-Jura in Les Rousses, T: 03 84 60 35 14.
Sightseeing: near Marchamp (on D87) is one of the richest fossil deposits (both fish and dinosaurs) in France.

FURTHER INFORMATION
Tourist offices: Bourg-en-Bresse, 6 av Alsace-Lorraine, T: 03 74 22 49 40; Champagnole, Hôtel de Ville, T: 03 84 52 43 67; Lons-le-Saunier, pl du 11 Novembre, T: 03 84 24 65 01; Poligny, rue Victor Hugo, T: 03 84 37 24 21; Pontarlier, 14 bis rue de la Gare, T: 03 81 46 48 33; St-Claude, 19 rue du Marché, T: 03 84 45 34 24.
CRT de Franche-Comté, Le St-Pierre, 28 rue de la République, 25025 Besançon, T: 03 81 47 85 47, F: 03 81 83 35 82, www.franche-comte.org.
Park office: headquarters at 39310 Lajoux, T: 03 84 34 12 30, F: 03 84 41 24 01.
Taped weather forecasts, T: 08 36 68 00 00.

CHAPTER 4

Central France

The angry sky reminded me of Robert Louis Stevenson's description of the Cévennes in *Travels with a Donkey*: 'On the opposite bank of the Allier the land kept mounting for miles to the horizon; a tanned and fallow autumn landscape with black blots of fir-wood and white roads wandering through the hills. Over all this the clouds shed a uniform and purplish shadow, sad, somewhat menacing, exaggerating height and distance and throwing into still higher relief the twisted ribbon of the highways. It was a cheerless prospect but one that is stimulating to the traveller.'

Stevenson made his trip through the Massif Central on his donkey, Modestine, more than a hundred years ago but his description of the scenery could have been written yesterday. The main difference now is that travelling in the Massif Central is altogether more comfortable than it was for Stevenson — and certainly for the artist, Eugène Delacroix, who complained of his journey there in 1855: 'I stood over my luggage for an hour in the mud and pouring rain before getting into a dreadful little conveyance, in which I had an unspeakable journey between a child that constantly relieved itself and three women who were sick.' Today smooth roads and railway tracks whisk you up the thickly wooded gorges and across the desolate plateaux.

The plateaux and gorges are the dominant features of the Massif Central and these landscapes could scarcely be more dissimilar. The plateaux are almost temperate deserts: often waterless, with few trees, and frequently buffeted by fierce

The Gorges de la Jonte are home to the griffon vulture. The gorges were formed when the River Jonte carved through the limestone plateaux of the Causses Noir at the end of the last Ice Age.

winds. Villages are few and far between and houses often turn out to be deserted. The gorges, on the other hand, are lined with trees, while water charges headlong through them, pausing only for the occasional hydro-electric dam. They contain many of the region's towns and the farmed terraces which local people have for centuries cut into the hillsides.

The Massif Central is a mix of granite and limestone. The granite centre is so old that there are no fossils, for the rocks were formed before identifiable life existed on earth. By contrast, the limestone plateaux, or *causses*, are littered with fossils, as well as ancient monuments, menhirs and stone circles built by early man. The *causses* lie in two distinct patches south and west of the granite Massif. Those in the southern part of the Cévennes, such as Méjean or Larzac, are known as the Grands Causses and those farther west, such as Quercy and Périgord, are known as the Petits Causses. In geological terms these are recent rocks, about 200 million years old, and formed the sea-bed until the formation of the Alps thrust them 300 metres (1,000 feet) or more upwards. Aesthetically speaking, the *causses* form some of the most desolate wilderness in France: wild and rugged landscapes of rock and coarse grass, which soon turn yellow in summer from lack of water and revert to being cold and inhospitable in winter.

The aridity of the plateaux is caused by surface water seeping through the porous limestone to form underground water courses. The Massif Central is thus also renowned for its springs (many of which are tapped for mineral water) and for being the source of some of France's major rivers, which radiate like arteries: to the west flow the Dordogne and the Tarn; to the north the

Loire and its tributaries. The eastward-flowing streams, such as the Ardèche, lead to the Rhône, while to the south the Hérault and the Orb funnel down to the Mediterranean.

The west-flowing rivers cut through the limestone *causses* towards the Dordogne and Périgord. Along with Armagnac, which lies further south, these regions constitute the gentler, lusher landscapes of Central France. If the Massif Central is the heart of France, then these are the lungs. Their green forests and meadows offer welcome respite to the mountain traveller.

The observer of wildlife in Central France must be discerning in choice of location, time of day and season. The lack of cover in the uplands makes bird-watching less rewarding than in the narrow valleys. Some of the richest bird-watching I experienced was not in the remotest areas but in the relatively well-populated valley of the River Allier. Chief among the attractions is the griffon vulture *(Gyps fulvus)*, which inhabits the gorges of the Tarn and Jonte. Other birds of prey in the region include Montagu's harrier and peregrine falcon.

As for mammals, the mountains provide sanctuary for boar and wildcats, though both are largely nocturnal, meaning that you will need good fortune and persistence to glimpse either. One method is to pick up their tracks in the snow in winter, work out a pattern and hope to see one of the animals on an expedition for food. The wolf is now extinct in central France, although its somewhat mythical presence is conveyed through stories that are still told today, such as the tale of the 'Bête du Gévaudan', a 'beast' that allegedly killed 50 women and children. When Stevenson made his journey through the Cévennes, he kept a revolver under his pillow in case wolves attacked him.

GETTING THERE

By air: international airports include Lyon (see p57); St-Etienne, T: 04 77 36 54 79; Toulouse, T: 05 61 42 44 00; and Montpellier, T: 04 67 22 85 00. Internal services go to Clermont-Ferrand, Limoges and Nîmes. Contact Air France, T: 08 02 80 28 02, www.airfrance.com, or the French airports web-site: www.aeroport.fr.

By car: the A6 Autoroute du Soleil is the main route from Paris south to Lyon. The more direct (and less crowded) alternative is to aim for Clermont-Ferrand, taking the A10 out of Paris, followed by the A71 south of Orléans; or N7 out of Paris, switching to N9 at Moulins. For the western portion of Central France exit from A71 on to N20, which runs down to Limoges, Cahors and Toulouse.

By rail: TGV services run from Paris-Gare de Lyon to Lyon and St-Etienne in the east of the region and to Nîmes, Montpellier and Béziers in the south. TGVs also go from Paris-Gare Montparnasse to Agen and Toulouse in the south-west. SNCF trains leave from Paris-Gare d'Austerlitz for towns in the west such as Limoges, Brive and Cahors and from Gare de Lyon for towns such as Clermont-Ferrand. Contact SNCF, T: 08 36 35 35 35 (French)/ 39 (English), www.sncf.fr.

By bus: Eurolines, T: 08 36 69 51 51, www.eurolines.fr, has services to towns including Clermont-Ferrand, Brive, Limoges, Cahors, Toulouse, Béziers, Montpellier, Nîmes and St-Etienne. Tourist offices will provide information on local services.

WHEN TO GO

Summers tend to be stultifyingly hot, winters freezing cold. Spring and autumn make better times for visiting.

WHERE TO STAY

The main centres are Clermont-Ferrand in the centre, Limoges in the west, the Rhône Valley in the east and Toulouse in the south. Local tourist offices will provide brochures and help with reservations. Alternatively, you could contact any of the accommodation agencies listed in USEFUL ADDRESSES (p215).

ACTIVITIES

Walking: there are some stiffish climbs in the Massif, from valley bottom to plateau table, but for the most part the walking is easy. The long-distance *grande randonnée* footpaths are a trusty guide to the best scenery. See IGN map No. 903, *Grande Randonnée.*

Cycling: the *France à Vélo* series includes *Auvergne, Languedoc-Roussillon* and *Midi-Pyrénées.* Several long-distance cycle routes pass through the region; for details see IGN map No. 906, *VTT & Randonées Cyclos.* Most towns will have cycle-hire outlets.

Riding: there are plenty of opportunities for riding, and it's also possible to rent a *calèche*, a horse-drawn wagon. For details of local and regional equestrian centres contact Association Régionale de Tourisme Equestre, Zanières, 63420 Apchat, T: 04 73 71 84 30, F: 04 73 71 83 48; ARTE de Limousin, 19470 Le Lonzac, T: 05 55 98 20 23, F:

The rare night heron inhabits river banks and lake shores.

05 55 97 90 29; for Midi-Pyrenées and Languedoc-Roussillon, see p117 and p194.

Climbing: the Club Alpin Français (see USEFUL ADDRESSES, p215) maintains some refuges in the region; local offices are listed in individual exploration zones.

Caving: the underground rivers and tunnels of the *causses* are classic sites for caving. Get in touch with the Fédération Française de Spéléologie (see USEFUL ADDRESSES).

Fishing: salmon can be fished in the Allier and Garonne during spring, and most rivers have trout. Get information on restrictions and licences from Le Conseil Supérieur de la Pêche (see USEFUL ADDRESSES) or local tourist offices.

Adventure holidays: UCPA (see USEFUL ADDRESSES) offers hill-walking, hang-gliding and cycling holidays at half a dozen centres in Central France; details are given in exploration zones. Loisirs Accueil can book activity holidays in the various *départements.*

Skiing: the mountains of the Auvergne and the Cévennes have cross-country skiing trails, notably around Mont-Dore, the Cantal and the Massif Lozère. Visit France's skiing web-sites: www.skifrance.com and www.ski-nordic-france.com.

SAFETY

The weather can change alarmingly fast in the mountains of the Massif Central, even in summer. A waterproof, warm clothing and sturdy footwear are essential.

FURTHER INFORMATION
Tourist offices: CRT
d'Auvergne, 44 av des Etats-
Unis, 63057 Clermont-Ferrand,
T: 04 73 29 49 49, F: 04 73 34
11 11, e-mail: documentation
@crt-auvergne.fr, www.crt-
auvergne.fr.
  CRT de Limousin, 27 blvd de
la Corderie, 87031 Limoges, T:

05 55 45 18 80, F: 05 55 45 18
18, e-mail: tourisme@cr-
limousin.fr, www.cr-limousin.fr.
  CRT de Languedoc-
Roussillon, 20 rue de la
République, 34000 Montpellier,
T: 04 67 22 81 00, F: 04 67 58
06 10, e-mail: contact.crtlr
@cnusc.fr, www.cr-
languedocroussillon.fr.

  CRT de Midi-Pyrenees, 54
blvd de l'Embouchure, BP
2166, 31022 Toulouse, T: 05 61
13 55 55, F: 05 61 47 17 16.

FURTHER READING
P. Puytorac et al, *L'Auvergne*, in
Bibliothèque du Naturaliste
series (Editions Delachaux et
Niestlé).

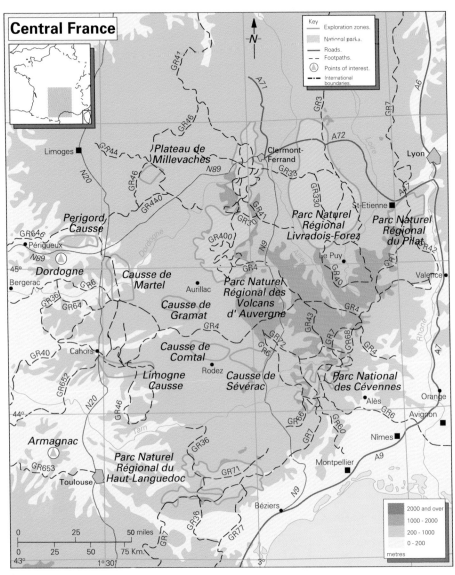

Les Volcans d'Auvergne

*Plateaux and peaks of volcanic rock;
France's largest* parc naturel régional
*ZICO
3,950 sq km (1,525 sq miles)*

While the volcanic peaks of the Auvergne no longer rain down lava, brooding thunder clouds can build up suddenly over this dramatic landscape and then open up with Wagnerian force. I learned this to my cost once when I ignored a hotel barometer I assumed was stuck on 'variable' and set off for a long walk. After an hour the heavens opened. Low hills had masked the dark clouds from me until it was too late. The nearest habitation was at least a couple of miles back, so I took shelter in a stunted beech grove in a hollow. The trees did me proud for half an hour, but soon rivulets of water began to trickle around my ankles. I consulted my map. By a stroke of luck a small building was located a couple of hun-dred yards away. I made a dash for it and sat out the rest of the storm there. When I later made my way back, the hot sun re-emerged just as I had the hotel within sight. By the time I got back to my room, my sodden clothes were steaming and I smelt like a kipper. This is a cautionary tale: the weather can change very quickly in the mountains, and a forecast that talks of occasional thunder storms should be heeded.

The Parc Naturel Régional des Volcans d'Auvergne stretches south from Clermont-Ferrand for 120 kilometres (75 miles) to Aurillac. As the name of the park suggests, extinct volcanoes dominate this stretch of land. Three million years ago its volcanoes erupted regularly, throwing out streams of molten lava which have moulded the landscape. To sit in the middle of Clermont-Ferrand surrounded by these peaks (*puys*), is like being at the theatre. The scenery is awe-inspiring, a perfect setting for an otherwise rather ordinary town. In *Fat Man on a Bicycle*, the author Tom Vernon describes it vividly: '...and suddenly there before me were the real mountains, the volcanoes of

The lunar landscape of the Auvergne was formed by the lava of now-extinct volcanoes.

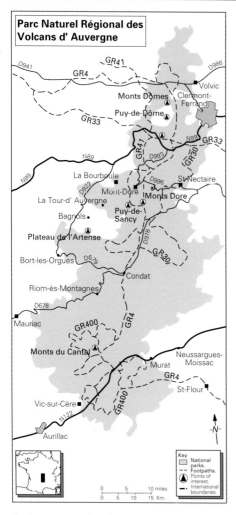

Parc Naturel Régional des Volcans d' Auvergne

rounding landscape. The summit is often missing, blown off by some ancient eruption. The resultant craters have filled with water, creating calm lakes where lava once spurted. Unfortunately, few of these lakes are wild, having been taken over by pedal-boats or anglers.

At the southern end of the park lie the Monts du Cantal, which were formed by cooling lava and have since been reworked extensively by glacial and water erosion. The Cézallier plateau, linking the Cantal with the northern *puys*, is also volcanic. Its chief town, Bort-les-Orgues, is so named because the cooled lava solidified into a ridge of basalt resembling organ pipes.

The landscape of the Volcans d'Auvergne bears the signs of long habitation by man. Stock-raising is an important way of life here and much of the farming land is given over to pasture. Because the herds are allowed to graze freely, there are few fences to impede ramblers and one of the characteristic sounds you will hear on a walk in these pastures is the musical chiming of brass cowbells. Many lizards can be seen lying on stone, soaking up the sun — they will scramble away at the slightest hint of human footsteps. If you are lucky you may also catch a glimpse of the short-toed eagle, whose staple diet is small reptiles.

The edge of the park produced some superb bird-watching when I last visited. I saw a huge variety of birds in one short afternoon walk. A Montagu's harrier flew past, larks rose from fields, and in a thicket a great tit sang loudly and persistently. The reason soon became clear: a red-backed shrike was sitting on a dead branch in a thorn thicket, surveying its prospects. Suddenly it swooped down on some unfortunate victim before taking it off to its larder. The shrike is known as the 'butcher bird' because of the way it stores its food. It impales its carrion on thorns, coming back when ready to eat. Nowadays, the skewer is as likely to be a barbed-wire fence. Later a golden oriole flew past. Despite its striking yellow markings, this bird is rarely seen because it blends in surprisingly well with sunlight and leaves. To cap the afternoon's entertainment I caught sight of a couple of kestrels and a red kite.

the Auvergne, mist-shrouded in the distance even in the sun, layer upon layer of blue shapes stretching back like stage mountains, cut-outs behind successive layers of gorse.'

The main volcanic peaks lie in the north of the park, between Volvic and Mont-Dore. Puy-de-Dôme, 12 kilometres (seven miles) west of Clermont-Ferrand, is the most celebrated (the climb to its summit is one of the most gruelling in the Tour de France), while Puy-de-Sancy is the highest, at 1,886 m (6,190 ft), and also contains the source of the Dordogne. The peaks have a characteristic shape, rising cone-like from the sur-

BEFORE YOU GO
Maps: IGN 1:100,000 No. 49; IGN 1:25,000 Nos. 2432 ET, 2434-35, 2531 OT and 2534 OT.

GETTING THERE
By car: from Clermont-Ferrand N89 then D983 head to Mont-Dore. Farther south, D996 cuts across the park. Turning left on to D978 takes you over the top of the hills to Condat; D679 continues to Bort-les-Orgues, D678 to Mauriac. At the park's southern boundary, D122 from Aurillac to Murat takes a scenic route up the valley that divides the Cantal massif.
By rail: trains from Clermont-Ferrand to La Bourboule and Mont-Dore in the north of the park; from Aurillac to Mauriac and Bort-les-Orgues in the west and St-Flour and Neussargues-Moissac in the south. The journey from Aurillac to Neussargues is one of the most spectacular in Europe.
By bus: regular buses connect with trains at Ussel and run to Bort-les-Orgues. There is also a service (not Sun) from Clermont-Ferrand to La Tour d'Auvergne and Bagnols.

GORGES OF THE MASSIF CENTRAL
One of the natural glories of France is its gorges. The Gorges du Tarn, in particular, number among the country's best-known tourist sights, a Gallic version of the Grand Canyon. The scenery is staggering: the colour of the cliffs changes when sunlight reflects from the minerals in the limestone sides.

It is possible to travel up most of the gorges by car and some have quiet roads well suited for cycling. Surprisingly few are scaled by long-distance footpaths, although there is a scenic path that runs along the Gorges du Chavanon. The optimum view of the Gorges du Allier is from the railway.

However, the best place to feel the full majesty of the gorges is from the water. It is worth renting a canoe, although some stretches of rapids are strictly for the experienced.

WHERE TO STAY
Clermont-Ferrand is central, but not particularly attractive. The main alternatives are scattered around the park periphery: Mauriac, La Bourboule, Murat, St-Flour and touristy Aurillac. Mont-Dore, Neussargues, Riom-ès-Montagnes, St-Nectaire and Vic-sur-Cère are the best options inside the park.
Outdoor living: there is no restriction on camping in the park. The Aubazines Leisure Complex near Bort-les-Orgues, T: 04 55 96 08 38 (in season)/T: 04 73 34 75 53 (out of season), has a camp-site and *gîtes* beside a large artificial lake.

ACTIVITIES
Walking: 4 long-distance footpaths cross the park: GR4, GR30, GR400 and GR41.
Cycling: contact Ligue Régional d'Auvergne de Cyclotourisme, rue Guérat, Saulcet, T: 04 70 45 56 87. You can rent bicycles at the railway stations of Aurillac, Mont-Dore and St-Flour.
Riding: information from ADTE du Cantal, BP 9, 15800 Polminhuc, T: 04 71 47 41 23, F: 04 71 47 45 71.
Climbing: contact the CAF d'Auvergne, 3 rue Maréchal Joffre, 63000 Clermont-Ferrand, T: 04 73 90 81 62.
Adventure holidays: contact Loisirs Accueil Cantal, 28 av Gambetta, 15015 Aurillac, T: 04 71 46 22 46, for information.
Skiing: the biggest ski resort is Le Lioran, T: 04 71 49 50 08. For cross-country skiing, contact Montagne Auvergne, 23 pl Delille, Clermont-Ferrand, T: 04 73 90 23 14.
Viewpoint: Puy-de-Dôme offers superb views of the volcanoes (you can see about 70 peaks in all) and has Roman ruins. A cable car runs to the summit of Puy-de-Sancy, south of Mont-Dore, T: 04 73 65 02 23.
Sightseeing: the Route des

CAUSSES OF THE MASSIF CENTRAL
The vast upland limestone plateaux of the Massif Central, known as *causses*, form one of the most striking landscapes in France. Many are characterized by scrub and scattered small trees: white oaks and Scots pines mingle with junipers, box, hazel and brambles. Others are covered by vast areas of heath: low spiny shrubs grow alongside an open-ground flora of herbs and grassy tussocks.

Montagu's harriers and chough fly over this seemingly barren landscape. Across the open heathland plateaux are little bustards and vast numbers of larks. The stony and thorny scrub habitats, on the other hand, are favoured by reptiles: the impressive ocellated lizard is very much at home in these hot dry areas, while the smaller, brown Iberian wall lizard has been found on the eastern side of the *causses*. Insects include grasshoppers and crickets, several species of which occur here in complete isolation from their main range.

In addition to the Grands Causses of the Cévennes, smaller *causses* lie to the north-west: the Causse de Sévérac and the Causse du Comtal (known as the Petits Causses), and the Causses de Quercy.

Châteaux d'Auvergne tours Auvergne's stunning castles; a guide is available from 17 rue des Minimes, Clermont-Ferrand, T: 04 73 29 49 49. For details of the various spas, contact the CDT du Cantal in Aurillac, T: 04 71 46 22 00, www.cdt-cantal.fr.
Museum: Vulcania, a European centre of volcanology, is due to open in 2000 in Chamalières near Clermont-Ferrand.

FURTHER INFORMATION
Tourist offices: Aurillac, pl du Square, T: 04 71 48 46 58; Bort-les-Orgues, pl Marmontel, T: 04 55 96 02 49; La Bourboule, 15 pl de la République, T: 04 73 65 57 71; Clermont-Ferrand, pl de la Victoire, T: 04 73 98 65 00; Mauriac, 1 rue Chapelle d'Auteroche, T: 04 71 67 30 26; Le Mont-Dore, av Libération, T: 04 73 65 20 21; Murat, rue du fbg Notre-Dame, T: 04 71 20 09 47; St-Flour, cours Spy des Ternes, T: 04 71 60 22 50.
Park offices: Montlosier, T: 04 73 65 64 00; Murat, T: 04 71 20 22 10; Château St-Etienne, Aurillac, T: 04 71 48 68 68; at the summit of Puy-de-Dôme, T: 04 73 62 21 45 (May-Nov).
86

Livradois-Forez

Land of blond soil and black forests, lying between the Allier and Dore valleys; parc naturel régional *320,000 ha (790,000 acres)*

The Parc Naturel Régional Livradois-Forez takes its name from two principal massifs: the Monts du Livradois, lying between the Allier and Dore river valleys; and to the east of the Dore, the Monts du Forez, which extend their imposing mass over a distance of 100 km (60 miles). The landscape is pastoral. Isolated farmsteads lie in the valleys surrounded by fields and meadows, while a mixed woodland of oak and pine covers the hills.

The day I chose to explore the countryside of the Forez it was blisteringly hot: our shoes left footprints in the tar of the road. The countryside was so sleepy that when we walked through a tiny hamlet, we woke

The Massif de Sancy lies among ancient volcanic mountains, well known for their spring water.

up the local cock: it was the crack of noon.

Tranquil though it may appear, Livradois-Forez needs to be treated with at least a modicum of respect. A good test of an area's wilderness rating is how easy it is to get lost. And we got lost pretty easily. Our chosen walk — climbing one of the hills — was part of a local ramble, but we missed our intended turning off a hillside road and ended up tramping half-way round the hill and fighting our way through a dense thicket of conifers before thankfully regaining the path that led to the summit. Once there we could look back across the agricultural plain of the Dore valley and see the distant deep purple peaks of the Volcans d'Auvergne lining the horizon. **Before you go** *Maps:* IGN 1:100,000 Nos. 42, 43, 49 and 50; IGN 1:25,000 (OT & ET) Nos. 2630-34, 2730-34 and 2830-34. **Getting there** *By car:* from Clermont-Ferrand, take

A72 towards Lyon, exiting at Thiers for the north of the park, or A75 towards Montpellier, exiting at Issoire for the middle and south of the park. D906 runs north-south through the park and D996 cuts across it east-west. *By rail:* services from Clermont-Ferrand and St-Etienne to (from north to south) Thiers, Vic-le-Comte, Issoire and Brioude. A 'discovery train' runs along the River Dore in the centre of the park from Courpière to Sembadel; contact the railway station at Ambert, T: 04 73 82 43 88. *By bus:* SNCF has buses from Thiers to Arlanc and La Chaise-Dieu. 'Voyages Maisonnière', T: 04 73 82 18 04, runs services to Arlanc and Ambert. **Where to stay:** Hôtel Robert at Vollore-Ville, T: 04 73 53 71 27, is welcoming and right in the middle of the park. Other convenient centres are La Chaise-Dieu, Ambert, Thiers, Le Puy and Brioude. Tourist offices have lists of camp-sites. **Activities** *Walking:* GR3 skirts the eastern edge of the park. *Cycling:* the Randonnée des Monts de Forez passes through the east of the park. Cycle-hire outlets in Ambert, St-Anthème, Aubusson d'Auvergne, Le Pays-Neuf and Chomelix. *Riding:* contact ADTE de Haute-Loire, Labauche, 43320 Vergezac, T: 04 71 08 08 81, F: 04 71 08 05 00. *Aerial sports:* the Aéro Club du Livradois, T: 04 73 72 27 09, offers a range of activities. *Adventure holidays:* 'Chamina' in Clermont-Ferrand, T: 04 73 92 81 44, has information on cycle paths and riding and ski trails. Loisirs Accueil Haute-Loire, 12 blvd Philippe Jourde, Le Puy-en-Velay, T: 04 71 09 91 50, is another option. *Skiing:* 90 km of pistes. Alpine skiing at St-Anthème, T: 04 73 95 40 20; cross-country skiing trips organized by Jean-Paul Mullié in Valcivières, T: 04 73 82 31

92. *Sightseeing:* you can take a tour of the park's châteaux, museums and craft shops; contact 'Route des Métiers' in St-Gervais-sous-Meymont, T: 04 73 95 58 04. *Museum:* Ambert has a museum of old agricultural machinery appropriately sited in rue de l'Industrie, T: 04 73 82 43 88. The museum also organizes summer train tours through the Auvergne and Cévennes; pick up the train at Ambert or Clermont-Ferrand. **Further information** *Tourist offices:* Ambert, 4 pl de l'Hôtel-de-Ville, T: 04 73 82 61 90; Brioude, T: 04 71 74 99 49; La Chaise-Dieu, pl de la Mairie, T: 04 71 00 01 16; Courpière, T: 04 73 51 20 27; St-Anthème, T: 04 73 95 47 06; Thiers, pl du Pirou, T: 04 73 80 65 65. *Park office:* St-Gervais-sous-Meymont, T: 04 73 95 57 57, www.parc-livradois-forez.org.

ONF Auvergne, site de Marmilhat-Sud, BP 106, 63370 Lempdes, T: 04 73 42 01 00.

Parc Régional du Pilat

Rounded hills between Lyon and St-Etienne; parc naturel régional *70,000 ha (175,000 acres)*

Muffled thunder sounded in the distance as I set out along the footpath into the hills of Pilat. By mid-morning it was already hot and humid, the heat being intensified by the mirror-like mica over which we were climbing. Several pairs of black redstarts — amazingly unconcerned by my presence — scurried ahead of me. Small streams cut across the path, which in places doubled as a watercourse. As I approached a

Spectacular rock formations rise from the granite plateaux of the Monts du Forez.

wood the clouds at first loomed larger, then retreated. But the thunder continued to rumble, as though Thor was grumbling under his breath.

I sat down on the edge of the wood for a picnic of bread and cheese. A Montagu's harrier circled below before diving into the valley in pursuit of prey.

The Parc Naturel Régional du Pilat is a welcome survival in an area once threatened by the urban sprawls of St-Etienne and Lyon. An eastern outpost of the Massif Central, it shares its geological features. Weather has shaped the landscape over a long period of time, wearing away the sharp edges and smoothing off the corners. Mixed forests of conifers and deciduous trees cover many of the higher hills, intermixed with pasture and arable farming on the lower slopes.

This wild part of France is holding its own. Deer had vanished from the park; they have now returned. Wild boar, too, can be glimpsed.

Before you go *Maps:* IGN 1:100,000 Nos. 50 and 51; IGN 1:25,000 (OT & ET) Nos. 2933-34 and 3032-34. **Getting there** *By car:* the park lies in a triangle bounded on 2 sides by *autoroutes*; A7 and A47. The N82 from St-Etienne to Annonay cuts through the park. *By rail:* the best approach is the line from Lyon to St-Etienne, which follows the border of the park. **Where to stay:** the 1-star Lion d'Or is an old coaching inn in St-Chamond, T: 04 77 22 01 38. Lyon, St-Etienne and Vienne are nearby; Annonay, Givors and Roussillon are smaller alternatives. Bourg-Argental is the best bet inside the park. **Activities** *Walking:* the park office has details of possible walks, including an 18-km (11-mile) botanical tour; 2 long-distance footpaths, GR7 and G42, cross the park. *Riding:* contact CDTE de la Loire, 36 rue du Bois d'Avaize, 42100 St-Etienne, T: 04 77 52 80 52. *Canoeing:* courses are held on the artificial River St-Pierre-de-Boeuf, T: 04 74 87 16 09. *Outdoor sports:* contact Loisirs Accueil Loire, 5 pl Jean Jaurès, 42021 St-Etienne, T: 04 77 43 24 42. *Skiing:* details from Loire Ski du Fond, 1 rue Emile Combe, St-Etienne, T: 04 77 32 23 40. **Further information** *Tourist offices:* Annonay, pl des Cordeliers, T: 04 75 33 24 51; St-Etienne, 3 pl Roannelle, T: 04 77 25 12 14. *Park offices:* Pélussin, Moulin de Virieu, T: 04 74 87 52 00; Bourg-Argental, 8 pl de la Liberté, T: 04 77 39 63 49; Condrieu, T: 04 74 56 62 83; St-Sauveur-en-Rue, T: 04 77 39 20 33.

Les Cévennes

Arid plateaus and moors in the south-east of the Massif Central; parc national ZICO, Biosphere Reserve 91,000 ha (225,000 acres)

ꕔ ꕔ ꕔ

One good way to discover France's wild places is to make for the high ground. From Villefort, in the valley of the Allier, a Grande Randonnée climbs up into the hills which closely surround the town. The path rises steeply: a 225-metre (750-foot) climb in less than three kilometres (two miles). At one point, I stopped to watch as two large green lizards tussled beside the path, totally oblivious to my presence. The dried leaves from last year's fall rustled and crackled as the pair thrashed about. Was this love or war? It was impossible to tell. The lizards suddenly realized they had an audience and scuttled off separately into the undergrowth.

The woodland changes as you climb. At

THE GRIFFON VULTURE

The griffon vulture (*Gyps fulvus*) is an immense bird. Even with a wing-span of up to 2.8 m (9 ft) it still welcomes the updraught of a thermal to help it fly. Consequently, it tends to favour warm cliffs and sunny gorges, where the sun warming up the valley bottom creates an updraught as the hot air rises.

There were griffon vultures in the Gorges du Tarn and de la Jonte until 1940. Hunters were partly responsible for their subsequent demise, but farmers caused just as many problems. They began to send their dead cattle to renderers, rather than leaving the carrion to be picked clean, while at the same time systematically poisoning wolves, which meant that what carrion there was in turn poisoned the scavenging vultures.

The griffon vulture was once common in mountainous areas through southern and central Europe. But by the late 1960s the population was down to a few pairs, scattered across the Mediterranean countries and holding on in North Africa. However, thanks to successful reintroduction programmes, numbers are increasing: there are now 30 nesting pairs in the Gorges du Tarn and de la Jonte and 75 pairs in the park as a whole.

first it is mostly deciduous. Farther up it becomes mixed, as conifers take over. Gradually it turns almost entirely to pines, interspersed with small birch trees. Finally you emerge, above the tree-line, on to a moor.

Before you reach the tree-line, you are climbing blind, with only glimpses through upper branches to a distant hill on the other side of the valley. The view at the top, though, repays all your patience and exertion. Snow still covers the distant peaks at the end of May. All around, almost as far as the eye can see, a plateau stretches into the distance, slashed by valleys, changing hue from green and brown to grey and purple on the horizon: a wasteland virtually devoid of any sign of human presence.

Much of this land lies within the Parc National des Cévennes, which was created in 1970. The park's central zone is the high ground that runs more or less south-south-west in a line between Mende and Villefort, roughly as far as Le Vigan, covering an area of over 900 square kilometres (350 square miles). The buffer zone forms a crude pentagon, from Mende to Les Vans, to Alès, Alzon, La Malène and back to Mende.

The park's central zone falls fairly naturally into three parts: the Mont Lozère massif, the massif of Mont Aigoual and the Grands Causses. The rounded old granite of Mont Lozère, in the north of the park, close to the town of Villefort, is the highest point, at 1,699 metres (5,570 feet), and is snow-covered for more than a quarter of the year. The massif of Mont Aigoual, south of Mont Lozère, is a mixture of granite and schist. Here the climate and plant life are almost Mediterranean; sweet chestnut trees prosper in the long dry summers. These areas of older rocks are shaped like an hourglass on the map, pinched into a slender neck at Barre-des-Cévennes.

To the south and west of Lozère and Aigoual are a series of limestone plateaux defined by gorges that form their natural boundaries: the *causses* of Sauveterre, Méjean, Noir and Larzac — collectively known as the Grands Causses. Apart from rocky quarters where there is not enough soil to support even a blade of grass, they are great grassy expanses, broken only by an occa-

The short-toed eagle is a specialist hunter of snakes and lizards.

sional stone wall or building, which farmers use for summer pasture. These *causses* are high, reaching an altitude of more than 1,000 metres (3,300 feet) at the eastern end of the Causse Méjean. The climate up here is extreme: the winters are freezing cold, and by late summer the baking heat has turned the pasture brown, forcing the farmers to move their herds to lower grazing.

Despite the high rainfall on the *causses* there is little groundwater, save the odd dew pond. Any rain immediately seeps into the rock underground, carving vast sculptured caverns filled with stalagmites and stalactites. Sometimes the roof of one of these caverns caves in, creating a sinkhole — a sudden drop from the plateau into the underworld.

With their networks of natural tunnels and channels, the *causses* are frequently likened to a Gruyère cheese. They are in fact the home of another type of cheese — Roquefort — made from the milk of ewes that graze on the plateaux. The cheese is stored in the caves above the village of Roquefort, close to the Causse du Larzac.

The caves at Aven Armand, on the Causse Méjean, are among the most celebrated in France. They make fascinating viewing: more than 400 stalagmites, often in excess of 20 metres (66 feet) high, glimmer with the remarkably delicate shadings caused by traces of minerals in the limestone deposits.

The variety of climate and habitat in the Cévennes gives rise to an impressive fauna. The holes and small caves on the limestone *causses* are convenient dwellings for a host of mammals including rabbits, foxes and mice. The black woodpecker nests in the park as does the short-toed eagle, which feeds on reptiles, a Cévennes speciality. The warmer southern slopes represent the northernmost range of the typically Mediterranean Montpellier snake, while altitude separates the two vipers: the more common asp frequents forest-edge habitats up to about 1,000 metres (3,300 feet), while the rarer adder is found from about 900 metres (3,000 feet) to the upper tree-line. The Cévennes is also one of the few places where the smooth snake and southern smooth snake occur together.

The park has pursued an active programme of reintroducing species that used to live in the Cévennes. It has successfully reintroduced European beavers into the rivers of the Tarn and the Tarnon, and griffon vultures into the Gorges de la Jonte and Gorges du Tarn. Several threatened birds of prey, including the golden eagle, also nest in the Gorges du Tarn.

BEFORE YOU GO
Maps: IGN 1:100,000 Nos. 58, 59 and 65; IGN 1:25,000 Nos. 2641 OT & ET, 2640 OT, 2739 OT and 2740-41 ET.

GETTING THERE
By car: take A75 south from Clermont-Ferrand, picking up N106 to Mende, which wends through the Cévennes to Florac and Alès. For a more scenic route, turn off N106 on to D907 about 5 km (3 miles) south of Florac, then D983. At St-Laurent-de-Trèves, D9 cuts through the pass of Faisses and continues to the village of St-Roman-de-Tousque.

By rail: the railway from Clermont-Ferrand to Alès takes a more northerly route than the 2 roads running the length of the park; there are stops at Lagogne and Villefort. Trains also run up into the hills from Alès to Bessèges.

By bus: there are regular services from Alès to Florac and St-Jean-du-Gard; Le Puy to Langogne and Mende; Florac to Mende, Millau and Génolhac; and Nîmes to Le Vigan. Buses also run from Sévérac to Rodez, and on to Millau, Cahors and Espalion.

WHERE TO STAY
Villefort is a good base; the 2-star Hôtel Balme, pl du Portalet, T: 04 66 46 80 14, has an excellent restaurant. Alès makes another convenient base. More central possibilities include Florac, Génolhac, Meyrueis and Les Vans.
Outdoor living: camping is forbidden in the park's central zone; there are plenty of campsites on the periphery.
Refuges: there are 118 *gîtes d'étape* or refuges and 655 *gîtes ruraux* in the park. Details from the park office.

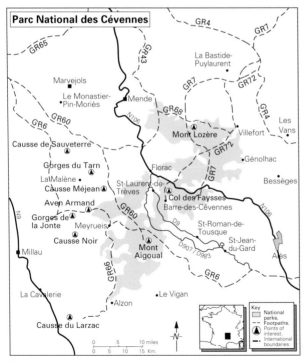

Parc National des Cévennes

In the Cévennes mountains, deciduous trees blend with evergreen pines.

Plateau de Millevaches

Remote granite plateau on the north-west edge of the Massif Central
ZICO

I set off from Merlines along the Tour d'Eygurande long-distance footpath. About an hour's walk out of the town the footpath picks up the route of a disused railway, following the woody gorges of the River Chavanon. Beneath the path vigorous waters gushed over the rocky river bed, while shafts of sunlight glinted on the water.

After a while the sky darkened and fine droplets began to fall, so I pressed on hurriedly to find shelter. As the drizzle turned to rain, I rounded the bend to see a deserted wayside station with a 'For Sale' notice on it. The glass platform canopy was still intact and I waited under it for the storm to pass. Soon the rain eased off and I made tracks, hopeful of seeing some bird life: the clear period after rain is often a good time for spotting birds as they emerge from their shelters to look for food. The practice was up to the theory: in the space of a few minutes, a lesser spotted woodpecker and a merlin flew past me.

For most of its route the path is on the plateau of Millevaches ('a thousand cows'). At first sight the name is an absurdity. This infertile and remote upland is far from the gadding waters of the river valleys and supports few cows. However, its name has nothing to do with cattle but is a corruption of a Celtic word for spring (*batz*). This immediately makes sense — a thousand springs. The

ACTIVITIES

Walking: GR7 runs most of the length of the park, while GR70 follows Stevenson's walk; call the Association sur le Chemin de R. L. Stevenson in Pont-de-Montvert, T: 04 66 45 86 31.

Cycling: bicycles are available at the railway stations of Alès, La Bastide-Puylaurent, Langogne, Marvejols, Mende and Villefort. There are 200 km (125 miles) of cycle trails in the park, including parts of the Toboggan Cévenol and Autour de Millau long-distance routes.

Riding: contact ADTE de Lozère, La Périgouse, 48210 Ste-Enimie, T: 04 66 48 53 71, for local equestrian centres.

Adventure holidays: contact Loisirs Accueil Lozère, 14 blvd Henri Bourrillon, 48001 Mende, T: 04 66 48 48 48, for details of treks on the park's 600 km (375 miles) of bridle paths and canoeing on some excellent stretches of river. UCPA centres at Florac, T: 04 66 45 05 49, and Mont-Lozère, T: 04 66 48 62 81, offer walking, cycling, gliding and other sports.

Skiing: there are 100 km (63 miles) of cross-country piste; contact Lozère Ski de Fond, 2 pl De Gaulle, Mende, T: 04 66 49 12 12.

The Corsican *mouflon* inhabits upland areas of mainland France.

Sightseeing: there are many museums in the park; the Ecomusée du Mont-Lozère, T: 04 66 45 80 73, is a good place to start. There are also a dozen dolmens and 5 menhirs. The park office will help you locate all of the above.

Viewpoints: a 38-km (23-mile) tour of the ridges (D998 from Génolhac to Les Bastides, returning on D35 and D906) takes in splendid views. The whole of the park can be seen from the Can de L'Hospitalet, south of St-Laurent-de-Trèves.

FURTHER INFORMATION

Tourist offices: Alès, pl Gabriel Péri, T: 04 66 52 32 15; Florac, av J-Monastier, T: 04 66 45 01 14; Mende, blvd Bourrillon, T: 04 66 65 02 69; Villefort, rue de l'Eglise, T: 04 66 46 87 30.

The Cévennes web-site is www.cevennes.net.

Park office: le Château, BP 15, 48400 Florac, T: 04 66 49 53 01, F: 04 66 49 53 02, e-mail: pnc@bsi.fr, www.bsi.fr/pnc.

FURTHER READING

R. L. Stevenson, *Travels with a Donkey in the Cévennes* (Marlboro Press, 1996).

The lesser-spotted woodpecker is an elusive but widespread species in broad-leaved forests.

plateau is the source of several important rivers, including the Vienne and the Creuse, as well as a couple of tributaries of the Dordogne.
Before you go *Maps:* IGN 1:100,000 No. 41; IGN 1:25,000 Nos. (OT & ET) 2231-32 and 2331-32. **Getting there** *By car:* N89 from Clermont-Ferrand to Ussel and Tulle is the plateau's southern boundary. A series of turnings off N89 cross the plateau: D982, D979 and D36. *By rail:* the railway line from Clermont-Ferrand to Brive passes through Ussel and Tulle. The line from Ussel to Bugeat, Eymoutiers and Limoges crosses the plateau. There is a service from Ussel to La Courtine. *By bus:* bus services from Ussel north to various destinations on the plateau.
Where to stay: Ussel is the hub of both road and rail services in

the area. La Courtine, Egletons, Felletin, Merlines, Meymac, Tarnac and Treignac are other options. **Activities** *Walking:* GR46 and GR440 cross the plateau ending up at Limoges. The Tour d'Eygurande runs along the eastern side of the plateau; pick up the footpath at Merlines or Ussel. *Cycling:* bicycles are available at Meymac station. **Further information** *Tourist office:* Ussel, pl Voltaire, T: 05 55 72 11 50. ONF Limousin, 40-42 av des Bénédictins, 87000 Limoges, T: 05 55 34 53 13, F: 05 55 43 57 93.

Dordogne

Fertile river valleys between Limoges and Bordeaux

Woodpeckers had been quite elusive on this trip to France. Occasionally you would hear one chuckling in the woods, a joke at my expense, but that was that. According to the bird books you ought to be able to see not only green woodpeckers, but also the lesser spotted and black species.

My quest for woodpeckers of any sort seemed fruitless, until I returned from a walk after a heavy shower. I was only a few hundred yards away from Déganac, the village where I was staying, when a black

woodpecker flew across the road, followed by two more. This proved again that bird-watching is often at its best immediately after rain.

The Dordogne may not be the wildest part of France, but it is exceptionally rural, a tranquil mixture of woodland and agriculture. It is a gentle and rich landscape of low hills, where herds of deer peer warily at passing strangers from the safety of the woods. The Dordogne river runs through the centre of this countryside, flowing from the granite of the Auvergne, cleaving the Causse de Martel, then meandering west to the Atlantic. 'Just to glimpse,' as Henry Miller observed, 'the black, mysterious river at Domme from the beautiful bluff at the edge of town is something to be grateful for all one's life.'

On its way west, the river passes through Périgord Noir: the name is supposed to reflect the darkness of the oak trees in the area, though they seem green enough to most. Neighbouring Périgord Blanc, north of the River Isle, takes its name — with a bit more accuracy — from the whiteness of its limestone. A particularly prized product from this region is the truffles which are hunted out in winter by pigs and specially trained dogs.

Another attraction of the Dordogne is the prehistoric cave paintings at Les Eyzies and Lescaux. The paintings at

---

TRUFFLES AND MUSHROOMS

Limousin and Périgord are noted for their immense variety of wild fungi. Most distinguished is the truffle, of which a dozen or so species occur in Périgord. Most widespread is the truffle *Tuber melanosporum*. It generally occurs around field edges where the ploughed and hard soils meet but is not particularly easy to locate because it is usually underground. Look for circular patches where the soil is bare and looks freshly dug, with stones paler than elsewhere: but in the end, it is far easier to train an animal to sniff them out for you.

Lascaux were discovered by accident in 1940 by four boys searching for a lost dog. Drawn by people living in the caves in the middle of the last Ice Age, they depict bison, reindeer and mammoths. They are remarkable not only for their vivid portrayal of these Stone Age animals but also for their uncanny state of preservation over 20,000 years. This is due to the evaporation of water which covered the walls with a kind of lacquer.

Before you go *Maps:* IGN 1:100,000 No. 48; IGN 1:25,000 Nos. 1834-37, 1934-38, 2034-39 and 2134-39.

Getting there *By car:* roads radiate from Sarlat; D47 leads to Périgueux while D703 heads west to Bergerac, east to Souillac. *By rail:* trains run south from Périgueux to Les Eyzies and Le Buisson. The line east from Bergerac follows the River Dordogne to Le Buisson and Sarlat. Main-line trains from Paris run through Brive to Souillac and Cahors. *By bus:* daily buses link Souillac to Sarlat. **Where to stay:** L'Auberge sans Frontière at Dégagnac, T: 05 65 41 52 88, is a splendid village hotel, and a good base for tours. The main towns are Périgueux, Brive-la-Gaillarde, Bergerac and Sarlat; other possibilities include Les Eyzies, Montignac, Domme and St-Cyprien. *Outdoor living:* practically every town has a municipal camp-site. **Activities** *Walking:* several Grande Randonnée paths cross this lovely walking country: GR6, GR46, GR36, GR646 and GR652. *Cycling:* railway stations at Bergerac, Cahors, Les Eyzies, Périgueux, Sarlat and Souillac rent out bicycles. The Chemins de Compostelle, Rose des Vents Briviste and Côteaux de Dordogne routes wind through the region. *Riding:* information from ADTE de Dordogne, 4-6 94

pl Francheville, 24016 Périgueux, T: 05 53 35 88 88. *Adventure holidays:* UCPA has a centre at Lacave, T: 05 65 37 01 45. Loisirs Accueil at CDT de la Dordogne (see below) will help organize activities in the region: canoeing down Dordogne's rivers is particularly memorable. *Sightseeing:* the hilltop village of St-Cirq-Lapopie is one of the best preserved in France. Les Eyzies is famous for its many prehistoric sites. **Further information** *Tourist offices:* Bergerac, 97 rue Neuve d'Argenson, T: 05 53 57 03 11; Les Eyzies-de-Tayac, pl de la Mairie, T: 05 53 06 97 05 (summer only); Périgueux, 26 pl Francheville, T: 05 53 53 10 63; Sarlat, pl de la Liberté, T: 05 53 31 45 45; Souillac, blvd Malvy, T: 05 65 37 81 56. CDT de la Dordogne, 25 rue Wilson, 24000 Périgueux, T: 05 53 35 50 00/05 53 35 50 24, www.perigord.tm.fr. *Park office:* 24300 Abjat-sur-Bandiat, T: 05 53 60 34 65.

Armagnac

Rural gem in south-west France; frequently overlooked by travellers speeding to the Pyrenees

Armagnac is most famous for the drink of the same name (a southern rival of Cognac) but has much more than brandy to offer. The region lies to the east of the vast forested tracts of Les Landes in Gascony and is sandwiched between the River Garonne to the north and the Pyrenees to the south.

A series of rivers stretch out like fingers to cross Armagnac, rising in the mountains of the Pyrenees and heading north

Poplar trees grow along the bank of the Dordogne near Beynac.

towards the valley of the Garonne, which is also the route of the Canal du Midi. The Garonne is clean enough to have salmon.

Armagnac is lush and green and is covered by a number of forests, including the 2,000-ha (5,000-acre) Forêt de Bouconne, west of Toulouse, and the Forêt de Berdoues, south of Mirande and close to the nature reserve of Puntous.

Armagnac is far from being the wildest part of France. It is, nevertheless, off the beaten track: the countryside is rustic, quiet and relatively free of tourists — certainly by comparison with the Dordogne to the north.

Before you go *Maps:* IGN 1:100,000 No. 63; IGN 1:25,000 Nos. 1542-45, 1642-45, 1742-45, 1842-45 and 1942-45. **Getting there** *By car:* A62 runs up the Garonne valley from Bordeaux to Toulouse, and is the region's northern boundary. N124 cuts across Gascony from Toulouse to Auch. Main north-south roads are N134 (Aire to Pau) and N21 (Tarbes to Auch). *By rail:* TGV services from Paris-Gare Montparnasse to Toulouse, Pau and Tarbes. Local trains from Toulouse to Auch. *By bus:* Auch is the centre for local buses; routes radiate to Agen, Lannemezan, Tarbes, Mont-de-Marsan, Condom, Barbotan-les-Thermes and Montauban. **Where to stay:** Pau and Tarbes border the Pyrenees; other options are Auch, Aire, Condom, Mirande and Mont-de-Marsan. *Outdoor living:* local tourist offices have lists of camp-sites. **Activities** *Walking:* GR65 runs from Roncevaux in the Pyrenees to Eauze and La Romieu, the starting point for the tour of Coeur de Gascogne, to Auch and back. GR653 heads from Toulouse to Auch and Maubourguet. Tourist offices have details of local walks. *Cycling:* rent bicycles at the stations of Auch and Tarbes. The Randonnée de l'Armagnac is a circular tour of the region which can be picked up in Auch. *Riding:* information from ADTE du Gers, Chambre d'Agriculture, route de Mirande, 32003 Auch, T: 05 62 63 16 55. *Outdoor sports:* Loisirs Accueil Gers is based in Auch, T: 05 62 61 79 00. **Further information** *Tourist offices:* Auch, 1 rue Dessoles, T: 05 62 05 22 89; Condom, pl Bossuet, T: 05 62 28 00 80; Mont-de-Marsan, 6 pl Général Leclerc, T: 05 58 05 87 37; Pau, pl Royale, T: 05 59 27 27 08; Tarbes, 3 cours Gambetta, T: 05 02 51 30 31; Toulouse, pl Charles-de-Gaulle, T: 05 61 11 02 22.

CDT du Gers, 7 rue Diderot, BP 106, 32002 Auch, T: 05 62 05 95 95, www.gascogne.com. ONF Midi-Pyrénées, 23 bis, blvd Bonrepos, 31000 Toulouse, T: 05 62 73 55 00.

Haut-Languedoc

Surprisingly verdant upland forming southern rim of the Massif Central; parc naturel régional
ZICO
187,000 ha (462,000 acres)

I sat down to lunch in a hillside meadow full of dandelions, by some woods overlooking a deep valley. Wild roses lined the woodland edge. The smell of wild thyme sweetened the air and the loudest sound was the chattering of the cicadas. Two jays settled in an oak tree just beneath where I sat. When they spotted me they exited squawking, upset by this unusual human intrusion. This was rural bliss, its tranquillity assured by the protection of park boundaries.

The Parc Naturel Régional du Haut-Languedoc lies in the south-western extremity of the Massif Central. The valley of the River Thoré and the industrialized plain of Castres separate the park into two distinct areas. The southern section includes a range of hills known as the Montagne Noire ('black mountain'), while the northern part of the park consists of a granite plateau known as the Sidobre. This forested upland is scattered with enormous rounded blocks of granite, sculpted by millons of years of erosion, which seemingly defy all laws of gravity. The projection of human imagination on to their fantastic forms gave birth to a local mythology in which each monolith was given a name.

The Sidobre has an almost Mediterranean climate, yet its vegetation remains surprisingly lush due to the good supply of groundwater. The explanation for the plentiful supply of water is not hard to find. This is a climatic frontier, where the warm Mediterranean air meets the moist westerlies from the Atlantic. The clouds float in on the westerly winds, rise up when they meet the hills, and promptly dump their cargo of rain. The mountains of Lacaune, to the north and east of the park boundary, have some of the highest rainfalls in France.

The combination of Mediterranean sunshine, water, shade, hills and trees means that Haut-Languedoc has a touch of Greece about it. The valley of the River Orb, which runs through the south-eastern corner of the park past the Massif du Caroux-Espinouse, could be the river valley at the foot of Mount Olympus: the trees are stacked up the valley sides so densely that when seen from afar the roots of one appear to be supported by the boughs of that beneath. Rocky outcrops, too steep for soil to cling to, show through gaps in the vegetation.

Despite the poorish soil, the Caroux-Espinouse hills bristle with oaks, sweet chestnuts and mountain ash; firs crown many of the hilltops. It is the climatic watershed that allows this opulent landscape of shaggy woodland to flourish.

The bird life in Haut-Languedoc is not easy to spot because of the denseness of the vegetation, but just occasionally a buzzard will rise above the tree-line to survey its domain. For the most part, however, prey and predator alike stay hidden in the foliage, only their songs betraying their presence.

The valleys are considerably less wild, being intensively cultivated. The sport is to spot a square foot of soil without a vine on it. The local villages, whose economy depends heavily on viticulture, have a certain Greek flavour complementing that of the landscape. St-Pons-de-Thomières, located in the centre of the park, is a good example. Whitewashed houses spread up the hillsides, their Mediterranean red-tiled roofs glowing in the sun. The streets wind upwards, twisting and turning. The local stone is manifest in the architecture; even the streets of St-Pons are paved with marble.

Ancient civilization left its mark on the area in the form of sculptured menhirs and other megaliths. The region's many caves were inhabited as long as 3,000 years ago. They were rediscovered by Edouard-Alfred Martel, the founding father of speleology in France. Haut-Languedoc has since become a mecca for potholers.

BEFORE YOU GO
Maps: IGN 1:100,000 Nos. 64 and 65; IGN 1:25,000 Nos. 2244, 2343-44, 2443-44 & 2543.

GETTING THERE
By car: the park lies 30 km (18 miles) north of the A61. At Carcassonne, D620 branches off into the park, where it turns into the D920 as far as St-Pons. D907 from Lacaune to St-Pons crosses the heart of the park.
By rail: trains link Toulouse with Castres and Mazamet, on the edge of the Montagne Noire. There is a Béziers-Bédarieux service for the east of the park.
By bus: buses connect St-Pons with Toulouse, Montpellier, Bédarieux and La Salvetat.

WHERE TO STAY
The 1-star Hôtel Pastré in St-Pons, T: 04 67 97 00 54, is delightfully eccentric. Other convenient centres include Lamalou-les-Bains, Olargues, Roquebrun, La Salvetat, Anglès and Brassac.

ACTIVITIES
Walking: long-distance footpaths GR7, GR36, GR653, GR71 and GR77 traverse the park. The park office has details of shorter tours, such as the path of St-Jacques-de-Compostelle (from St-Gervais-sur-Mare to Sorèze).
Cycling: the Brevet du Haut-Languedoc cycle route can be joined at St-Pons.
Riding: contact CDTE de l'Herault, av des Moulins, BP 3067, 34034 Montpellier, T: 04 67 67 64 65, F: 04 67 67 71 97.
Adventure holidays: the Mons-la-Trivalle Base de Plein Air near Olargues, T: 04 67 97 72 80, offers canoeing, caving, climbing, rafting and other activities. Loisirs Accueil Hérault, av des Moulins, 34034 Montpellier, T: 04 67 67 71 40, will help with bookings.
Sightseeing: the Route des Bois takes in the forests and villages of the Montagne Noire, giving spectacular views over valleys and gorges; contact Mazamet tourist office (see below).
Archaeology: there is a regional museum of prehistory in St-Pons, T: 04 67 97 22 61.

FURTHER INFORMATION
Tourist offices: Castres, 3 rue Milhau-Ducommun, T: 05 63 62 63 62; Mazamet, rue des Casernes, T: 05 63 61 27 07; Revel, pl Philippe-VI-de-Valois, T: 05 61 83 50 06; St-Pons, pl Foirail, T: 04 67 97 06 65. Haut-Languedoc has a useful web-site: www.guide-haut-languedoc.com.
Park office: 13 rue du Cloître, St-Pons-de-Thomières, T: 04 67 97 38 22, F: 04 67 97 38 18.

CHAPTER 5

The Loire and Burgundy

Most of the time the Loire is deceptively placid as it meanders languidly between the *levées*, the raised embankments which were constructed to contain its course. Herons poise on banks in the middle of the river while kingfishers dart up and down its length. But the river is capricious and in full flood it is an awesome sight. The waters, swollen by the melting snows of spring far upstream in the Massif Central, angrily swirl around any obstructions placed in their path, such as the piers of Decize's medieval bridge. Downstream the river sometimes breaks its banks, spilling over riverside pastures and forcing sheep and cattle (and people) to retreat to higher ground. Weeping willows stand proud amid the murky floodwater, marking the line of the bank.

In recent years, the Loire has been at the centre of an ecological dispute, precisely because of its volatile nature. The French government has tried to tame the river with a series of barrages and dams, defending this policy by pointing to the devastation caused by flooding. Environmentalists, on the other hand, claim that the Loire is the last truly wild river in Europe — it is one of France's last breeding places for salmon — and should not be tampered with. They accuse the government of having a more cynical motive: namely, to prevent the river drying up in summer so as to ensure that the four nuclear power stations on its banks have a constant supply of cooling water.

The Loire is France's longest river,

This clearing in the woods of the eastern Sologne has a typical heathland character, bright with heather, broom and gorse.

rising in the Cévennes and following a 950-kilometre (600-mile) course to the Atlantic coast. It grows from a swift-flowing stream into a bloated giant, which winds slowly through flood plains past myriad woods, vineyards and châteaux until it reaches the sea. Between Nevers and Orléans the river sweeps around to the west, crossing the limestone plateau of Berry and forming the northern boundary, on two sides of a triangle, of the marshy area known as the Sologne. This sharp change in direction is unusual; geologists believe that the Loire once flowed north, joining up with the Seine.

For much of its length canals run parallel to the river. Once arteries of commerce, these canals are discovering a new lease of life serving the pleasure-cruise market. One in particular, the Canal de Briare (which connects the Loire at Briare with the Loing, a tributary of the Seine), manages to support colonies of the European beaver as well as holidaymakers.

The most interesting refuges for wildlife along the valley of the Loire are the Brière marsh (see BRITTANY AND NORMANDY, p28), at the river's mouth on the Atlantic, and the Sologne. This huge area is the remains of a freshwater swamp, ill-drained and relatively inaccessible — though the A71 *autoroute* has been extended through its middle, to the dismay of environmentalists.

The Loire valley is also notable for a series of forests. The 5,000-hectare (12,000-acre) Forêt de Chinon and the hunting Forêt de Chambord lie on the left bank, while the forests of the Nivernais (the region around Nevers) and Orléans are on the right. Another string of forests follows the valley of the Claise, a tributary of the Creuse, from the confluence of these rivers to Châteauroux and onwards over the Berry plateau and up the valley of the River Cher. Among the more interesting woodlands here are the Forêt de Tronçais and, near Châteauroux, the Forêt de Lancosme, home to honey buzzards and hen harriers which perform aerial courtship displays in spring. At night the forests resound with the haunting calls of tawny and long-eared owls.

The area around the River Claise, known as the Brenne, is a smaller version of the Sologne. Its rivers and its lakes filled with water-lillies are renowned as the last French stronghold of the European pond terrapin, the only freshwater turtle found in France. They are also exceptionally rich in bird life; marsh harriers are resident throughout the year, while migrating ospreys regularly stop by. There are numerous other waterfowl, and black and moustached terns are a summer speciality.

Another place to escape to, away from the châteaux and tourists, is the Morvan plateau. This rural fastness, home to birds of prey such as hawks, buzzards and falcons, lies to the east of the Loire valley, in the heart of Burgundy. It has several 900-metre (3,000-foot) peaks, and is linked geologically to the Massif Central. The rock is granite, in contrast to the chalky earth of the Parisian basin farther to the north, and to the limestone strata around Nevers and to the east around Autun.

Between the Loire and the Morvan hills stretches the limestone plateau of the Nivernais, a country of hedgerows and distinctive white cattle, known as *charolais*, which are raised over much of Burgundy. In former times Burgundy was an independent duchy, a curious, shifting realm that drifted across the pages of history, occasionally becoming independent and then being reunited with France, gaining and losing possessions to the south and to the north.

Modern Burgundy is the one stretch of land that was common to this migratory state. From Nevers on the Loire the region today stretches east to Dijon, south to Mâcon. Its northern boundary ends just short of Fontainebleau.

In eastern Burgundy, towards Dijon and the valley of the Saône, lies La Côte d'Or (the Gold Coast). With its roll-call of famous vineyards, such as Gevrey-Chambertin and Nuits-St-Georges, this is the land of the Burgundy reds.

Burgundy was once on the historic trade route running north from Italy and the Mediterranean to Flanders. It still lies on the main north-south route, although these days journey's end is more likely to be Paris or the Riviera. In the 1960s the Autoroute du Soleil carved a swathe across the east of the region. Then came the *train à grande vitesse* (TGV), whistling past at more than 250 kph (150 mph). Fortunately, most of the people on these great routes shoot straight through Burgundy, leaving much of the country undisturbed.

GETTING THERE
By air: international services go to Paris-Charles de Gaulle and Paris-Orly (see p33). You can also get flights to Nantes (for the western Loire) and Orléans. The French airports web-site is www.aeroport.fr.
By car: A10 runs from Paris to Orléans and downstream to Tours. The A6 leads from Paris into the heart of Burgundy but is extremely busy at the beginning of Aug. A right fork south of Fontainebleau on to the N7 takes drivers into the Loire valley and on to Nevers.
By rail: for details of the Eurostar service to Paris, see THE NORTH-EAST (p33). TGVs run from Paris-Gare Montparnasse to Angers and Nantes at the western end of the Loire. Frequent trains go from Paris-Gare d'Austerlitz to Orléans and on down the Loire to Tours. Regular services run from Paris-Gare de Lyon to Fontainebleau, Gien, Nevers and destinations in Burgundy. Contact SNCF, T: 08 36 35 35 35 (French)/39 (English), www.sncf.fr.
By bus: Eurolines, T: 01 49 72 51 51, www.eurolines.fr, has international services to Paris, Versailles, Orléans, Tours, Angers and Nantes. Busabout, www.busabout.com, runs coaches to Paris and Tours.

WHEN TO GO
The Loire attracts tourists throughout the year, but most come for the châteaux and wine, leaving long stretches of river undisturbed. Burgundy is less crowded, except in Aug, when some roads are packed with French families *en route* for the Mediterranean.

WHERE TO STAY
There is a wide range of accommodation along the Loire and throughout Burgundy. Details can be found in the individual exploration zones, through tourist offices in the area or by contacting one of the national agencies listed in USEFUL ADDRESSES.

ACTIVITIES
Walking: this is one of the best means of seeing the area. Apart from the marshes the terrain is easy, and there are no stiff climbs. Several GR footpaths cross the region, many running south or east from Paris.
Cycling: several long-distance cycle routes traverse the region; see IGN map No. 906, *VTT & Randonnée Cyclos*.
Riding: contact Association Régionale de Tourisme Equestre of either Bourgogne, Mairie, Corbigny, T: 03 86 20 10 74, or Ile-de-France, 1 rue Barbès, Beaumont-sur-Oise, T: 02 34 70 05 34, for details of riding holidays. The Fédération Française d'Equitation (see USEFUL ADDRESSES) publishes a free booklet, *Tourisme et Loisirs Equestres en France*.
Fishing: for a map, *La Pêche en France*, and information on restrictions and licences contact Le Conseil Supérieur de la Pêche (see USEFUL ADDRESSES).
Boating: there are several canals and 3 navigable rivers in the area. Contact Nièvre Voies Navigables, 2 rue des Patis, Nevers, T: 03 86 71 71 71, or Loisirs Accueil Yonne, 1/2 quai de la République, Auxerre, T: 03 86 72 92 10, who will book cruises.
Canoeing: Canoë Découverte, Levée-des-Tuileries, La Chaussée-St-Victor, T: 02 54 78

The royal fern is a rare species found in sheltered damp conditions.

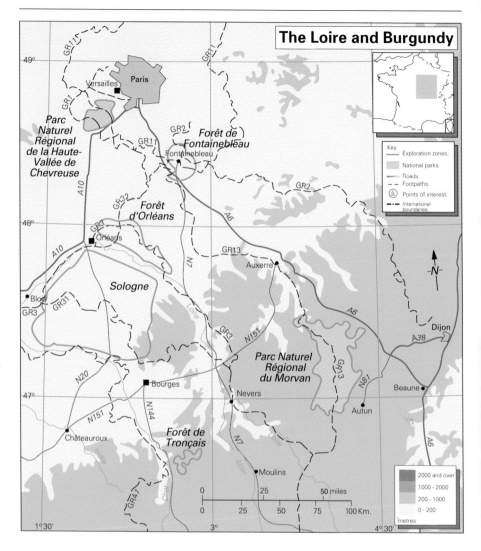

The Loire and Burgundy

Key
— Exploration zones.
National parks.
- - Roads.
- - Footpaths.
Ⓐ Points of interest.
- ▪ - International boundaries.

2000 and over
1000 - 2000
200 - 1000
0 - 200
metres

67 48, arranges trips on the Loire. Try also the Comité Régional du Centre de Canoë-Kayak, 6 rue Jeanne d'Arc, Orléans, T: 02 38 77 08 87.
Adventure holidays: the Loisirs Accueil service (see USEFUL ADDRESSES) will help book activity holidays.
Wine-tasting: the Bureau Interprofessionnel des Vins de Bourgogne, 12 blvd Bretonnière, Beaune, T: 03 80

25 04 80, www.bivb.com, will advise on visiting Burgundy's many vineyards.

FURTHER INFORMATION
Tourist offices: CRT de Bourgogne, BP 1602, 21035 Dijon, T: 03 80 50 90 00, F: 03 80 30 59 45, www.bourgogne-tourisme.com.
 CRT de Centre-Val de Loire, 10 rue Etienne Dolet, Orléans, T: 02 38 70 32 74, F: 02 38 70

33 80, www.loirevalleytourism. com.
 CRT d'Ile de France, 26 av de l'Opéra, 75001 Paris, T: 01 42 60 28 62, F: 01 42 60 20 23, www.cr-ile-de-france.fr.
 CRT de Pays de la Loire (see p145).

The sun sets over the Etang de Combreux, one of many small lakes which make up the wetland wilderness of the Sologne.

Sologne

*Marsh and woodland directly south of
Orléans, rich in water-loving flora and fauna
ZICO, World Heritage Site
5,000 sq km (1,900 sq miles)*

The European pond terrapin, a shy inhabitant of
freshwater lakes and marshes, has declined due to
pollution and discarded fishing tackle.

When I think of the Sologne, I think of
the smell of wood fires and the sound
of gunfire. There are few dwellings in this
vast area of flat, marshy woodland but when
you do come across one, you are likely to
smell the wood smoke before you see the
house and its smoking chimney. The gunfire
is the sound of hunting, which is common
throughout the Sologne. It is wise not to
stray from the paths: signs warning of private property and hunting grounds spell
danger not just for sundry wildlife — ramblers, too, are at risk.

The Sologne is wilderness regained. First
the Romans drained the swamps and developed agriculture: the region became the
bread-basket of Roman Gaul. After the fall
of the Roman empire the drainage system
became neglected and agriculture run down.
Monks endeavoured to recultivate the area
in the Middle Ages, but this attempt fell
apart during the religious wars that con-
vulsed France in the 16th and 17th centuries.
By the end of the 17th century the Sologne
was almost deserted.

In the mid-19th century, under Emperor
Napoleon III, a fresh attempt was made to
control the area: Scots pines were planted
and canals and drainage ditches were dug.
The effects of this are still visible but today
only small areas of the Sologne are given
over to agriculture or forestry: most of the
land is the preserve of hunting. And here lies
the irony. For although the hunters have ex-
terminated whole species and threaten the
survival of others, it is hunting, mostly for
rabbits, pheasants and waterfowl, that has
preserved the Sologne's natural habitats and
created a refuge for wildlife.

Most of the Sologne is woodland. The
trees are largely deciduous: silver birches
and oaks are common. The Scots pines,
which were planted in the 19th century and
continue to be planted today, rather spoil
the effect. However, the Sologne woodland
is far from commonplace. In other forests
the trees may give way to clearings and
glades. In the Sologne, as like as not, the
trees give way to lakes, ponds or the Loire,
which cradles the Sologne in its crooked
arm. The dampness of the soil shows
through on the forest floor, which is carpeted with a mixture of moss and ferns.

There are 2,000 lakes in all, covering
12,000 hectares (30,000 acres). Most are
found in the west, where the soil is a mixture
of clay and sand. Together with the wet,
warmish climate at the border between Atlantic and continental influences, the soil
creates the conditions needed for the area's
rich flora. White water-lilies, orchids and
rare ferns, including the tall royal fern, flourish in the lakes and valleys. One particularly
interesting plant found here is the rare
bird's-nest orchid, the plant realm's equivalent of a scavenger. It has no chlorophyll (the
pigment that makes leaves green) but instead
feeds saprophytically on decaying vegetable
matter in the soil.

The attraction of the Sologne for wildlife
enthusiasts is the mosaic of habitats jumbled
together in an intricate network of weed-
covered ponds with reedy fringes; these harbour rare aquatic flora and provide food for
a wide variety of aquatic invertebrates, especially dragonflies — the hawks of the insect

world. Bitterns and little bitterns lurk in the reeds, perfectly camouflaged against the streaky background. The only signs of bird life may be the constant scratchy chattering of reed and sedge warblers, and the occasional flypast of the majestic marsh harrier. The thousands of ducks that winter here are best seen on the *étangs* of Grande Corbois, Courcelles, Bièvre and Marcilly; the last of these is one of the principal sites for the huge breeding colonies of black-headed gulls, a feature of the Sologne.

On the western border of the Sologne is the Forêt de Chambord. This 5,400-hectare (13,000-acre) forest, a former royal hunting preserve, became the property of the state in 1932. It is populated by a wide variety of animals, including deer and a thousand head of wild boar, while the most common of the smaller predatory mammals is the polecat, though its numbers have declined considerably due to trapping.

The drier habitats in the east of the Sologne contrast with those in the west. They are covered with dense oak and hornbeam woods, which are inhabited by many deer, most visible during the autumn rutting period. Many clearings retain a heathland character, thick with heather, broom and gorse; this environment is home to Dartford warblers, as well as a rich variety of uncommon plants typical of sandy, poor soils.

BEFORE YOU GO
Maps: IGN 1:100,000 Nos. 26 and 27, also 1:100,000 map of the Sologne; IGN 1:25,000 Nos. 2120-23, 2220-23, 2320-23 and 2421-23.

GETTING THERE
By car: the A71 and N20 run south from Orléans through the heart of the Sologne. From the N20 the D922, D101 and D61 penetrate the marshland.
By rail: the main line from Paris-Gare d'Austerlitz runs through Orléans, Blois and Tours to the north and west of the Sologne. Local trains run south from Orléans to Salbris and Romorantin-Lanthenay, south-east to Sully-sur-Loire and Aubigny, and from Tours to Vierzon.
By bus: main routes from Blois operate to Chambord and Lamotte-Beuvron; to Nouan-le-Fuzelier and Salbris; and to Romorantin-Lanthenay and Villefranche-sur-Cher.

WHERE TO STAY
Romorantin-Lanthenay and La Ferté-St-Aubin are the main centres. Romorantin is on the expensive side, but the 2-star Le Colombier, 10 pl du Vieux-Marché, T: 02 54 76 12 76, is a comfortable base. Aubigny-sur-Nère, Bourges, Blois and Orléans are other options.
Outdoor living: there are about 30 camp-sites in the area; tourist offices have a list.

ACTIVITIES
Walking: GR41 runs along the southern edge of the Sologne from Tours to Vierzon. GR3 runs out of Tours along the south bank of the Loire and offshoots branch out into the interior of the marshes. GR31 can be picked up at Lamotte-Beuvron, from where it runs into the south-east of the area.
Cycling: this is pleasant cycling country. The Randonnée des Châteaux en Sologne and Tour Cyclo du Loir-et-Cher both meander around the Sologne.
Riding: contact the CDTE du Loir-et-Cher, 11 rue des Petits-Champs-Fy, St-Gervais-la-Forêt, T: 02 54 42 87 91.
Fishing: the lakes, river and

105

Extensive water-lily pads and dense reed-beds illustrate the typical wetland vegetation found in the lakes of the Sologne.

canal provide an immense variety of angling. You can buy day licences at the 60 towns or so in the area. Contact Loir-et-Cher fishing federation in Blois, T: 02 54 74 45 39.

Field studies: Sologne Nature Environnement in Nouan-le-Fuzelier, T: 02 54 88 79 74, organizes nature walks and guided tours of the Sologne's diverse habitats.

Viewpoints: about 1,500 hectares (3,700 acres) of the Forêt de Chambord are open to the public. There are a number of hides where visitors can observe animals in their natural environment.

FURTHER INFORMATION

Tourist offices: Bourges, 21 rue Victor Hugo, T: 02 48 23 02 60; Blois, 3 av Jean-Laigret, T: 02 54 90 41 41; Orléans, pl Albert-1er, T: 02 38 24 05 05; Romorantin-Lanthenay, pl de la Paix, T: 02 54 76 43 89; Sully-sur-Loire, pl de Gaulle, T: 02 38 36 23 70; Vierzon, 26 pl Vaillant Couturier, T: 02 48 52 65 24.

Association pour la Fondation Sologne, Domaine du Ciran, Ménestreau-en-Villette, T: 02 38 76 90 93.

106

Forêt d'Orléans

Fabled forest, France's fifth largest, on the upper reaches of the Loire, 120 km (70 miles) south of Paris
ZICO
35,000 ha (86,000 acres)

In his book *Gargantua*, François Rabelais tells how the great forest above Orléans used to be 105 miles long and 51 miles wide 'or thereabouts'. Since that time, it has greatly decreased in size. Rabelais himself offered this reason: Gargantua, 'after drinking, as you will understand,' was journeying to Paris through the forest on his giant mare. In order to ward off hornets the mare swished her tail vigorously, demolishing the trees as a scythe cuts grass. That which remains, to follow this line of fiction, is the wood the mare's tail missed.

The Forêt d'Orléans today is only a quarter of the size it was in the Middle Ages, but it is still the largest of the string of forests that line the banks of the Loire, and cover the right bank from Orléans to Gien.

The forest is mainly a mixture of oak and beech, with hornbeam and silver birch as well as more recently planted conifers, such as Scots pine. Despite the disturbance caused by hunting and a number of roads that cross the forest, deer and wild boar still roam free. **Before you go** *Maps:* IGN 1:100,000 Nos. 20 and 27; IGN 1:25,000 Nos. 2219, 2319 and 2320. **Getting there** *By car:* Orléans is on A10; N60 runs up the right bank of the Loire as far as Châteauneuf-sur-Loire, D952 continues to Gien. Roads crossing the forest include D97, N152, D921 and D961. *By rail:* local services run from Orléans (west of the forest) to Châteauneuf-sur-Loire and Sully-sur-Loire. *By bus:* buses go from Orléans through the forest to Pithiviers; and from Orléans to Vitry-aux-Loges in the middle of the forest. **Where to stay:** Orléans is boring and industrial; Châteauneuf, Gien and Pithiviers are better bets. *Refuges:* a refuge has been created near the lake of La Vallée for naturalists and ramblers who want to spend more time in the forest. *Outdoor living:* tourist offices have a list of local camp-sites. **Activities** *Walking:* there are many well-trodden footpaths — GRP (offshoot of GR3) from Orléans runs alongside first the Loire and then the Canal d'Orléans, as far as Fay-aux-Loges where it strikes north across the forest. GR3 from Orléans heads straight into the forest. From Sully-de-Loire follow 3 waymarked circuits: Val de Loire (5 km/3 miles, 1¼ hrs), Forêt de Sully (10 km/6 miles, 2 hrs) and Val de Loire/Sologne (15 km/9 miles, 3 hrs). *Cycling:* bicycles are available at railway stations of Gien and Orléans. *Riding:* information from Association Départementale de Tourisme Equestre du Loiret, Le Chereau, 45600 Viglain, T: 02 38 37 21 77. *Watersports:* trips on the boat *L'Oussance* down the Canal d'Orléans from Fays-aux-Loges, T: 02 38 57 04 74, and from Combleux. Wind-surfing, canoeing and sailing Mar-Oct on La Vallée lake, Combreux, T: 02 38 59 49 82; supervised swimming in the lake June-Sept, T: 02 38 59 42 85. *Outdoor sports:* Loisirs Accueil Loiret, 8 rue d'Escures, Orléans, T: 02 38 62 04 88, will organize activities such as canoeing. *Ecology:* wildlife courses at Ménestreau-en-Villette, T: 02 38 76 90 93. There is a 9-ha (23-acre) arboretum at Grandes Bruyères, near the village of Ingrannes, situated just off

Pink fox-gloves burst out among the ferns of the Morvan hills.

D921, T: 02 38 57 12 61. **Further information** *Tourist offices:* Châteauneuf-sur-Loire, 3 pl Aristide-Briand, T: 02 38 58 44 79; Gien, pl Jean Jaurès, T: 02 38 67 25 28; Orléans, pl

Albert-1er, T: 02 38 24 05 05; Pithiviers, Mail-Ouest, Gare Routière, T: 02 38 30 50 02.

Morvan

Range of hills in the heart of Burgundy, 270 km (170 miles) south-east of Paris; varied terrain of meadows, heathland, lakes and pine and mixed deciduous forest; parc naturel régional
World Heritage Site
196,000 ha (484,000 acres)

On my most recent visit to the Morvan I took the dawn train from Autun up the eastern side of the park. The train is slow and the line winds its way up the best part of 300 metres (1,000 feet) above the Arroux valley on to the granite plateau of the Morvan. As the train approached the little station of Brazey-en-Morvan I saw my first kestrel some 50 metres or so away, sitting on top of a fruit tree. Barely a mile further on, I saw the second of these park janitors, this time sitting on a fence post alongside the line. As the train passed, this magisterial bird observed it scornfully, not deigning to move an inch from its perch.

Later that day, I observed a buzzard take its sacraments. Having cycled well inside the park, I had stopped to pump up my tyre, which had developed a slow puncture. I looked up to see the silhouette of two massive wings, flapping. The bird soared, taking advantage of some indiscernible thermal, and plummeted on to an unsuspecting victim. Mercifully, for me that is, the bird's body obscured my vision of the gory details.

Parc Naturel Régional du Morvan

107

The pale and delicate silver birch makes a pleasing contrast when found among more sombre conifers.

It rose, flapped its wings a few times and settled a few feet away. It then noticed me and took off, prey in beak.

The landscape of the Morvan hills is a pleasant mixture of forest, moors and lakes, of pastures and heath; the meadows are full of wild flowers in spring and dry stone walls pattern the countryside. The hillsides are covered by deciduous trees, which yield to conifers near the summit. From afar the hills seem dark, even on sunny days. The rock underlying the mountains is granite, and the planting of conifers emphasizes the darkness of the summits.

The name Morvan in fact means 'black mountain' in the language of the Gauls, the tongue that was spoken in France before the Roman invasion. Their legacy can also be recalled on the hill of Le Beuvray in the

108

south of the park, which was the site of an old Gaulish fortress. The fort, originally called Bibracte, is now buried beneath beech trees. A paved road enables motorists to drive to the top of the hill, but the walk produces a better appreciation of the view from this strategic site overlooking the valley of the Loire.

The footpaths that cross the Morvan are also resonant of the past. They were once the main thoroughfares linking villages and moorland farms. The age of these footpaths can be gauged from their shape. The tramp of time has created U-shaped hollows with banks on either side.

The most famous path takes in the many lakes of the Morvan. The lakes — some natural, some the result of human intervention, created to provide the power for watermills — are a joy. There are also smaller meres worth seeking out, or you may chance upon a brook running across, or even along, a footpath. The area is also littered with dew ponds: small pools, natural or man-made, which provide drinking water for cattle and wild animals such as deer.

The advantage of these smaller water holes is that they are not as overrun with tourists as the lakes, such as the Lac des Settons: anywhere with pedal-boats can scarcely be wild. One escape is to do as I did and rent a bicycle, but according to locals the best way to immerse yourself in the wild woods — and actually stand a chance of seeing some of the many wild animals inhabiting their depths — is to explore on horseback. In this way you may see red and roe deer, wild boar and badgers, and possibly in the half-light of dawn or dusk catch sight of the secretive genet, wildcat or beech marten.

The landscape in the north of the park is gentler and more pastoral than in the south. The hills around the charming town of Vézelay contain some of the most beautiful countryside in Burgundy. There are none of the dark tones of the black mountains here; the wooded countryside gently rolls away into the distance, clothed in its summer green. The broad-leaf combination of beech and oak warms the woods and strikes a verdant contrast with the gaunt pine-topped hills farther south.

BEFORE YOU GO
Maps: IGN 1:100,000 Nos 28, 36 & 306; 1:25,000 Nos. 2722-25, 2822-25 and 2922.

GETTING THERE
By car: the A6 Autoroute du Soleil passes 20 km (12 miles) to the east of the park. N6 goes to Avallon and Saulieu. From Auxerre N151 heads south to Clamecy, and D985 continues to Corbigny. D978 links Nevers to Autun by way of Château-Chinon. To tour the park leave Avallon on D10, then take D211, D236 and D193 or D37.
By rail: services run from Paris-Gare de Lyon to Avallon, Saulieu and Autun. Local trains go from Auxerre to Clamecy, Corbigny and Château-Chinon in the west of the park.
By bus: there are daily services from Nevers and Autun to Château-Chinon; buses also link Tamnay-Château with Nevers, Château-Chinon, Cercy-la-Tour, St-Honoré-les-Bains and Rémilly.

WHERE TO STAY
The following towns are good bases: Arnay-le-Duc, Autun, Avallon, Château-Chinon, Dun-les-Places, Lormes, Montsauche-les-Settons, St-Honoré-les-Bains and Vézelay. The park authorities have a list of *gîtes* and camp-sites.

ACTIVITIES
Walking: the GR13 footpath from Ile-de-France to Burgundy passes through the park for more than 100 km (60 miles). There is also a 220-km (130-mile) circular tour of the park and its lakes. A booklet entitled *Tour du Morvan par les Grands Lacs* maps out the route and its *gîtes*. Obtain details of this and other shorter strolls from the park office.
Cycling: the Monts du Morvan route circles the south of the park and the Chemins de

Compostelle route from the Pyrenees ends at Vézelay in the north of the park. The park booklet *Le Morvan en VTT* has details of 1,400 km (870 miles) of marked routes.
Riding: the CDTE de la Nièvre in Château-Chinon, T: 03 86 85 29 09, will give details of equestrian centres. The Centre Equestre de Montcharlon in Chiddes, T/F: 03 86 30 42 78, and Tout Crin in Mhère, T: 03 86 22 73 19, organize treks in the park.
Climbing: you can climb at Anost and Dun-les-Places. Contact CAF de Yonne-Nièvre, 15 chemin de la Guimbarde, Joigny, T: 03 86 62 07 19.
Canoeing: for trips on the rivers Cure or Chalaux, contact Loisirs Accueil Nièvre, 3 rue du Sort, 58000 Nevers, T: 03 86 59 14 22. There are lessons for beginners on the Lac de Chamboux; contact Centre Social de Saulieu, T: 03 80 64 20 46.
Skiing: downhill and cross-country skiing is available in the south, around Arleuf, Glux-en-Glenne, St-Prix and Le Haut-Folin. Haut-Folin has 8 cross-country routes.
Museums: there is an interesting geological museum at St-Léger-sous-Beuvray, T: 03 85 82 51 01, and Musée de la Résistance en Morvan in St-Brisson, T: 03 86 78 72 99.

FURTHER INFORMATION
Tourist offices: Autun, 2 av Charles-de-Gaulle, T: 03 85 86 80 38; Auxerre, quai de la République. T: 03 86 52 06 19; Avallon, 6 rue Bocquillot, T: 03 86 34 14 19; Nevers, rue Sabatier, T: 03 86 68 46 00; St-Honoré-les-Bains, 13 rue Henri Renaud, T: 03 86 30 71 70; Saulieu, 24 rue d'Argentine, T: 03 80 64 00 21; Vézelay, rue St-Pierre, T: 03 86 33 23 69.
Park office: 58230 St-Brisson, T: 03 86 78 79 00, F: 03 86 78 74 22, www.parcdumorvan.org.

Forêt de Tronçais

Part of a chain of woodlands stretching across the geographical centre of France, midway between Bourges and Montluçon

Through the mists of the forest, Le Grand Meaulne, the eponymous hero of Alain Fournier's novel, discovers a magical château, full of music and dancing. When he next returns to the château it is closed and shuttered. The book was made into a film called *The Wanderer* or *The Lost Domain*, depending on whether you saw it in Britain or America. The novel is based in the country to the south of Bourges. Meaulne is the name of a village barely 5 km (3 miles) from the forest, while Fournier himself lived as a child in Epineuil, a couple of kilometres farther up the River Cher. You stand little chance of finding such a castle in the Forêt de Tronçais, but the wood is quiet enough to recreate the mysterious atmosphere of the film, which was shot in the area.

Even on the ditchwater dull day when I last visited the Forêt de Tronçais, it still had its quota of magic. The clouds glowered and threatened rain, soon making good the threat. Then three black kites flew past, doubtless surprised to be disturbed on such a day. The quixotic April weather turned sunny and then back to rain again but not before the sun had disclosed the newly sprouted oak leaves.

The Forêt de Tronçais is the easternmost of a series of forests that stretches in a belt from the Brenne round to the Loire at Nevers. The Forêt de Lancosme, beside the Brenne lakes, is on the western edge of

this belt. Further east lie the Forêt de Châteauroux (near Châteauroux itself) and the Bois de Meillant (near St-Amand-Montrond) on a limestone plateau known as the Champagne Berrichonne, where the woodland is sliced by rivers, roads and agricultural land. This area contains the geographical centre of France, a distinction claimed by several of the local communes.

The Forêt de Tronçais, with its dense stands of oak and beech, is particularly noteworthy as the westernmost outpost of the black woodpecker. Raptors, too, are a great speciality: in addition to typical arboreal species such as goshawk and honey buzzard, the attentive observer can hope to find short-toed and booted eagles, both on the edge of their zoological ranges here.

More than 5 ha (12 acres) of the forest are a biological reserve, set up to protect the oaks planted more than 300 years ago under the reign of the Sun King, Louis XIV. **Before you go** *Maps:* IGN 1:100,000 No. 35; IGN 1:25,000 No. 2426 OT & ET. **Getting there** *By car:* exit A71 on to D300 to St-Amand-Montrond, south of Bourges, and then on to N144 (which runs from Bourges through St-

Red deer browse undisturbed deep in the mixed deciduous forests.

Amand). Head south towards Urçay; 15 km (9 miles) from St-Amand, the D978 takes you into the forest. *By rail:* regular trains from Paris-Gare d'Austerlitz to St-Amand-Montrond. Alternatively, get off at Ainay-le-Vieil or Urçay and walk into the forest. *By bus:* there is a daily bus from St-Amand-Montrond to St-Bonnet-Tronçais, and another to St-Bonnet from the railway station at Moulins-sur-Allier. **Where to stay:** Urçay has 2 pleasant hotels; the Etoile d'Or, T: 04 70 06 92 66, is recommended. St-Amand and Montluçon have plenty of hotels. Lakeside *gîtes* are open year-round at St-Bonnet. *Outdoor living:* summer only at St-Bonnet, Pirot, Ainay-le-Château, Cérilly, Hérisson, Meaulne, Urçay and Vallon-en-Sully. **Activities** *Cycling:* rent bicycles at St-Bonnet. The long-distance Chemins de Compostelle route passes through St-Amand. *Riding:* contact CDTE du Cher, 7 rue de Beaulieu, 36100 Segry, T: 02 54 21 90 82/02 48 60 68 46. *Fishing:* possible on the lakes and the rivers Aumance and Cher. Details from the Cher

fishing federation, 103 rue de Mazières, 18000 Bourges, T: 02 48 67 92 22, or Association du Pays Tronçais, Cérilly, T: 04 70 67 55 89. *Adventure holidays:* contact Loisirs Accueil Cher, 5 rue de Séraucourt, 18000 Bourges, T: 02 48 67 01 38; or Loisirs Accueil Allier, 12 cours Anatole France, 03016 Moulins, T: 04 70 46 81 60. *Field studies:* contact the Centre Permanent d'Initiation à l'Environnement, Tronçais, St Bonnet-Tronçais, T: 04 70 06 14 69, for details of nature walks in the forest. *Sightseeing:* Ainay-le-Vieil has a medieval castle. To the north-west, near Drevant, are ruins of Roman baths, an amphitheatre and a temple. **Further information** *Tourist offices:* Bourges, 21 rue Victor-Hugo, T: 02 48 23 02 60; Montluçon, pl Piquand, T: 04 70 05 11 44; St-Amand-Montrond, pl de la République, T: 02 48 96 16 86.

Forêt de Fontainebleau

Extensive forest surrounding Napoleon's favourite hunting lodge, lying 65 km (40 miles) south-east of Paris
ZICO, World Heritage Site
170 sq km (65 sq miles)

One of Paul Cézanne's better known landscapes is *Les Rochers de Fontainebleau*, which now hangs in New York's Metropolitan Museum of Art. Cézanne's painting dates from the early 1890s, but the rocks still hold something

Sunlight struggles to penetrate the dense deciduous forest, home to deer and wild boar.

of the same mystery as they did then. Paths lead between them, with sudden turns revealing unanticipated glades. Nowadays, though, the element of surprise is likely to include stumbling over an apprentice rock climber.

The Forêt de Fontainebleau is the sixth largest forest in France, a relic of the ancient wood that once covered the Paris basin. Like many hunting forests, it has been thinned out considerably, to load the dice in favour of the hunter rather than the hunted. Almost half the trees are oaks, and the southern end has some magnificent oak copses. The other important deciduous tree is beech.

Thanks to its limestone rock and sandy sub-soil the forest is fairly dry, so you can leave your rubber boots behind. The other side of the coin is that the undergrowth tends towards scrub: brambles and ferns abound. Since the 1830s Scots pines have been planted on the more arid soils to such an extent that they are now as common as oaks. Larger clearings have developed a heath-like vegetation, which helps to provide variety and balance to the ecology.

It is estimated that upwards of 10 million visitors a year troop round the forest and the authorities have reacted by creating zones of silence to mitigate the effects of tourism.

It was during the mid-19th-century reigns of Louis-Philippe and Napoleon III that the forest first became popular with walkers. Hunting, that sport of kings, is still widespread, which is one of the forest's more disappointing aspects.

In spite of the press of visitors, however, the occasional gunshot is often the only sound to be heard in the forest. Even in spring, barely a bird breaks the silence in many areas. This cathedral-like atmosphere belies the wealth of birds and other animals which manage to live here. The forest hosts a full range of the typical forest birds of northern France, including redstart, five species of woodpecker and, most notably, pied flycatcher. Nesting raptors include the honey buzzard and hobby.

Before you go *Maps:* IGN 1:100,000 No. 21; 1:25,000 No. 2417 OT. **Getting there** *By car:* from Paris take either A6 (turning off on to N7) or N7 all the way. Parking is restricted on forest roads. *By rail:* frequent local trains from Paris-Gare de Lyon to Fontainebleau-Avon; journey time about 1 hr. *By bus:* town buses (*les cars verts*) run from outside the railway station. The walk to the centre of Fontainebleau takes 20 mins. **Where to stay:** Fontainebleau and Avon are the twin local towns, and as good a starting point as any for touring the

forest. Barbizon, on the forest's western edge, is close to the zones of silence. *Outdoor living:* there is a camp-site on the edge of the forest near Samois-sur-Seine, T: 01 64 24 63 45.

Activities *Walking:* there are over 300 km (180 miles) of forest paths reserved for pedestrians, cyclists or horse-riders. Contact the Amis de la Forêt (see below) for detailed walking itineraries. GR11 passes through the forest. *Cycling:* bicycles can be hired at Fontainebleau station. *Riding:* the Société Hippique Nationale, T: 01 60 72 22 40, the Poney Club de Fontainebleau, T: 01 64 22 63 49, and the Poney Club d'Avon, T: 01 60 72 53 70, organize outings into the forest. Attelages de la Forêt de Fontainebleau, T: 01 64 22 92 61, offers tours of the forest in horse-drawn carriages. *Climbing:* more than 130 climbs are listed by the tourist office in Fontainebleau. *Adventure holidays:* UCPA centre at Bois le Roi, T: 01 64 81 33 00, offers riding, cycling and other sports. TopLoisirs in Fontainebleau, T: 01 60 74 08 50, offers climbing, canoeing, cycling and orienteering. Loisirs Accueil Seine-et-Marne, 11 rue Royale, 77300 Fontainebleau, T: 01 60 39 60 39, F: 01 60 39 60 40, has an information and booking service for activity holidays. *Viewpoints:* Croix-du-Calvaire has a good view over the forest; there are also several picturesque gorges and a ruined hermitage which in the 18th century was a refuge for bandits. **Further information** *Tourist office:* Fontainebleau, 4 rue Royale, T: 01 60 74 99 99.

Office National des Forêts, blvd de Constance, 77300 Fontainebleau, T: 01 60 74 92 40.

Association des Amis de la Forêt, 26 rue de la Cloche, Fontainebleau, T: 01 64 23 46 45.

WILD BOAR — *SANGLIER*

The wild boar, which is the ancestor of the domestic pig, is not a rare creature. It ranges over much of the country, inhabiting the vast forest areas of the north and the *maquis* in the south, and may attain quite high population densities. However, because it is widely hunted, it is a furtive and timid creature and, being nocturnal, it is a very rare sight. Your closest contact is more likely to be signs of its activities on the ground. Wild boar are particularly fond of digging for bulbs and tubers, leaving large irregularly churned patches of ground in woodland clearings.

Haute-Vallée de Chevreuse

Wooded valley at the southern edge of the Parisian commuter belt; parc naturel régional *29,340 ha (72,500 acres)*

On the train running through the Legoland of suburbs that has developed to the south of Paris over the last 40 years, it was hard to believe that anything remotely wild might lie at the end of the line. True, Jean Racine, who lived in the area, could write of the giant oaks and lindens with their ornate arms; but that was 1656, nearly 150 years before the French Revolution. I had left Paris armed with my 1930 guide-book that still spoke of the 'beautiful Chevreuse valley', but 1930 fell a good half-century before the age of the *autoroute*. Could the valley have survived the southward sprawl?

As the train neared the end of the line the answer became clearer. Trees began to intervene between the houses, then whole woods appeared on the hilltops. Once out of the train, I found much to explore. The valleys are covered by a mixture of housing and agricultural land, but the hills and valley sides are largely wooded; some are accessible, many more are reserved for hunting. The trees are predominantly deciduous — beech and oak, as well as chestnut, hazel and silver birch — although there are also some plantations of Scots pine. The woods are heavily coppiced and surprisingly deserted given their proximity to Paris — provided you are prepared to

hike out of the valley bottom, away from the main roads.

The park of the Haute-Vallée de Chevreuse was created in 1984 by the regional council of the Ile de France in order to stave off the pressure of urbanization and maintain Paris's green lung. The council talks of achieving this aim by creating a sustainable mixed economy of agriculture and, of course, tourism.

Before you go *Maps:* IGN 1:100,000 No. 20; IGN 1:25,000 Nos. 2215, 2315 OT. **Getting there** *By car:* N10 runs from Paris to Rambouillet; D906 runs from Rambouillet to Chevreuse. *By rail:* local services link Paris-Gare Montparnasse with Rambouillet. A better option, which lands you in the middle of the park, is to take the RER line B to St-Rémy-ès-Chevreuse, or RER line C to St-Quentin-en-Yvelines. Call the RATP 24-hr enquiry line on T: 08 36 68 77 41 14 (English) for details of RER services. *By bus:* local buses run (infrequently) from Versailles (Rive Gauche) to St-Rémy and from St-Rémy to Chevreuse, Cernay-la-Ville and Rambouillet. **Where to stay:** widest choice in Paris and Versailles; or try Dampierre

The wild boar, though rarely seen, leaves heavy footprints and large areas of scuffled ground.

and Chevreuse in the park itself. Rambouillet, just outside the park boundary, is another option. *Outdoor living:* lists of camp-sites from local tourist offices. **Activities** *Walking:* 2 long-distance footpaths traverse the park: GR1 and GR11. Shorter trails include the 15-km (9-mile) Chemin Jean Racine from Chevreuse to Port-Royal. Details from the park office. *Cycling:* cycle-hire outlets at Dampierre, T: 01 30 52 56 40, and Rambouillet, T: 01 34 86 84 51. The Paris-Bordeaux cycle route passes through the middle of the park. *Riding:* horseback tours of the Chevreuse are organised by Les Ecuries de la Charpenterie in Les Breviaires, T: 01 34 84 14 09. *Field studies:* the Espace Rambouillet, T: 01 34 83 05 00, is a 250-ha (620-acre) wild animal reserve. **Further information** *Tourist offices:* Rambouillet, pl de la Libération, T: 01 34 83 21 21; St-Rémy-ès-Chevreuse, 1 rue Ditte, T: 01 30 52 22 49. *Park office:* Château de la Madeleine, BP 73, 78460 Chevreuse, T: 01 30 52 09 09, F: 01 30 52 12 43.

113

CHAPTER 6

The Pyrenees

The mountain range of the Pyrenees defies comparison, although it has often been described as a lesser cousin of the mighty Alps. Those who have been to the Pyrenees often prefer them because they are wilder, less developed and no less challenging than the Alpine peaks. I have visited these mountains in every season of the year, travelled across them from one side to the other, and on every visit I have found some previously hidden corner awaiting exploration.

The Pyrenees run 400 kilometres (250 miles) north-west to south-east across the neck of land that bars France from Spain between the Atlantic and the Mediterranean. The range does not contain great mountains — there are only three peaks over the 3,000-metre (9,900-foot) mark, and the highest of these lies in Spain. Where the Pyrenees excel is in the great variety and ruggedness of the terrain, which changes constantly, from the green hill country of the Basques in the west to the sun-scorched mountains in the east above the wine plains of Roussillon, with great valleys, high cols and snow-fields coming up all along the way.

The mountains have marked the Franco-Hispanic frontier since the Treaty of the Pyrenees was agreed in 1659, but the separation is by no means absolute. Nationality does not always follow the crest of the mountains. There are Spanish enclaves on the French side of the natural divide, most noticeably on the Cerdagne plateau; in the co-principality of Andorra, sovereignty is shared between France and Spain; and at both ends of the range strong cultural links bring together Basques and Catalans

Sheep graze on the fertile upland pastures of the Pyrenees near Arreau.

living on either side of the frontier.

The French Pyrenees differ from the Spanish in various ways, some plainly visible: the French side is greener and steeper, the mountains rising sharply from the plain. The barrier straddling the border is easily penetrated through a series of deep valleys, two of which follow the ancient pilgrim routes to Compostela. The modern motorways which carry commercial and tourist traffic across the border do so at either side of the range. As a result the broad central core is relatively undisturbed, so that even today it is possible to walk south to Spain on tracks and mule trails that have not changed for centuries.

The French Pyrenees can be divided into three regions: the Pays Basque, the Hautes-Pyrénées and Roussillon. On the Atlantic coast, the range begins in the hill country of the Basques, starting south of Les Landes and rising up through the valley of the Bidassoa. From here tumbled green hills stretch inland, punctuated by two great valleys, one of which leads into Spain over the famous pass of Roncesvalles, where Roland fell fighting with Charlemagne's army against the Basques.

The pattern of rising mountains cut by valleys and passes becomes more pronounced in Béarn, in the modern Hautes-Pyrénées. A notable feature of these central Pyrenees is the number of mountain lakes, which feed the mountain streams. All the streams are full of trout, and some shelter the rare desman, a kind of aquatic mole similar to the platypus but with a long tail and webbed hind feet, which I have never seen in spite of many attempts to do so.

Farther east the mountains stop briefly at the Val d'Aran. The Pyrenees are divided in two by the cleft of this valley, through which the Garonne river flows out of Spain on its way to the Bay of Biscay. The pattern of mountain and valley begins again in Ariège, north of Andorra. Beyond, Roussillon begins on a spectacular note, with Pic Carlit rising 2,921 metres (9,587 feet) above the great plateau of the Cerdagne, which, at 1,600 metres (one mile) above the plain, is fresh and green even in the hottest months of summer. Still farther east Mont Canigou, the great mountain of the Catalans, soars up to 2,784 metres (9,137 feet) before the Pyrenees fall away at last down the dwindling peaks of the Albères into the Mediterranean.

The high mountain chains of Europe have served as vital refuges for innumerable plants and animals ever since the glaciers receded at the end of the last Ice Age, and in this respect the Pyrenees are no exception. The diversity of the Pyrenean flora owes much to the different climatic influences which coincide here. Oak forests dominate the foothills, with the common and white oak in the more maritime western areas and cork and evergreen oaks in the drier Mediterranean east. Above 800 metres (2,600 feet), the true mountain forest begins, with beech and, eventually, fir dominating the higher ground. Seemingly silent at first, these forested areas are full of the high-pitched contact notes of coal tits, crested tits, goldcrests, treecreepers and chaffinches. Then there is the urgent tapping of the real forest specialities: the black, whitebacked and middle-spotted woodpeckers. Above 1,500 metres (5,000 feet), the forest gives way to an open zone of scattered pines and juniper shrubs, then to Alpine meadows beneath the bare rock faces and snow. These upper reaches provide a habitat for water pipits, Alpine accentors, rock thrushes and, in some places, the snow finch. Raptors such as golden eagles, lammergeiers and griffon vultures soar above the peaks on strong thermals.

GETTING THERE

By air: the main airports are Toulouse, T: 05 61 42 44 00, and Perpignan, T: 04 68 52 60 70, serving the west-central Pyrenees and Roussillon respectively. For the Pays Basque, take an internal flight to Bayonne-Biarritz-Anglet airport, T: 05 59 43 83 85.

By sea: the Spanish ports of Bilbao and Santander are convenient. P&O European Ferries, T: 08 03 01 30 13, www.poef.com, runs ferries from Portsmouth to Bilbao; and Brittany Ferries, T: 08 03 82 88 28, www.brittany-ferries.com, has a Plymouth-Santander service.

By car: the French Pyrenees are well served by the *autoroute* network either via the Rhône valley on A9 or on the western side via A62 or A63. The central Pyrenees are reached via Pau or Tarbes.

By rail: TGV services run from Paris-Gare de Lyon to Perpignan, and from Paris-Montparnasse to Toulouse or to Dax; from Dax the line branches west to Bayonne and stations south to the Spanish border, or east to stations including Pau and Tarbes. From main-line stations at Bayonne, Pau, Tarbes, Toulouse, Foix and Perpignan, local trains serve many of the valleys. Contact SNCF, T: 08 36 35 35 35, www.sncf.fr.

By bus: Eurolines, T: 08 36 69 52 52, www.eurolines.fr, has services to St-Jean-de-Luz, Pau, Lourdes, Tarbes, Toulouse and Perpignan.

WHEN TO GO

The climate varies considerably, being generally milder in the west and drier east of the Val d'Aran. Snow lies on the Pyrenees Dec-early Apr and may be expected anywhere above 1,800 m (5,900 ft). Most of the mountain passes are kept open throughout the winter.

The elusive desman inhabits fast-flowing mountain streams.

WHERE TO STAY

See individual exploration zones or ask the national accommodation agencies listed in USEFUL ADDRESSES, to recommend suitable bases.

ACTIVITIES

Walking: easier routes lie at either end of the range; harder, steeper and more exposed routes are in the centre. The main organizations for walkers and climbers are the Randonnées Pyrénéennes and CIMES Pyrénées (Centre d'Information Montagne et Sentiers), both based at 4 rue Maye Lane, 65421 Ibos, T: 05 62 90 09 92, F: 05 62 90 67 61, www.rando-editions.com; and the Fédération Française de Montagne et d'Escalade, 47 rue du IV Septembre, 65000 Tarbes, T: 05 62 44 11 87.

Cycling: the Raid Pyrénéen route stretches over 18 cols between the Atlantic and the Mediterranean; although spectacular, it is only suitable for experienced cyclists.

Fishing: there is good trout and char fishing throughout the range and salmon fishing around Navarrenx in the Pays Basque. Fishing is allowed in the national park with a permit, available from fishing tackle shops and *bureaux de tabac* (newsagents); the fishing season runs Mar-Sept.

Skiing: the ski season runs Dec-Apr. Resorts are smaller than those in the Alps, but offer good scope for off-piste skiing and ski mountaineering. The CAF, which has many branches in the Pyrenees, runs mountain refuges and offers information on skiing and other mountain activities; see individual zones. For Andorra, contact Ski Andorra, T: 86 43 89, www.skiandorra.ad.

Adventure holidays: for information and to book holidays, contact Loisirs Accueil Ariège Pyrénées, 31 bis av du Général de Gaulle, 09004 Foix, T: 05 61 02 30 80, F: 05 61 65 17 34, or Loisirs Accueil Hautes Pyrénées, 6 rue Eugène Tenot, 65004 Tarbes, T: 05 62 56 48 00, F: 05 62 51 96 88.

FURTHER INFORMATION

Tourist offices: Maison des Pyrénées, 15 rue St-Augustin, 75002 Paris, T: 01 42 86 51 86, F: 01 42 86 51 65; CRT Midi-Pyrénées, 54 blvd de l'Embouchure, 31022 Toulouse, T: 05 61 13 55 55, F: 05 61 47 17 16; Agence de Tourisme du Pays Basque, 1 rue Donzac, 64108 Bayonne, T: 05 59 46 46 64, F: 05 59 46 46 60.

Park office: 65000 Tarbes, 59 rte de Pau, T: 05 62 44 36 60, F: 05 62 44 36 70, www.parc-pyrenees.com.

Pays Basque

The modern département of Pyrénées-Atlantiques, redolent with Basque and Navarre associations, covers the area from the Atlantic to the first Pyrenean peaks
ZICO

This was the first part of the Pyrenees I ever visited, and the impact of that visit has never left me. It is a striking countryside, the hills a rich billiard-table green, seamed with deep valleys from which the mist rises thickly in the early morning, shredding up into the trees in the sunlight. In the valleys nestle villages of whitewashed houses topped with slate roofs. The climate is wetter than in other parts of the range; the rivers are usually full and rushing torrents, cutting deeply through forests, plateaux and hills.

The hills around the peak of La Rhune (900 m/2,950 ft) make for excellent walking, full of open ridges, stunning views and breezy paths through the meadows and copses. You can also explore on small,

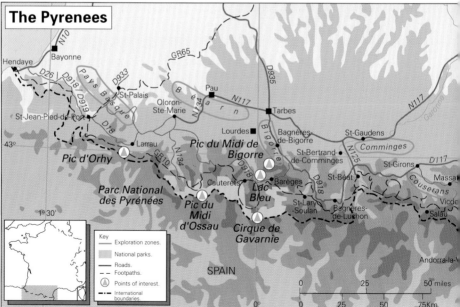

The Pyrenees

Brown bear and lynx still find refuge in the remoter forests and peaks of the Basque Pyrenees.

piebald local ponies known as *pottocks*. A ride into the hills on one of these shaggy ponies is memorable, but hard on the knees; you'll soon be more than ready to walk.

The hills rise as you move east, and you encounter a mixture of moorland and forest. The Forêt d'Iraty, at the heart of the Basque Pyrenees, is a vast terrain of beech and pines, a marvellous spot for birds, notably tits and woodpeckers. The Plateau d'Iraty is covered with sheep browsing in the bracken. North of Iraty lie two more beech forests, at Ahusquy and Arbailles, the latter draping a limestone plateau cut with sheer valleys.

The first major peak in the Pyrenees, the Pic d'Orhy (2,017 metres/6,620 feet), lies to the south of Arbailles, rising above the valley of the Gave de Larrau. If you are extremely lucky, you may see a griffon vulture around the peak, soaring on the summer thermals, recognizable by its black wings and white neck. The largest bird in the Pyrenees is the bearded vulture, or lammergeier, a magnificent bird with a wing-span of up to 2.8 metres (nine feet), making it the largest of all the European raptors.

Just to the north-east of the Pic d'Orhy lie the forked valleys of the Haute-Soule, one of which, the Gave de Ste-Engrâce, leads to the Gorges de Kakouetta. These gorges are a spectacular sight, narrowing to ten metres (33 feet) in width, dropping to 250 metres (800 feet) or more in places, and ending with a great waterfall. Air descending into the gorge cools and becomes clammy and thick with moisture, a complete change from the heat in the hills outside. The change is so marked that a micro-climate exists, and in the humus created by fallen beech-leaves, orchids grow amid the rocky crevices.

BEFORE YOU GO
Maps: IGN 1:100,000 No. 69; IGN Randonées Pyrénées (RP) 1:50,000 Nos. 1 and 2.

GETTING THERE
By car: take N10 south from Bordeaux to Bayonne and Hendaye. From the east, follow A64 or N124/N10 westwards from Toulouse to Bayonne. From Bayonne, the D932/D918 to St-Jean-Pied-de-Port, and then the D18/D19 lead south to the Forêt and Plateau d'Iraty. **By rail:** trains run from Paris-Gare Montparnasse to Hendaye and to Tarbes; both lines link up with local services. From Bayonne, trains run all year round to St-Jean-Pied-de-Port, stoppping at Cambo-les-Bains, Itxassou and Bidarray. **By bus:** there are services into the hills from Hendaye, Bayonne, Orthez and Pau. Le Basque Bondissant, T: 05 59 26 25 87, runs a service Apr-Oct between St-Jean-de-Luz and Col de St-Ignace, from where La Rhune is accessible either on foot or by a 4-km cog-wheel railway; the service also stops at Ascain, and at Sare and its caves July-Aug only. TPR, T: 05 59 82 95 85, runs buses between Pau and Bayonne or Mauléon.

WHERE TO STAY
Two options are the Hôtel Etchpare in Itxassou, quartier la Place, T: 05 59 29 75 14, and Hôtel Ramuntcho in St-Jean-Pied-de-Port, 1 rue de la France, T: 05 59 37 03 91.

Outdoor living: try Camping Caravaning Hiriberria in Itxassou, T: 05 59 29 98 09, or Camping Mendy in St-Jean-Pied-de-Port, T: 05 59 37 11 81.

ACTIVITIES
Walking: the 170 km (100 miles) of GR10 from Hendaye to La Pierre-St-Martin would take a fit walker 11 days. Shorter walks can be found around most towns. Contact CIMES (see p117). **Caving:** a good cave system is Oxocelhaya near Isturits, T: 05 59 47 07 06; it has a small museum. The caves at Sare, T: 05 59 54 21 88, have a sound and light show and guided visits as well as a museum. A former smugglers' path links these caves to others at Urdax and Zugarramundi (Navarre). **Fishing:** there is good fishing in all the rivers of the Pays Basque, mostly for trout, but also for salmon, eels, pike, gudgeon, minnows and perch. For the fishing guide published by the *département*, call T: 05 59 30 01 30.

FURTHER INFORMATION
Tourist offices: Agence de Tourisme du Pays Basque, 1 rue Donzac, 64108 Bayonne, T: 05 59 46 46 64; St-Jean-Pied-de-Port, T: 05 59 37 03 57; Mauléon, T: 05 59 28 02 37.

For taped weather forecasts, call T: 08 36 68 08 08. For mountain rescue services, call T: 05 59 39 86 22.

THE PYRENEAN BROWN BEAR
The last of the European big game, the brown bear is now reduced to relict populations in remote mountain forests across the Continent. They are confined to the forests between 900 and 1,500 metres (3,000 and 5,000 feet). Merely walking through such a 'bear forest' generates a sense of excitement, although it is unlikely that the king of the Pyrenees will grant you an audience. The only signs of his presence are likely to be scratch marks on a tree or footprints in the mud.

The Pyrenean brown bear can grow to 2½ metres (8 feet) in height, and weigh from 120-200 kg (260-440 lb). It is an extremely powerful animal: a single blow can despatch a donkey. The bear is also a tireless walker, covering 25 km (15 miles) in a single nocturnal prowl. When the mood takes it, it can run at speeds up to 40 kph (25 mph).

In France bears were widespread in the Middle Ages, but by the end of World War II there were less than 100. Now there are only 12 individuals: 6 are genuine Pyrenean bears and 6 have been introduced from Slovakia. Although these figures are bleak, there is a glimmer of hope for the brown bear — a cub was born in 1995 and has since been successfully reared.

Béarn

Series of deep valleys flanked by high-mountain country, stretching south-west from Pau to the Spanish frontier; contains part of the Parc National des Pyrénées

The medieval *comté* of Béarn, birthplace of Henry of Navarre, *le grand Béarnais*, lies behind the city of Pau in the Hautes-Pyrénées. A ramble in the forests and Alpine meadows of these high hills will create lasting impressions. Indeed, it is fair to say that Béarn contains a lot of all that is best in the entire range: great mountains, rushing rivers, spas, excellent walking, good climbs on the higher peaks and a wonderful variety of wildlife. This is the place to see izard scrambling on the rocks, and wild pig or boar rootling in the undergrowth. It is also one of the last refuges of the Pyrenean brown bear. Above, great eagles and vultures wing their way about the peaks, while bitterns and herons fish in rocky ponds. Many of these species are summer residents only, but throughout the year you can expect to see many of the raptors for which the Pyrenees are most famous: black and red kites, goshawk, sparrowhawk, buzzards, booted eagles and even the mighty golden eagle, as well as the extremely rare Egyptian vulture and bearded vulture.

Heading south-west from Pau, the first major valley you come to is the Vallée d'Aspe. The valley is a place of grassy meadows, shady trees, warm breezes and tinkling streams, which are home to the elusive desman. If you keep your eyes peeled, you may spot his curious webbed tracks. The road follows the fast-flowing River Aspe up the valley towards the dramatic pass at Col du Somport (1,632 metres/5,356 feet), which forms the border with Spain. In the Middle Ages, the col was traversed by pilgrims *en route* to Compostela.

Many tracks and footpaths cross the mountainous divide between this valley and the Vallée d'Ossau to its east. Paths are marked from 1,400 metres (4,600 feet) up to

In contrast to its ferocious reputation the brown bear, now extremely rare, is principally vegetarian.

the 2,884-metre (9,465-foot) Pic du Midi d'Ossau, which dominates the southern end of the valley. Farther north, near the village of Béon, lies the 82-hectare (200-acre) Réserve Naturelle de La Vallée d'Ossau, which was established to protect the griffon vulture, one of Europe's largest raptors. The reserve's sheer limestone cliffs support a number of these birds. Naturalists encourage them to stay by placing carrion at feeding places; this is a vulture that feeds exclusively on dead meat.

To penetrate deeper into Béarn, follow the D918 corniche road, one of the most spectacular routes in the Pyrenees, leading east out of the Vallée d'Ossau at Laruns, passing meadows, dramatic cols and ski-style slopes before descending to the ski resort of Argelès-Gazost, on the edge of the Bigorre region. From here, a road leads up to Pont d'Espagne, the main entrance to the national park. Another, running more south-easterly, climbs through Luz-St-Sauveur to the fabulous Cirque de Gavarnie. This cirque, or mountain amphitheatre, together with the neighbouring Cirque de Troumouse, is a stunning sight when seen from the track that leads up from the village of Gavarnie. From a distance it appears to be a sheer wall, but as you draw closer, either on foot or taking the popular option of riding up on a donkey or a horse, you'll see that it rises up in a series of gigantic steps, each marked out, even in summer, by a wide belt of snow; from the top, waterfalls plummet thousands of metres into the valley.

Gavarnie is widely noted for its location on a migration route for both birds and butterflies, although it is for the former that most visitors come. You have to be up early and actually at the crossing point at the col to see the birds in flight, but it is well worth the climb. Raptors draw the most attention, for there are few sights more inspiring than large numbers of eagles, buzzards, hawks, kites, vultures and falcons passing over this magnificent range.

BEFORE YOU GO
Maps: IGN 1:100,000 Nos. 69 and 70; IGN (RP) 1:50,000 Nos. 3 and 4.

GETTING THERE
By car: the area can be approached from the south over the Somport pass (where a tunnel is under construction), following N134 along the Vallée d'Aspe towards Oloron-Ste-Marie, or, in summer only, over the Pourtalet, following

D934 through the Vallée d'Ossau towards Pau. From the north, roads delve deep into the valleys from Pau or Tarbes.
By rail: TGV and AutoTrain services run from Paris Gare-Montparnasse to Tarbes. Provincial services from Bayonne to the west and Toulouse to the east pass through Tarbes, Lourdes and Pau. From Pau, a service runs south to Oloron-Ste-Marie.
By bus: SNCF buses run

between Lourdes train station and Cauterets. Buses run June-Sept from Cauterets to Pont d'Espagne; call Excursions Bordenave, T: 05 62 92 53 68.
 SNCF buses run infrequently from Oloron-Ste-Marie, following N134 along the Vallée d'Aspe and up to the Col du Somport.

WHERE TO STAY
Gavarnie, Luz-St-Sauveur and Cauterets are convenient places to find hotels.
Outdoor living: camping is not permitted within park boundaries.
Refuges: there are refuges by the Brèche-de-Roland on the Cirque de Gavarnie, and several CAF refuges in the national park. Contact the CAF in Lourdes, pl de la République, T: 05 62 42 13 67; or in Tarbes, 46 blvd du Martinet, T: 05 62 36 56 06.

ACCESS
Public access to the Réserve Naturelle de la Vallée d'Ossau is prohibited. However, griffon vultures can be observed at La Falaise aux Vautours museum, T: 05 59 82 45 49.

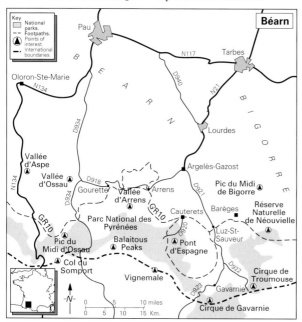

Snow melt-waters carve their way through the rich pastures below the Pic d'Anie. The wide variety of flora is characteristic of undisturbed upland areas.

ACTIVITIES

Walking/climbing: climbers should head for the Balaïtous peaks on the frontier, or cross to the Vignemale south of Cauterets. Good walks include one from the village of Gavarnie to the cleft of the Brèche de Roland; and east from Accous in the Vallée d'Aspe, across the mountains to the Gorges de Bitet in the Vallée d'Ossau.

Skiing: for information on skiing and other adventure activities, contact Tourisme Environnement-Hautes Pyrénées, 6 rue Eugène-Ténot, 65004 Tarbes, T: 05 62 56 48

03, F: 05 62 93 69 90.

Viewpoints: from boulevard des Pyrénées in Pau you can see 83 peaks if the weather is clear. Cable cars at Gourette lift walkers to Pic de Ger (2,613 m/8,576 ft); the Téléphérique du Lys at Cauterets runs during the ski season and mid-June to mid-Sept to the Cirque du Lys (1,850 m/6,000 ft). From here the Télésiège du Grand Barbat continues to the Crêtes du Lys (2,300 m/7,550 ft).

Ecology: the Maison du Parc in Cauterets, pl de la Gare, T: 05 62 92 52 56, is open all year and has a free exhibition on Pyrenean flora and fauna.

The small yellow-faced Egyptian vulture inhabits a wide variety of terrain, but is particularly at home on rocky escarpments.

FURTHER INFORMATION

Tourist offices: Cauterets, pl Maréchal Foch, T: 05 62 92 50 27; Gavarnie, T: 05 62 92 49 10; Laruns (Vallée d'Ossau), T: 05 59 05 31 41; Luz-St-Sauveur, T: 05 62 92 81 60; Oloron-Ste-Marie, T: 05 59 39 01 96.

Park office: headquarters at 59 rte de Pau, 65000 Tarbes, T: 05 62 44 36 60.

Weather service, T: 08 36 68 02 65; mountain rescue service, T: 05 62 92 41 41.

Bigorre

Dramatic mountainous region extending south from Lourdes; largely protected by parc national *or* réserve naturelle

🏔🏔🏔

Bigorre contains much of the most spectacular scenery in the entire Pyrenean range. The mountains are snow-tipped even in summer, and the land below them is a

spread of grassy mountain meadows where sheep and cattle are sent for summer pasture. These meadows are well irrigated by snow-melt from the heights above, and this steady supply of water keeps the countryside green, the trees flourishing and the streams filled even in the driest summer.

Some of the best scenery lies either side of the Vallée de Gripp in the west of Bigorre. On the northern side are the rugged Pic du Midi de Bigorre (2,872 metres/9,422 feet), one of the great mountains of the French Pyrenees, and the Lac Bleu, which nestles in the fold of the hills as if an azure carpet had been spread across the rocky slope.

The Vallée de Campan, further east, is one of the wider valleys of the central Pyrenees, running north-west to south-east and lined on either side by grassy mountain meadows which are knee-deep in flowers throughout the summer months. The flora includes the yellow turk's cap lily, one of the most extravagantly coloured plants in the Pyrenees. Beyond the Vallée de Campan lies the Vallée d'Aure, which can be reached over the Col d'Aspin (1,489 m/4,896 ft).

These three valleys form an arc around the north of the Massif de Néouvielle. Adjoining the north-eastern boundary of the national park, this massif harbours the Réserve Naturelle de Néouvielle ('Old Snow' Nature Reserve), the third oldest nature reserve in the country, and arguably the most impressive both for scenery and wildlife. It covers 2,313 hectares (5,715 acres), ranges from 1,800 to 3,091 metres (5,910 to 10,145 feet) in altitude and is notable for the 15 lakes and numerous ponds it contains. The reserve experiences a mixture of climatic influences, which accounts for the proximity of unlikely neighbours, such as the cross-leaved heath of Atlantic origins, the arctic marsh cinquefoil and several Mediterranean species. There are several bogs, which together support some 22 species of sphagnum moss. Altogether the reserve has 94 species of lichen and 1,238 high plant species. More than 250 types of beetle find nourishment on this varied feast.

The wildlife harboured by the Réserve de Néouvielle is almost as diverse — and unexpected — as the flora. It is remarkable to find the midwife toad here, for at this altitude its tadpoles take a good 20 years to complete their development. The most notable reptile is the rare Seoanei's viper. The thriving population of this species comes as a surprise to those who associate reptiles with hot environments. More appropriately, perhaps, a wide selection of typical Alpine birds can be found here, including the wallcreeper, ptarmigan, capercaillie and the rare Pyrenean race of common partridge. There are no longer thought to be any bears, though suitable areas of habitat do remain. However, otters, hares, foxes and the unique desman are still present.

The Pic de Néouvielle gives great views over Monte Perdido to the south, across the border in Spain, and the Pic du Midi de Bigorre to the north. All around the rippling hills run down to the Col de Tourmalet, at the head of the Vallée de Gripp, and to the Vallée de Campan; rocky slopes fade into meadows in the farther distance and everywhere the panorama is flecked with the deep blue of mountain lakes.

BEFORE YOU GO
Maps: IGN (RP) 1:50,000 No. 4; IGN 1:25,000 Nos. 1647 ET, 1747 ET and 1748 OT & ET.

The midwife toad, though mainly a lowland species, is found at over 2,000 m (6,600 ft) in the Pyrenees.

GETTING THERE
By car: the best route is to follow N21/D921 south from Lourdes to Luz-St-Sauveur; then take the scenic D918, cutting across the range and leading through the Vallée de Campan towards Arreau and the Vallée d'Aure.
By rail: trains run to Tarbes and Lannemezan.
By bus: buses serve all the valleys from Lourdes and Tarbes. SNCF operates buses from Tarbes to Bagnères-de-Bigorre and from Lannemezan to Arreau and St-Lary-Soulan.

WHERE TO STAY
Good places include: Hôtel Trianon, pl des Thermes, Bagnères-de-Bigorre, T: 05 62 95 09 34; Hôtel Richelieu, Barèges, T: 05 62 92 68 11; La Sapinière, Espiaule, St-Lary-

(*Overleaf*) A light dusting of snow adorns the impressive high peaks of the central Pyrenees.

Soulan, T: 05 62 98 44 04.
Outdoor living: tourist offices
have lists of camp-sites;
Bagnères-de-Bigorre has
several options.

ACTIVITIES
Walking: the classic walk is
from Fabian in the Vallée
d'Aure, up to the Massif de
Néouvielle. For guided walks,
contact the Association
Départementale des

Accompagnateurs en
Montagne, 2 pl Lafayette,
Bagnères-de-Bigorre, or the
Compagnie des Guides
Pyrénéens, Strattem, 21 Point
Sud, Soulom, T: 05 62 92 20 78.
For information on activities
and refuges, contact the CAF, 1
rue Blanche Odin, Bagnères-de-
Bigorre, T: 05 62 91 04 83.
Cycling: a challenging
expedition is the one along the
Route des Cols on D918/D618.

Ecology: the Maison de l'Ours
in St-Lary-Soulan, T: 05 62 39
50 83, offers an exhibition on
Pyrenean brown bears; closed
Nov and Tues out of season.

FURTHER INFORMATION
Tourist offices: Arreau,
Château des Nestes, T: 05 62 98
63 15; Bagnères-de-Bigorre, 3
allée Tournefort, T: 05 62 95 50
71; St-Lary, 37 rue Principale,
T: 05 62 39 50 81.

Comminges

*Forested south-east corner of the Hautes-
Pyrénées département, where the Garonne
enters France through a lush valley*

I first made the journey up the Vallée du
Lys, in the southern Comminges region, at
the end of the 1950s, when the Pyrenees were
distinctly wilder than they are today. It was
late February, and when I left the town of
Bagnères-de-Luchon it was growing dark
and starting to snow; by the time I got about
a kilometre out of town I was wishing I had
stayed overnight. I pressed on into the bliz-
zard, however, which was now hurling snow
across the mountains, got gloriously lost,
and was just thinking of pitching my tent
and waiting it out until morning when out of
the dark loomed the Hospice de France. It
was a hostel open to all comers in those
days, and was positively crammed with people: French, Spanish, some English, a few
Germans, walkers and climbers, even a few
muleteers. They all shifted up on the bench-
es, passed the jugs of wine and the mountain
ham and rough rye bread, and in half a
dozen languages we passed the night away.

The Comminges countryside represents a
change from its lofty and imposing neighbours; the terrain is greener and more forested, and the mountains a jumble of lower
peaks rather than majestic ranges. In geographical terms, Comminges is a curious
part of the French Pyrenees because it is

here that the Val d'Aran thrusts north across
the mountains from Spain and places the
Franco-Hispanic frontier well north of the
watershed, with the result that the border
lies directly to the east as well as south of
Bagnères-de-Luchon. It is through the Val
d'Aran that the infant River Garonne,
known there as the Garona, begins its long
journey to the Atlantic.

The Comminges region can be approached either from the west, crossing from
Bigorre, or from the north, where the main
road running along the foothills of the Pyrenees, the N117, provides a natural starting
point. The road follows the Garonne up its
valley from Toulouse all the way to St-Gaudens, the capital of Comminges. Wild explorers will be itching to turn off and head
for the high ground to the south. From St-
Gaudens, the twisting N125 leads up to St-
Bertrand-de-Comminges, a town whose
abbey is a celebrated place of pilgrimage. Ec-
clesiastical buildings built between the 11th
and 16th centuries stand peacefully in their
green and pleasant setting, with high mountains rippling away on either side and the
valleys of the Plateau de Lannemezan fan-
ning out to the north.

After St-Bertrand, you have two dramatic
routes to choose from. At Fronsac, near the
little fortress town of St-Béat, the D618
turns off to the eastern Comminges. This
spectacular corniche road winds upwards,
cutting here and there across the Comminges hills, before climbing steadily to the
pass of the Col de Portet d'Aspet, the eastern boundary of the region. For the southern Comminges, the D125 splits off from the

N125 at Chaum, at the confluence of the Garonne and its tributary the Pique, and follows the Pique south to Bagnères-de-Luchon, close to the Spanish border.

The way in to Comminges from the west brings you to Bagnères-de-Luchon over the Col de Peyresourde, a ski centre in winter. The great contrasts you can find in the French Pyrenees are never more obvious than here in the high country around Luchon. This is a region of sharp peaks, small lakes, thickly wooded valleys and a distinct lack of footpaths and signposts. It is a frontier region, with no roads across save a few old smugglers' tracks, and there is nothing to stop you crossing the frontier through the Port de Vénasque and scrambling on the lower slopes of the Spanish Pic d'Aneto.

South-west of Bagnères are some of the region's steep-sided valleys and high mountain lakes. Most notable is the Lac d'Oô, backed by a 271-metre (900-foot) high waterfall. The Vallée du Lys, to the east of Lac d'Oô, sports another great waterfall, the Cascade d'Enfer. South of Bagnères, the country is in the main gentle, but if you should happen to walk up the Vallée du Lys and on to the Hospice de France you leave civilization rapidly behind, as I found out all those years ago.

BEFORE YOU GO
Maps: IGN 1:100,000 Nos. 70 and 71; IGN (RP) 1:50,000 No. 5; IGN 1:25,000 1847 OT, 1848 OT and 1947 OT.

GETTING THERE
By car: N125 by St-Bertrand runs south to Chaum, where the D125 splits off to Bagnères-de-Luchon, and then turns out of the Luchon valley near St-Béat and enters Spain through the Val d'Aran.
By rail: SNCF trains and buses operate between Toulouse and Bagnères-de-Luchon, usually via Montrejeau; trains between Toulouse and St-Gaudens.
By bus: SNCF buses go from Toulouse and Montrejeau to Marignac, near St-Béat. Services from St-Gaudens run up the 2 main valleys to St-Béat and Bagnères-de-Luchon.

WHERE TO STAY
The best centres are St-Béat for the Val d'Aran; St-Gaudens for the northern Comminges; and Bagnères-de-Luchon for expeditions to the frontier.

ACTIVITIES
Walking: local trails abound but the most exciting walks are from Luchon up D125 past the Hospice de France and then on footpaths into the Malditos, the Val d'Aran and Pic d'Aneto. Lac d'Oô can be reached via the Vallée du Lys, and there are good walks east of St-Bertrand.
Climbing: information from the CAF, 18 rue Guillemin Taraye, Toulouse, T: 05 61 63 74 42.
Fishing: trout and salmon can be caught in the Garonne and in the high lakes beyond Luchon. Contact the Haute-Garonne fishing federation, 50 blvd des Récollets, 31400 Toulouse, T: 05 61 52 03 00.
Skiing: try cross-country and alpine skiing at Superbagnères and at Peyragudes, the newest ski resort in the Pyrenees, near the Col de Peyresourde. Season runs Dec-Apr; snow cannons guarantee plentiful snow.
Viewpoints: try the cols on D618, the grassy slopes below Superbagnères and Col du Portillon above the Val d'Aran.

FURTHER INFORMATION
Tourist offices: Bagnères-de-Luchon, 18 allée d'Etigny, T: 05 61 79 21 21; St-Gaudens, 2 rue Thiers, T: 05 61 94 77 61, www.st-gaudens.com; St-Béat, av Galliéni, T: 05 61 79 45 98.

PARC NATIONAL DES PYRENEES

The Parc National des Pyrénées was created in 1967 to join up with the Parque de Ordesa just across the Spanish border. It runs east-west along the mountains for 100 km (60 miles) between the valleys of the Aure and Aspe, and is between 3 km (2 miles) and 15 km (10 miles) wide. Together with the smaller Réserve Naturelle de Néouvielle in its north-east corner, this park encompasses a superb mountain area of 45,700 ha (113,000 acres), straddling the *départements* of Pyrénées-Atlantiques and Hautes-Pyrénées. Thanks to the varied altitudes and nature of the soil, the park is a zoologist's paradise, and contains many of the rarest Pyrenean species: izard, the Pyrenean chamois, marmots, aquatic desman, pine marten and red squirrel. Unfortunately, however, the most threatened species of the region and symbol of the park, the brown bear, does not occur within its boundaries. The equally fragile mountain flora includes rare Alpine lilies and several varieties of orchid.

Ariège

The rushing River Ariège gives its name to the sparsely populated département *on the borders of Andorra*
ZICO

The Ariège marks the point where the central Pyrenees begin to assume a more Mediterranean air. The change is noticeable as soon as you cross the border from the Comminges, in the Hautes-Pyrénées *département*, to the Couserans district of western Ariège. The air dries out and the soft grass gives way to short, tufty tussocks. This is a region that offers great variety of landscape within a comparatively small area, and what is more, the scenery changes enormously according to the time of year. Trout streams still course through the valleys, but move on to the upper slopes in summer and the land becomes bleak, rocky and uncomfortably hot. In winter the snow comes early and lies late and many of the villages are ski centres. Even the geology is varied, a mixture of granite in the Barguillère and limestone in the valley south of Foix.

Until Napoleon decreed that all *départements* created since the Revolution should, where possible, bear the name of the main local river, Ariège was known as the country of Foix, home to an ancient line of warlike nobles. Hemmed in by Andorra to the south and the high plateau of the Cerdagne to the east, looking out over the Toulouse plateau to the north, modern Ariège is a shadow of its former self, its villages abandoned and roads virtually deserted.

The Couserans region in particular, has suffered severely from emigration: its largest town, St-Girons, has a population of only 7,000 — less than half the 1850 figure. Wildlife, however, has thrived in direct proportion to the human exodus; as you rove

The Cascade d'Oô in the Montagnes de Luchon is one of the spectacular waterfalls which, together with the mountain lakes and torrents, are some of the best sights of the Comminges.

about the hills above St-Girons you will see marmots, mountain goats and large numbers of rabbits, prey for the ever-watchful eagles, buzzards and other raptors. East of Mont Vallier, the highest peak (2,838 metres/9,314 feet), several former mule trails make excellent walking tracks up to the frontier, taking you into some of the emptiest country of the Ariège.

Picturesque scenery can also be found in the small valleys between Foix and Andorra. The lush valley of the Vicdessos lies beneath a long ridge running east from the Pic des Trois Seigneurs, which shelters it from the north and allows it a mild micro-climate. The valley runs up through mainly empty country to the bare peaks and ridges along the Franco-Spanish-Andorran frontier. The area has no towns, few villages and very few hamlets. This is hardly surprising as there are no roads, only a few tracks to take walkers and campers deeper into the hills. The great joy of this wild, barren borderland is its large number of lakes, many created by glaciation and feeding mountain streams full of rainbow trout and char.

East of a line between Foix and Tarascon-sur-Ariège, the country is green, open and studded with half-deserted villages. Here walkers and backpackers can explore fascinating places such as famous Montaillou, once inhabited by the heretical Cathars. This sect, whose believers were also known as Albigensians, viewed the world as the creation of the Devil and set about purifying themselves without the intercession of the Church. An anti-Cathar crusade in the early 13th century dealt cruelly and mercilessly with this proto-Reformation, which at one point had converted much of south-west France. Many of the Cathars withdrew to remote hilltop castles, such as Montségur, Puivert and Puilaurens: when finally captured, they were burned at the stake and their last outposts razed to the ground. Nature has begun to reclaim these former citadels, and ravens, choughs and crows nest among the ruins.

Other notable features of the Ariège include the Pic de St-Barthélemy (2,348 metres/7,706 feet) in the Monts d'Olmes and the hills west and south of Ax-les-Thermes, an area virtually without roads now that the villagers' homes have been abandoned and the byways which lead into the hills have crumbled into tracks. East of Ax the country is open, but the hills are steep, ideal for skiing in winter and ridge-walking in summer.

NATURE RESERVES OF THE EASTERN PYRENEES

Le Massif de la Carança nature reserve is located between the valleys of the Têt and the Tech. Landscape and vegetation is typically Pyrenean, including a selection of endemic plants in the high Alpine zone: saxifrages and the Isard parsley. Another local botanical speciality is the tall herbaceous community known as 'megaphorbiae', among which grow the Pyrenean lily, *Eryngium bourgatii*, mountain delphinium and a mountain form of angelica of more Mediterranean origin, *Molopospermum peloponnesianum*.

Such a varied flora naturally hosts an abundance of insects: beetles, moths and butterflies are particularly well represented. Notable among the latter are the distinctive and large Apollo, and two small, brown species, Lefebre's ringlet and the Gavarnie ringlet, which both inhabit the high alpine meadows above 1,800 m (5,900 ft).

The two adjoining reserves of the Massif de Madres and the Mont Coronat cover 3,160 ha (7,810 acres) north of the Têt valley. The vegetation is typical of limestone mountains but with a strong Mediterranean influence from the warm air blown up the Têt valley. On the plateaux of red limestone are great carpets of bearberry, a spreading, mat-forming shrub with shiny, leathery, oval leaves. Naturalists can enjoy the area for its reptiles, which in turn attract the short-toed, or snake eagle. There are also a couple of pairs of golden eagles and a pair of eagle owls.

Invertebrates are abundant, including marbled skipper and mountain small white butterflies, and the rare blind scorpion *Belisarius xambui*. Perhaps most notable, though, are the mammals, with wildcat, genet, izard, wild boar, red deer and, according to recent reports, sightings of lynx.

Maps: IGN 1:100,000 No. 71;
IGN 1:50,000 Nos. 6 and 7.

GETTING THERE
By car: the most direct route
into Ariège is the N20, which
leads through Foix, Tarascon-
sur-Ariège and Ax-les-
Thermes; minor roads branch
off to the Vicdessos and other
valleys. St-Girons is centrally
located in the Couserans on
D117 from Foix.
By rail: trains operate between
Toulouse and Foix; a regular
service links Foix and Ax-les-
Thermes. Trains link Toulouse
with Boussens, from where a
bus service runs to St-Girons,
Foix and the valleys.
By bus: bus services run in
summer between Foix and Ax-
les-Thermes and into some of
the main valleys.

WHERE TO STAY
There are plenty of hotels in
Foix, Ax, Tarascon, St-Girons
and the larger villages and
main valleys. One of the better
ones is Hôtel Audoye Lons, 6
pl Georges-Dutihl, Foix, T: 05
61 65 52 44.

ACTIVITIES
Walking: an excellent trek
heads south from Laramade in
the Vicdessos to a point near
the Pic du Pas de Bouc (2,602
m/8,539 ft) on the Spanish
frontier. Ax-les-Thermes has
many local trails up to the Tute
de l'Ours (2,255 m/7,400 ft);
others extend to the west of this
peak. Several disused mule
tracks lead up to the Spanish
frontier from Mont Valier. For
more information on walking
in Ariège, contact the Comité
Départemental Ariégeois de la
Randonnée, Hôtel du
Département, 09000 Foix, T: 05
61 02 09 09.
Riding: donkeys can be hired to
carry your children or bags on
mountain hikes. Try
RandoCouser'Anes, T: 05 61 96

Honey buzzards feed on honey
from the nests of wasps and bees.

44 32, in Betchat and Guzet,
June-Sept. La Ferme aux Anes
in Unac, T: 05 61 64 44 22, also
has donkeys available at the
Lac d'Appy and the entrance to
the Réserve d'Orlu.
Caving: the grotto and caves of
Mas d'Azil, north-east of St-
Girons, are justly famous —
their soaring height rivals that
of some of the country's
cathedrals. The caves at Niaux
are full of prehistoric paintings,
while those at Bédeilhac and
Lombrives sheltered Cathars.
Ecology: the Maison des Loups
at Les Forges, Orlu, T: 05 61 64
02 66, offers a forested park
where visitors can watch
European and North American
wolves with their cubs.

FURTHER INFORMATION
Tourist offices: CDT Ariège-
Pyrénées, 31 bis av du Général
de Gaulle, 09004 Foix, T: 05 61
02 30 70, F: 05 61 65 17 34; Ax-
les-Thermes, pl du Breilh; Foix,
45 cours Gabriel Fauré, T: 05
61 65 12 12; Luzenac (Vallées
d'Ax), 6 rue de la Mairie, T: 05
61 64 60 60; St-Girons, pl A-
Sentein, T: 05 61 96 26 60;
Tarascon-sur-Ariège, av des
Pyrénées, T: 05 61 05 94 94.
  For Ariège mountain rescue
services, call T: 05 61 64 22 58.

Andorra

*Tiny principality in the
French Pyrenees; haven for
botanists
468 sq km (181 sq miles)*

Andorra is first and foremost a
skiing area, and in winter
tourists flock there in their
thousands. But when the snow
has gone the mountains open
up to other types of outdoor
lover, the wild-flower enthusiast
and mountain walker.
  The country is barren and
desolate and has only two main
roads. One runs across from
France to Spain, linking the
main centres of population,
while the other much smaller
road leads north from the
capital, Andorra-la-Vella, to
the ski resort at El Serrat.
Outcrops of alkaline rocks line
this route, and it is among these
rocks that you will find the
widest variety of Andorra's
famous flora. Over 1,000
species of flowering plants have
been identified in the
principality, making it one of
the best areas in the Pyrenees
for the botanist. For the walker,
there are plenty of tracks
running north and south, once

off the road, many of which are still used as smuggler's trails by people taking tax-free goods from Andorra to France and Spain.

Andorra lies in the Pyrenees north of the French border, but it is not French. Its independence was guaranteed by a treaty of 1278 between the Spanish Bishop of Urgel and the Counts of Foix. The latters' responsibilities have long been assumed by the President of France; in 1993 the current Andorran constitution was signed by the incumbent Bishop of Urgel and François Mitterand. Andorra is the only country in the world where Catalan is the official tongue. **Getting there** *By air:* the nearest airports are at Barcelona (in Spain), T: 93 298 3838, Toulouse or Perpignan (see p117). *By car:* the main road across Andorra is CG1/CG2, which runs from Pas de la Casa in the north to the old cathedral city of La Seu d'Urgell in Spain. *By rail:* from Barcelona there are trains to Puigcerdà on the Spanish-Andorran border, and buses from there to Andorra la Vella, via La Seu d'Urgell. From Toulouse there are trains to

L'Hospitalet and Latour-de-Carol, with daily bus links to Andorra, and Ax-les-Thermes, with daily buses May-Oct. *By bus:* Alsina Graells, T: 82 73 79, operates regular services between the bus station in Andorra la Vella and the Estació del Nord in Barcelona, and has buses between Puigcerdà and La Seu d'Urgell, from where a service runs several times daily to Andorra la Vella. Samar, T: 82 62 89, operates buses linking Andorra with Zaragoza and Madrid, the east coast of Spain and also Toulouse. From Toulouse, Intercars, T: 05 61 58 14 53, operates buses to Ax-les-Thermes and Pas de la Casa, offering easy access to Andorra. **Activities** *Walking:* Andorra is wild, tough country, suitable only for well-equipped walkers. You can make a circuit up the Valira d'Ordino to El Serrat and then up to the Pic de l'Estanyo (2,912 m/9,557 ft). Information and maps from the Secretary of State for the Environment, T: 82 93 45, the Andorran Trekking Federation, T: 86 74 44, F: 86 74 67, or the Andorran Trekking Club, T: 82 28 47. *Cycling:* Andorra offers plenty of scope for mountain-

biking, and details of itineraries are available from the Andorran Cycling Federation, T: 82 96 92, F: 86 44 41. Bikes can be hired in most places, including Soldeu-El Tartar, La Massana, Encamp, Sant Julià de Lòria and Ordino. *Riding:* many centres offer trekking excursions; contact Andorran Horse-Riding Federation, T: 82 00 19, F: 83 92 43. *Skiing:* Andorra has the highest and largest area for skiing in the Pyrenees; its 6 resorts, at Pal, Ordino-Arcalís, Soldeu-El Tartar, Pas de la Casa-Grau Roig, La Rabassa and Arinsal, have 152 runs over 147 km of piste. Pas de la Casa-Grau Roig is the highest and largest resort; you can try monoskiing, snowboarding, skiing and sleighing at night on the floodlit Font Negre run. Call T: 80 10 60 for details. **Further information** *Tourist offices:* Andorra la Vella (national tourist office), calle Dr-Vilanova, T: 82 02 14, F: 82 58 23; Andorra la Vella, plaça de la Rotonda, T: 82 71 17.

The Giro footpath in the Vallée d'Aspe is one of many paths with stunning views of this ever-changing landscape.

FOOTPATHS OF THE PYRENEES

Grande Randonnée 10, which spans the Pyrenees from Hendaye in the west to Banyuls on the Mediterranean, is one of the great footpaths of France. The 400-km (250-mile) long-distance footpath is covered by five well-illustrated *topo-guides*, which break the journey into sections. GR10 is certainly a challenge, but the rewards for taking it up are considerable. The trail across the Hautes-Pyrénées is wildly beautiful and alert walkers will see a considerable array of wildlife (including Egyptian vultures, booted eagles and the Pyrenean chamois), a host of Alpine plants and, in the meadows below the bare upper slopes, a riot of flowers and butterflies.

Higher and even harder than the GR10 is the Haute Randonnée Pyrénéenne, much of which lies at altitudes above 1,800 m (6,000 ft). To complete the whole of this splendid challenge will take at least five weeks. For long sections the walks are far from any habitation, so thorough planning is essential, as is a knowledge of weather lore and map and compass work. There is no real climbing involved but plenty of scrambling, with the trail running along knife-edged ridges and over 2,400-m (8,000-ft) high cols — not places for the inexperienced walker. The best guide to the route is *Pyrenees High Level Route* by Georges Véron, published by West Col.

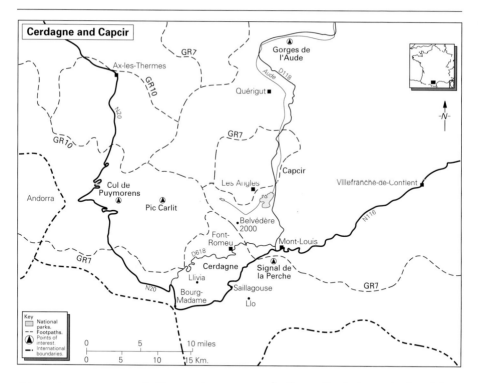

Cerdagne and Capcir

Gorges de
l'Aude

Ax-les-Thermes

GR7

GR10

Quérigut■

N20

GR7

GR10

Capcir

Col de
Puymorens

Les Angles

Villefranche-de-Conflent

Andorra

Pic Carlit

Belvédère
2000

N116

Font-
Romeu

Mont-Louis

GR7

D618

Cerdagne

Signal de
la Perche

Llívia

GR7

N20

Saillagouse

Bourg-
Madame

Llo

Key
National
parks.
Footpaths.
Points of
interest.
International
boundaries.

| 0 | 5 | 10 miles |
| 0 | 5 | 10 | 15 Km. |

Cerdagne and Capcir

Fertile, cool plateau and steep-sided valley lying between Andorra and the dusty plain of Roussillon

If I were pressed to declare which part of the Pyrenees I prefer above the rest, I would put forward the Cerdagne and the area which abuts it, the Capcir. Perhaps the main reason for this choice is that when you enter the Cerdagne from the west, you leave France behind and come into the country of the Catalans: Roussillon. Yet the Cerdagne is a complete contrast to the hot, dusty, vine-draped plains of Roussillon far below. The vast rolling plateau is a place of farms and meadows, surrounded by snow-capped mountains; the air is cool and sweet and cattle graze on rich, belly-high meadow grass.

The road leading to the Cerdagne from Andorra in the west or from Ax-les-Ther-

mes in the north climbs up to the plateau over the Col de Puymorens (1,915 metres/6,285 feet), from which there are good views across to the highest peak of the Cerdagne, the Pic Carlit (2,921 metres/9,587 feet). Once past the col, the road rises steadily, coming into the Cerdagne by the enclave of Llívia, which, under the 1659 Treaty of the Pyrenees, remains a Spanish town within the frontiers of France.

A road encircles the Cerdagne, and the simplest way to explore the region is to follow this road east from Bourg-Madame, past Hix and along the meadows and valleys leading up to the Spanish frontier; it continues through Saillagouse, over the Col de la Perche and past the viewpoint at the Signal de La Perche to Mont-Louis, a fortified town at the point where the Cerdagne tips down into the steep, narrow valley of the Conflent gorge. Along this road to Mont-Louis you get marvellous views over the line of peaks and cols which mark the frontier.

This part of the Cerdagne is open meadowland for the most part, seamed with half-

136

hidden streams tucked away amid the grassy tussocks. After Mont-Louis, the road loops round and heads back towards Bourg-Madame, skirting the foothills of the Pic Carlit. Here the countryside is steeper, glorious short-grass country with springy turf. There are small lakes and ponds, and lots of streams for fishing and bathing. Wildlife is abundantly present: izard on the slopes of Carlit, goats browsing in the meadows, otters splashing in the streams and a wealth of bird life, particularly in summer when the songbirds flourish in the tall grasses. Butterflies are another feature of the Cerdagne; black-veined white, swallowtails and purple

emperors, the fritillaries and blues.

Of equal interest is the Capcir valley, which runs off the Cerdagne to the north, descending to the gorges of the River Aude. The Capcir has a fascinating array of wild flowers and orchids. If you follow some of the marked trails up the steep valley you will see the full range of plant life, with certain species thriving only in the narrowest of altitude bands — prolific in one meadow and non-existent ten minutes later in your climb. There are good walks up from the Lac de Bouillouses to the Pic Carlit: from its summit there are great views over the plateau and surrounding lakes.

BEFORE YOU GO
Maps: IGN 1:100,000 Nos. 71 and 72; IGN 1:50,000 No. 8.

GETTING THERE
By car: from Perpignan, take N116 west up the Têt valley to Villefranche-de-Conflent and on to the Cerdagne. The Capcir is served by D118 between Mont-Louis and Quérigut.
By rail: from Perpignan a regular service runs along the Têt to Villefranche from where the *petit train jaune*, which terminates at Latour-de-Carol, climbs to the Cerdagne, stopping at Font-Romeu-Bolquère, and to the Capcir, stopping at Mont-Louis La Cabanasse. Main-line services also run between Perpignan or Toulouse and Latour-de-Carol.
By bus: the region's erratic services originate in Perpignan.

WHERE TO STAY
Accommodation is not a problem in the Cerdagne-Capcir region, even in winter, as the villages operate as both summer and ski resorts. Try Le Coq Hardi in Odeillo, near Font-Romeu, T: 04 68 30 11 02.

ACTIVITIES
Walking: marked trails cover this area; 3 of the most rewarding walks extend from Lac des Bouillouses to the Pic

In spite of its name, the scarce swallowtail is common in southern France and is frequently seen feeding beside footpaths.

Carlit; across the Pyrenees from Llo to Nuria; and across the Cerdagne from Carlit to Canigou (allow 5 days).
Skiing: established resorts are Font-Romeu, Belvédère and Les Angles. For information on cross-country skiing, contact the Association de Ski de Fond for the Pyrénées Catalanes, Maison de la Montagne, 66210 Matemale, T: 04 68 04 32 75.

Viewpoints: there are remarkable views from the Pic Carlit, Belvédère 2000 and the Signal de La Perche.

FURTHER INFORMATION
Tourist offices: Les Angles, 2 av de l'Aude, T: 04 68 04 32 76; Font-Romeu, av Emmanuel-Brousse, T: 04 68 30 68 30; Mont-Louis, rue du Marché, T: 04 68 04 21 97.

(*Overleaf*) Dense pine forest is mirrored in the still waters of the Lac des Bouillouses on the Cerdagne plateau.

Conflent and Vallespir

*Two dramatic valleys of the easternmost
Pyrenees; a varied countryside of
waterfalls, steep gorges, vineyards and
orchards*
ZICO

The Conflent and the Vallespir are the two major valleys of the Pyrénées-Orientales *département*, the first to the north, the second to the south. Between them they cradle the last rocky thrust of the Pyrenees and the mighty bulk of the Pic du Canigou (2,784 metres/9,137 feet), the highest mountain of the Catalans. The valleys stop some way short of the coast, leaving their rivers Têt and Tech to continue across the Roussillon plain, overlooked to the south by the Chaine des Albères, whose descending hills reach out and dip their rocky fingers into the Mediterranean near Port-Vendres. Both valleys support vineyards and orchards, the fruit trees bright in spring with cherry, apple and almond blossom; and both look up to the soaring peaks on either side.

The entrance to the Conflent valley lies on the edge of the Cerdagne plateau at the town of Mont-Louis, where the road and railway plunge down a steep gorge. Waterfalls burst from the gorge's rocky sides and send their spray tumbling down for hundreds of metres, and there are remarkable feats of engineering to see, notably the bridge of the Pont Sejourné. From this point on plenty of options open up for exploration on foot or by car. Steep though the gorge is, there are tracks leading up it, giving access to the Capcir valley and the Vallée de Rotja, which skirts the eastern slopes of Canigou. From the main town, Villefranche-de-Conflent, a network of minor roads leads into the southern mountains where you can find the spa at Vernet-les-Bains and the monastery of St-Martin-du-Canigou, at the foot of the massif. Canigou is a great bulk of a mountain, the dominant feature of the landscape. A footpath runs up to the top, where it joins others coming in from the Cerdagne.

The walk from the Pic Carlit in the Cerdagne, along the Spanish frontier and up to the top of Pic du Canigou is not a trip to be undertaken lightly. I went with a companion one wild October, choosing autumn as we thought the weather would be pleasantly cool by then. We calculated the expedition would take about five days of slow, pleasant walking. Unfortunately winter started early that year. When we emerged from our tent on the first morning, we found ourselves ankle-deep in snow. Later in the day this turned to sleet and rain, driving us off the frontier's ridge and down into Spain to the little village and monastery at Nuria, where we stayed the night.

The next day we climbed again to the ridge, but were trapped by low cloud, and when my companion walked off a corniche, which was completely invisible in the whiteout, we decided we should descend the northern slope of the mountain and seek what shelter we could find below the crest. That descent of a snow-filled couloir remains lodged in my memory as one of my less pleasant experiences in the Pyrenees. Inevitably, when we got to the bottom of the slope, the skies cleared. We camped that night by a small mountain lake in a truly dream-like setting of rocks and mountains and blue lakes, with a great red sunset to round it off.

It took three more days to get to the top of Canigou. I remember falling headlong on ice-covered rocks early in the morning and wading for hours waist-deep in a stream, which seemed to be the only way we could make progress along a valley, since all the little bridges had been washed away. When we finally crawled exhausted on to the summit we were greeted by two sprightly gentlemen in their eighties who had climbed the mountain from its northern side and, like a couple of spring lambs, led us down to civilization.

Running down the Conflent valley is the Têt, one of those rushing, stony, mountain rivers, which you can follow eastward as far as Ille-sur-Têt. Here the valley widens and the landscape becomes tame compared with what has gone before. Mountain lovers have another chance to find excitement by turning south towards the Vallespir valley and up into the Aspres, the last outpost of the main Pyrenean range.

Vallespir is nothing if not spectacular, full of trails and small hamlets, with the Gorges de la Fou alone making the visit worthwhile. There is no road into the Haut-Vallespir from the west, only a track along the spine of the Pyrenees, where peak follows peak at about 2,500 metres (8,200 feet), descending into the valley by La Preste, where the track gradually broadens into a road and meets the main route coming in from Spain at Prats-de-Mollo. Continuing east the road runs along beside the Tech to Amélie-les-Bains, and out on to the Roussillon plain by the town of Céret.

Here we might end, but rather than driving across the plain to reach the Mediterranean the wild traveller has one last hilly option to exercise, taking the route through the Albères. Apart from the main road and the *autoroute*, which cross into Spain by the Col du Perthus, only minor roads, little more than tracks, run into these hills. The peaks are already down to 1,000-1,200 metres (3,300-3,900 feet), gentler country now, and the best way through to the sea is to follow the *grande randonnée* down to Banyuls, a fine spot at which to end a 250-mile journey through the wild Pyrenees.

BEFORE YOU GO
Maps: IGN 1:100,000 Nos. 71 and 72; IGN (RP) 1:50,000 Nos. 10 and 11.

GETTING THERE
By air: the nearest airport is Perpignan (see p117).
By car: from Toulouse N113 or A63 *autoroute* runs past Carcassonne; then take D118 south to Quillan and into the Capcir and Cerdagne-Conflent. N116 and D115 run up the Têt and Tech valleys respectively, giving access to the Conflent and the Vallespir. N116 continues directly to Perpignan.
By rail: a train from Perpignan runs up the Têt valley to

Villefranche-de-Conflent.
By bus: buses run infrequently to Prats-de-Mollo.

WHERE TO STAY
Four possibilities are Castel Emeraude in Amélie-les-Bains, T: 04 68 39 02 83; Les Glycines in Arles-sur-Tech, T: 04 68 39 10 09; Hôtel Princess in Vernet-les-Bains, T: 04 68 05 56 22, Hostellerie La Relais in Prats-de-Mollo, T: 04 68 39 71 30.

ACTIVITIES
Walking: one of the most exhilarating walks is that from St-Martin-de-Canigou to the summit. There are marked trails around all the main

towns, and particularly good trails from Prats-de-Mollo.
Riding: the CDTE Pyrénées Orientales, 4 rue du Mûrier, 66740 Montesquieu-des-Albères, T/F: 04 68 89 85 20, will provide information on horse-riding in the area.
Ecology: around the Canigou massif are several nature reserves: Py, Mantet, Conat, Nohèdes and Jujols.

FURTHER INFORMATION
Tourist offices: Céret, av G-Clemenceau, T: 04 68 87 00 53; Prats-de-Mollo, pl El Firal, T: 04 68 39 70 83; Villefranche-de-Conflent, pl de l'Eglise, T: 04 68 96 22 96.

The Iberian lynx hunts at dusk for rabbits and other small mammals which form its staple diet.

CHAPTER 7

The Atlantic Coast

About 35 years ago I nearly drowned off the coast near Arcachon. It was a perfect June day — a clear blue sky, gentle waves lapping at the beach, a backcloth of sand dunes and pine trees. The calmness of the sea's surface belied a vicious undertow that dragged me relentlessly down the coast, even though I was barely 50 metres from the shore. Luckily I survived but the experience left me with a healthy respect for the power of the ocean.

The French Atlantic coastline forms a giant arc from the Pointe du Raz on the westernmost tip of Brittany, down to Basque country and the foothills of the Pyrenees. It can be split conveniently into three parts, divided by the great estuaries of the Loire and the Gironde: the rugged cliffs of southern Brittany, the indented coastline between the two estuaries and the ruler-straight sandy shoreline of Aquitaine further south.

The area south of the Loire estuary is rich in wetland habitats, such as the bird-haunted Lac de Grand-Lieu, where eel-fishermen still make a precarious living. To the west of Grand-Lieu lies the wide expanse of the *marais* of Machecoul and Challans: drained salt marshes where cattle browse under an immense canopy of sky, with hardly a tree to lessen the force of the west winds blowing off the Atlantic. The marshes stretch right down to the shores of the wide Baie de Bourgneuf, sheltered along much of its western side by the long finger of the Ile de Noirmoutier. Further

The open coast of the Bassin d'Arcachon is exposed to the fierce attrition of wind and wave from the Atlantic Ocean. New pools, rivulets and channels are formed daily in the shifting sands.

south lie the tidal flats of the Anse de l'Aiguillon, the drained Marais Poitevin, stretching far inland, and the sheltered waters of the bays and estuary creeks around La Rochelle, which are famous for their flourishing oysters. These coastal flats lie at the junction of the two major migration routes from Greenland and Siberia and consequently see some of the largest concentrations of birds in Europe. Clouds of knot and dunlin wheel in tight formation over the barren, estuarine mud and herons flap across the shallows or lumber heavily back to their untidy nests.

As you progress south from the Loire towards the Gironde, the landscape changes gradually from a northern to southern character. The grey slate roofs of Brittany give way to the orange-red pantiles of the south, more and more of the countryside is given over to vineyards, and the crops are further advanced — by late May in the Vendée, hay-making is finished and the wheat is knee high. The area south of the Ile de Noirmoutier especially is famous for the mildness of its climate, which allows subtropical plants to grow.

The Atlantic coast's second great water barrier, the Gironde, cuts into the shoreline like a downward-slanting axe-stroke. Unlike the Loire, which runs almost east-west between Nantes and the sea, the Gironde's estuary is virtually north-south. On either side lies a gently rolling landscape of vineyards producing the classic red wines of Bordeaux.

East of the Gironde, almost every farmhouse you pass calls itself a *château* and has a sun-bleached roadside notice inviting you to turn into its courtyard and sample its home-bottled vintage. On the western bank are the Médoc vineyards where great wine names, such as Mouton-Rothschild, Margaux, Pauillac and St-Estèphe, stud the map.

The Médoc lies at the northern tip of Les Landes, a seemingly endless forest of pine trees. This million-hectare (2.4-million-acre) expanse is Europe's largest forest and is shaped like a huge isosceles triangle, with its base along the foothills of the Pyrenees and its sides bounded by the Atlantic and the Garonne.

If you follow any of the minor roads from one village to the next, you will pass half-timbered farmhouses, with low-pitched red-tiled roofs, surrounded by outhouses and wood-stores built in the same harmonious style. Down some narrow lane you may find a time-worn church standing among the trees, on the medieval pilgrim route to the shrine of Santiago de Compostela in northern Spain. A 12th-century guide-book for pilgrims called it a 'desolate country, lacking everything, where there is no bread, no wine, no meat, no fish, no water, no spring.' That was before the 19th-century planting of conifers, which have brought another desolation. From the map, the forest looks as though it would be monotonous to explore, but despite its flat dark-green vistas, it enjoys a certain quality of stillness that the French term *le calme*.

The forest also hides numerous winding rivers. In the half light under the tangled canopy of willows, birches and alders draped with lianas and sprouting a profusion of epiphytic mosses and ferns, you feel a world apart from the orderly plantations only yards away. The river erosion on the soft, sandy banks exposes the multitude of tree roots, creating the impression of being in some exotic mangrove swamp.

As you head west across Les Landes towards the sea, the sand takes over completely. The pines thin out as the coastal dunes approach, and are gradually engulfed as the wind blows the sands inland. This phenomenon can be seen at its most dramatic at the huge Dune du Pilat at the entrance to the Bassin d'Arcachon. This Sahara-like mountain of sand, at 117 metres (384 feet) the highest dune in Europe, is advancing relentlessly inland at the rate of a metre a year. Though its surroundings are hardly wild — on either side are some of the most civilized summer resorts along the Atlantic coast — it is worth seeing for itself, and worth struggling to the top for the marvellous view north across the Bassin d'Arcachon and inland over the tree-tops of Les Landes.

GETTING THERE

By air: the coast is well served by international airports at Nantes-Atlantique, T: 02 40 84 80 00; and Bordeaux-Merignac, T: 05 56 34 50 50; internal flights go to La Rochelle-Ile de Ré, T: 08 03 80 58 05; and Biarritz-Bayonne-Anglet, T: 05 59 43 83 85.

By sea: ferry services to St-Malo provide access to the northern Atlantic coast (see BRITTANY AND NORMANDY, p13); for the southern Atlantic coast, ferries to Santander or Bilbao are an option (see THE PYRENEES, p117).

By car: from St-Malo, the most direct route to the Atlantic coast is the N137 through Rennes to Nantes, from where roads radiate southwards. Alternatively, go to Rennes, then cross-country on D roads via Redon and Pontchâteau to the St-Nazaire toll bridge; from here you can follow the coast southwards.

By rail: TGV services run from Paris-Montparnasse to Nantes, Bordeaux and Bayonne, all important rail centres with connections to places along the coast. Motorail services run from Calais to Bordeaux and Biarritz, saving motorists a long drive; AutoTrain services run from Paris to Nantes. Between Nantes and Bordeaux a line meanders via La Roche-sur-Yonne, La Rochelle and Saintes, with spurs to Les Sables d'Olonne and other seaside resorts. Les Landes has a single north-south line between Bordeaux and Bayonne, with only a single coastal spur, to Arcachon.

By bus: Eurolines (see p13) operates long-distance coaches to destinations including Nantes, La Rochelle, Bordeaux Angoulême, Arcachon, Castets and Bayonne.

WHEN TO GO

This is an excellent area for watching migrating and wintering birds; the best time to see them is between Oct and Mar. Most of the year temperatures along the coast are moderate, though in Les Landes it can be blisteringly hot and sultry even in May.

WHERE TO STAY

Most inland towns and large villages have at least 1 comfortable hotel. Seaside hotels are packed in summer, but out of season may be virtually empty or closed; many do not open until May or June.

Camp-sites are plentiful, although many open only from spring to early autumn.

ACTIVITIES

Walking: coastal routes include the GR364, leading from St-Jean-de-Monts to Les Sables d'Olonne before heading east to Poitiers; GR4 and GR360, which take in the coast near Royan; and GR8, which follows the coastline from Arcachon to near Bayonne.

Cycling: the Fédération Française de Cyclotourisme (see USEFUL ADDRESSES, p215) publishes *La France à Vélo* series, which includes *Pays-de-Loire; Poitou-Charentes* and *Aquitaine.*

Watersports: a wide range of activities is on offer, from punting on the Marais Poitevin to canoeing down the Leyre valley or surfing on the Aquitaine coast.

FURTHER INFORMATION

CRT Pays-de-la-Loire, 2 rue de la Loire, 44204 Nantes, T: 02 40 48 24 20, F: 02 40 08 07 10, www.cr-pays-de-la-loire.fr.

CRT Poitou-Charentes, BP 56, 86002 Poitiers, T: 05 49 50 10 50, F: 05 49 41 37 28, e-mail: poitou-charentes.tourisme@ interpc.fr.

CRT Aquitaine, Cité Mondiale, 23 parvis des Chartrons, 33074 Bordeaux, T: 05 56 01 70 00, F: 05 56 01 70 07, e-mail: tourisme@crt.cr-aquitaine.fr.

The rare butterfly iris grows in the Marais Poitevin.

The Atlantic Coast

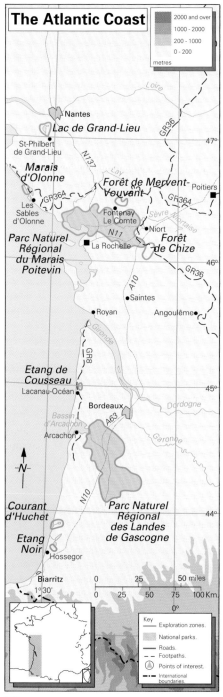

■	2000 and over
■	1000 - 2000
■	200 - 1000
□	0 - 200
	metres

Key
— Exploration zones.
■ National parks.
— Roads.
-- Footpaths.
Ⓐ Points of interest.
-·- International boundaries.

Lac de Grand-Lieu

Inland lake 15 km (9 miles) south-west of Nantes; réserve naturelle
Ramsar, ZICO

Although Nantes was nearby, the Lac de Grand-Lieu seemed a thousand miles from civilization, as a cold wind ruffled the water and herons picked their way through the shallows, stabbing their bills downwards as they hunted for the lake's abundant fish.

According to legend, the lake came into being to swallow up a town notorious for its evil ways; on Christmas night Grand-Lieu fishermen have been known to hear the ghostly chimes of its underwater bells. By day, the lake resounds to the sound of thousands of wintering waterfowl, waders and raptors, including grebes, ducks, buzzards, kites, plovers and spoonbills.

This rich aquatic ecosystem also supports the largest heronry in France, some years attaining 1,300 breeding pairs. Other waders commonly found on the lake include purple herons, little bitterns, bitterns and little egret. Amongst the mammals, otters survive here, although some fail to run the gauntlet of nets and the long, conical, black-tarred fish-traps that fringe the lake and become trapped. Altogether 226 bird species have been recorded, along with 43 species of mammals, including muskrat and fox, 19 reptiles and amphibians — notably frogs, toads and newts — and 19 fish.

With such a vibrant natural community in evidence it is hard to appreciate that the lake is slowly dying. Swelled by winter rains, it expands to more than 6,000 hectares (14,800 acres), making it one of the largest lakes in France, but in the summer months, its surface area drops to about 4,000 hectares (9,900 acres). Each year the marsh vegetation reaches out a little farther into the open water, while in turn the damp margins give way to scrub and then woodland. Herons nest in sallows, which grow as floating forests on former reed beds, while genet, honey buzzard and hobby inhabit the drier

forest. But once the open water disappears, choked under a blanket of water-lilies, reedmace and sedges, there will be nowhere for the specialized aquatic fauna to go.

The central part of the lake lies within the confines of a nature reserve: access is limited to 10 local fishermen, whose traditional punts, known as *yoles*, can still be seen

The Lac de Grand-Lieu supports an exceptional range of wildlife, including numerous waterfowl.

drawn up in the shallows. The primitive square sails, held up not by a proper mast but by two poles on either side of the punt, used to be preserved by being dipped in copper sulphate from the local vineyards.

BEFORE YOU GO
Maps: IGN 1:100,000 No. 32; IGN 1:25,000 No. 1224 OT.

GETTING THERE
By car: St-Philbert and Passay are the closest towns. St-Philbert is on D117 half-way between Nantes and Machecoul. For Passay, head north from St-Philbert on D65, then turn left on D62 in La Chevrolière. It is possible to drive around the periphery of the reserve on a series of minor roads. Clockwise from St-Philbert, these are: D61, D64, D264, D85 and D65.
By rail: the nearest station is at Nantes, 25 km (16 miles) away.
By bus: buses run from Nantes to St-Philbert.

WHERE TO STAY
Try Les Champs d'Avaux, Bouaye, T: 02 40 65 43 50, F: 02 40 32 64 83.
Outdoor living: La Boulogne camp-site is in St-Philbert, T: 02 40 78 88 79.

ACCESS
Public access to the centre of the lake is not permitted.

ACTIVITIES
Walking: a footpath encircles the lake.
Riding: the Comité Départementale de Tourisme Equestre for Loire-Atlantique, at 30 rue des Champs Menauds, 44115 Basse Goulaine, T: 02 40 06 02 75, will provide details of local equestrian centres.
Watersports: St-Philbert offers canoeing, kayaking, windsurfing and pedalo hire; boat trips can be taken on the Boulogne river in summer.
Museums: St-Philbert's Musée

147

du Lac, Site l'Abbatiale, has a collection of stuffed birds and audio-visual displays on the lake's flora and fauna; open all year but closed Mon-Tues in Oct-Apr. La Maison du Pêcheur museum in Passay, T/F: 02 40 31 36 46, has exhibitions on the history of local fishing (open all year).

Bird-watching: there is an observatory at Passay, equipped with powerful binoculars and video links to the birds outside (open all year).

Sightseeing: St-Philbert has a magnificent 9th-century abbey church in the town centre where regular concerts are held in summer.

FURTHER INFORMATION
Tourist office: St-Philbert-de-Grand-Lieu, Le Prieuré, T: 02 40 78 73 88, F: 02 40 78 83 42.
  Grand-Lieu nature reserve, 15 rue de la Châtaigneraie, 44830 Bouaye, T: 02 40 32 62 81.

Marais d'Olonne

Salt-marsh, lake and bird sanctuary north of Les Sables-d'Olonne

The Marais is a narrow stretch of salt-marsh, about 5 km long by 1 km (3 miles by half a mile wide), stranded 5 km (3 miles) inland. During the Middle Ages it stood on the edge of a bay, but the sea retreated and the bay dried out, leaving behind a salt-marsh lake, now in part neatly embanked, elsewhere choked with reeds and undergrowth. The Marais is separated from the sea by the pine woods of the Forêt d'Olonne. On hot summer afternoons you can stroll down to the dune-lined beach along any number of shady, resin-

---

> ## THE OTTER
>
> At the turn of the 20th century otters inhabited every *département* in mainland France outside Paris, and their numbers were estimated at 30-50,000. By 1986 this secretive mammal was common in only ten *départements*, mostly along the Atlantic coast. With a population of between 500 and 1,000 animals, this represented a 95% decrease since 1900. However, in recent years the population has experienced an encouraging and unexpected increase, and at present stands at 1,500.
>
> To describe the habitat of the otter would be to list virtually all aquatic environments from mountain lakes to salt marsh, but today they are not necessarily found in their most favoured environment — slow-moving rivers — but rather in areas that have been least disturbed by modern development. For the otter is above all a shy creature, and many naturalists have done detailed research on the species without ever having seen one in the wild. Bearing in mind the otter's huge territorial areas — a male may patrol a 20-40-kilometre (15-25-mile) stretch of river — you can appreciate how fortunate you must be to see one.

---

scented paths through the pine trees.

The Marais ranks as one of the Atlantic coast's most important sites for both migrant and resident species. It is home to France's largest colony of avocets: in May, I watched a dozen or so of these smart black-and-white birds, with their long upturned bills, as they picked their way over the mud, accompanied by their fluffy fledgelings. Other birds that can be seen in the Marais include cormorants, egrets, herons, black-winged stilts, shelducks and, in autumn, large numbers of passage waders. Another impressive spectacle can be witnessed a little farther down the coast in summer when several thousand Manx shearwaters assemble offshore at the Plage de Sauveterre.

Before you go *Maps:* IGN 1:100,000 No. 32; 1:25,000 No. 1227 OT. *Guide-books:* M Bournerias, C. Pomerol & Y. Turquier, *La Côte Atlantique de la Loire à la Gironde* (Delachaux & Niestlé). **Getting there** *By car:* take D32 north from Olonne-sur-Mer; after 2 km (1 mile) turn left along D38

towards L'Ile d'Olonne, which lies east of the marsh. *By rail:* Les Sables-d'Olonne has SNCF services from Paris-Gare Montparnasse via Nantes. *By bus:* service from Les Sables-d'Olonne to the Marais. **Where to stay:** as a major seaside resort, Les Sables-d'Olonne has hotels and guest-houses of every category. They include the Chêne Vert, 5 rue de la Bauduère, T: 02 51 32 09 47, and the Hôtel d'Angleterre, 15 quai Guiné, T: 02 51 21 03 28. **Activities** *Walking:* the GR364 long-distance footpath between St-Jean-de-Monts and Poitiers crosses the Marais d'Olonne. *Cycling:* bicycle rental at Les Sables-d'Olonne station. The long-distance cycle path La Route des Fleurs passes through Les Sables-d'Olonne and skirts the Marais. *Watersports:* Les Sables-d'Olonne is a good base for watersports and has a sailing school. *Bird-watching:* the bird sanctuary of L'Ileau, on the left before L'Ile d'Olonne, has a bird observatory. **Further information** *Tourist office:* Les Sables-d'Olonne, av du Maréchal Leclerc, T: 02 51 32 03 28, F: 02 51 32 84 49.

Marais Poitevin

Mixture of verdant waterways, reclaimed estuary marsh and sheltered coastline north of La Rochelle; parc interrégional ZICO
96,000 ha (237,000 acres)

The otter is an extremely rare sight in France, having disappeared from nearly all lowland rivers.

Off the wind-swept promontory of the Pointe d'Arçay the gulls wheel and scream, while far inland, on the tree-shaded canals of France's Venise Verte ('green Venice'), flat-bottomed punts glide silently between fields yellow with buttercups — as great an environmental contrast as can be imagined, yet both coast and canals come under the protective umbrella of the Parc Interrégional du Marais Poitevin.

The Marais has three main divisions: the Venise Verte or Marais Mouillé ('wet marshland') in the east, which covers about 16,000 hectares (40,000 acres); the western part, mainly agricultural, known as the Marais Desséché ('dried-out marshland') covering 56,000 ha (138,000 acres); and a stretch of coastline which includes the Anse ('bay') de l'Aiguillon.

The Venise Verte lies roughly between the villages of Coulon in the east and Maille in the west. Here the lower courses of the Autise, the Sèvre-Niortaise and a tangle of lesser streams are linked by canals large and small, dating back to the days when all transport in the Marais was water-borne.

As with Venice proper, the only way to see the Venise Verte is from the water — though here you do not glide past crumbling palaces and churches, but beneath a canopy of ash trees, willows and poplars, between fields where cream-coloured Charolais cattle graze among the buttercups. As you drift along, your punt (*plate*) brushes past reeds and yellow flag irises, and over a carpet of water-lilies. Fishermen line the banks, waiting patiently for a bite from the pike, tench, eels and carp that thrive in the muddy waters, while countless dragonflies dart and hover over the calm surface. The change-over from farming to tourism is highlighted by the abandoned condition of the smallest canals, which are largely silted up and overgrown now that they no longer have any practical purpose. These undisturbed backwaters are hiding places for polecats and beech martens, both highly secretive creatures. The Marais Poitevin, and the Venise Verte in particular, is also one of Europe's last strongholds for the otter. Although they rarely show themselves, their tracks can be seen from time to time in the mud. The otter population is vulnerable here, as elsewhere, to the traps and poisons put out for the far more ecologically harmful coypus and musk-rats.

I went out in a punt from the jetty — flatteringly called the Grand Port — below the pretty little town of Maillezais, within sight of one of the most beautiful ruined medieval abbeys in the whole of France. Our boatman was one of the last of the older generation still working on the canals of the Venise Verte, where vacationing students have largely taken over. He handled his punt-pole (*pigouille*) like a virtuoso. Apart from the swishing of the punt through the water, all we could hear was the sound of bird-song in the trees overhead, interrupted from time to time by the clanking of pedal-boats, the only form of mechanical transport allowed on the canals.

The Marais Poitevin was in former centuries a huge bay stretching 50 km (30 miles) inland almost as far as the town of Niort. Since the Middle Ages the bay has been gradually reclaimed for agriculture. The reclamation began in the 13th century, when five wealthy abbeys collaborated on a major drainage project: a canal on the western side of the Marais still called the Canal des Cinq Abbés. In the 17th century, as happened in England's Fens, Dutch experts were called in to carry on the work: their name survives in the Canal de la Ceinture des Hollandais, a 20-km (13-mile) masterpiece of land-drainage engineering between Luçon and Velluire. Successive generations of canal-builders continued the project, creating the Marais Desséché. This area is still farmed extensively, upsetting the hydrology of the marshes as a whole. For this reason, the Marais Poitevin was downgraded from *parc naturel régional* to *parc interrégional* (in reality a meaningless designation).

Because the Marais Desséché is mainly agricultural, it is much less interesting than the Venise Verte from the wildlife and scenic point of view. All around are wide fields planted with wheat, fruit trees and *mojettes*, the local type of green bean.

The Marais Desséché has one small nature reserve, just east of the village of St-Denis-du-Payré. Set up in 1976 on 200 hectares (500 acres) of pasture, it has been allowed to revert to its natural condition. To the south a *réserve nationale de chasse* — where hunting is forbidden — effectively extends the protected area. Unfortunately, these two parcels of land are divided by a canal and dyke, the Chenal Vieux, along which hunting is still allowed, making it a real trap for any bird passing over the supposedly green corridor. Nevertheless, the reserve retains an excellent flora and fauna. The wettest areas are enlivened by several rare and spectacular flowers, such as the thrumwort, a floating annual with whorls of white flowers on leafless stalks, and the largest remaining colony in the region of the rare butterfly iris; marsh mallows can be found in more brackish places. In summer the drier areas are dotted with the delicate

The marshland of the Venise Verte comprises a labyrinth of canals and streams which create a romantic world of dappled green light and verdant waterways.

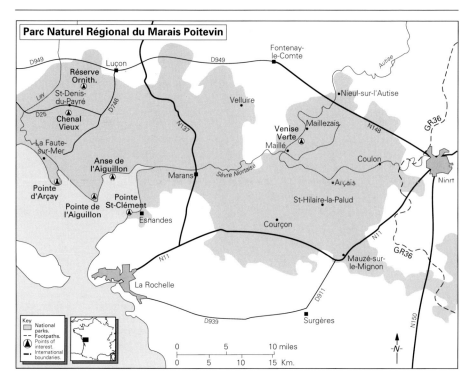

pink spikes of the pyramidal orchid and the unusual grey flowers of the lizard orchid. This botanical paradise resounds to the reedy cries of some 40 pairs of black terns and the shriller notes of the rarer whiskered tern and plays host to the courtships of three of the most elegant wading birds: black-winged stilts, black-tailed godwit and ruff.

The third main division of the Marais Poitevin is the coastline, which runs south from the resort of La Faute-sur-Mer, around the Anse de l'Aiguillon, to the Pointe St-Clément, a few kilometres north of La Rochelle. About 10 km (6 miles) south-west of St-Denis-du-Payre, stretching south from La Faute-sur-Mer, lies the Pointe d'Arçay, much of which is protected as a *réserve nationale de chasse*. This narrow, tree-covered peninsula features a magnificent beach, which runs for 8 kilometres (5 miles) along its western shore and is a haven for wildlife. Stranded cuttlefish, razor-shells, seaweed and the inevitable plastic bottles mark the tideline. Flocks of sandpipers scuttle busily

about the sand in search of food, while buzzards float lazily above the pine woods.

The Anse de l'Aiguillon forms a large horseshoe between two prominent headlands, the Pointe de l'Aiguillon and the Pointe St-Clément. The sand-bars and silt deposits at the mouths of the rivers Lay and Sèvre-Niortaise are a paradise for aquatic birds of all kinds — and an ideal environment for growing the mussels served in the local restaurants. At low tide the bay is almost empty of water, and its muddy expanse attracts almost every kind of wading bird. Species that winter here in their thousands include knots, dunlins, redshanks, black-tailed godwits and Brent geese; the 5,000 wintering avocets are the second-largest concentration in Europe.

Out at the Pointe St-Clément you can see where mussel cultivation is carried out. Off the headland and far out into the shallows are acres of black stakes (*bouchots*) driven into the mud. These stakes are festooned with ropes, to which the mussels cling.

152

BEFORE YOU GO

Maps: IGN 1:100,000 Nos. 33, 39 and 40; IGN 1:25,000 Nos. 1328 OT & ET, 1329 ET, 1428 OT & ET, 1429 ET, 1528 OT & ET and 1529 OT & ET.
Guide-book: J-L. Eulin and F. Rousseaux, *La Nature dans le Marais Poitevin* (Ouest-France).

GETTING THERE

By car: the *parc interrégional* is roughly bounded on the north by D949/N148 from Les Sables-d'Olonne to Niort; east by N150 from Niort to St-Jean d'Angély; and south by D939 from St-Jean d'Angély via Surgères to La Rochelle. N11 cuts across its centre from La Rochelle to Niort.
By rail: TGV services run to Niort, Surgères and La Rochelle; from La Rochelle trains run to Fontenay-le-Comte and from there to Niort and Mauzé. Car rental is available at Niort, Surgères and La Rochelle stations.
By bus: Eurolines (see p13) runs long-distance buses to La Rochelle. Bus services operated by SNCF or Sovetours connect La Rochelle, Les Sables-d'Olonne, Niort, Luçon, Fontenay-le-Comte and other villages of the Marais Poitevin.

WHERE TO STAY

Most people visiting the Marais Poitevin want to stay in the Venise Verte, but there are not many hotels here; try the Logis de France in Maillezais, rue du Dr-Daroux, T: 02 51 00 74 45, or in Coulon, 48 quai Louis Tardy, T: 05 49 35 90 43, or the Hôtel de l'Union in St-Hilaire-le-Palud, T: 05 49 35 32 25. Surrounding towns (Luçon, Fontenay, Niort, Surgères) offer a wider choice, as do L'Aiguillon-sur-Mer and other seaside resorts. During summer, book in advance; if you arrive without a booking, try La Rochelle.

ACTIVITIES

Walking: a GRP route leads through the middle of the Marais; the long-distance GR36 skirts the eastern edge of the park near Niort and the GR364 crosses the northern boundary near Fontenay-le-Comte. Short-distance paths lead out from most of the villages; La Faute-sur-Mer has a 13-km (8-mile) way-marked forest walk.
Cycling: the long-distance cycle Tour des Deux-Sèvres takes in part of the Marais Poitevin; see IGN map No. 906, *VTT & Randonnées Cyclos*. Local circuits link the villages of Epannes, Fougerit, Les Touches and Vallans; 6 circuits head out from Maillezais. Cycle hire is widely available.
Riding: to explore the Marais on horseback, contact the Relais Equestre Equinoxe at La Grande Moucherie, 79000 St-Liguaire (near Niort), T: 05 49 79 45 67; or the Ecurie du Marais at Pot Grenouillet, 85420 Ste-Christine, T: 02 51 52 98 38.
Watersports: canoes and punts can be hired in many of the villages, including Coulon, La Garetter-Sanais, Le Vanneau and Magné, where there is a Base Nautique, T: 05 49 35 78 14. Pedalos can be rented in Maillezais.
Sightseeing: minibus tours of the Venise Verte are available from Le Grenouillen, pl de l'Eglise, Coulon, T/F: 05 49 35 08 08; for a tour by scenic railway, take *le petit train Pibalou*, 6 rue de l'Eglise, Coulon, T: 05 49 35 02 29. Canal trips are organized from Coulon (the main centre), Damvix, Maillezais, St-Hilaire-le-Palud, Le Vanneau and several other villages.
Museums: at Nieul-sur-l'Autise, the old village watermill has been restored as the centre-piece of the Maison de la Meunerie (Milling Museum),

T: 02 51 52 47 43, F: 02 51 52 43 23. The Maison des Marais Mouillés museum in Coulon, T: 05 49 35 81 04, F: 05 49 35 83 26, shows a film on the history of the marshes and has exhibits on boat-building and fishing, as well as providing general tourist information. The Musée de la Mytiliculture in Esnandes, T/F: 05 46 01 34 64, is worth a visit for its displays on the history of mussel-growing and on the topography and biology of the Anse de l'Aiguillon.

FURTHER INFORMATION

Tourist offices: L'Aiguillon-sur-Mer, av de l'Amiral-Courbet, T: 02 51 56 43 87; Coulon, pl de l'Eglise, T: 05 49 35 99 29; La Faute-sur-Mer, Rond-Point Fleuri, T: 02 51 56 45 19; Fontenay-le-Comte, quai Poey-d'Avant, T: 02 51 69 44 99; La Rochelle, pl de la Petite Sirène, T: 05 46 41 14 68.
Park office: Maison des Marais Mouillés, 79510 Coulon, T: 05 49 35 86 77.

The rare lizard orchid (left) and more common bee orchid (right) are both found amongst the sand dunes of the Atlantic coast.

Forêt de Mervent-Vouvant

Small hilltop forest north of Fontenay-le-Comte

The Forêt de Mervent-Vouvant crowns one of a string of forested hills (*massifs forestiers*) that surround the Marais Poitevin. This crescent of forest, on a granite plateau, is hardly more than 16 km (10 miles) across, yet in its limited area you will find deep tree-covered ravines, a reservoir and wide clearings that in spring are full of spiky pink asphodel and yellow-flowered broom. Its trees include beech, oak, hornbeam and chestnut. In summer the ground below the trees is rich in edible fungi, much prized by local gourmets.

The reservoir was created in the 1950s when a dam (the Barrage de Mervent) was built across the River Vendée to provide fresh water for the nearby town of Fontenay-le-Comte. The reservoir and the streams that drain into it are full of carp, pike, eel and bream, while frogs (including the edible variety) and toads breed in the shallows. Birds include kingfishers, black kites, two rare varieties of magpies and the even rarer short-toed eagle which feeds on snakes and lizards. Among the mammals are badgers, roe deer and pine martens and a few wild boar are said to lurk in the depths of the forest.
Before you go *Maps:* IGN 1:100,000 No. 33; IGN 1:25,000 Nos. 1427 ET and 1527 OT. **Getting there** *By car:*

from Nantes, take N137 as far as Ste-Hermine, then turn left on N148 to Fontenay-le-Comte. The forest begins 6 km (4 miles) north of Fontenay, on D938. *By rail:* Fontenay has services from La Rochelle and Niort. *By bus:* local services run from Fontenay to the small town of Mervent in the middle of the forest, and Vouvant at its northern end. **Where to stay:** Ermitage de Pierre-Brune, Mervent, T: 02 51 00 25 53; Auberge de Maître Pannetier, Vouvant, T: 02 51 00 80 12.
Activities *Riding:* horseback excursions available from Sarl l'Etrier Fontenaisien, 4 rue Ernest Cousseau, Fontenay-le-Comte, T: 02 51 51 11 34. *Sightseeing:* the forest has its own little religious sanctuary in a cave, known as the Grotte du Père de Montfort, off D99A, set in the hillside above a small lake. **Further information** *Tourist offices:* Fontenay-le-Comte, quai Poey d'Avant, T: 02 51 69 44 99; Vouvant, pl du Bail, T: 02 51 00 86 80.

Forêt de Chizé

Magnificent oak and beech woodland lying to the south-east of the Marais Poitevin
10,000 ha (25,000 acres)

The Forêt de Chizé is a remnant of the vast Forêt d'Argenson that once covered the whole region. It is dotted with small villages and delightful open glades. Most of it is protected from hunting as a *réserve nationale de chasse*.

The forest marks the transition between northern and Mediterranean tree types, with beech growing alongside Montpellier maple. Among its arboreal curiosities is an extraordinary oak tree down a track just north of the village of

Chizé. Known as Les Sept Chênes ('seven oaks'), it is not in fact seven separate trees, but a single oak with seven trunks growing from the same base.

The mammals that breed in the forest include roe deer, badger, marten, wild boar and dormouse. But what most people come to Chizé to see is not wild but captive: the *baudet de Poitou* ('Poitou mule'). This animal, much taller and hairier than an ordinary donkey, has a shaggy, dark brown coat and a large and lugubrious head that would make the ideal model for Bottom in Shakespeare's *A Midsummer Night's Dream*. Male *baudets* are crossed with Poitou mares to produce a large and powerful type of mule, which has been used on farms in Poitou since the Middle Ages. The mules lost their practical purpose with the advent of mechanized farming in the 1950s, but they and their offspring have been preserved and can still be seen frisking about a large meadow at the peaceful farm of La Tillauderie near Dampierre-sur-Boutonne. They are amazingly friendly — as soon as you walk into the field they nuzzle you and follow you around. The boy who looks after the farm told me, 'they don't want sugar, they just want to be stroked'.
Before you go *Maps:* IGN 1:100,000 No. 40; IGN 1:25,000 Nos. 1529 ET and 1629 OT. **Getting there** *By car:* from Niort, head south along N150 for 17 km (10 miles) to Beauvoir-sur-Niort, then turn east into the forest along D1. The Paris-Bordeaux A10 skirts the forest's western edge. *By rail:* Niort is on the Poitiers-La Rochelle line. *By bus:* local buses run from Niort to Virollet, Chizé and the other main forest villages. **Where to stay:** Hôtel Terminus, Niort, T: 05 49 24 00 38; Auberge des Cèdres, Villiers-en-Bois,

The wooded slopes and deep ravines of the Forêt de Mervent-Vouvant harbour an outstanding range of animals and plants.

Beauvoir-sur-Niort, T: 05 49 09 60 53. *Outdoor living:* Camping Municipal de Noron, T/F: 05 49 79 05 06. **Activities** *Riding:* several way-marked tracks through the forest. *Field studies:* the Maison du Baudet de Poitou (see below) is run by the Parc Interrégional du Marais Poitevin. It is open all year, 9 am-7 pm, and has exhibitions on breeding and commercial uses of the mule. **Further information** *Park office:* Maison du Baudet de Poitou, La Tillauderie, 17470 Dampierre-sur-Boutonne, T/F: 05 46 24 07 72.

Etang de Cousseau

Secluded woods and lake between the larger lakes of Hourtin and Lacanau;
réserve naturelle
600 ha (1,480 acres)

The Etang de Cousseau is a small link in the chain of lakes that runs down the length of the Aquitaine coast between the sea and the forest of Les Landes, a few kilometres inland. The *étang* is the central feature of one of the most peaceful and remote nature reserves on the Atlantic coast. The protected area includes three principal habitats: the mixed oak woods on the former dunes to the west; the open waters of the shallow *étang*, and, most importantly, the extensive reed beds of the Marais de Talaris, which supports a strong colony of the great fen sedge and some giant specimens of the imposing royal fern.

The reserve can be reached from the coast along a forest path, which is easy to follow as it consists of a narrow strip of concrete laid for cyclists. The

path runs first beneath tall pine trees, some of which are scarred with the long gashes cut in their bark by resin collectors. Beyond the trees it crosses a clear-felled expanse, where plants that have colonized the ground in succession to the pines include seedling oaks, heather, gorse, rock-rose and scabious.

The reserve lies about half an hour's walk down the path. Once you are inside, the ground cover consists mainly of dead leaves and sand beneath an arching canopy of holly, pine and evergreen oak. The path drops down to a clearing beside the *étang* where you can look across the water to the reeds and sedges of the Marais de Talaris on the other side.

A large part of the *étang* in

summer becomes speckled with the white and yellow flowers of water-lilies, while beneath the surface grow a couple of species of the delicate and now quite rare bladderwort. Several pond terrapins and also a few otters live among this verdant growth, dining sumptuously on some of the uncommon fish which inhabit the lake. Around 70 bird species nest here, among them birds of prey such as short-toed eagle and honey buzzard, and many woodland species including wren, nightingale and crested tit. **Before you go** *Maps:* IGN 1:100,000 No. 46; IGN 1:25,000 Nos. 1336 ET and 1434 OT. **Getting there** *By car:* from Bordeaux follow N215/D6 via Ste-Hélène and Lacanau to Lacanau-Océan. In

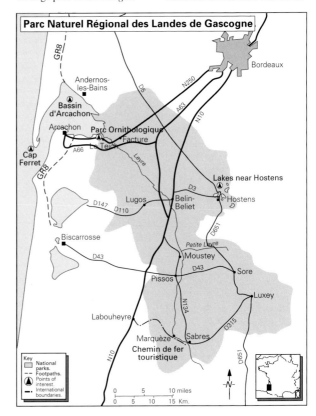

Parc Naturel Régional des Landes de Gascogne

the hamlet of Le Huga, 1 km (½ mile) east of Lacanau-Océan, take D6E1, which runs north to D207. *By rail:* the nearest station is at Bordeaux, with frequent main-line services and TGV connections to Paris-Montparnasse. *By bus:* buses connecting in Bordeaux with the airport (see p145) and the train station run to Lacanau and Lacanau-Océan. *By bicycle/on foot:* the path to Cousseau, giving pedestrian or bicycle access only, begins at Marmande on the D6E1, where there is a small car park. The path is well marked and has

information posts documenting the life of the forest and the *étang.* **Where to stay:** Etoile d'Argent, Lacanau-Océan, T: 05 56 03 21 07; Hôtel de l'Océan, Carcans-Maubisson, T: 05 56 03 31 13. *Outdoor living:* there are numerous camp-sites on the coast and around the Etang de Lacanau. **Access:** bicycles must be left in bicycle parks at Règue-Verte or Dune de l'Esperon and are not permitted in the *réserve naturelle.* **Activities** *Walking:* the GR8 long-distance footpath from Arcachon to near Bayonne runs through

Carcans-Plage and Lacanau-Océan, passing the *étang.* *Cycling:* the Lacanau-Océan tourist office (see below) will supply a map showing the footpaths and cycle-tracks in and around the Lac de Lacanau. *Nature walks:* guided walks to the Cousseau reserve run mid-June to mid-Sept; out of season, walks can be arranged for groups through SEPANSO, 1 rue de Tauzia, 33800 Bordeaux, T: 05 56 91 33 65. **Further information** *Tourist office:* Lacanau-Océan, 438 pl de l'Europe, T: 05 56 03 21 01, www.lacanau.com.

Landes de Gascogne

Vast pine forest south-west of Bordeaux; parc naturel régional
206,000 ha (500,000 acres)

Although this huge park is almost exactly the same size as the Marais Poitevin, it would be hard to imagine two equally grand areas with greater differences. While the Marais Poitevin is infinitely varied, the Landes de Gascogne park is virtually homogeneous. Apart from a short stretch of coast on the Bassin d'Arcachon, it consists exclusively of pine forest, broken here and there by large clearings where crops such as asparagus are grown. Villages are often as much as 16 kilometres (ten miles) apart, where three or four is the average in France. Save for a small man-made lake at Hostens, the Gascogne forest does not include any of the wide stretches of water that break the monotony of the rest of Les Landes.

For centuries this was a region of large-scale sheep-farming. The local shepherds, known as *échassiers*, used to follow their flocks over the flat, shrub-covered grazing lands on stilts, in order to keep their animals within view. This traditional way of life changed in the 19th century. Maritime pines were planted to drain the marshy land and to fulfil a demand for turpentine and rosin, products made from their resin. Rosin in its

pure form is used by violinists to give the correct friction to their bows; it can also be used in varnish, lipstick, plastics and washing powder. However, by the 1950s the resin industry had virtually disappeared. White spirit took over from turpentine as a thinner for paint, and rosin is now mainly imported from China and Portugal. You will still see trees here and there with resin oozing slowly from gashes in their bark. Though few are nowadays tapped commercially, the pines are still being exploited for their timber.

Through the centre of the park runs the River Leyre, whose two branches — the Grande and Petite Leyre — meet at the village of Moustey. Fringed by alders, oaks and chestnuts, it was formerly the region's main transport artery, though nowadays it is

The Aleppo and stone pines (left and right) are the principal pine species of the region, each creating its own distinct vegetation community.

The white stork is one of the most conspicuous birds of Le Teich reserve, known for its habit of building large nests on man-made structures.

used only by canoeists and fishermen. Most of the villages are built along its banks, and appear like oases in the hot monotony of the countryside. The largest is the double village of Belin-Béliet, where the park authorities have their headquarters in the old town hall opposite the southernmost church.

The variety of habitat in the Gascogne is as limited as you would expect from hundreds of square kilometres of conifers planted on soil that is little more than sand. There is virtually no undergrowth to provide food and shelter for mammals and birds. But despite this apparent inhospitality and the unnatural origins of the forest, nature has managed to reassert itself. At the edges, where sunlight penetrates to the ground, the natural flora has been able to develop, much to the benefit of the huge range of insects for which this area is noted. The variety of dragonflies is particularly dazzling and enlivens all the ditches and watercourses. There are even a good number of wild creatures such as boar, hare, fox and introduced deer somewhere out there in the vastness of the forest.

The park has one centre of outstanding wildlife interest, the large bird reserve of Le Teich on the southern shore of the Bassin d'Arcachon. Protected on all sides, with a single narrow entrance guarded by the arm of Cap Ferret, the tidal mud-flats attract some 280 bird species each year; about 200 are migratory, while 80 nest and breed here.

Set up in 1972, the reserve covers 120 hectares (300 acres) and is laid out to cater for different degrees of bird-watching enthusiasm. Nearest the entrance are enclosures for exotic species such as emus and golden pheasants, together with a 'hospital' aviary where birds of prey, wounded by hunters outside the reserve, are nursed before being returned to the wild. Just beyond, nesting platforms at tree-top level have been set up for families of storks: visitors can watch the adults flapping down to land on their untidy heaps of twigs while their young throw their heads backwards and clatter their bills in anticipation of food. Beyond the storks, the reserve extends out into the bay. You can enter it on a broad causeway, protected on either side by hedges. Spaced along it are hides, from which you can look across a narrow stretch of water to a massive heronry, and see herons and egrets probing the shallows for food.

The dense canopy of the forest of Les Landes prohibits luxuriant undergrowth, but numerous insects thrive in the flora of the forest margins.

BEFORE YOU GO
Maps: IGN 1:100,000 Nos. 46, 55 and 62.

GETTING THERE
By car: the park has many access points. From Bordeaux, you can reach its headquarters at Belin-Béliet on either A63 or N10; the N10 gives a far better view of the Landes countryside. For Le Teich bird reserve, take N250 from Bordeaux to Facture, from where D650 leads to the *parc ornithologique*.
By rail: TGV services run to Bordeaux and Arcachon from Paris-Montparnasse. There is a ruler-straight branch line from Facture down to Dax, passing the western side of the park, with stations at Morcenx and Mont-de-Marsan. The SNCF station at Le Teich, 1 km ($\frac{1}{2}$ mile) from the *parc ornithologique*, on the Bordeaux-Arcachon line, has frequent services. From Sabres, a tourist steam train runs the 4 km ($2\frac{1}{2}$ miles) to the museums at Quartier Marquèze (see below).
By bus: there are infrequent bus services throughout the park, but the places to see do not necessarily have connections and are so scattered that bus travel between them is not a practical proposition.

WHERE TO STAY
Auberge des Pins, Sabres, T: 05 58 07 50 47; La Bonne Auberge, Lugos, T: 05 57 71 95 28. Further afield, there are hotels of every grade in the resorts around the Bassin d'Arcachon and down the coast at Biscarosse.
Outdoor living: at Le Teich, Camping Ker Helen, T: 05 56 66 03 79.

ACTIVITIES
Walking: there are trails to suit every walker. A coastal path follows the banks of the Bassin d'Arcachon through the Delta

de la Leyre; you can pick it up at Le Teich or Audenge. An Itinéraire Départemental route crosses the Val de l'Eyre from east to west over 150 km (95 miles) of marked paths, giving access to numerous local circular walks based around villages. The walking and hiking leaflet-guides *Val de l'Eyre*, *Lande Girondine* and *Chemins du Parc* are available from tourist and park offices (see below).
Cycling: tourist offices supply a leaflet (*Landes Itinéraires Cyclo*) with 25 recommended itineraries covering the whole of the Landes, including a 329-km (205-mile) circular tour of the park. Belin-Béliet, Saugnac, Mios, Hostens and Sabres are just some of the villages where cycle hire is available.
Riding: there are 8 equestrian centres scattered through the park; you can find their addresses in a *Guide Pratique*, available from park headquarters. Alternatively, contact the CDTE for Landes, Chambre d'Agriculture, 40005 Mont-de-Marsan, T: 05 58 85 44 43; or for Gironde, Maison des Sports de la Gironde, 153 rue David Johnston, 33000 Bordeaux, T: 05 56 00 99 28.
Watersports: Le Teich, Mios, Belin-Béliet, Saugnac, Moustey and Pissos all offer canoe hire and guides; for sea-kayaking, contact the Maison de la Nature du Bassin d'Arcachon in Le Teich, T: 05 56 22 80 93. The Graoux activity centre, T: 05 57 71 99 29, offers outdoor pursuits including canoeing on the Leyre.
Museums: the Ecomusée de la Grande Lande encompasses 3 museums based around Sabres. The best of these is the Marquèze museum, a faithful reconstruction of a traditional 19th-century rural Landes settlement; access is via a tourist steam train from Sabres, open Mar-Nov.

Ecology: Le Teich bird reserve is signposted by the church and is open all year 10 am-6 pm (except July-Aug, 10 am-10 pm); guided tours for groups can be arranged in advance. No dogs or bicycles are permitted within the reserve.

FURTHER INFORMATION
Tourist offices: CDT des Landes, 4 av Aristide Briand, 40012 Mont-de-Marsan, T: 05 58 06 89 89, F: 05 58 06 90 90; Relais Nature du Delta de la Leyre, Pont de Lamothe, Le Teich, T: 05 56 22 61 53 (open daily mid-June to mid-Sept, rest of year open Wed-Fri).
Park offices: headquarters at 22 av d'Aliénor, 33830 Belin-Béliet, T: 05 58 07 52 70, F: 05 58 07 56 85, www.parc-landes-de-gascogne.fr; Maison de la Nature du Bassin Arcachon, 33470 Le Teich, T: 05 56 22 80 93, F: 05 56 22 69 43.

Courant d'Huchet

An 8-km (5-mile) waterway between Lac de Léon and the sea; réserve naturelle

Twice a day from Easter to the end of September a flotilla of small rowing boats sets out across the wide Etang de Léon for a trip down one of the natural wonders of the Atlantic coast. As they glide down the Courant d'Huchet — not a river but a channel for overflow water from the lake — they pass through several different types of environment, marked by striking changes in terrain and vegetation.

The Courant begins its seaward journey at a stretch of reed-covered marshland, fringed by willows and alders, on the southern side of the lake. Known as the Cout de Mountagne, it covers about 140 ha (350 acres). Until the 1960s the marsh vegetation was grazed down by the cattle which browsed around its edges, but since their disappearance the reeds have grown unchecked, though areas have been cleared to provide open water for ducks, moorhens, herons and other water-birds.

Beyond the marsh, the Courant runs under an arcade of willows and alders, past giant fronds of royal ferns, lady ferns and a host of exotic plants such as the Brazilian water-milfoil and the rosy hibiscus. Strangest of all are the bulbous pneumatophores (aerial roots) of the rough-barked Arizona cypress trees growing in the shallows.

Downstream, near the little seaside resort of Huchet-Plage, the tree canopy opens out round a small lake, the Marais de la Pipe, where young eels that have swum thousands of miles across the Atlantic from the Sargasso Sea feed on the rich growth of plankton.

Both otter and genet occur here, but do not receive any formal protection which, on top of their natural shyness, means they are only rarely sighted. Herons and bitterns can be found in the marshy areas; but much the most likely sighting will be the vivid flash of azure blue as a kingfisher darts along the river.

From the Marais de la Pipe the Courant meanders south, separated from the Atlantic by a wide sand-bar, and reaches the sea near Moliets-Plage. The dunes at Moliets were stabilized as long ago as 1832 by dumping clay on the shifting sand, which was then planted with marram grass. **Before you go** *Maps:* IGN 1:100,000 No. 62; IGN 1:25,000 No. 1341 ET. **Getting there** *By car:* take N10 to Castets, then D142 to Léon,

A New World exotic, the swamp cypress has now adapted to wet woodland habitats in Europe.

following signposts to Lac de Léon. *By rail:* the nearest main-line station is at Dax, 30 km (18 miles) away. *By bus:* an infrequent service operates to Léon from Soustons. **Where to stay:** Côte d'Argent, Vieux-Boucau, T: 05 58 48 13 17; Hôtel du Centre, Léon, T: 05 58 48 74 09. *Outdoor living:* Lou Puntaou camp-site is beside the lake, T: 05 58 48 74 30; Les Cigales at Moliets-Plage, T: 05 58 48 51 18. **Access:** to protect the fragile ground cover of the dunes at Moliets, access is restricted. **Activities** *Boating:* boat trips down the Courant start from the beach. **Further information** *Tourist offices:* Castets, 30 av Jean Noël Serret, T: 05 58 89 44 79; Vieux-Boucau, T: 05 58 48 13 47; *Park office:* contact the Réserve Naturelle du Courant d'Huchet, T: 05 58 48 73 91, for information on guided visits on foot; to book guided boat trips down the *courant*, call T: 05 58 48 75 39 (advance booking is required).

Etang Noir

Tiny lakeside marsh; réserve naturelle

This magical little reserve lies just outside the village of Seignosse and consists of a tract of marshland that seems in parts like a miniature humid jungle or primeval swamp.

More than 430 plant species have been found here, including many rare sorts of mosses, ferns, algae and aquatic microflora, though the reason for the site being classified is its population of 'monster' frogs. These edible amphibians suffer from a genetic mutation, whose effects range from an extra toe to a complete realignment of the skeletal system in both pairs of limbs.

The reserve is called the 'black lagoon' because of the dense layer of sludge which gives the water a menacingly opaque and sombre tint. A raised wooden walkway extends out over the marsh. It leads first to a viewing platform looking across a small lake, then over a tangle of roots, decaying vegetation, yellow irises and reeds, where frogs croak and tadpoles flicker in the stagnant pools.

Before you go *Maps:* IGN 1:100,000 No. 62; 1:25,000 No. 1343 OT. **Getting there** *By car:* leave N10 at St Vincent-de-Tyrosse, 22 km (14 miles) west of Dax, and take D112 to Seignosse. The Etang Noir is just north of the village. *By bus:* buses run from Dax and Bayonne to Hossegor, from where services go to Seignosse. **Where to stay:** Les Hélianthes, 156 av de la Côte d'Argent, Hossegor, T: 05 58 43 52 19; L'Océan, Capbreton, T: 05 58 72 10 22. **Further information** *Tourist offices:* Hossegor, pl des Halles, T: 05 58 41 79 00; Seignosse, av des Lacs, T: 05 58 43 32 15.

The Eastern Mediterranean and Corsica

My first day in Provence was memorable. I arrived at the natural history museum in the quaint old quarter of Aix, expecting to stretch my basic French to the limit in interrogating the country's leading expert on the natural ways of tortoises. He had other plans, however, and no sooner had we said *bonjour* than I was whisked off on a hair-raising car dash to catch a ferry for the island of Porquerolles, just off the coast near Toulon. By mid-afternoon he was trying to teach me the art of lassoing wall lizards by creeping up slowly behind them on all fours and dangling a noose of cotton thread around their necks, so they could be yanked clear from cover. Having laboured a good few hours in the heat to capture some specimens, my colleague measured each one with great precision and then took a photograph of their undersides, explaining that he was studying variations in island populations on the basis of differences in size and belly patterns.

Of course, I had no right to think this bizarre. Why should it be only English naturalists who get involved with minute studies on some rather esoteric subject? It was simply that I had not expected Provence to be such a hotbed of ecological research, and it felt even more out of place as we returned to base past shoals of bronzing tourists, baring as much as they dared, along one of the island's fine sandy beaches.

Rugged massifs and low oak scrub dominate the Provençal landscape above the Gorges du Verdon. This spectacular limestone canyon marks the meeting point of Mediterranean France and the Alps.

I did eventually get taken to see the tortoise area in the Massif des Maures my colleague had promised me. The countryside was incredibly lush and green, and there on a damp, drizzly and very un-Mediterranean Sunday afternoon, I saw my first wild French tortoise, resting motionless underneath a tree heather shrub. At this my colleague felt he had done his job, so he took his leave. I did not feel up to negotiating accommodation in the nearby village so I camped out in an old stone barn on the edge of a vineyard. As darkness fell the sombre forest came to life. The nightingales became more vocal, a background chorus of tree frogs took up their cue and in the dim distance a nightjar commenced its churring call. A bit nearer, another low but penetrating sound became noticeable — a scops owl calling from a telegraph pole along the roadside; I felt a million miles from home.

My purpose in going to the Massif de Maures was to study tortoises as part of a research project for the University of Kent. All this was incomprehensible to the inhabitants of the tiny village I chose as my base; but they were admirable hosts. Although I arrived unannounced the mayor quickly resolved my accommodation problems by offering me the use of the château! It was a large, abandoned house with few amenities, set apart from the village among its own olive groves and flanked by three huge stone pines; a naturalist's paradise.

Early every morning a flock of golden orioles would do a tour of the village and visit my pine trees. I shared the château with swifts, swallows and martins, and in the evenings I often had a Moorish gecko for company; sometimes skulking furtively in some nook or cranny, other times out in the open clinging to the ceiling. I could sit on the balcony and admire a nuthatch

despatching another pine kernel, or across the olive grove I might spy a redbacked shrike, or even a hoopoe.

But I had to track down some more tortoises. After a week of stomping through dense, thorny scrub I had only found a dozen or so animals — hardly the stuff of great research. Once again the locals came to my rescue, and showed up the experts in the process.

An old lady who had spent her whole life working in the fields and orchards around the village advised me to take a walk beyond the back of the village — exactly the opposite direction from that instructed in the scientific literature. Following her advice I climbed through a dense forest of sweet chestnuts, slipping frequently on piles of dead leaves and, as the path became steep and rocky, wondering how on earth tortoises were supposed to cope with such gradients. Eventually the slope levelled off and I emerged from the forest into a small clearing where I stood transfixed. In front of me was a neatly tended olive grove, set out on terraces carved from the forested hillside and retained by dry stone walls. Beyond, the hills stretched for miles, covered with an uninterrupted expanse of dense evergreen forest.

A rustling sound caught my attention. Little more than an arm's length away, yet hidden under tall herbage, two creatures were in earnest pursuit, oblivious to my presence. A sudden, dull and twice-repeated thudding sound followed by a thin, desperate squeaking confirmed it was a pair of tortoises in frantic courtship, well before they emerged into a more open patch of the clearing. The image of a tortoise as a free-living wild animal does not come easily to people used to them simply as sluggish garden pets. But here they were in their natural element, re-enacting a ritual evolved over tens of millions of years, and showing a turn of speed and vitality unimaginable to anyone who has never witnessed them in the wild.

A second rustling sound, much closer this time, distracted me. Another tortoise had been basking beside me, immobile and unseen, its ochre and black patterned shell camouflaging it against the dry leaves on which it rested. Now it had had enough and it scurried, again with startling rapidity, into thick cover under a bramble shrub. I turned back to watch the first two but there was no trace of them. 'They can't have just vanished,' I told myself.

A slight movement glimpsed in the corner of my eye made me look up. At the same instant a large Montpellier snake, all of two metres (6½ feet) long and thick as an arm, froze rigid and fixed me with a penetrating gaze. It was half-way down the terrace wall, a couple of metres in front of me. The head was arched up slightly, pointing in my direction, the heavy ridges of its brow emphasizing its menacing expression. Remaining motionless, I studied its minutest details, but it was those challenging yellow eyes that focused my attention: the stare of a truly wild animal alert to all dangers. Strange as it may seem, I was the threat, not the snake, a

The liquid call of bee-eaters, high in the Provençal sky, is one of the memorable sounds of summer.

resident of this ancient world into which I had stepped uninvited.

Reptiles are not the only exciting creatures of the Mediterranean forest, but for me they represent that special element of primitive wildness which gives this area such a feeling of being untamed and remote despite being so close to civilization. The last wild lands of Mediterranean France, with their mantle of thorny *maquis* and evergreen forest, their wealth of flowers, large insects in all shapes and colours, birds and reptiles, are an essential part of Europe's natural heritage: to enter these forests is to open a living history book of one of the continent's oldest landscapes.

GETTING THERE

By air: the region's main airports are Nice-Côte d'Azur, T: 04 93 21 30 30, and Marseille-Provence, T: 04 42 14 14 14. Corsica receives daily internal flights from Paris and international flights from major European cities (see p188). The French airports web-site is www.aeroport.fr.

By sea: SNCM (see p188) runs ferries to Corsica from Marseille, Nice and Toulon.

By car: the A8 *autoroute*, La Provençale, and N7 running parallel, cross the Riviera from

Aix-en-Provence to the Italian border at Menton. A52 branches off at Aix for Toulon. A50 runs along the coast from Marseille to Toulon, as does D559, which then continues as N98 through all the coastal resorts to the Italian border. This is a very scenic drive but extremely busy June-Sept. On Corsica, there are 2 main north-south roads: the east coast N198 is flatter and easier than the central route (N197/193 and N196), which offers highly dramatic views but is often steep and tortuous.

By rail: TGV services run from Paris-Gare de Lyon to stations on the Riviera coast including Marseille, Toulon, Hyères, Cannes and Nice; services to Fréjus-St-Raphaël go via Les Arcs Draguignan. Motorail services, where passengers travel with their cars, run from Calais to Nice; AutoTrain services, where cars and passengers travel on separate trains, run from Paris to Marseille, Toulon, Fréjus-St-Raphaël and Nice. All major towns are well served by coastal train services. On Corsica, 2

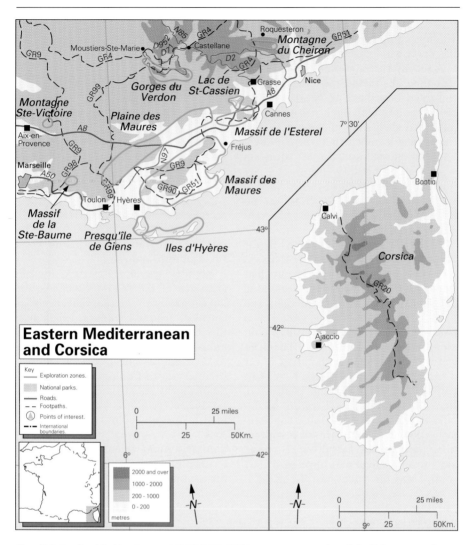

Eastern Mediterranean and Corsica

Key
Exploration zones.
National parks.
Roads.
Footpaths.
Points of interest.
International boundaries.

0   25 miles
0   25   50Km.

2000 and over
1000 - 2000
200 - 1000
0 - 200
metres

-N-   -N-

0   25 miles
0   9°   25   50Km.

lines link Bastia with Ajaccio and Calvi. Contact SNCF (see p13).

By bus: Eurolines (see p13) runs international services to Nice, Marseille, Aix-en-Provence, Toulon, Fréjus and Cannes. Busabout, www.busabout.com, also has a service to Nice. Timetables of local services are available from the main bus station in Nice, T: 04 93 85 03 90, or, in Corsica, from local tourist offices.

WHERE TO STAY
The French Riviera has no shortage of hotels, inns, hostels, *gîtes ruraux*, apartments and camp-sites, although they will be more pricey than elsewhere in France. Reservations are essential in the peak summer season. For brochures of places to stay, contact local tourist offices or national agencies (see USEFUL ADDRESSES, p215).

Outdoor living: many towns have a municipal camp-site,

though facilities may not be as good as at privately owned ones. During July-Aug it is advisable to reserve in advance.

ACTIVITIES
Walking: the hills behind the coast are spectacular, if strenuous. They are best tackled in the cooler months or in the early morning or evening during summer. Long-distance footpaths include the GR51, roughly following the coast

between Toulon and the border with Italy; the GR9, GR90, GR98 and GR99 cover the coastal area between Marseille and St-Tropez. See IGN map No. 903, *Grande Randonnée*. A large number of footpaths and excellent hiking trails have been developed in Corsica, most of them taking in the regional park. The Maison d'Informations Randonnées du Parc Naturel Régional de la Corse (see p189) provides free brochures with marked trails.

Cycling: bicycles are available at railway stations, camp-sites and private hire shops, though most routes are hilly and the roads by the coast are often crowded. For long-distance routes, including A Travers le Var and Route de la Lavande, see IGN map No. 906, *VTT & Randonnées Cyclos*. The Fédération Française de Cyclotourisme (see USEFUL ADDRESSES, p215) publishes *La France à Vélo* series, which

includes *Provence-Côte d'Azur* and *Corse*.

Riding: there are many opportunities for horse-riding in the wildest parts of Provence, such as the Parc du Verdon or the Massif de l'Esterel. Contact the Association Régionale du Tourisme Equestre Provence-Côte d'Azur, Mas de la Jumenterie, 318 rte de St-Cézaire, 06460 St-Vallier-de-Thiey, T: 04 93 42 62 98.

Watersports: sailing and wind-surfing are popular on the Mediterranean and the lakes, and wind-surf boards are easily obtainable at beaches all along the coast. Yachts and motor-boats can be rented, with or without crew, at harbours including Cannes, Nice and Toulon; on Corsica at Ajaccio, Calvi and Bonifacio. Corsica also has numerous diving clubs.

Adventure holidays: the Côte d'Azur and Corsica have several UCPA centres, offering a range of activities from diving

and sea-kayaking to canyoning and horse-riding. Loisirs Accueil Bouches-du-Rhône office, Domaine du Vergon, 13370 Mallemort, T: 04 90 59 49 39, will book activity holidays.

FURTHER INFORMATION
Tourist offices: Comité Régional du Tourisme Riviera-Côte d'Azur, 55 promenade des Anglais, BP 1602, 06011 Nice, T: 04 93 37 78 78, F: 04 93 86 01 06, www.crt-riviera.fr.
   CRT Provence-Alpes-Côte d'Azur, Espace Colbert, 14 rue Ste-Barbe, 13231 Marseille, T: 04 91 39 38 00, F: 04 91 56 66 61, www.cr-paca.fr.
   Fédération Régionale des Offices de Tourisme et Syndicats d'Initiative, 1 pl Foch, 20181 Ajaccio, T: 04 95 51 53 03, F: 04 95 51 53 01.

A dense layer of bracken carpets the cork-oak forest on the slopes of the Massif des Maures.

Massif des Maures & Plaine des Maures

Imposing headlands and rugged open land on the coast between Toulon and Fréjus
ZICO

I have always been captivated by the nocturnal cacophony of wildlife in the Maures. The night air hums with the incessant chirping of grasshoppers, tree frogs and crickets, the most notable being the famous *cigale* (cicada), a large beast reaching a good 7½ centimetres (three inches) in length and capable of a strong and sustained rasping noise as it calls from a perch high up a maritime pine. Away from the disturbance of mankind, you feel alone with mother nature and her unseen orchestra: a mere spectator before some great natural stage.

The Massif des Maures is the most impressive example of wilderness in Mediter-

Hermann's tortoise, the most famous reptile of the Massif des Maures, can measure up to 20 cm (8 in) and rarely weighs more than one kilo (2½ lb).

ranean France. Although not attaining great altitudes (La Sauvette at 779 metres/2,555 feet marks the highest point), it presents itself as a formidable dark wall from whichever direction you approach it. On the seaward side the massif provides a steep backdrop to some of the most attractive Riviera towns: for most people, their closest encounter with the Maures is the high, red cliff-face known as the Rocher de Roquebrune, which overlooks the Fréjus Plain. But if you venture further into the interior, you would think yourself many miles from civilization among some of the country's most rugged hills and dense evergreen forest and *maquis*.

The mountains owe their name to this dark mantle of evergreen forest; Maures is derived from an old Provençal word meaning 'the dark massif'. The landscape bursts into flower for a few weeks in spring, first with the delicate blossoms of the tree heather, which are soon followed by masses of white, yellow and blue from rock-roses, broom and lavender. But by midsummer the rolling expanse of *maquis* can seem empty in the debilitating daytime heat, save for the constant buzz of grasshoppers and crickets.

The Maures and its sister massif, the Esterel, are composed of siliceous rocks, and as such they possess a very distinctive vegetation which offers a complete contrast to the limestone flora of the massifs to the west. The most characteristic feature of these mountains is the cork-oak forest, which covers the lower slopes, mostly below 300 metres (1,000 feet). The forest provides shade from the intense summer sun, and here, too, much of the area's wildlife makes its home. The canopy is not dense and plenty of light reaches the ground, allowing a thick layer of shrub to grow. This provides ideal cover and food for Hermann's tortoise, here surviving in its last stronghold in France. The patient observer may be rewarded by hearing a slow, deliberate rustling of the dry leaf litter, indicating one of these ancient creatures is on the move.

Sound is very important for identifying life in the forest, since the dappled light and dense vegetation makes it hard to spot the animal residents. While the tortoise is measured in its movements, a sudden, short burst of leaves rustling probably betrays a wall lizard, or if it sounds heavier, a green lizard. Snakes are different again, making a more constant, crashing noise in the leaves. Then there is a whole range of bird calls to learn, such as the harsh grating call of the various warblers. The forest is also home to crested tits, short-toed treecreepers and the ubiquitous nightingale; there are even a few goshawks and sparrowhawks.

Some of the most rewarding places to go bird-watching are the low slopes, where the cork-oak forests merge with great stands of ancient sweet chestnuts, and small vegetable plots and olive groves have been maintained in woodland clearings. Serins, cirl buntings and golden orioles are constantly calling from their tree-top perches and the forests contain green, great and lesser-spotted woodpeckers as well as nuthatches and jays. The old olive groves and grassy clearings are rich in butterfly and plant life. For those short on stamina, the chestnuts offer even cooler shade than the cork oaks, though their dense foliage blocks out more light, which means that the undergrowth is less well developed. Still this is one of the best places to look for the delicate flowers of the Provence orchid (*Orchis provincialis*), and wall lizards thrive here.

Exploring the Massif des Maures is not difficult. Innumerable narrow tracks head off into the bush. Many are made by hunters and are therefore only ever used during the autumn and winter. Others are made by the hunters' usual quarry, the wild boar. These are truly wild creatures and extremely wary of approaching danger. Boars are mostly nocturnal, but some days you strike lucky, as I did once when I was heading briskly along a track and stumbled across a mother and her two young foraging in a clearing. I stopped, hardly daring to breathe, and watched the family group carry on their routine without the slightest concern. They may not have been the most attractive looking beasts, but somehow seeing them in the wild made the encounter thrilling.

Between the Massif des Maures and the foothills of the high Var lies the Plaine des Maures. This sedimentary plain is the largest remaining single area of prime lowland *maquis* and open cork-oak and pine forest in France. Impressions of its wild, colourful scenery remain in the mind long after a visit: the short *garrigue* dotted with the curiously gnarled outlines of burnt, but living, cork oaks, and the deep red siliceous rocks formed into sweeping pavements and bold outcrops. Across this arid undulating

---

VILLAGE DES TORTUES

The 'Tortoise Village', near Gonfaron in the Var, is the only one of its kind in the world. Its role is to breed and rear Hermann's tortoises for release back into the wild as part of a project to restore the natural populations of tortoise in the Massif des Maures. Visitors will find a nursery for hatchlings and juveniles, a clinic for sick and injured tortoises, breeding enclosures, a diorama featuring the natural life cycle of tortoises, and a lecture theatre where videos and slides are shown regularly. There is also accommodation for researchers and students.

CHAPTER 8

FOREST FIRES

Forest fires are an ever-present danger in the Mediterranean countryside, especially during the hot summer months. The worst blazes occur when the strong Mistral winds fan the flames and push the fire forward at frightening speed. Some fierce fires have devastated thousands of acres in the space of a few days, and the scars endure for many years; one such fire occurred in 1990. At this time of year many of the remote forest tracks are marked *Route Barrée* ('no thoroughfare'). For your own safety, as well as for the sake of the forest, do not use these routes.

landscape flow several sparkling streams with luxuriant fringes.

The eastern plain is dominated by a majestic forest of stone pines, while on the western side Aleppo pines preside over a dense undergrowth of *maquis*. The central area is covered with open cork-oak forest and mixed *maquis* and *garrigue*: it boasts an array of vibrant bird species, including the gaudy bee-eater, golden oriole, hoopoe and roller, plus woodchat shrike, woodlark, nightjar, ortolan and melodious warbler.

Dirt tracks lead into the wilds of the plain, to spots where the rock lies near the surface and the vegetation is no more than a short turf. These places are swathed with orchids, particularly the delicate green-winged orchids and mixed patches of two or more species of Seraphias orchids. Butterflies abound, as do dragonflies and damselflies, and the air is full of the sound of crickets and cicadas. But the most striking insect is the ascalaphid, which resembles a large lacewing with black and yellow patterning on its wings and long black antennae.

The plain is also important for wild tortoises, and there are terrapins in the streams. Ocellated lizards and ladder snakes are among the spectacular reptiles. At night the herpetofauna really comes into its own. An incessant chorus is struck up by the stripeless tree frog, joined by the equally vocal marsh frog calling beside ponds and the lake of Escarcets.

The wild flowers of the *maquis* provide a riot of colour against the dark forest backdrop of the Massif des Maures.

BEFORE YOU GO
Maps: IGN 1:100,000 No. 68; IGN 1:25,000 Nos. 3445 OT, 3446, 3544 and 3545 OT.

GETTING THERE
By car: leave the A8 at Le Cannet-des-Maures exit between Brignoles and Fréjus; from here, D588 to Grimaud leads across the massif.
By rail: local services run to Hyères and St-Raphaël from Toulon and Marseille; trains from Paris-Gare de Lyon go direct to Hyères and, via Les Arcs Draguignan, St-Raphaël.
By bus: Sodetrav, T: 04 94 12 55 12, operates buses between Toulon and St-Raphaël, calling at other towns along the coast.

WHERE TO STAY
The coastal resorts have a large choice of hotels but are very busy: reservations are advised June-Sept. There is less pressure on accommodation inland.

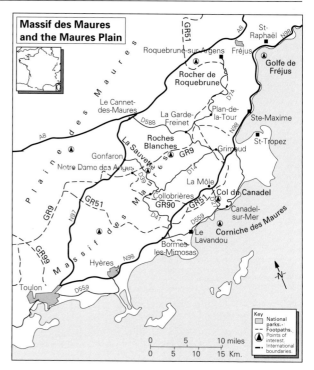

Massif des Maures and the Maures Plain

Key
- ▢ National parks.
- -- Footpaths.
- ▲ Points of interest.
- -·- International boundaries.

0   5   10 miles
0   5   10   15 Km.

ACTIVITIES
Walking: you get spectacular views from the footpaths across the massif, and there are plenty of old villages to explore such as Grimaud and Collobrières. The wooded slopes around the Rocher de Roquebrune, and the valleys of the rivers Argens and Aille to the west, are among the best spots for searching out wildlife. GR9 and GR51 cross the massif from east to west and GR90 north to south.
Cycling: there are numerous marked trails on the massif.
Riding: the Relais Equestre de la Ferme in Hyères, T: 04 94 66 41 78, offers day excursions on horseback into the massif.

FURTHER INFORMATION
Tourist offices: Fréjus/St-Raphaël, rue Waldeck-Rousseau, T: 04 94 19 52 52, www.st-raphael.com; Le Lavandou, quai Gabriel-Péri, T: 04 94 71 00 61; Hyères-les-Palmiers, Rotonde Jean-Salusse, T: 04 94 65 18 55, F: 04 94 35 85 05, www.ville-hyeres.

Presqu'île de Giens & Iles d'Hyères

Sunny peninsula and secluded islands in waters off Toulon; includes Parc National de Port-Cros
ZICO

One warm spring day not so long ago, I went on a bird-watching trip to the Salins des Pesquiers, a series of salt-pans and *étangs*, backed by palm trees, on the Presqu'île de Giens.

The *étangs* are up to a metre (40 inches) deep. A submerged plant, *Ruppia maritima*, covers their base and harbours vast numbers of fish, particularly eels and mullet, making them an ideal location for observing all manner of waders and wildfowl. Cooled by a gentle breeze, I stood and looked out over one of the *étangs*, where a small flock of flamingoes was resting. Avocets and black-winged stilts were out there too, and over-head I was buzzed by a couple of agitated little terns. The birds are attracted by the climate which is reputedly the warmest in France: in winter the temperatures are normally a few degrees warmer here than elsewhere on the coast. In fact, whenever there is a cold snap at the Camargue, thousands of birds move to Giens for refuge.

The Presqu'île de Giens projects into the Mediterranean south of the ancient town of Myère near Toulon. Giens is basically an island connected to the mainland by two parallel sandy spits, created by a combination of changing sea levels, currents and alluvial deposition from two rivers, the Gapeau and Roubeau. The spits are separated by a marshy depression, where the *étangs* and salt-pans are found.

The geological quirks of Giens have created a variety of habitats. At the landward end of the peninsula, around Toulon-Hyères airport, are several freshwater marshes which host a good population of amphibians, including the western spadefoot toad. In winter there are also several secluded pools with different depths of water, providing a range of conditions suitable for egrets and herons, not to mention terrapins. In summer they are mostly dried out and covered with the typical salt-marsh plant, glasswort.

At the extreme tip of the peninsula, on what used to be the Ile de Gien, are some low sea cliffs topped by a forest of Aleppo pines, which at night resounds with the plaintive call of the scops owl, distinctly audible above the background noise of croaking marsh and tree frogs. The cliffs are the best vantage point for observing sea-birds: both the Mediterranean Manx shearwater and Cory's shearwater are found here, as are blue rock thrush and pallid swift. You might also catch sight of the occasional whale or school of dolphins out at sea.

Just off the coast are the Iles d'Hyères. Although belonging to the same small archipelago, the three main islands are remarkably different in character. The largest, Porquerolles, is the most varied, with a patchwork of cultivated fields in the lower-lying areas, surrounded by a dense forest of Aleppo pines and a *maquis* vegetation on the higher and rockier parts. To the east, the smallest of the three islands, Port-Cros (which is a *parc national*), is cloaked in an

The haunting call of the diminutive scops owl may be heard over long distances on still nights.

evergreen forest of holm oak and Aleppo pine. The easternmost island, Levant, is almost entirely covered with *maquis*, interrupted only by a few fire breaks.

It is a particular treat to find all three species of gecko present on the islands. The Moorish and Turkish geckos are the commonest and inhabit buildings. The much rarer leaf-toed gecko, which is found only on Port-Cros and its small outlier La Gabinière, sticks to natural habitats, principally crevices in juniper bark. The islands are also notable for their bird life. In spring they are about as good a place as any in southern France to find the elusive great-spotted cuckoo, and breeding birds include the peregrine falcon and all three species of swift.

173

BEFORE YOU GO
Maps: IGN 1:100,000 No. 68; IGN 1:25,000 No. 3446.

GETTING THERE
By air: internal flights can be taken to Toulon-Hyères airport, T: 04 94 00 83 83.
By sea: ferries go to the islands of Porquerolles, Port-Cros and Le Levant from La Tour-Fondue, at the end of the Presqu'île de Giens. Boats also run from Le Lavandou all year round to Port-Cros and Le Levant, and in July-Aug to Porquerolles. Services run from Cavalaire, Toulon, Bormes and La Londe to Porquerolles only in July-Aug. Contact Compagnie des Iles d'Or, T: 04 94 71 01 02, or Compagnie TLV, T: 04 94 57 44 07.
By car: from Marseille, take A50 to Toulon and then either D559 through Carqueiranne or N98 to Hyères, turning on to D97 to travel along the narrow Giens peninsula.
By rail: the nearest station is Hyères, with regular trains from Toulon and Marseille and TGV services from Paris.
By bus: Sodetrav, T: 04 94 12 55 12, has regular services linking Hyères with Toulon and St-Raphaël; Tropezavia operates a shuttle bus linking Toulon-Hyères airport with Hyères, Toulon and St-Tropez.

WHERE TO STAY
The best choice of hotels is in Hyères, where 2-star choices include Du Parc, 7 blvd Pasteur, T: 04 94 65 06 65, and Mozart, 26 av Denis, T: 04 94 65 09 45. Porquerolles also offers a choice of hotels, but accommodation on Le Levant and Port-Cros is limited.
Outdoor living: camp-sites abound in the area, particularly along the east side of the Presqu'île de Giens: it is best to book ahead in summer. A 3-star site is La Presqu'île de Giens, 153 rte de la Madrague, T: 04 94 58 22 86, open Apr-Sept. There are 2 sites on Le Levant, including La Pinède, T: 04 94 05 90 47.

ACTIVITIES
Walking: 3 walks are recommended by the Port-Cros park authority: a gentle walk from the port to the Plage du Sud (30 mins); the Circuit des Crêtes et Vallon de la Solitude (3 hrs); and the Circuit de Port-Man (4 hrs).
Field studies: there is an underwater route at the Plage de la Palud on Port-Cros; for guided tours, ring T: 04 94 01 40 72. For a discovery boat with a glass bottom, call T: 04 94 05 92 22. On Porquerolles, the Centre IGESA, T: 04 94 12 31 80, runs nature courses.

FURTHER INFORMATION
Tourist offices: Toulon, pl Raimu, T: 04 94 18 53 00, www.toulon.com; Hyères, Rotonde Jean-Salusse, T: 04 94 65 18 55; Carqueiranne, pl de la Libération, T: 04 94 58 72 06.
The Porquerolles office is at the port, T: 04 94 58 33 76.
Park office: (Port-Cros) 50 rue Ste-Claire, 83418 Hyères, T: 04 94 12 82 30, F: 04 94 12 82 31.

Massif de l'Esterel & Lac de St-Cassien

Coastal massif overlooking Cannes and extending to the nature reserve of the Lac de St-Cassien

Driving into the Massif de l'Esterel, I was, as ever, struck by the austere beauty of the red porphyry rock formations and the clear profile of the landscape as I looked back across the Golfe de Napoule to Cannes. All was space and tranquillity. A lone raven circling overhead, and later a peregrine flying along a valley ridge, added a certain wild grandeur to the scene.

The massif was originally covered by pine, oak and eucalyptus trees but a series of fires in 1985 and 1986 devastated the area, leaving a charred ruin of what had been a magnificent landscape. Today, though, the massif is coming back to life.

I found a rough forest track, the Piste de Belvédères, and followed it through some typical *maquis* of tree heather, spiny broom and strawberry tree, with small clusters of cork oaks and a typical assortment of aromatic herbs such as rock-rose and lavender. Nightingales and Sardinian warblers called from the undergrowth and a Montpellier snake cruised across the path in front of me. Cleopatra and false ilex hairstreak butterflies were on the wing, as were a couple of the gaudy two-tailed pasha.

If the dry heat of the Esterel becomes too much for you, there is always Lac de St-Cassien for respite. Located just north of the

After a series of devastating fires, the Massif de L'Esterel is recapturing its rugged beauty.

Esterel, this man-made lake is six kilometres (3½ miles) end to end, and provides nearly 30 kilometres (20 miles) of shoreline.

The north-western arm of the lake falls within the Réserve Biologique de Fondurane. This area covers 43 hectares (100 acres) of the lake, including the largest reed-bed in the Var *département*, where 170 species of birds have been recorded.

Nowadays, nature trails wind around the lake edge and bird hides overlook the reeds, but when I was last there bird-watching was still hard work: it was a case of fighting through a dense fringe of the very attractive but fiercely spiny Christ's thorn (*Paliurus spina-christi*), only to land knee-deep in a marshy field. It was worth it though. All around there were frequent bursts of song from both Cetti's warblers and nightingales. Frogs croaked and turtle doves cooed. A kingfisher streaked past in a flash of azure blue and a little grebe uttered its laughing call from deep inside the reed-bed. The damp meadow was full of butterflies: southern white admiral, marbled white, great-banded grayling and some large fritillary species fluttered around me.

I retreated from the scene and carried on round to the opposite side of the lake where a dense forest of white oak, maritime pine, tree heather and rock-rose grows right down to the shore. A track follows the entire western side of the lake — passing through the forest — until you are brought back to reality in the heart of yet another tourist complex at the southern end of the lake.

BEFORE YOU GO
Maps: IGN 1:100,000 No. 68; IGN 1:25,000 Nos. 3543 ET and 3544 ET.

GETTING THERE
By car: leave the A8 at Fréjus, Les Adrets-de-l'Esterel or Mandelieu to join N7, which crosses the Massif de l'Esterel. For the Lac de St-Cassien leave A8 on D37 at Les Adrets. The N98 coast road skirts the massif on the south, passing through several small resorts west of Cannes.
By rail: the nearest station is St-Raphaël, which has regular services from Paris-Gare de Lyon (connections at Les Arcs Draguignan) and direct AutoTrain services from Paris-Bercy. Direct trains also run from Nice and Marseille.
By bus: take local services from Fréjus and Cannes.

WHERE TO STAY
One of France's most famous seaside resorts, Cannes has everything from top-class hotels to small *pensions*, although, as with most other resorts, it can get very busy in summer. St-Raphaël is another good coastal choice. In Valescure, near St-Raphaël, try La Cheneraie, 167 av des Gondins, T: 04 94 95 03 83, F: 04 94 19 49 23. Les Adrets has a choice of hotels.
Outdoor living: among the area's numerous camp-sites, you may want to try Les

REPTILES OF MEDITERRANEAN FRANCE

Perhaps the most striking aspect of Mediterranean wildlife is the abundance and variety of reptiles. Lizards are most abundant in Corsica, where the walker scarcely dares to tread for fear of stepping on one of the local species, the Tyrrhenian wall lizard, *Podarcis tiliguerta*.

Green lizards are very common on the mainland in rough scrubby areas, field margins and along forest edges. The most spectacular and rarest lizard, though, is the large ocellated lizard, which can reach over half a metre (20 in) in length.

Even more exclusive to the Mediterranean region are three species of gecko: the Moorish gecko is most abundant, the Turkish gecko less common and the most restricted and special of all is the European leaf-toed gecko, which is found only on the Iles d'Hyères, a few smaller islets off the French coast and Corsica.

Snakes are a common sight, although the average visitor is more likely to encounter them as road victims than alive. The most commonly seen species is the impressive Montpellier snake, whose adults often attain sizes in excess of 1½ m (5 ft). Other common reptiles are the natracine snakes — the grass (*Natrix natrix*) and the viperine (*Natrix maura*) — which commonly occur along streams and beside other bodies of water. A walk into the *maquis* is a must if you want any chance of seeing the southern smooth snake or the ladder snake, while the dense oak forests are home to the Aesculapian snake.

Undoubtedly the most famous of all the region's reptiles is Hermann's tortoise, which is restricted to the Massif des Maures and its environs.

Philippons in Les Adrets, T: 04 94 40 90 67, which has 150 places.

ACTIVITIES
Walking: the ONF provides guided tours of the massif, with 85 km (53 miles) of pathways and 15 circuits to explore. For bookings, or to obtain a map and guide to the massif, contact the St-Raphaël tourist office (see below). The GR49 and GR51 long-distance footpaths also cross the massif.
Cycling: there are more than 42 km (26 miles) of tarmac roads within the massif and cyclists also have access to numerous mountain-biking trails. Cycles can be hired from Mountain Bike, Ferme de Grenouillet, T: 04 94 82 81 89; Maison Cap Esterel, T: 04 94 82 50 00; and Lucky Bikes, rue Waldeck Rousseau, St-Raphaël, T: 04 94 95 86 35. The route A Travers le Var runs through the massif and can be picked up at St-Raphaël. The tourist office in St-Raphaël sells a guide detailing other mountain-biking routes.
Riding: 1-hr, 2-hr and half-day organized treks are available over 50 km (31 miles) of bridle paths within the Esterel massif. Contact Les Trois Fers, T: 04 94 82 75 28; Ecoloisirs Développement, T: 04 94 40 58 06; or Ranch de l'Esterel, T: 04 94 82 80 41.
Ecology: Ecoloisirs Développement (see above) operates tours to see the flora, fauna and geology of the mountains; English- and German-speaking guides are available.

FURTHER INFORMATION
Tourist offices: the Cannes tourist office is at the railway station, T: 04 93 99 19 77, F: 04 92 99 84 23; Fréjus/St-Raphaël, rue Waldeck-Rousseau, T: 04 94 19 52 52, F: 04 94 83 85 40, www.st-raphael.com.

Gorges du Verdon

A spectacular canyon, 100 km (60 miles) north-west of Cannes; part of Parc Naturel Régional du Verdon

Describing the wonders of the Gorges du Verdon in 1928, the French explorer E. A. Martel wrote: 'You have to visit the Canyon at least twenty times before you can dare say that you have seen it. It is a marvel without equal in Europe, the largest, the wildest and the most varied of all the great faults in the Old World.'

The gorge is composed of Jurassic and Cretaceous limestone, dating back 100 to 200 million years. As the sheer sides of the narrow gorge are 600 m (2,000 ft) high, there are times of the year when the sun does not penetrate directly to the valley floor. The rugged topography, with its dramatic range of heights and exposure, provides a wide array of microclimatic conditions which support a corresponding profusion of plant types.

The gorge is very much a frontier site, marking the point where Mediterranean France meets the foothills of the Alps. As a result, there are all sorts of odd combinations of semi-montane, temperate and Mediterranean vegetation. The hillsides around the top of the gorge are dominated by box, a shrub associated with temperate Europe, which grows alongside prickly juniper, a typically Mediterranean species. The heat-loving evergreen oak is found on the upper south-facing slopes, while beech trees profit from more humid conditions nearer the valley bottom: normally, it would be the oak at lower levels. And, given the isolating

Wallcreepers with their brilliant crimson wings are secretive birds of high mountain cliffs.

effects of such extreme relief, there are several very rare and in some cases endemic plants, such as the fern, *Asplenium jahandiezi*, and a species of sandwort, *Moehringia dosyphylla*.

Bird life is an equally varied mix. Species include golden eagle, buzzard, peregrine, black woodpecker, rock thrush, wallcreeper and citril finch. The wood warbler also flourishes, well removed from its more temperate habitat in the beech forests of western France.
Before you go *Maps:* IGN 1:100,000 No. 68; IGN 1:25,000 Nos. 3342 ET, 3442 OT and 3542 OT. **Getting there** *By car:* leave A8 at Brignoles and head north on D554 to Barjols; then follow signs for Montmeyan and Aups. If you are coming from the east, take

(Overleaf) The Gorges du Verdon has an unusually varied flora.

N85 north from Grasse to Castellane and D21 turn-off for Comps-sur-Artuby. From Moustiers, on D952 north of the Gorges du Verdon, a circuit is possible in either direction. *By rail:* the nearest station is at Les Arcs Draguignan; direct services from Nice, Marseille and Paris-Gare de Lyon. *By bus:* Autocars Sumian, T: 04 42 67 60 34, operates buses between Marseille and Castellane, stopping in Aix-en-Provence, La Palud-sur-Verdon and Moustiers. From Nice, VFD, T: 04 93 85 24 56, operates a service to Grenoble calling at Grasse and Castellane. A shuttle service runs around the gorge July-Aug; call Navettes Autocar, T: 04 92 83 40 27, for details. **Where to stay:** Castellane has a wide range of accommodation, including 2 *auberges*, the Bon Accueil, T/F: 04 92 83 62 01, and the Teillon, T: 04 92 83 60 88. Details of refuges and hostels from the Comité Départemental de Randonnée Pédestre, l'Hélianthe, Toulon, T: 04 94 42 15 01, F: 04 94 41 63 41. *Outdoor living:* several camp-sites in the Castellane area, including the Camp du Verdon, rte des Gorges du Verdon, T: 04 92 83 61 29, with 420 places. **Activities** *Walking:* a 25-km (15-mile) footpath runs along the bottom of the canyon. The GR4 long-distance footpath traverses the Parc Naturel Régional de Verdon and follows the gorge as far as Castellane. *Rafting:* Aqua Viva Est, T/F: 04 92 83 75 74, based in Castellane, offers a range of half-day to week-long rafting and canoeing expeditions in the Gorges du Verdon. **Further information** *Tourist offices:* Castellane, rue Nationale, T: 04 92 83 61 14, www.castellane.org. *Park office:* Mairie, BP 14, 04360 Moustiers-Ste-Marie, T: 04 92 74 63 95, F: 04 92 74 63 94.

The large Montpellier snake is extremely nervous and flees at the first hint of human approach.

Montagne du Cheiron

A curious east-west massif supporting varied flora and fauna; often overlooked by visitors to nearby Nice ZICO

The Montagne du Cheiron, situated between the valleys of the Loup and the Var, and centred on the village of Roquesteron, is relatively unexplored and ideal for anyone who likes to wander off the beaten track. Unlike most of the other massifs around Nice, the Cheiron is orientated east-west, so its slopes are north- and south-facing. The consequent differences in climate create a variety of plant and animal life. The vegetation passes through a series of stages from the low-altitude evergreen-oak forest, up to beech and fir woods with hop hornbeam at higher altitudes (the summit of Cheiron reaches 1,780 m/5,840 ft) and on north-facing slopes. There are also vast areas of open country carpeted with a form of *maquis* consisting of box, lavender and broom, interspersed with dry grasslands full of interesting aromatic herbs and orchids.

Many elements of the Mediterranean reptile fauna occur, such as the Montpellier snake, green and ocellated lizards and southern smooth snake. These are found together with more northern species such as asp viper, and on higher ground live a few colonies of the rare and strictly protected Orsini's viper.

As with the reptiles, there is a *mélange* of northern, montane and Mediterranean bird species. Few areas of a similar size can match the Cheiron's motley assortment of birds: chough, black grouse, black woodpecker, Tengmalm's owl, blue rock thrush, black-eared wheatear and up to six warblers of the genus *Sylvia*. Cheiron also forms the hunting zone for a pair of golden eagles.

Before you go *Maps:* IGN 1:100,000 No. 61; IGN 1:25,000 Nos. 3542 OT & ET, 3543 OT & ET, 3642 ET and 3643 ET. **Getting there** *By car:* from Nice, drive north through Vence along the spectacular D2 over the Col de Vence to Coursegoules and Gréolières; the road skirts the Montagne du Cheiron. There are equally scenic routes from Grasse via D3 and D5. From the north, join D2 from N85, the famous Route Napoléon between Digne and Cannes. *By rail:* the nearest main-line station is at Nice. *By bus:* there are local services around Nice run by Sunbus, T: 04 93 16 52 10. **Where to stay:** Nice is one of the country's largest resorts, with everything from top-class hotels to small *pensions*, as well as apartments and villas. Inland are smaller towns and villages with interesting small *auberges*; try the Villiard, T: 04 92 64 17 42, in St-Auban. Details of refuges and hostels from the Comité Départemental de Randonnée Pédestre, l'Hélianthe, Toulon, T: 04 94 42 15 01, F: 04 94 41 63 41. *Outdoor living:* there are numerous coastal camp-sites, fewer inland. St-Antoine is a 2-star site at Coursegoules, T: 04 93 59 12 36. **Activities** *Walking:* the GR4 long-distance footpath, which crosses the Montagne du Cheiron from Grasse to Entrevaux in the Var valley, is accessible Mar-Nov. *Cycling:* the long-distance Tour des Alpes Maritimes and Route de la Lavande cycling itineraries skirt the Montagne du Cheiron. *Riding:* many itineraries are possible in the area. Contact the Comité Départemental d'Equitation de Randonnée des Alpes-Maritimes, T: 04 93 42 62 98, F: 04 93 42 64 73, for further details. **Further information** *Tourist offices:* Nice, 5 promenade des Anglais, T: 04 92 14 48 00, F: 04 92 14 48 03, www.nice-coteazur.org; Vence, pl du Gd-Jardin, T: 04 93 58 06 38, F: 04 93 58 91 81.

Massif de la Ste-Baume & Montagne Ste-Victoire

Rocky escarpments overlooking the approaches to Aix and Marseille
ZICO

Lavender, marjoram and mint are some of the herbs which produce the heady aroma of the *maquis*.

Anyone entering Provence via Aix or Marseille cannot fail to be impressed by the brilliant white limestone massifs of Ste-Baume and Ste-Victoire, which rise above these towns. The two great rocky escarpments form the principal refuges for the larger rare birds of the area, notably Bonelli's eagle, short-toed eagle and eagle owl.

Their southern slopes harbour typical Mediterranean vegetation such as evergreen oak, Aleppo pine and a dense *maquis* of spiny shrubs, lentisk and strawberry tree. The less arid northern slopes are different, combining elements of both Mediterranean and alpine flora.

The forests of the Ste-Baume are more humid than those of Ste-Victoire: they are composed of beech, white oak, lime and maple, and offer a great harmony of colour in autumn. The deciduous white oak creates the impression that you are somewhere further north in a more temperate climate; this feeling is accentuated by the huge sizes of both yew and holly growing in the shadow of the great northern cliff face. The rich humus of the forest floor supports a wide array of herbs, including Solomon's seal and the saprophytic bird's-nest. **Before you go** *Maps:* IGN 1:100,000 No. 67; IGN 1:25,000 Nos. 3243-44, 3245 ET, 3344 OT and 3345 OT. **Getting there** *By car:* Montagne Ste-Victoire is a short drive east

---

BUTTERFLIES OF PROVENCE

The abundance of butterflies along the country lanes and in the *garrigue* and forest clearings is wonderful to see. There are scores of species in the region: in one commune area in the Massif des Maures, over 60 species have been recorded.

The largest and strongest flying butterfly is the two-tailed pasha (*Charaxes jasius*), which has a brightly and intricately patterned underside contrasting with a more uniform dark upperside with orange bands along the tips. Even more complicated is the patterning on the festoon butterflies (*Zerynthia* species), two species of which appear in early spring on wooded slopes. Two species of swallowtail are also easy to find in a wide range of situations including the rare *Iphiclides podalinius*.

The russet hues of the fertile plain give way to the white escarpments of Montagne Ste-Victoire, home to many of the larger raptors.

from Aix-en-Provence on D10 or D17. For the Massif de la Ste-Baume, take A8 from Aix and then A52, leaving it at Aubagne. From Aubagne, D2 runs across the massif. *By rail:* Aix-en-Provence has frequent services from Marseille. *By bus:* there are local services to Aix from Arles, Avignon, Marseille and Toulon. Call bus information service, T: 04 42 27 17 91. **Where to stay:** Aix is a

charming spa town with a selection of 1- to 4-star hotels. The 3-star Relais Ste-Victoire, T: 04 42 66 94 98, is just outside at Beaurecueil. There is also the Jas de Bouffan *auberge de jeunesse*, 3 av Marcel Pagnol, T: 04 42 20 15 99, situated 2 km to the west of Aix town centre. The 2-star Lou Pebre d'Aï, rte Pic de Bertagne, T: 04 42 04 50 42, lies at the foot of the Massif de la Ste-Baume in Plan d'Aups. *Outdoor living:* Aix has 2 camp-sites, including the Aérotel Camping Chanteclerc, av du Val St-André, T: 04 42 26 12 98. Near the massif is Le

Clos, in Gémenos, T: 04 42 82 06 29. **Activities** *Walking:* there are marked footpaths in both areas. GR9 crosses the Montagne Ste-Victoire; GR98 and GR9 cross the Massif de la Ste-Baume. **Further information** *Tourist offices:* Aix-en-Provence, pl du Général-de-Gaulle, T: 04 42 16 11 61, www.aixenprovencetourism. com; Aubagne, av Antide Boyer, T: 04 42 03 49 98.

The olive, extensively cultivated over the centuries, is considered by many to be the definitive Mediterranean tree.

Corsica

France's 'île de beauté' 160 km (100 miles) offshore; diverse landscape of deserted coastline, soaring granite mountains, flatland marshes and maquis-*covered hills. Ramsar, ZICO, Biosphere Reserve, World Heritage Site*

In the diffuse light of dawn, the island emerged over the horizon and began to take form. As I headed smoothly across the sea, I felt as though I was being drawn towards it by magnetic force. Corsica held me under its spell for the duration of my stay.

For such a small island, measuring a mere 75 kilometres (45 miles) at its widest by 180 kilometres (110 miles) long, Corsica is an amazing kaleidoscope of landscapes and images. It has twenty peaks higher than 2,000 metres (6,600 feet), 900 kilometres (560 miles) of tortuous rocky coastline and miles of sandy beaches marking the edge of the long ribbon of the eastern plain. This coastal strip merges into the forests and *maquis* cloaking the roughly angled hills and precipitous valleys of the island's interior, reaching up to the bare rocks and alpine grasslands of the great mountains with their permanently snow-capped summits.

Formerly, Corsica and Sardinia, its closest neighbour, were thought to be the remaining fragments of a sunken continent, Tyrrhenia. Now it is believed more likely that the Corso-Sardinian land mass broke away from France at the beginning of the Tertiary period and rotated south-east to its present location.

Corsica's long isolation from the continental land mass is reflected in its unique flora. It supports some 2,000 species of plants, of which 8 per cent are endemic to the island. In the higher Alpine zones nearly half of all the known species are endemic, and of the others, very few can be found on the mainland. Some of these Corsican specialities therefore have a world distribution of only a handful of square kilometres, yet within their restricted niches they are often very abundant. Apart from its own home-grown specialities, Corsica is host to many plants that occur in Spain, or Italy, or even North Africa, but which do not reach mainland France. The island boasts some 1,200 species of lichen, hundreds of species of moss and over a thousand kinds of fungi.

Corsica also has an exceptional variety of fauna, including nearly 130 breeding species of bird. The island has a rich supply of endemics, some being full species, others just special island races of commoner mainland forms. My first exciting discovery happened before I had even stepped off my boat. As we drew into Bastia harbour, I was casually focusing my binoculars on some sea gulls, when I realized that one of the group flying past the harbour wall was an Audouin's gull, one of the rarest gulls in the world, confined to a few Mediterranean islands.

As you might expect from an island with a largely undeveloped coastline, plus numerous surrounding islets, Corsica has its fair share of sea-birds. Most can be found on the island's impressive rocky cliffs, particularly the northern and western sides of Cap Corse in the extreme north, the coastal stretch within the Parc Régional de Corse on the west side between Calvi and Capo Rosso, and the breath-taking limestone cliffs upon which the ancient fortress town of Bonifacio is precariously lodged. The old ramparts, which were not enough to deter marauding Turks in the 16th century, provide a perfect vantage point from which to admire the flying skills of all three species of swift — common, alpine and pallid — as they hawk incessantly at great speed, diving, tumbling and darting after their airborne insect prey.

For sheer variety, though, the most important section of coast is in the Réserve Naturelle de Scandola, north of Porto on the western side of the island. Shags and herring gulls nest on the cliff-faces, also frequented by the wild rock doves that make up the major part of the diet of the now rare peregrine falcon. Scandola is also one of the last Mediterranean stations for the osprey.

In winter, cormorants, gannets and various sea ducks float offshore at either end of the island, and for lucky observers there is always a chance of seeing wallcreepers and alpine accentors along the cliffs, having come down from their summer retreats in the mountains to escape the winter freeze.

In contrast to the vertiginous cliffy coastline of the north and west of Corsica, much of the eastern seaboard is open and sandy, backed in places by large, brackish, reed-fringed *étangs*, such as those at Biguglia near Bastia, and Diane, Urbino and Palo on the Plaine d'Aléria. In winter and during the passage seasons these *étangs* are alive with waterfowl and waders, and in the breeding season you can hope to find red-crested pochard, purple heron, moustached warbler and little ringed plovers. Once, on a glorious mid-June morning, I followed the deserted coast from Etang d'Urbino to Ghisonaccia. In all the hours it took me to progress slowly along the upper beach and through the flanking forest of tall pines, I saw only two people: one a fisherman, the other a wood cutter. My only company along the route consisted of a couple of Dartford warblers in the scrub, a Kentish plover flitting along the beach in short runs, only occasionally taking to the wing if I came too close, and finally a woodlark and a red-backed shrike.

Just behind the beaches grows a littoral *maquis* consisting mostly of the co-dominant junipers, *Juniperus oxycedrus* and *J. phoenicia*, which provide a natural home for the extremely scarce leaf-toed gecko. I did not find any of these particular reptiles but much more abundant and easy to find is the Italian wall lizard which, contrary to what its name suggests, is perfectly at home on the hot dunes. It shows a turn of speed probably greater than any other lizard in the region — the ones I saw certainly left me standing.

For most people the epitome of Corsica is its expanse of *maquis*-covered hills, changing in parts to dense evergreen-oak forest, with cork oaks dominant in areas of siliceous soils. The *maquis* evokes countless stories and legends, and is said to be bandit country. It has also played an important role in the island's rural economy — as an abundant source of firewood, browsing for goats (which has kept the forest in check) and numerous useful fruits and berries. Junipers are used for a potent liqueur, and at Asco it is a tradition for the priest to place a bucket

The Corsican nuthatch is found in the pine forests of the central and western mountains.

made from juniper wood on the head of the bridegroom during the marriage ceremony.

The *maquis* supports numerous small warblers of the *Sylvia* genus; Dartford and Sardinian warblers are the most common, but the most eagerly sought by bird-watching visitors is the Marmora's warbler, which is also quite common and widespread here, although it is hard to catch a good enough glimpse of it to tell it apart form the very similar looking Dartford warbler. I earned numerous scratches on my legs from the less forgiving of the *maquis* shrubs in vain attempts to get a decent view of these small birds as they called from dense thickets.

The *maquis* is also home to Hermann's tortoise, ostensibly the same race as that on the French mainland, but with subtle differences in coloration and shell morphology.

Sadly for the tortoise, and all the other wildlife associated with this classic habitat, forest fires have had devastating effects on vast areas, while the lowland Plaine d'Aléria has been converted to agricultural use. Indeed, Corsica has at times the look of a dying country. The desolate fire-torn landscape of the south-eastern quarter is all the more forlorn for the innumerable wrecked

The famous cliffs of Bonifacio, on Corsica's southern tip, are a favourite haunt of swifts.

cars dumped haphazardly throughout the countryside, while the *étangs* and their maritime fringes on the east coast have come under threat from tourist development. The beauty of still pristine areas, such as near Porto-Vecchio, only serves to emphasize the extent of the loss.

Thankfully, the centre of the island presents a largely unspoiled world of high jagged mountains clothed in pine and fir forests and traversed by great torrents that have carved magnificent deep gorges through the ancient rocks. Much of central Corsica is uninhabited and lies within the large Parc Régional de Corse. The only town of any consequence inside the park is Corte.

While in the interior I was determined to spot the endemic Corsican nuthatch, known to favour the high conifer forests. I began my search in the pine forest of Asco since this also promised one of the most spectacular drives on the island. The approach road winds up through a steep, rugged gorge to the small village of Asco, and then on an-

other 15 kilometres (9 miles) to Haut-Asco, a small ski station set at 1,500 metres (4,900 feet) at the base of some of the island's most formidable peaks, including the 2,710-metre (8,894-foot) Mont Cinto, Corsica's highest point. Up on the peaks above the tree-line lies the mountain domain of alpine choughs and accentors, as well as the very rare lammergeier or bearded vulture.

Walking through the ancient forest was sheer joy. The scent of pine wafting through the crisp mountain air, and the sense of being close to my quarry, the elusive nuthatch, made me extra alert. But I had to be content with coal tits, goldcrest and spotted flycatcher. Lizards turned out to be the real highlights. Every step sent them scurrying, and when I sat down for a few minutes, all around they began to reappear from their hideaways: at any one time there would be at least a dozen of these brightly patterned creatures furtively patrolling the forest floor.

Further downhill I searched again along

The cool mountain forests in north-west Corsica provide a glorious contrast to the lowland plains on the eastern side of the island.

The Corsican hellebore, which grows profusely in scattered clumps, is one of the most striking flowers on the forest floor of the Gorges de Lasco.

bonsai in scale. The dominant herb, with its characteristic robust tufts, was the Corsican hellebore (*Helleborus lividus corsicus*), a primitive-looking plant, known for its poisonous properties. At this point I came across a melanistic whip snake (*Coluber viridflavus*) stretched out across the stony path; it slithered into cover as I approached.

My final attempt to find the nuthatch was in the Forêt de Valdo-Niello, at a spot lying just above 1,000 metres (3,000 feet). The forest looked just perfect with many well-spaced, mature pines covered in craggy bark, a scatter of dead trunks still standing and plenty of young pines and birches coming through. There seemed to be no shortage of bird life. I found serin, chaffinch, coal tit, goldcrest and tree creeper, and in a clearing within a section of fir woodland, a flock of citril finches. But still my quarry eluded me so I retired for lunch by a small rivulet crossing the forest track.

one of the many foaming torrents tumbling down the mountainside. A dipper and grey wagtail, both looking delicate and powerless against the incessant surge of white water, were perfectly at home. The stream drowned out any sounds from the surrounding forest, so I moved away and up through the steep valley sides. Shafts of sunlight poured through the canopy, emphasizing the height of the tall, straight pine trunks, making me feel dwarfed. Even the ground flora seemed

Nature has a habit of springing surprises. You go in search of one creature and likely as not something else equally interesting turns up. This day was one such occasion. I had tossed a peach stone into the stream when I noticed something move in the water. I peered into the pebbly stream-bed to find a small, brown, superbly camouflaged newt-like creature: a Corsican brook salamander, another of the island's elusive endemics.

BEFORE YOU GO
Maps: IGN 1:100,000 Nos. 73 and 74; IGN 1:25,000 Nos. 4149-4154 OT, 4249-4252 OT, 4253 ET & OT, 4254 ET & OT, 4255 OT and 4347-4352 OT.

GETTING THERE
By air: there are airports at Ajaccio, T: 04 95 23 56 56, Bastia, T: 04 95 54 54 54, Calvi, T: 04 95 65 88 88, and Figari, T: 04 95 71 10 10, with direct flights daily from Paris, Nice and Marseille; Air France (see p13) operates flights to Corsica from major European cities.
By sea: SNCM, T: 08 36 64 00 95, www.sncm.fr, has regular services from Marseille, Nice and Toulon to Ajaccio, Bastia,

Calvi, L'Ile-Rousse, Porto-Vecchio and Propriano; journey-time 5-10 hrs. SNCM and Corsica Ferries also run an express service, the NGV, from Nice to Calvi (2½ hrs) and Bastia (3½ hrs).
There are regular car ferries to Bastia, Porto-Vecchio and Calvi from Genoa, Savona and Livorno in Italy: contact Corsica Ferries, T: 04 95 32 95 95, or Corsica Marittima, T: 04 95 54 66 95, in Bastia. Ferries also run between Corsica and Sardinia; call Moby Lines, T: 04 95 73 00 29, or Saremar, T: 04 95 72 00 96.
By car: driving is the best way of making the most of Corsica's scenery and exploring off the

beaten track; car rental is available in all main towns.
By rail: Chemins de Fer de la Corse (CFC), T: 04 95 32 80 57, based in Bastia, operates a scenic route through the mountains between Ajaccio, Corte and Bastia as well as along the coast between L'Ile-Rousse and Calvi. The train times co-ordinate twice daily, meeting at Ponte Leccia.
By bus: most towns are served by at least 1 bus a day, though services tend to be slow. The principal routes across the island are from Ajaccio, Bastia, Calvi, L'Ile-Rousse, Corte, Sartène and Porto-Vecchio. Most of the longer routes are run by Eurocorse, T: 04 95 71

24 64. Contact the bus station in Ajaccio, T: 04 95 51 55 45, for details of other services.

WHERE TO STAY
There is no shortage of hotels, apartments or *gîtes*, but prices tend to be higher than on the mainland. Hotel bookings can be made through the Association des Logis de France offices in Bastia, T: 04 95 54 44 30, and Porto-Vecchio, T: 04 95 70 05 93.
Outdoor living: there are many recognized camp-sites; though tempting, camping elsewhere is prohibited because of the risk of fires.

ACTIVITIES
Walking: a large number of footpaths and walking itineraries have been developed, particularly in the regional park, which is crossed by the GR20 long-distance footpath. The Maison d'Informations Randonnées in Ajaccio (see below) provides information on the park, maps of hiking trails and details of mountain refuges and *gîtes d'étape*. For guided hiking and cycling tours of the interior, try Objectif Nature, 3 rue Notre Dame de Loretta, 20200 Bastia, T: 04 95 32 54 34.
Cycling: bicycle tours, with luggage transported and accommodation arranged, are organized by Vivre la Corse en Vélo, Résidence Napoléon, 23 av Général-Leclerc, 20000 Ajaccio, T: 04 95 21 96 94. The Tour de Corse long-distance route can be picked up in the major coastal towns.
Riding: there are over 100 km (60 miles) of bridle paths. Contact the ARTE for Corsica, 7 rue Colonel-Ferracci, 20250 Corte, T/F: 04 95 46 31 74.
Watersports: sailing and wind-surfing is available at coastal centres, and there are many diving clubs. White-water rafting on the River Tavignano is possible Mar-Oct from

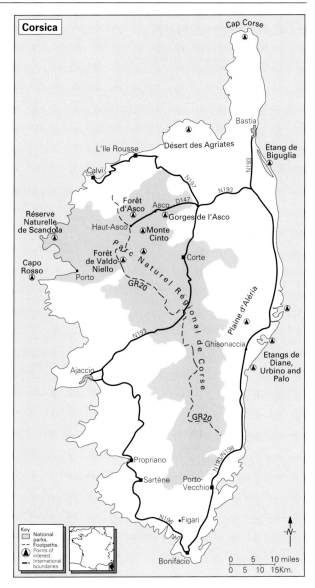

Corte; details from Corsica Adventure, Guincaggio, T: 04 95 48 82 06.

FURTHER INFORMATION
Tourist offices: Ajaccio, 1 pl Foch, BP 21, T: 04 95 51 53 03; Bastia, pl St-Nicolas, T: 04 95 55 96 96; Bonifacio, pl de l'Europe, T: 04 95 73 11 88; Calvi, Port de Plaisance, T: 04 95 65 16 67.
Park office: 2 rue Major Lambroschini, BP 417, 20184 Ajaccio, T: 04 95 61 79 10, F: 04 95 21 88 17.
  ONF Corse, T: 04 95 23 78 20, F: 04 95 20 81 15.

CHAPTER 9

The Western Mediterranean

The warm, tranquil, brilliantly sunlit land that follows the Mediterranean around from the Rhône delta to the Spanish border has long been tamed and civilized. So long, indeed, it is surprising just how much wildness survives at the uncultivable margins of this silent, forceful landscape. A sea of ancient vineyards covers the flatter country, and laps against the edges of unruly limestone hills cloaked with dense, evergreen forest. Overhead a blue silk sky is smoothed by bone-dry northern winds.

For much of the year the climate is extremely dry, with long, hot summers and short winters. The prevailing northerly winds — the famous Mistral and the Tramontane — mostly keep the air fresh and the skies clear. Both summer and autumn bring forceful storms, however, and in late winter, when the moist Marin wind drifts off the Mediterranean, there can be lengthy periods of heavy rain.

Most visitors stay within sight of the coast and its resorts, the majority of which were not here thirty-five years ago. Indeed, much of the Languedoc coast was barely inhabited before its broad beaches and relatively unpolluted Mediterranean waters became a tourist attraction. Despite the massive upsurge in tourism, Languedoc's *étangs*, the shallow saline lagoons strung along the seashore from the Camargue to the Pyrenees, retain a strange, inscrutable and remote character, totally out of keeping with the life of the holiday-makers. Mostly without any bathing

Dawn steals over the reed-beds of the Camargue, Europe's most famous wetland and a great inspiration for modern conservationists.

beach and sometimes hard to approach except on foot because of the enclosing grasses and succulents, these tideless expanses of water do not attract a great many visitors. As a result, they provide a fine breeding environment for numerous species of wildfowl, both resident and migratory, particularly waders. Most striking are the extraordinary pink flamingoes. Great groups of these colourful birds can be spotted standing one-legged in the shallows.

Behind the coast, stretching to the hazy Cévennes, lies the basking Languedoc plain. Though it has seen much turmoil in history, witness to movements of peoples and of armies, it is now utterly tranquil. Remarkably few tourists venture this far inland, except to a handful of interesting old towns and cities such as Arles and Nîmes. Its old villages of picturesque stone houses have been left much as they always have been, and in most of the rural backcountry, life continues unaffected by the summer holiday season.

Languedoc's rustic interior is characterized by an almost total monoculture of vines, although some diversification into fruit orchards or the cultivation of vegetables is now increasingly apparent. The traditional myriad haphazard patterns of fields — some large, some tiny, each striped with neat rows of grapevines — are one of Languedoc's most distinctive and appealing features. Standing on a hillside in the evening, it is wonderful to watch the sinking sun illuminate the pearly heat haze over these countless fields, changing the sky into a gigantic kaleidoscope of colour. For most residents these vines are the very basis of life. All work revolves around the annual cycle of the vineyard and most communities have their *cave coopérative*, where the local wine is made. The harvest, *les vendanges*, is the high

point of the year. All available hands are employed to help bring in the ripe grapes — post offices and shops will close to release staff if necessary — and roads are clogged with tractors hauling overflowing trailers. At this time, the grapevines are a spectacular sight, their green leaves turning an astonishingly brilliant crimson red and vivid yellow.

This traditional picture of Languedoc is changing. With EU incentives, farming has diversified: more and more, among the vineyards you can see fruit orchards, olive groves and fields of vegetables. Eventually such developments may alter the ecological balance; at present the vineyards, being heavily sprayed, are from the wildlife point of view almost like a desert.

In contrast, inland Languedoc's wild *garrigue* is extremely rich in Mediterranean flora and harbours numerous insects, reptiles and small mammals. The densest, wildest *garrigue* flourishes on the rocky slopes that mark the limits of the Languedoc plain and in the hilly, limestone landscapes spanning the northern halves of the Hérault and Gard *départements*.

Throughout Languedoc, whether in *garrigue*, vineyard or village square, insectivores are in their element. High-soaring swifts fill the air with their shrill whistling, while over the fields, swallows — including the rare, red-rumped variety — abound. At night the bats — Savi's and Kuhl's pipistrelles, as well as greater, lesser and Mediterranean horseshoes — dart about feasting on a multitude of flying insects.

One of the most characteristic sounds of the Languedoc countryside in summer is the monotonous stridulating of the cicada, accompanied by the croaking of frogs and the rasp of crickets. The best-known cicada is the large *cigale*, which lives on tree branches. Although the *cigale* manages simply on the sap of its host tree, many of the insects are themselves insectivores. Other notable insect-eaters include the older arthropods from which insects are descended. The scorpion is especially abundant, and often, while returning home along village lanes in late evening from a long day's walking, I have seen them climbing on house walls; during the day they can be seen hiding in the shade beneath flowerpots or tiles.

Although walking in the *garrigue* can be hot work, exploring brings great rewards. The heady scent of the air and the sight and sound of abundant wildlife create a feeling of peaceful isolation from the modern world.

GETTING THERE
By air: you can take international flights to Perpignan-Rivesaltes, T: 04 68 52 60 70, F: 04 68 51 31 03, or Montpellier-Mediterranée, T: 04 67 20 85 00, F: 04 67 22 02 12; more frequent services go to Marseille-Provence, T: 04 42 14 14 14, F: 04 42 14 27 24, which is nearest the Camargue; there are internal flights to Avignon, Béziers and Nîmes. The French airports web-site is www.aeroport.fr.

By car: A9 *autoroute* runs from the Spanish border across the Languedoc plain to the Rhône valley. Another *autoroute*, A61, comes into Languedoc from Bordeaux via Toulouse and Carcassonne. N9 and N113 run parallel to the *autoroutes*. From Lyon A7 runs south to Marseille; it joins the A9 at Orange, giving easy access to Avignon, Nîmes and the Camargue.

By rail: TGV services run from Paris-Gare de Lyon to Avignon, Nîmes, Montpellier, Sète, Béziers, Narbonne and Perpignan. Overnight Motorail trains offer a direct link from Calais to Narbonne or Avignon. The AutoTrain, on which cars and passengers travel separately, links Paris to Avignon and Marseille. For details contact SNCF (see p13).

By bus: Eurolines (see p13) has international services to Béziers, Narbonne, Perpignan, Montpellier, Nîmes, Avignon and Marseille. Busabout, www.busabout.com, runs to Avignon. Tourist offices in the region will provide details of local bus services.

WHEN TO GO
The best time to visit is in late spring and early summer: the summer birds will already have arrived (unlike the hordes of tourists) and the multitudes of flowering plants are mostly in blossom. If *les vendanges* appeal, plan to come in Sept.

WHERE TO STAY
Most larger towns on and around the Languedoc plain are historic and all have a selection of hotels in every price range. Nîmes and Montpellier are recommended, as are the smaller towns of Béziers and Narbonne. The most attractive coastal towns are Sète and Collioure.

ACTIVITIES
Walking: some rewarding long-distance footpaths traverse the *garrigue*-covered slopes rising from the Languedoc plain. GR6 meanders from the Alpilles across the Rhône and along the valley of the Gard north of Nîmes; GR60, GR74 and GR7 cross the hills north and west of Montpellier; GR77 lies inland from Béziers and Narbonne; GR36 explores the Corbières and climbs into the Pyrenees. Contact the Fédération Française de la Randonnée Pédestre, Sentiers et Randonnées, 64 rue de Gergovie, 75014 Paris, T: 01 45 45 31 02. When walking in the *garrigue*, it is advisable to protect head, arms and legs against the ravages of sunshine, plants and insects.

Cycling: there are several long-distance cycle routes, including the circuit De la Camargue à la Crau; see IGN map No. 906, *VTT & Randonnées Cyclos*. The Fédération Française de Cyclotourisme (see USEFUL ADDRESSES, p215) publishes the *France à Vélo* series, which includes *Languedoc-Roussillon*.

Riding: guided tours of the Camargue are offered by numerous stables near Les Stes-Maries-de-la-Mer. For details

The greater horseshoe bat is one of the larger species that thrive in the western Mediterranean.

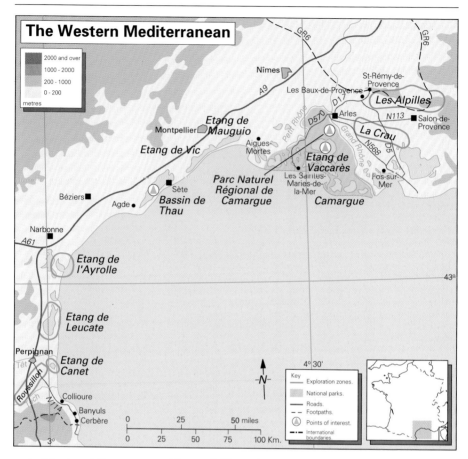

The Western Mediterranean

contact the Association Camarguaise de Tourisme Equestre, Centre d'Information de Ginès, rte d'Arles, Pont de Gau, T: 04 90 97 86 32, F: 04 90 97 70 82. The Association Régionale de Tourisme Equestre Cévennes-Languedoc-Roussillon, 14 rue des Logis, Loupian, 34140 Mèze, T/F: 04 67 43 82 50, will provide details of equestrian centres throughout the region.
Watersports: sailing schools and clubs are found at Les Stes-Maries-de-la-Mer, La Grande-Motte, Sète, Agde, Leucate and Port-Barcarès. Inland, there are similar facilities at Lac du Salagou, 3 km (2 miles) from Clermont-l'Hérault.
194

Adventure holidays: three UCPA centres in the region offer a wide range of outdoor activities; Loisirs Accueil centres provide information and booking services in Gard, 3 pl des Arènes, 30010 Nîmes, T: 04 66 36 96 30, F: 04 66 67 65 25, and in Hérault, Maison du Tourisme, av des Moulins, 34034 Montpellier, T: 04 67 67 71 40, F: 04 67 67 71 34.

FURTHER INFORMATION
Tourist offices: CRT de Languedoc-Roussillon, 20 rue de la République, 34000 Montpellier, T: 04 67 22 81 00, F: 04 67 58 06 10, e-mail: contact.crtlr@cnusc.fr, or www.cr-languedocroussillon.

fr/tourisme/.
  CDT de Bouches-du-Rhône, Le Montesquieu, 13 rue Roux de Brignoles, 13006 Marseille, T: 04 91 13 84 13, F: 04 91 33 01 82.
  Maison de la France, www.maison-de-la-france.fr, has links to all French tourist offices.
  For information on forests, contact the ONF Languedoc-Roussillon, 505 rue de la Croix-Verte, Parc Euromédecine, 34094 Montpellier, T: 04 67 04 66 99, F: 04 67 04 66 88.

Bulls roam through the Languedoc marshlands, grazing on grasses and herbs along the dykes.

La Camargue

Large, flat and marshy delta of the River Rhône; parc naturel régional
Ramsar, ZICO, Biosphere Reserve, World Heritage Site
100,000 ha (250,000 acres)

The Camargue has a romance and a haunting appeal matched by few other areas. A flat, windy, barely inhabited land of tall, swaying grasses, this lonely, bewitching place puzzles, astonishes, excites and even alarms the unaccustomed eye. In all its immense area the highest point is an imperceptible 'peak' just 4.5 metres (15 feet) above sea-level, a vestige of some former dunes.

The Camargue is one of Europe's major wetlands, with extensive areas of marsh and shallow *étangs* providing an unusually salty environment and a haven for wildfowl and sea-birds. The birds come in all shapes and sizes and they attract a similarly diverse bunch of tourists. Hundreds of binocular-toting naturalists and bird-lovers stalk about the edges of the Etang du Vaccarès, a nature reserve within the regional park, while scores of hunters come here as well — for outside the protected reserve hunting is legal and extremely popular. Other tourists take guided tours, riding the native white horses; buses pour into the area on daily excursions; and even larger numbers of people deposit themselves on the beach at the old coastal town of Les Stes-Maries-de-la-Mer.

Many visitors confine their exploration of the Camargue to the main road that plunges southwards across the delta from Arles to Les Stes-Maries. While this myopia prevents them from appreciating most of the area's natural habitats, it also serves as a form of protection for the Camargue's abundant wildlife. For although the Camargue attracts tens of thousands of tourists each year, most of it remains essentially unvisited and unknown. At first sight it reveals nothing of itself: almost everywhere tall, bamboo-like reeds, growing from roadside drainage ditches, act as a curtain drawn across the view. For a while you sense rather than see the wildlife that thrives behind this veil.

To escape the tourists and experience the wildlife properly, it is essential to get away from the Arles-Stes-Maries road by following one of the long, straight back roads and tracks which delve deep into the flat, almost eerie, emptiness of this strange land.

Once you have left the hustle and bustle of the main tourist spots, you will be able to observe the animals more closely. The famous white horses of the Camargue, though nearly all privately owned and branded, are for the most part left to live as wild. Do not, however, imagine proud, snow-white herds galloping exuberantly across the salty plains. The horses are small, docile and cautious, and only acquire their handsome white coat when five to seven years old. Even more wary of humans are the herds of *bouvines*, or native black bulls, which also live wild. Until the 19th century, the pure Camargue species was simply domesticated for farm work or killed for meat, but since then it has been cross-bred with Spanish bulls and periodically rounded up to perform in bullfights; it was Napoleon III's Spanish wife, the Empress Eugénie, who popularized the idea of the fighting bull. The bullfights of Languedoc and the Camargue, known as *courses à la cocarde*, involve trying to pluck coloured ribbons from the animal's horns. The spectacle has perhaps less grandeur than the Spanish *corrida*, but the bull is not killed in the *course*. For Spanish-style bullfights, which are also popular here, larger bulls are imported from Spain.

Such local traditions and customs are part of the Camargue's appeal. The herds, whether they be bulls or horses, are called *manades*, the ranchers are *manadiers* and the men — Camarguais 'cowboys' whose work revolves around herding, branding and keeping an eye on the animals — are known as *gardians*. Traditional *gardian* dwellings, or *cabanes*, dot the landscape: long, low, white-washed houses, with a cross raised at one end of the roof. But perhaps best known of all the Camargue's attractions is its Gypsy population. Swarthy black-haired Gypsies — the women clothed in vivid, multi-

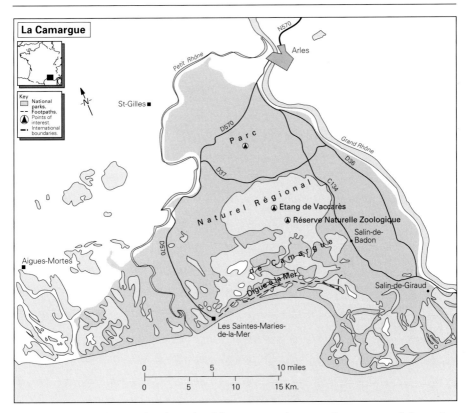

coloured long skirts and adorned with gaudy gilt bangles and bracelets — throng the picturesque, though commercialized lanes of Les Stes-Maries.

In many ways, though, the Camargue is not an ideal place to visit. It is too windy in winter, too shadelessly hot and sunny in summer, when busy with visitors. The worst of its disadvantages, especially in summer, is the incredible abundance of mosquitoes, flies, horseflies and other irritating insects. The only really enjoyable time to visit is spring — from say March to mid-May — when tourists and insects are both relatively scarce, temperatures are pleasant and colourful wild flowers abound in the drying salt-water marshes, wild irises flourishing beside the freshwater marshes and ditches.

In the past, one of the Camargue's most important features was that sea-water extended far inland, mixing with the silt-laden fresh water of the river. Since the late 19th century, however, large tracts of the region have lost their salty character due to the construction of a dyke to keep the sea-water out and the drainage and reclamation of vast spaces for arable farming.

In the northern part of the Camargue, closest to Arles and St-Gilles, completely drained areas support cereal and vegetable crops, while small rice paddies have been constructed within high banks. Farther south, you find wider areas of flat, uncultivated marsh. Some is freshwater marsh, where poppies and other wild flowers flourish in spring, but the most common is *sansouire*, formed by salt-water submersion every winter. During the rest of the year the surface dries out and becomes white with salt, supporting a vegetation adapted to such strongly saline soil and able to withstand the annual flooding. Here bird life is

(Overleaf) The Camargue is famous for its wild horses.

The bulls of the Camargue are fairly small, very robust and capable of living on poor pasture.

profuse: squacco, purple and night heron, marsh harrier, little egret, glossy ibis, coot, bittern, great crested grebe and many other marsh birds are regularly sighted. The night air resounds with the grunting and croaking of frogs and toads.

Another common terrain, the Camargue *pelouses*, are almost-dry expanses of sparse, low vegetation adapted to a salty soil that is not submerged. These areas, dotted with tamarisk and inhabited by wandering bulls and horses, are the haunt of a thrilling variety of birds. In addition to larks and an occasional rare stone curlew, pratincole, bee-eaters and rollers can be sighted. Usually, bee-eater colonies are found in sandy cliff faces, but in the Camargue they are sited on the ground.

Everywhere, between fields, beside roads, the land is criss-crossed by drainage channels, called *ronbines*. Both insects and birds thrive near these ditches, which are several feet wide, sometimes brim-full, extremely soupy and crowded with plant life and fish. Along them grows a kind of tall, bamboo-like reed (*Arundo donan*), used throughout the region for fences and shed roofs. Water

channels too deep for these reeds support masses of pondweed and water milfoil, and the coypu, a remarkably successful foreign immigrant, is well established here. Unfortunately, the native otter, becoming rarer and rarer, struggles to survive.

Central southern Camargue — largely taken up by the huge (6,500-hectare/16,600-acre) Etang de Vaccarès — has been designated as a zoological and botanical reserve. All development is prohibited and access is restricted, but the *étang* can be seen from various points on D37 (on the north shore) and D36C (on the east). Herring gulls and black headed gulls number in their thousands, and far out in the lake are numerous wading birds, including huge crowds of pink flamingo. Herons are plentiful, too — all eight western European species, including the rare spoonbill, nest here — while avocets, with their distinctively curved beaks, may also be sighted. It is best to come early in the morning to avoid the cars and buses which stop and disgorge on the lakeside, leaving their engines running and driving away all signs of the wildlife the tourists have come to see. Around the western and southern edges of the *étang*, footpaths — especially the walkway along the sea dyke — provide much better and quieter access.

BEFORE YOU GO
Maps: IGN 1:100,000 No. 66; IGN 1:25,000 (OT & ET) No. 2944.

GETTING THERE
By air: international airports at Montpellier and Marseille (see p193) give good access.
By car: head straight down the Rhône valley either on N7 (left bank), the busier N86 (right bank) or A7 Autoroute du Soleil. Beyond Avignon, minor roads continue to Arles and the Camargue.
By rail: TGVs run from Paris-Gare de Lyon to Avignon, Nîmes and Montpellier; Motorail services go from Calais to Avignon and Narbonne, AutoTrain from Paris to Marseille. Nîmes can also be reached on Le Cévenol, a train from Paris via the Massif Central — a longer but more scenic ride; change at Nîmes for Arles.
By bus: Les Courriers du Midi, T: 04 67 06 03 73, runs a service from Montpellier to Aigues-Mortes via La Grande-Motte, continuing on to Les Stes-Maries-de-la-Mer in July-Aug. Les Rapides de Camargue, T: 04 66 29 52 57, operates between Nîmes and Les Stes-Maries via St-Gilles June-Sept. Les Cars de Camargue, T: 04 90 96 94 78, runs several services daily from Arles to Nîmes and Marseille. It also has regular services linking Arles with Les Stes-Maries and Port St-Louis.

WHERE TO STAY
In and around Les Stes-Maries-de-la-Mer is a lot of over-priced accommodation, but the town is well situated for an early-morning visit to the *étangs*. A more pleasant base is Arles; try the modest Calendal, 22 pl Pomme, T: 04 90 96 11 89, or St-Trophime, 16 rue de la Calade, T: 04 90 96 88 38. Nîmes is farther afield, but well within reach.

ACTIVITIES
Walking: Arles tourist office has information on marked walks. The 7-km (5-mile) footpath along the Digue à la Mer — the sea dyke from Les Stes-Maries to the Gacholle lighthouse — gives the best views into the *réserve naturelle*. The GR653 long-distance path cuts across the northern part of the Camargue between Montpellier and Arles.
Cycling: the long-distance cycle route De la Camargue à la Crau passes through the park, running between Aigues-Mortes and Martigues before looping back through Arles. Cycle hire is available at Le Vélociste, T: 04 90 97 83 26, or Le Vélo Saintois, T/F: 04 90 97 74 56, both in Les Stes-Maries, av de la République.
Riding: Domaine de Méjanes, T: 04 90 97 10 62/60, and many other Camargue ranches offer riding holidays; enquire at tourist offices or contact the Association Camarguaise de Tourisme Equestre (see p194).
Watersports: a wide range of activities is available at Les Stes-Maries; contact the Ecole de Voile, Capitainerie de Port Gardian, T: 04 90 97 85 87.
Adventure holidays: contact Loisirs Accueil des Bouches-du-Rhône, Domaine du Vergon, 13370 Mallemort, T: 04 90 59 49 39.
Bullfights: gaudy posters in Arles and Les Stes-Maries give information about forthcoming bullfights, which are held

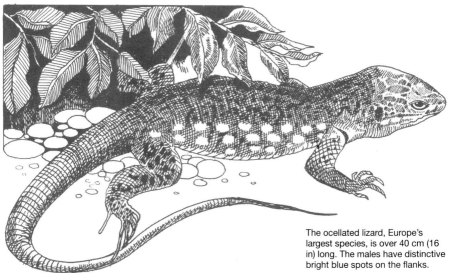

The ocellated lizard, Europe's largest species, is over 40 cm (16 in) long. The males have distinctive bright blue spots on the flanks.

Tall reed grasses are common in the ditches that line the roads and paths of the Camargue.

frequently in summer.

Exhibitions: the information centre of the *réserve naturelle* at La Capelière (see below) has a permanent exhibition illustrating the Camargue season by season; nearby are nature trails and three wildlife observation points.

Ecology: there is a *parc ornithologique* at Pont de Gau, T: 04 90 97 82 62.

FURTHER INFORMATION

Tourist offices: Arles, 35 pl de la République, T: 04 90 18 41 20; Les Stes-Maries-de-la-Mer, 5 av Van Gogh, T: 04 90 97 82 55, www.saintes-maries-camargue.enprovence.com; Aigues-Mortes, porte de la Gardette, T: 04 66 53 73 00; and Nîmes, 6 rue Auguste, T: 04 66 67 29 11.

Park offices: at Mas du Pont de Rousty, on D570, T: 04 90 97 10 82, or at Pont de Gau, Les Stes-Maries, T: 04 90 97 86 32. The Centre d'Information Nature is at La Capelière, by the eastern side of the Etang de Vaccarès, T: 04 90 97 00 97.

202

La Crau

A semi-arid desert of stones north-east of the Camargue; one of Europe's most important breeding sites for rare birds
ZICO

La Crau can hardly be called scenic. Totally flat and waterless, it consists of an immense sea of stones lying on top of a bone-dry silt. Not a single tree relieves the relentless monotony. It is a daunting sight, especially in the burning heat and blinding light of the baking southern sun.

Lying north-east of the Camargue and stretching from Salon-de-Provence almost to Arles, then down to Fos on the coast, this curious terrain is the unique surviving example of a once widespread landscape. In the Middle Ages, far more of southern France looked like this. Even as recently as the 19th century, La Crau was much larger and more arid. In

prehistoric times, the area was the estuary of the rushing Durance, still a turbulent and capricious river. Later the Durance abandoned this part of its course and moved north to join the Rhône, leaving behind an apparently lifeless and uncultivable landscape.

In fact it was neither lifeless nor uncultivable. Over the centuries farmers have managed to clear fields and plant crops. The process still continues today and La Crau is gradually disappearing. Already two-thirds of it is cultivated, and visitors will be astonished by the green meadows, olive groves and fields of cereal which enterprising farmers have planted. In the uncultivated parts, sheep are free to roam, though they find poor pasture.

In these untouched areas, scattered and close-cropped scrubby vegetation emerges from between the sun-baked stones, and there are tough thorny bushes of several types, including wild rose, which lends the odd flash of remarkable beauty. This type of scenery is known locally as *coussous*.

On the ground, living among

this meagre plant life, is a large population of insects, including locusts and curious giant, wingless crickets (*Prionotopis rhodanica*) moving awkwardly among the stones. Lizards thrive on the abundant insects. This is one of the principal French strongholds of the large ocellated lizard. Both insects and lizards make it possible for birds to find enough to eat in an otherwise unpromising habitat. But where on earth, you might wonder, do they nest? Sheep pens and old cairns installed during World War II to prevent Allied gliders from

landing, together with random piles of stones, apparently provide acceptable nesting sites in the absence of anything better. Both Calandra and short-toed larks, together with stone curlew and little bustard, manage to survive here. Black kite are common, too, and there are also a few pairs of red kite. If you are lucky, you may spot a lesser kestrel scanning the ground; the species is not found anywhere else in France. The roller, a beautiful, golden brown bird with a head of almost iridescent turquoise, also comes to La Crau though

The ancient village of Les Baux, carved into the limestone rock of Les Alpilles, stands sentinel over the dry plains of La Crau.

it is merely a day-tripper; it prefers to nest in the poplars at the perimeter, venturing into the desert to pick over the stones for food.

Another wonderful sight, much more frequent, is groups of hoopoe, with lovely crest and black-and-white striped feathers, loping along in their low, undulating flight. And the modest little pintailed sand-grouse chooses this area as its

203

The distinctive hoopoe is common throughout the Mediterranean.

exclusive French nesting site. Spring is the best time to visit, when the sand-grouse and little bustards are displaying.

Before you go *Maps:* IGN 1:100,000 No. 66; IGN 1:25,000 (OT & ET) No. 3043.

Getting there *By car:* N113, from Arles to Salon-de-Provence, passes through the village of St-Martin-de-Crau and skirts northern La Crau. A turning to the south, N568, crosses the southern part. *By rail:* trains run from Marseille-St-Charles to Miramas; from the west, the nearest station is at Arles. **Where to stay:** Arles, about 20 km (12 miles) away, is the obvious base; see the Camargue zone for hotels. There are a few hotels in the village of St-Martin-de-Crau; try Auberge des Epis, T: 04 90 47 31 17. **Activities** *Nature walks:* the Ecomusée de la Crau, near the church at St-Martin-de-Crau, organizes guided tours of the *coussous*.

Further information *Tourist offices:* Arles, 35 pl de la République, T: 04 90 18 41 20; Les Baux-de-Provence, Hôtel de Manville, T: 04 90 54 34 39.

The Société Nationale pour la Protection de la Nature at La Capelière, T: 04 90 97 00 97, has material on the wildlife of La Crau.

204

Les Alpilles

An isolated ridge of craggy limestone crests lying east of the Rhône
ZICO

The Alpilles present an extraordinary, beautiful and sometimes disturbing landscape of white rocks weatherworn to bizarre shapes. Although they cover just a small area, they represent a captivating and enchanted miniature world which feels lost in time and remote from anywhere.

The entire chain is a narrow strip barely 20 km by 4 km (12 by 2½ miles), which emerges abruptly from the flat country in the angle between the rivers Durance and Rhône. It rises in a series of hills to central summits of about 400 m (1,300 ft). In places these hills are barren, in places planted with olive groves, almond, cypress, fruit trees and vineyards, and elsewhere densely cloaked with wild evergreen Mediterranean vegetation. Typical *garrigue* plants abound — especially broom, the kermes oak with its prickly leaves, and the local gorse *ajonc de Provence* with its bright yellow, pea-like flowers — but pines, too, are abundant, and the air is fragrant with the warm tang of their resin.

The secret to visiting Les Alpilles is to travel along the chain (that is, east-west) rather than across (north-south). Drivers and cyclists can discover the area at a sauntering pace on enticing minor roads that thread between fields and forest. My own favourite route is the relatively traffic-free journey along the country lanes from

Maussane to Eygalières.

By far the best way to explore the Alpilles, however, is on foot. Warm, dusty paths criss-cross a peaceful, ever-changing terrain, and the air is alive with the creaky scratchings of insects and the aromatic scent of pine and wild herbs. You may be fortunate enough to catch a glimpse of the raptors which soar above these hills, including Bonelli's eagle and even the spectacular Egyptian vulture. Many interesting smaller birds can be seen too, such as rock sparrow, blue rock-thrush and Alpine swift. At the foot of the hills on the southern side are Camargue-type habitats: here warblers, roller and hoopoe may be glimpsed.

While walking, you are likely to come across the picturesque, characteristically southern villages that nestle in the Alpilles. There are also several Roman and medieval sites worth seeing. Foremost among these is the lofty fortified town of Les Baux-de-Provence, commanding a superb panorama of the rocky landscape. Destroyed in the 17th-century wars of religion, the town was almost deserted until restoration was undertaken in the 20th century. The older, ruined section of town provides excellent vantage points from which to view the landscape.

Before you go *Maps:* IGN 1:100,000 No. 66; IGN 1:25,000 (OT & ET) Nos. 3042 and 3043. **Getting there** *By car:* the Alpilles are almost too easily accessible by car: Les Baux is just a short drive from Arles (20 km/12 miles on D17), Avignon (20 km/12 miles on D571) and Nîmes (40 km/24 miles on D999). From Les Baux D5 skirts the west and D78/D24 skirt the south and east of the Alpilles. The roads to Les Baux, from either side of the hills, are very busy during peak holiday weekends and should be avoided. *By rail:* Arles station is accessible from Montpellier via Tarascon or Avignon, or on a direct line from Marseille; bikes and cars can be rented here. *On foot:* by far the best, if the most strenuous, access is the GR6 footpath, which runs right across the hills. **Where to stay:** hotels in Les Baux, Maussane, Eygalières and St-Rémy-de-Provence are predominantly up-market. Cheaper rooms can

be found in St-Rémy, just north of the hills. Try the Hostellerie Le Chalet Fleuri, T: 04 90 92 03 62, F: 04 90 92 60 28; Arts, T: 04 90 92 08 50, F: 04 90 92 55 09; or Cheval Blanc, T: 04 90 92 09 28, F: 04 90 92 69 05. **Activities** *Walking:* GR6 long-distance path runs through the Alpilles. *Cycling:* the long-distance route De la Camargue à la Crau skirts the Alpilles. *Sightseeing:* the ruins of Glanum, a Celtic, Greek and then Roman town, stands just south of today's St-Rémy. Main

features are the Triumphal Arch of 49 BC, the Mausoleum of about the 3rd century AD. Glanum also has the oldest surviving buildings in France, dating back to the Greek period around the 2nd century BC. Nearby, off D5, is the 12th-century priory of St-Paul-de-Mausole, which housed the mental institution where Van Gogh was a patient. **Further information** *Tourist office:* Les Baux-de-Provence, Hôtel de Manville, T: 04 90 54 34 39, F: 04 90 54 51 15.

Les Etangs du Littoral

A string of large, shallow, saline lagoons lying just behind the coast and separated from the sea by a narrow ribbon of sand
ZICO

The Languedoc coastline extends in a single sandy sweep from the Camargue to the Pyrenees — 200 kilometres (125 miles) of spectacular beach almost unbroken except by the volcanic rocky outcrops at Agde. The sand slopes shallowly into the warm Mediterranean under skies kept clear and blue by the refreshing Tramontane and Mistral offshore winds. Looking inland, almost nothing can be seen except grassy dunes and a vast, open sky.

Over the last four decades, new coastal resort towns have been built alongside the older, and more characterful, harbour towns — the result of an ambitious programme launched by the French government in the 1960s to promote tourism. The success of new towns such as La Grande-Motte and Cap-d'Agde has done much to revitalize the ailing local economy. Despite the upheaval the natural habitat has remained relatively unscathed, saved by the unwillingness of the tourists to stray far from the resorts. For long stretches the beach is almost completely deserted and is wonderfully free of the usual cafés, pedalos and surf-board rentals.

Behind the beach lie the *étangs*, connected to the sea by narrow channels (*graus*). The

étangs vary enormously in character. Some are unsavoury, malodorous, highly saline and coated with algae; others are cleaner and fresher, with attractive shorelines and good access on footpaths or tracks. Rarely more than a metre (three feet) in depth, they are separated from the sea by sand bars (*barres* or *lidos*), which have been created by natural Rhône alluvium and sand deposits. They are not very ancient, having formed mainly since the Roman period.

Between Agde and the intriguing Montagne de la Clape (near Narbonne), few *étangs* exist, as this stretch of coast has been more affected than the rest by the estuaries of three of Languedoc's larger rivers: the Hérault, Orb and Aude. The *étangs* are particularly shallow from Sète to the Rhône; there are also smaller, shallow *étangs* nearer Roussillon. The *bassins* of Thau and Leucate are deeper.

For many centuries the *étangs* made the seashore an insalubrious environment, shunned by man but favoured by myriad insects and birds. Chief among the insects was the mosquito, which multiplied in huge numbers in the stagnant waters. Today, spraying keeps their numbers down, despite concerns about the effect of a shrinking mosquito population on the area's bird life.

These concerns seem to be more theoretical than actual. From spring to autumn the air is filled with numerous small flying beetles, while the water harbours their larvae, together with annelides, leeches, tadpoles, young fish and molluscs, all providing ample

nourishment for an astonishing range of divers, waders and sea-birds. Large numbers of gulls squeal and turn above the water, sharing the plunder of insects and water creatures with moorhens, terns, crakes, bald coots, stilts, avocets and ducks.

Among the most striking of all the lagoon birds are the pink flamingoes and herons. You can get surprisingly good views from roads passing close to the *étangs*, or by approaching on foot over a shoreline thickly banked with saltworts, marsh samphires and small succulents, which form virtual cushions of vegetation.

The Etang de Mauguio, lying north of the busy main road from La Grande-Motte to Carnon, is a particularly good spot to see flamingoes, although it is in every other way among the least pleasant of the *étangs*, being highly saline and very marshy in places. Maybe this is why the birds remain here so tranquilly. A much more agreeable spot is the inland village of Villeneuve-lès-Maguelonne, from where small back roads lead down through the vines to the pretty shores of the Arnel, Moures and Vic *étangs*.

Right behind Villeneuve is the Etang de l'Estagnol, a small, freshwater marsh area designated a nature reserve. Its dense rushes harbour numerous duck and coot nests. The Etang d'Ingril, east of Frontignan, best seen from D60 on the south side, and accessible by paths on the north side, is another marshy area with large populations of most of Languedoc's coastal birds and plants.

Largest and deepest of the *étangs* is the Bassin de Thau, a 65-square-kilometre (26-square-mile) lake between the upland ridges of Sète and Agde. Its waters are relatively clear and clean, with large tracts near Sète devoted to oyster 'farms', where hundreds of wooden poles rise up out of the water. On the southern shore, a road runs along the 20-kilometre (12-mile) strip of sand-bar separating the *étang* from a fine sandy beach. On the eastern shore, vines skirt the water's edge and the inland hills are visible, dark and shimmering in the hazy distance.

The Etang de Vaccarès is the largest expanse of open water in the Camargue, and is noted for its huge numbers of wildfowl.

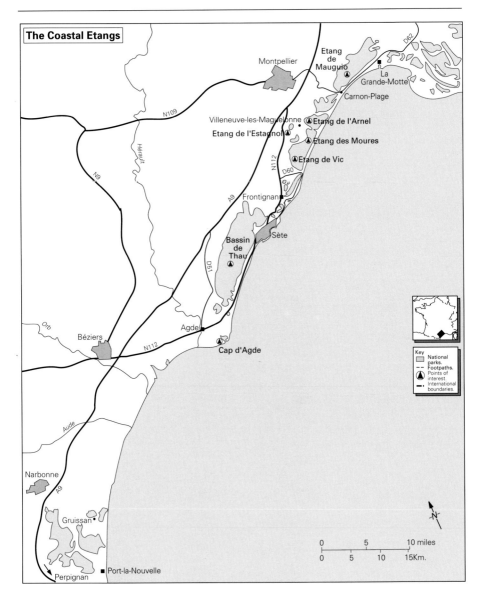

The Coastal Etangs

Montpellier
Etang de Mauguio
La Grande-Motte
Carnon-Plage
N109
Villeneuve-les-Maguelonne · Etang de l'Arnel
Etang de l'Estagnol ▲ ▲ Etang des Moures
▲Etang de Vic
Hérault
N9
N112
D60
A9
Frontignan
D51
Bassin de Thau ▲
Sète
Béziers
N112
Agde
Orb
Cap d'Agde
Aude
Narbonne
A9
Gruissan
Perpignan
Port-la-Nouvelle
D62

Key
National parks.
Footpaths.
▲ Points of interest.
International boundaries.

0   5   10 miles
0   5   10   15Km.

BEFORE YOU GO
Maps: IGN 1:100,000 Nos. 65 and 72; IGN 1:25,000 Nos. 2545 ET, 2546 OT, 2645 ET, 2743 ET and 2843 OT.

GETTING THERE
By air: international and internal flights go to Perpignan

and Montpellier (see p193).
By car: the Languedoc coast and *étangs* are easily reached, although there is no coast road as such. N112, N113, A9 and N9 cross the inland plain parallel to the coast; minor roads lead down to the *étangs*.
By rail: a fast, frequent service

runs parallel to the coast, with principal stations at Perpignan, Narbonne, Béziers, Sète, Montpellier and Nîmes; from Narbonne, services go to Agde.

WHERE TO STAY
Hotels on the coast tend to be expensive, but there are

exceptions as well as hundreds of low-priced camp-sites. Modern La Grande-Motte and Cap d'Agde have plenty of both kinds of accommodation. Sète is an interesting and appealing base; the Grand Hotel, T: 04 67 74 71 77, F: 04 67 74 29 27, has rooms at a wide range of prices.

ACTIVITIES
Cycling: from La Grande-Motte, 4 circuits take in the coastline, the town and the Camargue; leaflet from tourist office (see below).
Watersports: the Centre Nautique Municipal in La Grande-Motte, T: 04 67 56 62 64, F: 04 67 56 92 03, offers wind-surfing and sailing (catamarans are available); Locorama in Cap d'Agde, T: 04 67 26 26 45, F: 04 67 01 21 79, has motor-boats and jet-skis for hire; in Sète, Aqua Sète, T: 04 67 74 23 16, offers diving expeditions and there is a wide choice of sailing schools.
Adventure holidays: the UCPA centre at Montpellier Saint-Clement, T: 04 67 84 86 00, offers activities including horse-riding, mountain-biking and tennis. The new resorts, especially Agde, La Grande-Motte and Port-Barcarès, offer leisure pursuits with tuition, including archery, diving, parascending, riding, sailing, tennis and wind-surfing.

FURTHER INFORMATION
Tourist offices: Agde, espace Molière, 1 pl Molière, T: 04 67 94 29 68, F: 04 67 94 03 50; Aigues-Mortes, porte de la Gardette, T: 04 66 53 73 00, F: 04 66 53 65 94; La Grande-Motte, av Jean Bene, T: 04 67 56 40 50, F: 04 67 56 78 30, www.webmediterranee. fr/grandemotte/; Port-Barcarès, on the seafront, T: 04 68 86 16 56, F: 04 68 86 34 20; Sète, 60 grand rue Marie Roustan, T: 04 67 74 71 71, F: 04 67 46 17 54.

Flamingoes flock to the *étangs*, especially the Etang de Mauguio.

THE PINK FLAMINGO

By far the most evocative image of the *étangs* of the Camargue and the Languedoc coast is the exotic-looking flamingo, which gathers in huge flocks in these shallow waters. The average flamingo population here numbers 12,000 individuals. Day and night, flamingoes feed by trawling the bottom of the *étangs*, with their heads held almost completely upside down in search of vegetation and crustaceans, which they filter out of the silt. The bulk of their diet is made up of small aquatic invertebrates and it is the high level of carotinoids in these tiny creatures which gives the flamingo its distinctive colour.

During March and April, adults court with balletic movement of wings, neck and head. Nesting takes place in large groups, on islands. The nests themselves are raised platforms of mud, generally about 30 centimetres (12 inches) high, with a hollow on top in which a single egg is laid. The same nests endure and are used year after year, the result of constant repairs and rebuilding.

The flamingo is mainly a summer visitor, wintering on the Spanish coast or (more usually) in North Africa. However, an estimated 5,000 birds do not migrate and winter in the Camargue.

Roussillon

Grand, rugged shoreline stretching up into the eastern Pyrenees

As visitors travel south towards Spain through the vineyards and plain of ancient Languedoc, they pass the massive brick defences of the Fort de Salses to enter the land known as Roussillon. Initially the ruddy, sun-bathed coastal lowland seems very like the landscape of Languedoc, though flatter and less fertile. But soon the craggy peaks of the Pyrenees come into view, and the dramatic contrast between the two regions is apparent. High slopes and summits dominate Roussillon's inland horizons while, closer to the coast, green foothills climb into a calmer, wilder, wooded countryside.

Contained entirely within the Pyrénées-Orientales *département* on the Spanish border, the Roussillon region boasts the highest sunshine figures in France. Most of the inhabitants speak Catalan, many as a first language. For Catalans, the name Roussillon applies correctly only to the coastal plain around Perpignan (see Chapter 6, THE PYRENEES). South and west of the city the land rises to magnificent high ranges separated by broad basins and fertile valleys. The valleys of the rivers Têt and Tech, descending to the balmy coastal plain, are intensively cultivated with market gardens and orchards that supply the country with much of its early fresh fruit and winter vegetables. Only close to the coast does the blanket of vineyards reappear.

Stretching along the Spanish frontier, close to the Mediterranean, the Albères hills are perhaps the most pleasing part of French Catalonia, not only visually, but also culturally and gastronomically. The Albères have a cover of *garrigue* and evergreen forest with dense holm oak and abundant rock-rose and

The vineyards of the Roussillon plain provide a rich spectrum of autumnal tints contrasting with the drab backdrop of the *garrigue*-covered foothills.

broom, broken up by steep vineyards yielding fine red Côtes de Roussillon wines.

As you follow the hills inland, the lofty Pic du Canigou (2,784 metres/9,130 feet) comes into sight. Catalans hold this mountain in almost religious regard, and many foreigners have been deeply impressed by it too: Hilaire Belloc described it as 'the mountain which many people who have not heard the name have been looking for all their lives'. Its conical summit stands rocky and spectacular, sometimes shrouded in cloud, soaring far above a tangled landscape of forest and pasture. The view from the top stretches clear across Languedoc and Roussillon to the Cévennes.

The higher reaches of the Roussillon Pyrenees are hot and dry in summer but can be thickly snow-covered in winter. The vegetation on the mountain slopes is completely different according to whether it faces north or south. *A la baga* ('on the shady side'), as the locals say, pine and fir woods are broken by open pasture. *A la soulane* ('on the sunny side'), the woods are predominantly beech. Crisply cool lakes, enclosed by rushes, cotton grass and sedges, abound. Towards higher altitudes there is a chance of seeing —

if you are very lucky — a rare golden eagle soaring, a family of *sanglier*, wild boar, pushing through the undergrowth, a genet after dusk, marmot, small groups of izard (the Pyrenean version of chamois), or a herd of *mouflon* (the wild forerunner of today's sheep) nervously grazing on a distant slope.

Much more striking are Roussillon's sheltered valleys and open meadows. These large tracts are noted for amazingly luxuriant and colourful arrays of flowers. They can be quite dazzling, with great masses of buttercups and daisies mixed together with gentians, lilies and lupins, while underfoot lies a thick mat of fragrant thyme. On these lower slopes and the Roussillon plain, wildlife follows the Languedoc pattern. For the region's most distinctive fauna head down to the rocky coast, where the cliffs are draped with sea fennel, thrift and sea clover. Concealed beneath the waves of the offshore shallows lies one of the richest marine habitats in France. Accordingly, most of the coast between Banyuls and Cerbère — from Ile Grosse to Cap Peyrefite — has been designated an aquatic nature reserve, sheltering a wonderful profusion of warm-water molluscs and corals.

The genet has spread throughout France, being particularly numerous in the south-west.

BEFORE YOU GO
Maps: IGN 1:100,000 No. 72; IGN 1:50,000 Nos. 10 and 11; IGN 1:25,000 Nos. 2348-49 ET, 2448-49 OT and 2547-49 OT.

GETTING THERE
By air: Perpignan (see p193) has international and internal flights.
By car: Perpignan is easily reached on the A9 *autoroute* La Catalane and N9 from all points north. From Perpignan 3 main highways open up the region to the west: N114, N116 and D115.
By rail: frequent main-line trains link Perpignan with Paris via the Rhône valley. The line continues south down the Roussillon coast to Spain, offering frequent services to towns including Argelès, Collioure, Banyuls-sur-Mer

and Cerbère. *Le petit train jaune* takes a scenic route up the Têt valley from Perpignan to La Tour-du-Carol high in the Pyrenees.

WHERE TO STAY
A good hotel in Perpignan is the Park, 18 blvd J.-Bourrat, T: 04 68 35 14 14, F: 04 68 35 48 18. There are hotels and campsites at Canet, Argelès, Collioure and Banyuls. At Collioure, the quayside Les Templiers, T: 04 68 98 31 10, F: 04 68 98 01 24, is an option.

ACTIVITIES
Walking: GR10 and GR36 are the main long-distance footpaths, climbing up from the Roussillon lowland into the Pyrenees. There are shorter paths in the Roussillon hills, with several routes up from the Têt valley to the top of the Canigou massif. For details, contact the Centre d'Informations Montagne et Sentiers, Association Randonnées Pyrénéennes, 4 rue Maye Lane, BP 24, 65421 Ibos, T: 05 62 90 09 92, F: 05 62 90 67 61, e-mail: cimes @randopyrenees.com.
Cycling: the Randonnée des Pyrénées Catalanes tours the region.
Riding: the Comité Départemental de Tourisme Equestre for the Pyrénées Orientales, 4 rue du Mûrier, 66740 Montesquieu-des-Albères, T: 04 68 89 85 20, F: 04 68 89 85 20, will give details of equestrian centres.
Skiing: the higher Roussillon Pyrenees have some unpretentious downhill and cross-country ski centres. Contact the Confédération de la Neige Catalane, Office Municipal du Tourisme, Font-Romeu, T: 04 68 30 68 30, F: 04 68 30 29 70. The Club Alpin Français organizes a wide range of mountain sports; it has offices in Montpellier, T: 04

67 72 51 07, and Perpignan, T: 04 68 54 56 38.
Watersports: Collioure, Argelès and Banyuls are centres for every kind of watersport, including diving in the marine *réserve naturelle* off Banyuls.
Adventure holidays: the UCPA centre at St-Cyprien, T: 04 68 21 90 95, offers week-long activity holidays for tennis, sailing and wind-surfing.

MAQUIS AND GARRIGUE

Maquis is the name given to the impenetrably dense, rugged evergreen forest and shrubland that covers the region's low, rocky terrain. Principal shrubs include the kermes, holm and cork oaks, the arbutus (strawberry tree) and prickly juniper. Typical *maquis* undergrowth ranges from two to three metres (six to ten feet) in height, with some trees rising to four or five metres (13 to 16 feet). However, true *maquis* has nearly everywhere been replaced by a lower-growing heath and forest which naturalists refer to as secondary *maquis*. Here trees are generally more scattered and stunted, and bushes and herbs proliferate.

While climate is the overriding influence in the Mediterranean landscape, man's intervention has had a major effect on the region's vegetation. Once fire or deforestation has removed the dense woodland or *maquis*, a more varied community of wild shrubs and flowers can flourish. In areas where the soil has eroded as a result of repeated fires, or where it is naturally shallow and rocky, this more open vegetation becomes fully established as *garrigue*. *Garrigue* is also dominated by tough, tangled, prickly evergreen shrubs such as the kermes and holm oaks. But, interestingly enough, the wild forms of plant species cultivated in many gardens also grow here: in addition to cistus (rock-rose), juniper and arbutus, plants such as box, flowering viburnum, lentisk and terebinth (turpentine tree), their branches entangled with clematis and honeysuckle vines, thrive in the *garrigue*.

Beneath the taller shrubs pushes a thick undergrowth of thistles, myrtle, fragrant rosemary flourishing as small bushes, and larger bushes of several types of gorse and broom. Occasionally there are small woods and copses of parasol and Aleppo pines, their resin smelling sharply in the hot air.

The single most interesting feature, however, is the thick carpet of aromatic wild herbs. These include many varieties of thyme, savory, lavender and mint, together with rosemary, garlic and sage. In the Languedoc wilderness, powerful sweet and spicy aromas prevail, and the sense of smell can be as affecting and satisfying as the sense of sight. Wild plants release enticing fragrances at every step.

The *garrigue* type of vegetation bursts out wherever land is not in use, even in small borders between vineyards, or along roadsides, and larger areas of land which cannot be cultivated economically are given over entirely to *garrigue*.

FURTHER INFORMATION
Tourist office: Perpignan, quai de Lattre-de-Tassigny, T: 04 68 34 29 94, F: 04 68 34 71 01, e-mail: Tourisme.Roussillon. france@wanadoo.fr/; for region-wide information.

FURTHER READING
Chris Townsend, *Long Distance Walks in the Pyrenees* (Crowood, 1992).

GLOSSARY

ADTE/ARTE/CDTE/CRTE, Association Départementale/ Régionale de Tourisme Equestre/Comité Départemental/Régional de Tourisme Equestre, regional and departmental horse-riding associations and committees.

Auberge, inn, usually found in country villages.

Auberge de jeunesse, youth hostel.

Autoroute, motorway/highway requiring payment of tolls.

Biosphere Reserve, a site included in the UNESCO Man and the Biosphere (MAB) programme, which aims to develop reserves of sustainable biodiversity and promote interdisciplinary research and training. This project began in 1971 and by April 1996 covered 337 sites in 85 countries.

CAF, Club Alpin Français, organization responsible for the management of over 140 refuges; provides guided excursions and training for a wide range of mountain sports.

CDT, Comité Départemental du Tourisme, committee in charge of promoting tourism within a *département*.

Chambre d'hôte, bed and breakfast.

CIMES, Centre d'Information Montagne et Sentiers, organization providing information on walking and refuges in the Pyrenees.

CR, Conseil Régional, elected council in charge of regional administration.

CRT, Comité Régional du Tourisme, committee in charge of promoting tourism within a *région.*

Département, one of the 96 principal administrative divisions in mainland France and Corsica.

Gîte, privately owned self-catering accommodation to rent in rural areas, often

214

attached to owner's home.

Gîte d'étape, self-catering accommodation intended specifically for walkers, usually found in small villages.

GR, Grande Randonnée, part of a network of long-distance walking routes covering almost 60,000 km (37,500 miles); red and white waymarks.

GRP, Grande Randonnée de Pays, circular walking route allowing you to discover an individual region; yellow and red waymarks.

IGN, Institut Géographique National, produces a variety of map series. The most frequently cited in this book are the large-scale (1:25,000) and provincial (1:100,000) maps.

Loisirs Accueil, booking service operated by most *départements*, usually free of charge. They can reserve hotels, *gîtes* and camp-sites as well as activity holidays.

Michelin, produces 1:200,000 *Tourist and Motoring Atlas of France*, and other map series.

ONF, Office National des Forêts, national organization set up to manage state-owned woodland in France.

Parc National, national park, of which France has seven.

Parc Naturel Régional, regional nature park, of which France has 36.

Ramsar, wildlife designation providing protection under international law for wetlands, particularly those used by wintering wildfowl and wading birds. Sites worldwide provide a network of areas for migrating birds. Ramsar is the Iranian town where this convention was adopted in 1971.

RATP, Régie Autonome des Transports Parisiens, operates most of Paris's public transport system, linking underground, RER and bus networks.

Refuge, alpine hut that caters for climbers and walkers. Some are open and staffed all year round while some are left unstaffed but unlocked during

low season. Others can only be used if you pick up the key from a local village before you set off. Most are maintained by national park authorities or Club Alpin Français.

Région, comprises several *départements*; there are 22 *régions* in France, each with an elected council, set up for the purposes of regional co-ordination, although they lack direct administrative powers.

RER, Réseau Express Régional, a network of services that connect the suburbs with the centre of Paris, jointly run by SNCF and RATP.

Réserve Naturelle, a protected area notified for biological or geological interest.

SNCF, Société Nationale des Chemins de Fer, state-owned organization which runs the rail network, supplemented by buses where train lines have proved uneconomical.

TGV, Train à Grand Vitesse, high-speed train run by SNCF.

UCPA, Union Nationale des Centres Sportifs de Plein Air, organization which unites sports associations with ministerial bodies in order to offer affordable activity holidays to people aged 18-40; holidays range from weekend breaks to a fortnight's stay.

World Heritage Site, listed under the UNESCO Convention Concerning the Protection of the World Cultural and Natural Heritage. This international agreement, signed by more than 150 countries, was adopted by the General Conference of UNESCO in 1972.

ZICO, les Zones Importantes pour la Conservation des Oiseaux en France, a site covered by the 1979 EC Directive for the Conservation of Wild Birds, the French equivalent of a UK Special Protection Area or a Spanish ZEPA. Today 285 areas in France merit this distinction.

USEFUL ADDRESSES

IGN, Espace IGN, 107 rue la Boétie, 75008 Paris, www.ign.fr.
Maison de la France, 20 av de l'Opéra, 75041 Paris, T: 01 42 96 70 00, F: 01 42 96 70 71, www.franceguide.com, www.maison-de-la-france.fr, www.tourisme.fr, www.francetourism.com.
Maison de la France (UK), 178 Piccadilly, London W1V 0AL, T: (0891) 244123, F: (020) 7493 6594.
Maison de la France (USA), 444 Madison Ave, 16th floor, New York, T: (212) 838 7800, F: 838 7855; 9454 Wiltshire Blvd, Suite 715, Beverley Hills, Los Angeles, California, T: (310) 271 6665, F: 276 2835.
Michelin (France), pl Carmes-Déchaux, 63000 Clermont-Ferrand.
Michelin (UK), Tourism Department, Michelin Tyre plc, 38 Clarendon Road, Watford, Hertfordshire WD1 1SX, www.michelin-travel.com.

ACCOMMODATION

Fédération Française de Camping et de Caravaning, 78 rue de Rivoli, 75004 Paris, T: 01 42 72 84 08, F: 01 42 72 70 21, www.campingfrance.com.
Fédération Nationale des Logis et Auberges de France, 83 av de l'Italie, 75023 Paris, T: 01 45 84 70 00.
Fédération Unie des Auberges de Jeunesse, 27 rue Pajol, 75018 Paris, T: 01 44 89 87 27, F: 01 44 89 87 49, www.fuaj.org.
Maison des Gîtes de France et du Tourisme Vert, 59 rue St-Lazare, 75439 Paris, T: 01 49 70 75 75, F: 01 42 81 28 53, www.gites-de-france.fr.
Relais du Silence, 17 rue d'Ouessant, 75015 Paris, T: 01 44 49 79 00, F: 01 44 49 79 01, www.relais-du-silence.com.

NATURE ORGANIZATIONS

Centres Permanents d'Initiatives pour l'Environnement, 26 rue Beaubourg, 75003 Paris, T: 01 44 61 75 35, F: 01 44 61 75 36.
Conservatoire de l'Espace Littoral, 36 quai d'Austerlitz, 75013 Paris, T: 01 44 06 89 00, www.conservatoire-du-littoral.fr.
Fédération Nationale pour la Défense de l'Environnement, rue des Piles, BP 3046, 24750 Périgueux, T: 05 53 08 29 01, F: 05 53 09 52 52.
Fédération des Parcs Naturels Régionaux de France, 4 rue de Stockholm, 75008 Paris, T: 01 44 90 86 20, F: 01 45 22 70 78, e-mail: info@parcs-naturels-regionaux.tm.fr, www.parcs-naturels-regionaux.tm.fr.
France Nature-Environnement, 57 rue Cuvier, 75005 Paris, T: 01 43 36 79 95, F: 01 43 36 84 67, e-mail: fneparis@aol.com.
Ligue pour la Protection des Oiseaux, La Corderie Royale, BP 263, 17305 Rochefort, T: 05 46 82 12 34, F: 01 46 83 95 86.
Le Ministère de l'Amenagement du Territoire et de l'Environnement, 20 av de Ségur, 75032 Paris, www.environnement.gouv.fr.
Office National des Forêts (ONF), 2 av St-Mandé, 75012 Paris, T: 01 40 19 58 00, www.onf.fr.
Réserves Naturelles de France, BP 1, 21803 Quetigny, T: 03 80 48 91 01.

SPORTS ORGANIZATIONS

Centre d'Informations Montagne Et Sentiers (CIMES-PYRENEES), 4 rue Maye Lane, BP 24, 65241 Ibos, T: 05 62 90 09 92, F: 05 62 90 67 61.
Centre d'Informations Sentiers et Randonnées, 64 rue de Gergovie, 75014 Paris, T: 01 45 45 31 02.
Club Alpin Français (CAF), 24 av Laumière, 75019 Paris, T: 01 53 72 87 00, F: 01 42 03 55 60.

Le Conseil Supérieur de la Navigation de Plaisance et des Sports Nautiques, 3 square Desaix, 75015 Paris, T: 01 44 49 89 71, F: 01 44 49 89 70.
Le Conseil Supérieur de la Pêche, 135 av de Malakoff, 75016 Paris, T: 01 45 02 20 20.
Fédération Française de Canoë-Kayak, 87 quai de la Marne, 94340 Joinville-le-Pont, T: 01 45 11 08 50, F: 01 48 86 13 25.
Fédération Française de Cyclotourisme, 8 rue Jean-Marie Jégo, 75013 Paris, T: 01 44 16 88 88, F: 01 44 16 88 99.
Fédération Française d'Equitation, 30 av d'Iéna, 75116 Paris, T: 01 53 67 43 43, F: 01 53 67 43 45, www.dnse-ffe.com.
Fédération Française de la Montagne et de l'Escalade, 8 quai de la Marne, 75019 Paris, T: 01 40 18 75 50, F: 01 40 18 75 59, www.ffme.fr.
Fédération Française de la Randonnée Pédestre, 14 rue Riquet, 75019 Paris, T: 01 44 89 93 90, F: 01 40 35 85 48, www.ffrp.asso.fr.
Fédération Française de Ski, 50 av des Marquisats, 74000 Annecy, T: 04 50 51 40 34, F: 04 50 51 75 90, www.ffs.fr.
Fédération Française de Spéléologie, 130 rue St-Maur, 75011 Paris, T: 01 43 57 56 54, F: 01 49 23 00 95, www.ffspeleo.fr.
Fédération Française de Voile, 55 av Kléber, 75016 Paris, T: 01 44 05 81 00, F: 01 47 04 90 12, web-site: asso.ffv.fr.
Fédération Française de Vol Libre, 4 rue Suisse, 06000 Nice, T: 04 93 88 62 89, F: 04 93 16 15 62, www.ffvl.fr.
Fédération Nationale des Services de Réservation Loisirs Accueil, 208 blvd St-Germain, 75007 Paris, T: 01 44 11 10 44, F: 01 45 55 99 78.
Union Nationale des Centres Sportifs de Plein Air (UCPA), 104 blvd Blanqui, 75013 Paris, T: 01 43 36 05 20, F: 01 45 87 45 88, www.ucpa.asso.fr.

INDEX

Species are indexed only where information is provided in addition to general description and location, and where they are illustrated; page references in *italics* refer to illustrations.

PICTURE CREDITS
Front Cover — Images Colour Library. 10/11 — C. Guy, Campagne Campagne. 19 — J. Cornish, Landscape Only. 22 — Stephanie Pain. 23 — A. Clech, Campagne Campagne. 26/27 — C. Baudu, Campagne Campagne. 30/31 — H. Ouitlier, Campagne Campagne. 38 — A. Chartier, Campagne Campagne. 39 — P. Clatot, Campagne Campagne. 42/43 — Michael Busselle. 46/47 — A. Dagbert, Campagne Campagne. 50/51 — Meissonier, Campagne Campagne. 54/55 — E. Merlen, Campagne Campagne. 62/63, 66 — A. Chartier, Campagne Campagne. 67 — F. Puyplat, Campagne Campagne. 70/71, 74/75 — A. Chartier, Campagne Campagne. 78/79 — Michael Busselle. 86 — C. Guy, Campagne Campagne. 87 — G. Christian, Campagne Campagne. 91, 94/95, 98/99 — Michael Busselle. 103 — C. Siret, Campagne Campagne. 106 — T. Lamoureux,

Campagne Campagne. 107 — Michael Busselle. 110 — J. P. Fagard, Campagne Campagne. 111 — J. F. Girardel, Campagne Campagne. 114/115 — Michael Busselle. 118/119 — A. Chartier, Campagne Campagne. 123 — C. Waite, Landscape Only. 126/127 — A. Chartier, Campagne Campagne. 130/131 — Christophe, Campagne Campagne. 135 — J. Y. Uguet, Campagne Campagne. 138/139 — Gemo, Campagne Campagne. 142/143 — M. Mouchy, Campagne Campagne. 147 — G. Rabiller, Campagne Campagne. 150/151 — F. Puyplat, Campagne Campagne. 154 — Keith Spence. 159, 162/163 — A. Chartier, Campagne Campagne. 167 — J. Cornish, Landscape Only. 170/171, 175 — David Stubbs. 178/179 — Michael Busselle. 182 — C. Waite, Landscape Only. 183 — A. Chartier, Campagne Campagne. 186 — A.G.E. FotoStock. 187 — Archie Miles. 190/191 — C. Rouvet,

Campagne Campagne. 195 — C. Rivoire, Campagne Campagne. 198/199 — K. Graber. Campagne Campagne. 202 — C. Guy, Campagne Campagne. 203 — David Stubbs. 206/207, 210/211 — C. Rouvet, Campagne Campagne.

ACKNOWLEDGEMENTS
The contributors and editors wish to extend their grateful thanks to the following people and organisations for their assistance: Dr. Mark Adams, Dr. Jean-Christophe Balouet, David Black, Roger Boulanger, Brittany Ferries, Bernard Devaux, Gerry Dunham, I. P. Freely, Gillian Green and Pauline Hallam of the Maison de la France, John Harrison, Judith Harte, Richard Jones, Jillian Luff, Peter Mills of SNCF, Susan Mitchell, Neville Morgan, Stephanie Pain, Mme. Martine Renouard, Nina Shandloff, Penny Spence.